CITIZEN DWYER

Sean McCarthy

**NEW
ISLAND**

copyright page

*For my beloved wife
Annmarie Cotter*

CITIZEN DWYER
First published 2011 by
New Island
2 Brookside
Dundrum Road
Dublin 14
www.newisland.ie

ISBN 978-1- 8484-0122-8

British Library Cataloguing Data. A CIP catalogue record for
this book is available from the British Library

Typeset by Mariel Deegan.
Printed by Drukarnia Skleniarz

New Island received financial assistance from
The Arts Council (An Comhairle Ealaíon), Dublin, Ireland

10 9 8 7 6 5 4 3 2 1

Acknowledgements

Thanks are due to all the fine historians who have written on the events that inspired this fiction, and to the many curators and archivists who gave of their time and knowledge, but in particular I thank Rebecca Edmunds and Caleb Williams of the Police and Justice Museum in Sydney.

Thank you to Morgan O'Sullivan and the Wicklow Film Commission who were with me at the start of this journey. I thank Neil Donnelly for the intelligence and passion he brought to our many discussions, Dermot Bolger for his advice and direction, and Mary Stanley for reading the manuscript and offering insightful comment.

Many thanks are due to Dr Justin Corfield for being a thorough and sympathetic editor. Finally, I thank Edwin Higel and all at New Island.

PART 1

Of the Tree of liberty

What have you got in your hand?
A green bough.
Where did it first grow?
In America.
Where did it bud?
In France.
Where are you going to plant it?
In the Crown of Great Britain.

- From the Oath of the United Irishmen

Chapter I
Michael Dwyer speaks from out the darkness, and tells us how he wooed Mary Doyle of Donard

The twelfth day, as always, belonged to the women. The men did their chores. We were not adept at it, but pretended to be less able than we truly were. I did the milking, my father fed the hens, my brother John prepared the meal for breakfast, Peter swept the floor, but James put his foot down when my sister Etty asked him to wash a petticoat.

'You should do it, Jimmy. That's breaking the rule,' my sister Catherine said and Mary agreed with her.

'Tis not a rule,' my mother told them, 'only a tradition.'

'I'd say the rain will hold off,' my father declaimed as he came in. He was a man who didn't say much but every utterance was grave. Not that he didn't have a sense of humour, but the jokes were delivered with such seriousness that you'd miss them if you didn't know him. Dry is what you'd call the manner and dry is what the man was: skin like leather and tight as a drum. Didn't have much in the way of height and brawn, but I've met very few in the world as strong as him.

'We'll chance going west to Donard so?' I asked.

'Erra why not,' said he.

'Hurrah for cousins!' said young Mary Dwyer, who thrived in company, and the other two girls laughed and clapped along with her. All three of my sisters had freckles, which they hated, and black hair, which they loved. They felt it was unfair to be afflicted with freckles which properly belonged on foxy girls.

'You'll lose them in time,' my mother told them, 'I lost mine.'

'Then ye'll get even bigger ones,' said their father tapping one of his liver spots.

The stirabout that John made for breakfast was excellent. So good in fact that mother suggested he should make it every morning. You see that's what comes of not making a hames of your tasks at Women's Christmas. The day was cold and so we closed the door. Mind you we could still see out from the table or the hearth through the little round spy window by the door.

Our two-roomed house in Eadstown was stone-built, made with blocks of Wicklow granite, some dressed some rough. The thatch was of oaten straw and the rafters on which it rested of blackened oak. 'Twas a more substantial house than many lived in and the small farm sustained us. I was the eldest and would be twenty-six in the year that had just begun. The lease of our land was secure thanks to Thomas Addis Emmet, who was one of the leaders of the United Irish Men, an organisation of which I myself was a fully committed member.

Peter, who had been assigned clearing and washing up while I went to draw water, wanted to leave the tasks until we returned from Donard, so that we might get there and back in light. The women would not hear of it. Mother was concerned about securing the house while we were away, but my father said that locks and bolts would not keep them away if they wanted to attack the place and ransack it, and if they burned it to the ground itself, we'd just have to be thankful that we weren't in the place.

We made it to Donard in time for Mass and the little church was full. The men had to stand at the back but the women found seats. The priest talked about the three wise men from the east and the gifts they brought to Bethlehem. How it all started with a star in the sky and an infant in a manger.

Some say it is like a bolt of lightning. Now, it wasn't exactly that for me. Oh, I was struck all right but in a gentler way. It was like looking and knowing that I need look no further. She met my look as she walked from her seat, and she held it with something close to brazenness. Dark, dark skin and the bluest of blue eyes. Head and shoulders were covered with a shawl. Everything else dissolved from my vision: the great V of the timber roof, the stone-carved stations on the walls, the marble altar and the golden tabernacle itself. Oh, I knew; in my heart of hearts I knew. And audaciously, I believed, so did she.

I hurried out after her, trying to remain polite and not push people aside in the house of God. Thankfully, when I got outside she was there with her father, a big man made bigger by his tri-cornered hat and vast winter cloak, her mother, who had her back to me, and her teenage brother Kevin, who like so many youngsters had made approaches about wanting to join the organisation. They were talking to neighbours. All the talk outside the chapel concerned an unfortunate family in the parish of Donard who had been burned out of their house the day before because of their United sympathies. Thankfully they were unhurt and hopefully they had recognised some of the aggressors who would be brought to justice in time.

'Do you know them?' I asked my father pointing to the little group.

'The Doyles? I've met them yes.'

'Can you introduce me?'

'They'd have no time for the like of us.'

'Give it a try anyway.'

'Why, so?'

'I believe I've had an epiphany on the Epiphany.'

'This might not be the action of a wise man,' said my father as he walked towards the Doyles.

'Mister Doyle!' said he.

Doyle wheeled round and looked down at my father.

'Yes?' he kind of barked.

'John Dwyer, from beyond in Eadstown. We met in Ashford I believe.'

'Oh?'

'Terrible business over your way yesterday.'

The wife tut-tutted and blessed herself.

'What an outrage!' said she who had taken my heart.

'We do not discuss such matters,' said Mister Doyle.

'And it should not go unpunished,' said his daughter, looking directly at me.

She knows me, I thought, she knows who I am.

Mister Doyle pushed his daughter and wife ahead of him as he hurried away.

'Now there's a man with little respect for Women's Christmas,' said my father.

I heard Kevin Doyle say: 'do you *know* who that is?' as they moved on.

Donard is near the western end of the Glen of Imaal, where the land gets ever richer and greener as it starts to spread out towards the plains of Kildare. The farms were not any bigger than back to the east, but they were productive. So, there was a bit more fur and finery on display outside this church than there would be at our own.

Children ran wild, free from the constraints of sitting still for Mass. There were buggies and traps and horses and carts and asses impatient to get moving again in the cold. It all looked and sounded like a normal gathering outside any church after Mass, but in truth the people had to make an effort to keep up the appearance of normality. The talk was about the burning the day before; if you talked too passionately about it you might draw attention to yourself, but to say nothing on the subject could arouse even greater suspicion. Though there were many United men at that gathering, we had to take care to seem neither too friendly, nor to appear too unnaturally distant from each other. You never whispered in another man's ear, and that in itself was odd where young men were gathered in proximity to young women.

I liked a drink back then as much as the next man, if not more, but I was abstemious on that 6th of January. Now, there were two reasons for this: I was so elated I did not need a drink, and many Epiphanies in the past had been ruined by us men overindulging on the visit to the cousins and then being unable to complete the tasks that awaited us when we got back home.

The return journey was mostly silent. Twilight was beginning to close in and travelling too late in the day could be dangerous. Although the light was fading the countryside still sparkled. It was freezing and the grass glistened. There was glitter too on the granite of the walls between the fields and on the sides of the larger houses. Nearer to Donard there were fine long houses constructed of dressed stone and with sturdy, hipped roofs. But as we travelled east towards the mountains we saw a greater number of cabins and hovels. The thatches were scraggy and sodden, and some had sod walls at the gable, constructed out of layers of sods with marl and mortar in between.

Indeed we were thankful for the little we had.

Soon enough I'd have to leave the house in Eadstown and be 'out' for God alone knows how long. So what was I doing entertaining thoughts of romance in my head? What had I to offer a woman? Nothing more than a dream. No, not just a dream! Was it not a reality in France and America? Not a dream then, an ambition. Of course the house would be mine in time, if I wanted it, as I was the first born. But my parents had many good years in them yet. In time my sisters should find good matches, but that would not be easy because materially they had little or nothing to bring to a marriage. Few prospects other than soldiering existed for my brothers and, as they would not want to join the army of our oppressor, they'd have to travel to Europe and link up with one of the Irish regiments there.

All that would change. Now Christmas was over, and the new year of 1798 had begun, I hoped everything would change.

For now, my brother Peter remarked that there would be no need for me to cook supper when we got home because my goose was cooked already.

I was not entirely surprised when Kevin Doyle came to visit me. He found me in the field which was the farthest from the house. There was a wall there I was mending; a stone wall of course. Some folk call them dry stone walls, but here in west Wicklow you'd seldom get fine weather for long enough to keep the stones dry. One of the beasts, panicking for some reason it would seem, took a run at it. But as I started the work I suspected mischief because some of the stones had been scattered quite far. No point in conjecturing about the cause of it, I just had to get on and mend it. The boulders at the bottom were still in place but most of the other stones had fallen and the gap was about a yard wide.

'Mending a wall, I see,' Kevin said as he approached.

'God bless your eyesight and intelligence, young man,' I told him.

'Can I give you some help?'

'I doubt it.'

Straight away he started going round picking up stones and heaping them into the gap.

'Will ya stop!'

'What?

'Every stone has its place, lad.'

'Oh!'

''Course 'tis all hedges and fences where you are.'

'You have to find each exact stone for each exact place?'

'Not as precise as that, no. General rule is that the height should be the same as the width of the base and the top should be half the base width.'

'Oh, I see,' he said, but I don't think he saw at all.

'So, what brings you over this way?'

He was a gangly kind of a lad, but the face was rosy-cheeked and young. Could have been as young as fourteen, because he was definitely not a shaver, but given his height he'd try and pass for seventeen. Had the blue eyes right enough and perfectly curved dark eyelashes.

'Ah, ya know,' he answered.

'No I don't. But if it is to ask to be sworn in to some organisation, of which you think I am a member, then you are wasting your time.'

'Maybe.'

'Oh you are being mysterious now.'

He stared at me for a while, not giving much away, a few stones in each hand.

'You can put that one there,' said I, pointing to a stone and then a gap. We found another space for another of his stones and, to be fair, he wasn't long getting the hang

of it. He was a grand young fella and you couldn't but be
fond of him. I asked him about his family and in particular his father's politics. The man was, as I thought, a
royalist to the core.

'You see, straight away, you have a problem there!'

'But I do not agree with him. And the sins of the
father...'

I stopped him with a wave of my hand. 'This is not to
do with morality, or justice, or what is right or wrong. It
is about security, Kevin, and that is all.'

'I'll leave home. There's younger than me fighting in
armies.'

'I doubt it. Young man, this is an argument that is
going nowhere.'

'My sister disagrees with him too.'

'Go 'way?'

I had to tread very carefully now, letting the head rule
the heart, if at all possible. We worked in silence for a
while, gathering the stones and fitting them in. He'd stop
and look at the base from time to time and tried to measure each layer according to the rules I had told him.

'I thought you'd be interested in that,' he told me.

'Did you, now?'

'And she thought you might be interested too.'

I must have blushed because the boy laughed.

'I have another sister, Roisin. She's just a little one. But
Mary, that'd be my older sister, will be taking her to her
aunt's on Friday. At a certain time, she will be walking a
certain path by a certain stream. I think she thought you
might want to know that.'

'Did she now? And which time, which path and which
stream did she have in mind?'

'Hmm,' he purred, enjoying himself far too much.
'And then will you have me sworn in?'

'I'll have you booted all the way from here to Donard!'

He laughed heartily, but then revealed the time and the place.

I was champing at the bit right enough, raring to go, but then so was almost every able-bodied man in the country. We were waiting for the signal. Two years ago it should have happened but it didn't. A French fleet approached Bantry Bay, was tossed about in the waves for a while and then returned to France. They would be back. But now the leaders were not prepared to wait and this year we would rise, French or no French. You'd have to say that it was not the most appropriate time to be starting out on the romance of my life.

My good comrade Sam MacAllister laughed when I told him my predicament. Why does everyone find love funny? Sam was a gentle giant from the Country Antrim. Silent as many tall men seem to be, he could say more by raising one bushy eyebrow and looking down at you than many could with a lengthy speech. Or he'd run his bony hand down his craggy face, grip your shoulder and sigh. That is exactly what he did when his laughter subsided. This comforted me, but it did not solve my problem.

'Let you court away to your heart's content Michael. Make no promises mind, and be careful what you say about our business.'

'You think you need to remind me of that, Sam?'

'I do.'

That's the northern manner for you. No humming and hawing with apologies like you'd get in Wicklow, where we'd say anything except what we mean.

One spluttering candle lit the corner of the shebeen wherein we sat, and we were surrounded by whispering shadows. Sam was a Presbyterian and a steady drinker. He did it like a man, proud of his capacity, but never allowing himself to stagger or slur his words.

'Were you ever in love yourself, Sam?'

'There is only one woman in my life.'

'Your mother?'

'Now you have it.'

Sam was an only child. His father had died a young man, and his mother had to toil to feed him, clothe him and get him an education. She had some connections with our county and had moved south with Sam when he deserted from the Antrim Militia. He took the United oath and we were glad to have him. With the eye of an eagle, and some might say unkindly the beak of one as well, he could hit anything with a musket. I believe it was Sam's accuracy that would soon earn us the title 'Holt's sharpshooters', because he was as good a teacher as he was a marksman.

'I don't want to lose her.'

'Understood! But she'll have to wait.'

'Won't we all. What am I talking about? I haven't even met her yet. The family are ferocious royalists.'

'Tread carefully then.'

'Don't I always?'

Sam gave me one of his 'who-are-you-fooling' looks and I laughed.

I was never much of a one for reading. Oh, I had been taught and could manage what was necessary, but I never had the patience for it. Sam would not tolerate this. He had brought me the pamphlets of Mister Tom Paine on The Rights of Man, and he'd ask me when we met what I thought of this section or that section. So, I had no choice but to read them. And I tell you now I am mighty glad I did. Tom Paine was an honorary member of the United Irishmen and had lodged in Paris with our leader Lord Edward Fitzgerald. If I wasn't fired up for the cause before I read them, I surely was when I put them down.

So, there I was, zealous for revolution and zealous for love.

The day was cold, but dry, thank God. I was there a long time before the appointed hour. I leant against an old ash tree and watched the stream babble by, clear, clean and cold. I was tempted to take a drink from it, but resisted, thinking leaning against a tree a more dignified posture than crouching over a stream. I heard the voices of Kevin and the young girl I guessed was Roisin before I saw them. Roisin scampered into view first, but stopped when she saw me.

'It is all right,' Kevin told her as she skipped along. Always skipped, never walked. Her hair was a much lighter and more golden colour than her brother's or sister's, and curly. When she skipped, and it was a high skip, indeed more of a hop than a skip, her curls bounced from side to side. She has a niece now at the other side of the world, who hops and skips and bounces her curls in exactly the same way, but she is black as night and just as beautiful. Roisin curtsied when she came to me and I bowed as gracefully as I could.

Mary Doyle walked slowly towards me. She wore a long, hooded cloak, dark green in colour. Kevin stood between us.

'I believe you have met my sister Mister Dwyer!' he said.

'Not formally,' I replied.

'Michael Dwyer, Mary Doyle,' said the lad with a flourish.

'Delighted,' I said.

'Charmed,' she replied.

An awkward pause ensued. She broke the silence. 'What brings you to this path Mister Dwyer?'

I wasn't expecting that.

'I... eh... wished to look at the trees. To assess the suitability of some of the branches for making...'

'Pikes?' she asked.

'Hurleys.'

'And have you consulted with the owner of the trees?'

'They have an owner?'

'Why, His Lordship of course.'

'He owns the trees?'

'And the path we walk on and the stream that flows by.'

'And the rain that falls from the sky?'

'When it lands on his property, of course. But you would dispute that?'

'I do not hold with hereditary titles.'

'They are a fact of life. From God, some say. Once you have one you cannot relinquish it.'

'Lord Edward Fitzgerald repudiated his.'

'A lot of good his repudiation did if you still call him *Lord* Edward Fitzgerald.'

We laughed, and walked along, now more at ease.

'Is it right to tamper with the order of things?' she asked. 'God in his heaven, the King on his throne, the Lord in the Manor, the Bishop in his Palace, the Priest at the Altar? That is what my father has taught me. Is he wrong?'

'You will decide that with your own intelligence. You have no lack in that faculty.'

'Into what dangers would you lead me Mister Dwyer?'

'I hope none from which I cannot protect you.'

Her hands I saw only briefly during the walk, and I could not make out anything she wore beneath the cloak. Perhaps a waist-length jacket in a lighter green. As we strolled I talked and talked: about self-evident truths and inalienable rights, about liberty, democracy, freedom and equality. On and on! And she loved it: the words, the sound, the passion, and yes, the meaning too.

When it came time to part I had to explain that my first commitment was to the movement, and the defence of our people. Since martial law had been introduced a campaign of terror had been carried out in Wicklow, with half-hanging, pitch-capping, free quartering and plain murder being everyday events.

'For now,' I told her, 'we need to be patient. Keep our powder dry, so to speak. Defend whom we can when we can. But...'

I paused here but Kevin, who had been carried away by all this talk, interjected: 'You are waiting for the signal, and when it comes the whole place will go up.'

'Look to your brother,' I said. 'Such talk could have him up before a court martial.'

'You must do what you think is right, Mister Dwyer, but I do hope that we shall be able to meet again,' she told me, a little quaver in her voice.

'We will.'

I waved to Roisin, who smiled and waved back. I strode home elated, but like a walking boil that needed to burst.

'She'll have a mind of her own,' my mother said as we sat round the hearth.

'Don't they all?' my father mumbled.

My mother displayed great concentration on the threading of a needle, but we knew she was searching for a smart remark in reply to my father. She found it: 'Ah sure now, somebody has to do the thinking.'

My mother chuckled at that one for a while. God love her, she had hardly an intact tooth left in her head, and that made her look her older than she was. Her skin was remarkably smooth, considering the years of toil she had put in, and she was energetic. Always busy, I could not imagine her at rest, doing nothing.

'Something serious must be afoot to have those two running here!' my father said, looking out the spy window.

Sam MacAllister was at the door and he was followed by Hugh Vesty Byrne. Hugh Vesty was big bull of a man whose heart was twice the size of his brain. Fearless in battle, he would take on any enterprise as long as it didn't involve dogs, of which he had an irrational fear.

He stood in the kitchen, puffing, hands on his knees.

'We are undone Michael,' he gasped. 'A raid on the house of Oliver Bond in Dublin; most of the leaders have been taken.'

'Edward Fitzgerald?' I asked.

'He escaped,' Hugh Vesty told me.

Then Sam said: 'They have put a price of one thousand pounds on his head!'

I think we all gasped at the enormity of the sum.

'He won't last a wet day in Dublin with that on his head,' my father said.

I had already started to collect a few necessary items during this and my mother was filling me a bag of meal. Now I was unlikely to sleep in my own bed again until God's knows when, but I was determined not to have any emotional farewells. So I rolled what I needed in a cloth, picked up my blunderbuss and led the lads out the door with me bundle on me shoulder and the blunderbuss held aloft. Where would I be without it?

'You're a blunderbuss yourself!' said Sam.

'Hey, watch it now Sam.'

'Erra watch ye'r arse!'

That was Sam MacAllister all out, asking for the impossible and damning the plain and simple. Mind you he had a point. For the blunderbuss was me and I was the blunderbuss.

Wicklow rebels were meant to march on Dublin and join the United Men, who had come out there, to secure the Capital and hold it until the French arrived. But the work of the spies had probably spoiled that plan now.

'Any Catholic in Wicklow will be fair game now,' said Hugh Vesty.

'They want to make this religious,' said Sam. 'Divide the country along religious lines.'

'Oldest trick in the book!' I told him.

'Ironic when you think about it though,' he continued. 'There's you Catholics, and me a Presbyterian, and General Joe Holt, who will lead us, a member of the Established Church of Ireland.'

'I tell ye boy,' said Hugh Vesty, 'them French rebels knew what to do about the church. There was hardly a bishop or an abbot left with a head on his shoulders in all of France.'

'And rightly so!' asserted my Northern friend.

'None the less Sam there are priests joining our ranks now,' I told him.

'Well, there shouldn't be.'

'But it is only out of concern for what is happening to their people.'

'Now Michael, a true United Irishman must sacrifice his religion to his politics, and no priest will do that!'

'Ah, the ordinary priests I'm talking about Sam, who rolled up their sleeves and stood by the people through thick and thin!'

'They will lead us right into the trap that the enemy have set for us!'

He stopped and looked at me as he said this, but I made no reply because I was concerned that Sam and myself had started to nibble on the bait that the English had set out for us. We marched on in silence for a while, Hugh Vesty trudging behind. Sam had been shot in the hip following his desertion from the Antrim Militia and he walked with a limp. So that we might proceed in as soldierly a fashion as possible I marched in step with him, but when we had put a few perches behind us I noticed myself walking with a limp also. I had to ease myself out of this gait as quickly as possible because if my companion copped it, one of us might not have reached our pre-arranged destination.

Once we got there (it was just a dimly lit barn) we were told by our general, Joe Holt, that what we had to do now was wait and be prepared.

Some of our number went on night-time raids to houses where arms and ammunition were likely to be held. Mostly these were the houses of local yeomen. The general pointed out that the yeomen's arms had been paid for by the people's taxes and so the people were entitled to take hold of the same arms. I always admired the general's logic. Joe Holt was a small, rotund, ruddy-faced man, mostly bald, but what hair he had was very curly.

During this time of waiting we heard of the arrest and subsequent death of Edward Fitzgerald.

As summer came that year hope began to wane. The rebellion was to take place on the 23rd of May and the signal was to be the halting of the mail coaches. The rising in Dublin was foiled, however, and the original plan was now in ruins.

On the 24th of May in the town of Dunlavin in west Wicklow all the republican prisoners were brought from the jail, tied together in twos and threes, and shot on the village green. My cousin John Dwyer of Seskin was among them. There was talk of going to Wexford and talk of Kildare, but I knew that before I went anywhere I would have to contrive to see Mary Doyle one more time.

Setting up the rendezvous was more complex now, and the journey and the meeting much more dangerous. A head stuck on a spike was not an uncommon sight in the countryside, and I came across two of them on my way to meet Mary. Both young men had been known to me. I crossed myself and said a prayer for their souls, but such are the ways of war.

Mary, Kevin and Roisin sat on a rug by the same ash tree. The two girls, Mary in a light summer dress, Roisin in a pink dress and bonnet, were making a daisy-chain. Kevin lay stretched out on his back, hands behind his head. When I arrived he stood up. From time to time Roisin would remove the bonnet from her head determinedly, only for Mary to replace it. Roisin handed me the daisy-chain for inspection, and I told her that I was very impressed. She ordered me to sit and help with the rest of the chain, and she was not the kind of lady you disobeyed.

'Kevin,' I said, 'you see that tree?'

'The beech?'

'Aye. It looks like an easy climb. Go up as high as you can, so you have a view north and south. Watch out for forces of the crown. If you see anything do not cry out. Come down smartly and tell me.'

He stood to attention, gave me a salute, and ran to the tree.

Roisin chided me for my awkwardness in daisy-chaining because I kept cutting through the stem and not just making a neat hole for the next daisy to thread through. I soon got the hang of it and the child was pacified and occupied. I could now have a conversation with her sister.

'These times will pass, but not immediately,' I said.

She nodded.

'I'll have to go from here, and I do not know when we may meet again. Sorry, I make bold here. If it is your wish that we should meet.'

'It is.'

'You believe in the rightness of what I do? For me there is no option, you understand?'

'I believe, yes.'

'I think we may never get your father's blessing.'

'We will not.'

'Not how things should be, ideally. Not how I would wish things to be. This is not the courtship I would have wanted.'

'There will come a time for wooing.'

'I hope. But you must wait.'

'That I will, sir.'

That was as much conversation as we were permitted, because we now had to turn our attention to Roisin. That we did happily. Indeed there was nothing more to be said. Mary seemed content, and I was blissful. It was idyllic, the three of us on the rug by the ash tree on the river bank.

Kevin scampered down the tree and ran to us. Ashen faced he told us: 'A troop of Ancient Britons.'

'You sure it is them?'

'Plumes on the helmets, blue riding cloaks. Oh, it is them.'

The Cambrian Horse, known as the Ancient Britons, had ridden from Ulster, through Louth and Dublin into Wicklow, leaving in their wake a trail of carnage.

'Walking, trotting, what?' I asked him.

'Walking.'

'Then let us pack everything neatly, but quickly and we'd best make our way into the woods. No panic!'

As we picked up the few possessions, rug, shawl and bonnets, I could tell from the approaching horse hooves that it was no longer a walk, but a brisk canter. I tried to hurry them along calmly, and we barely made it into the woods before the troop came into view.

'My daisy-chain!' the child shouted.

'Leave it, we'll make another,' I said.

'No, we'll fetch it,' Mary said, picking up Roisin and running to the path. They made it safely to the tree, where Mary put Roisin down and the child picked up the daisy-chain. Then the little one walked straight onto the path as the troops rounded the bend at a gallop. Roisin stood stock still staring at the horses. Mary froze by the tree. The riders saw the child, but they made no attempt to pull up or veer to the right or left. They rode straight at her and she disappeared from my view. I could see neither Roisin nor Mary now, only the galloping horses, a big red-faced sergeant to the fore. They passed and through the dust I could see Mary on her knees screaming. Beside her on the grass the child lay, mangled.

I knew before I touched the child to check for pulse or breath that she was dead. Mary was screaming and beating the ground. I think she shouted: 'They saw her! They saw her!'

I held her as she sobbed, 'We must get her to a doctor.'

'There is no use,' I told her, 'I'm sorry.'

Kevin knelt by his little sister, bewildered. Mary crawled to her, kissed her through her tears and tried to lift her broken body.

'We must take her home,' I said.

Placing the lifeless Roisin on the rug, I lifted it and started to walk.

Doyle was in the farmyard when we arrived, and I walked straight past him into the kitchen to place the child on the table. Behind me I could hear Kevin and Mary telling of the Cambrian horse and what had happened. I stepped aside as the big man came to the table. He wept and prayed over his daughter. Finally he said: 'Go fetch your mother Kevin, I don't know where...' At this point he saw me, stared blankly at me for a moment and looked at Mary. Then the man lost all control, started to call me a murderer and grabbed me by the throat.

Mary shouting: 'No, no, no!' tried to pull him off me, and I managed to get free of his grip.

'Go, Michael,' she shouted, 'go!'

I walked away. Nothing more to do or to say, I walked away. I prayed. Prayed for the soul of the child and for succour for the family in their grief. And, yes, I prayed for justice.

In the early hours of the morning of the 25th of June our company was part of a force of fifteen thousand men and we took a position on Kilmacart Hill overlooking Hackettstown, which was our objective. The Shebagh Cavalry lined the opposite side of the rapidly flowing Dereen River. They were accompanied by a force of infantry made up of militia and yeomen, and it was from these fellas we took fire. In fording the river we lost many, but once we'd crossed it we weren't long in forcing the infantry to retreat towards the town.

Now I will not tell you here about my plan that dislodged the cavalry from their position and drove them back into Hackettstown to join their companions, because I know it is a story that has been told perhaps too frequently. Ah no, it is!

As a force of Wexford men attacked the town from another direction we soon cleared all the military off the streets and the town was ours apart from three positions which were heavily defended: a large private dwelling, the Malt House and the barracks. I learned a sore lesson that day about how difficult it is to dislodge a well-supplied force from stone structures unless you have artillery at your disposal, which of course we did not. Oh, now I was in a rage of frustration at having to abandon the project. That was our first engagement.

You see when we joined this war the Republic of Wexford was already in its last days, and we missed the great victories at Oulart Hill (where the republicans were led by a priest, despite the misgivings of the likes of Sam), Harrow and Eniscorthy. Of course we were also absent at the defeat in New Ross and the massacre at Vinegar Hill. Perhaps we would have made a difference in these engagements, but who is to say?

Now we were at Ballyellis, a mile from Carnew on the road to Monaseed with no accessible enemy to engage.

But doesn't the Lord always move in the strangest ways? This time he sent us a massive gift for which nobody but me had prayed.

A detachment of British cavalry had left Carnew intending to make Monaseed, and they included in their number the same murderous Ancient Britons. Joe Holt kept a clear head, which was just as well, because mine was now suddenly overcome with anger and vengeance. The road at Ballyellis is lined with thick bushes on both sides, making it ideal for an ambush. Holt ordered us on either side in such a way that we would not take our own fire. When we had fired a volley at them our pikemen tore into them immediately and soon there was hardly a single cavalryman left on a horse. Some of them did escape on foot into an adjoining field, but we were up and after them before Joe Holt had even given the order.

I saw my man among them—the big, red-faced bastard. I followed the bobbing plume of his helmet, which fell to the ground when I gave him a belt of the butt of my blunderbuss in the small of his back. 'I hope,' said I, 'that your head will come off as easily as your helmet.' It didn't. When I was halfway through the hacking and the sawing I realised that my own blade might not be equal to the task. So I threw it to one side and picked up his sabre. That wasn't long cutting through the meat. Fountains of blood spurted on the grass. I held the napper aloft. My comrades were overjoyed that for once we had one of theirs to stick on a spike! For myself I was just grateful the Lord had granted me vengeance.

On the day following the battle I wrote this letter to Mary Doyle. I would try to find a way to have it delivered personally to her in the townland of Knockandorragh in the parish of Donard.

Dearest Mary,

I felt compelled to write to you. Our acquaintance has been so brief and yet so desperately dramatic, marked as it was by that most terrible tragedy. Since that saddest of days I am haunted by the thought that if you had not met me, if I had not sought you out, if we had not been on that particular river bank on that particular day at that specific time, that the child might yet be alive. But, more certain than anything else, if that troop of Ancient Britons had not ridden that path or if they had chosen to halt their horse or veer to the right or to the left, then Roisin would still be with you.

It was nothing short of the murder of an innocent. We have recourse to no just law or court in these troubled times, and it is incumbent upon us to meet out our own justice, rough though it may be. In the case of your sister such justice has now been served. That troop of Ancient Britons has been destroyed, and the soldier who led them and perpetrated the murder has been executed by my own hand. His head is now impaled on a spike on the road at Bellyellis.

I know that is small consolation to you and your family in the agony of the grief you must now endure.

I wish I could be by your side and I hope that may be my situation one day. If only I could speak to your father and accomplish this in the correct way, but such an approach is closed to me. He blames me for the tragedy. True, we should not have met without his permission or spoken without his blessing. Yet, we did. Compelled by what? For myself I must now boldly declare that is was love for you. Oh, I wish that I could commence on a long and ardent courtship. The times prohibit this. I am a soldier in the midst of war, where time is amongst my many enemies. Tomorrow I may die. That is a fate, like any soldier, I am bound to accept. I cannot embrace it however without you knowing what I have declared herein. We will prevail in the fight. And if the feelings I have expressed are shared by you, then our love will also prevail.

It will not be long now my love until we walk unfettered from the pastures of west Wicklow into beloved Imaal, with

*Keadeen, Carrig and Brusselstown Hill guarding the north
and before us to the east, Table Mountain and the mighty Lug
na Coille. And through the townland of Camarra we shall
walk and ascend the great mountain itself and they will call
you 'Mountain Mary of Knockandorragh' betrothed to the
Wicklow chieftain Michael Dwyer. And we will wash in the
clear waters of the Ow that ripples through her own deep
valley. And we will ramble through Fairwood, and all the
forests from Blessington east to the Downs and Kilduddery, for
they will no longer be the preserve of Lords and Ladies
hunting with the hounds.*
Know that I will not rest until this be accomplished.
Pray for me my dearest Mary.

I hope this finds you,
May God bless and keep you,
With love and respect,
Michael Dwyer

After Hackettstown, Ballyellis and another brief engagement at Carnew, the General led us back to Whelp Rock
on Black Hill Mountain. The powers that be in the movement wanted us to go from there and invade County
Meath. But I was against this because it meant meeting the
enemy in flat, open country, however Joe determined to
go. We did not fall out on this matter and he agreed that
I should stay behind with part of our force, a continuing
presence being necessary in Wicklow.

Well Joe's sortie into Meath proved to be a disaster, and
indeed he was lucky to escape with his life. The poor man,
who suffered agonies from his stomach all his life, was in
a desperate state altogether when he returned to us. He
took command of us just the same and determined that
we fight on and hold out until the French arrived, which
we all believed would be soon and in great numbers.

The first French expedition had come within sight of Bantry Bay two years previously, but failed to land because of a storm. One of our number, Arthur Devereux, who was a cousin of mine, was familiar with the ways of the Directorate in Paris, and confident that the next French expedition was imminent. Arthur was the most serious man I ever met in my life, and for all the years I had known him I never once saw him crack a smile. Try as we might we could not knock a laugh out of him. Unlike other bases we would have Whelp Rock was not hidden and the presence of our force there was widely known. It was easy to defend, however and inaccessible even to a large force using artillery. It was not surprising then that Kevin Doyle found his way to the place. It was Martin Burke who brought him to me, along with two other teenagers, friends of Kevin. Lucky for them that Martin was the sentry who discovered them, because other fighters might not have treated them so gently. Martin was a fair-minded man of a calm disposition, but very precise, with a military bearing. He was, I suppose, what the women would call handsome. Good height, a fine crop of dark hair, and he had a pale, serene face.

'They say they know you,' he said.

'Kevin Doyle I know, but not the other two.'

'This is Fintan and this is Donal,' he told me, pointing to his companions. One of them, Donal, was a fussy, foxy ferret of a lad, and Fintan, who could have been a dreamy genius or a gom, was a very blond specimen bordering on the albino. He carried a hurley, and Fintan a pitchfork. Kevin had a rusty old flintlock which must have belonged to his father. No powder or ammunition of course.

I told them that they should not have come, but he remarked: 'Well they are with us now captain. They have seen the place and what's in it and they can't go back down.'

'True,' I said, and putting my arm round Kevin's shoulder: 'You take care of those two, I'll talk with this one.'

Now, I was angry with Kevin for having come to this place, but I was very pleased to see him.

'I'd say your family hate me enough without adding this adventure to it.'

'Believe me captain, my family could not hate you any worse.'

I smiled at his calling me captain like a regular fighter, and full member. It was my rank of course, a rank I had been given before the fighting ever started.

'How is she?'

'She's a pity. We all are. House of tears! She avoids my father now because it takes little or nothing to start him off. He blames her still, and you. Mary will not last long in that house. If my father has his way he'll marry her off immediately, but if there is any sign of that I'd say she'll run.'

'Does she know about Ballyellis and the fate of the Ancient Britons? Of my letter?'

'Oh yes, and how you took the head off the big fella. Yes, it made a difference to her knowing that justice had been done.'

So the three lads were set to work cleaning and cooking and making fires and Sam was to teach them how to prime, load and fire a musket. The young fellas went about their tasks with enthusiasm. In the case of Donal and Fintan this industry was motivated by fear of General Holt, and believe me this fear was not groundless. Joe was a ruthless man, who had once shot an eleven-year-old boy for giving information to the Yeos. That was Joe Holt for ye. Kevin Doyle stayed, out of commitment and admiration for the older fighters; in particular Sam MacAllister. He hero-worshiped him. Oh yes, if there was one person Kevin Doyle wanted to be, it was not Michael Dwyer but

Sam MacAllister. Sam never raised his voice to the boy but instructed him quietly in his low Ulster lilt, and, under his tutelage, Kevin was becoming an expert shot. The boy was never happier, but I wanted him home with his family, because I did not want to be responsible for the death of yet another of Mary's siblings. Every night I was haunted by the death of Roisin and I knew that the terrors Mary must be going through were even worse. How I wished we could share our grief. I confided in Sam, who chided me for being more interested in romance than revolution, but he did promise that he would guard and protect Kevin with his very life, and this was some consolation to me.

General Lake, who had commanded the British Forces in the Wexford campaign, instigated a reign of terror in County Wicklow, but this served only to harden the people's hearts and drove more young men into the ranks of the United Irishmen. The authorities were no fools and they replaced Lake with Cornwallis, who was committed to a policy of appeasement.

In July, proclamations appeared in the press offering 'protections' to those who surrendered their arms and 'returned to their allegiance'. General Holt read out for us the text of one of these so-called 'certificates of protection':

> *This is to certify that the Bearer hereof..........................of the Parish of................. County............. by occupation.............
> has surrendered himself, confessed his being engaged in the present Rebellion and............ has given up all his arms, and discovered of those which he knew to be concealed; has taken the Oath of Allegiance to His Majesty, His Heirs and Successors, and has abjured all former Oaths and Engagements in any wise whatsoever contrary thereto, and has bound himself to behave for the future as a peaceable and loyal Subject; in consequence whereof this certificate is given to the*

*said............ in order that his person and his property may not
in any wise be molested. And all His Majesty's Officers,
Magistrates, and other His Majesty's loving subjects, are
hereby enjoined to pay due Attention thereto, in Pursuance of
the Proclamation issued............. General.......... dated the.....
of............. 1798; and this Certificate to be in full force so long
as the said......... continues to demean himself as a peaceable
and loyal Subject.
Dated at...........the...... Day of........ 1798.*

Now here was a way to get Kevin Doyle back to his
family. It was immediately and generally agreed that no
United Man could sign this pardon and remain part of the
movement; however Arthur Devereux called for silence.
He held up his finger for a moment and turned his head
slightly, showing most of us his profile. It looked as
though he might have been posing for a portrait but we
knew he was just thinking matters through.

'You could, if you didn't mean it.'

At this Hugh Vesty Byrne bellowed: 'You can't take an
oath of allegiance to the King!'

'I'm only saying that it could be of tactical value to us,'
Arthur told him.

'An oath is an oath,' said Hugh, 'and it is calling on
God to witness. On God, mind!'

Arthur just shrugged.

Before Joe Holt came out with a definitive ruling on
the matter I knew that I would be helpful to get Hugh
Vesty on my side.

'But sure you're only signing a piece of paper, Hugh
Vesty,' I said. 'It is not as though you have one hand on
the Bible and the other raised to the Lord. If people want
to go back to their families and their farms, then they
should be given the opportunity to do that. I'm thinking
especially about the young lads here. I think it is too much
to ask that they stay with us for the long haul, and this is

an opportunity for them to go back to their parents without being thrown in jail, or pitch-capped or piked or whatever. And also, if we are going to conduct a war in this countryside we are going to need the help of the people, and these good lads can be our eyes and ears among them. We all know that the place is crawling with spies and we have to be on our guard. What do you say General?'

Joe himself was a married man with children and, although he was tough, he had a heart.

'I'll leave it up to the lads,' he said. 'Donal!'

Donal had a hoarse voice which did not seem to have fully broken yet, so in one sentence he could go from boy treble to basso profundo. He was the butt of cruel japes and the source of much merriment. 'Yes sir (high). Please sir (very low). (a cough) I'd like to go home sir!' he said, standing rigidly to attention. The fair-haired Fintan spoke in rapid bursts: 'Well, yes, I suppose, all things considered, eh, what would be best for all concerned, not just for myself I mean, but to go home, yes.'

'As you wish,' said the General. 'That leaves only Kevin. Well?'

Kevin stood before the General, but he looked at Sam. I tell you, I was annoyed by this. Call it jealousy if you wish, but I did not care for the way Kevin always deferred to Sam, and that habit was making this moment much more awkward for me. Of course I admired Sam and I trusted him, but I needed him to be supportive of me and firm with Kevin in this circumstance and he let me down. Instead of telling the boy to go back to his family he turned away and removed himself from the scene. Inevitably, Kevin said: 'If you please General, I would like to stay sir.'

'But your parents need you,' I said. 'After all they've been through recently! And now you are going to heap further stress and worry on them!'

'I'll be flogged as soon as I cross the threshold,' Kevin told the assembly. 'My parents are royalists. They hate the rebellion and the United Irishmen. If they had their way they would turn us all over to the authorities. I believe in what we are doing and I must stay. My parents are wrong and my place is here.'

I thought he'd get a round of applause from the rest of them.

'Well spoken lad. You can stay and welcome,' Holt told him.

'The boy is needed at home,' I tried again. 'Of course you might get a slap or two from your father, but if you pretend to him that you have seen the light and wish to follow the King he'll go easy on ye, and think of the value you could be to us, stationed in the ranks of the enemy.'

'That is a good point you make there,' said Hugh Vesty.

'I want to fight. I don't want to spy!' said Kevin.

'You'll do what is best for the movement!' said I.

'Indeed he must,' said Hugh Vesty, but then unfortunately added: 'Mind you, 'tis for the General to decide that.'

'Well, young Kevin, I think you have the makings of a good soldier,' said Holt. 'And he's making progress, with the firearms MacAllister, yes?'

Sam nodded.

Later that morning Fintan and Donal went to the British Army camp to get General Moore to sign their Protections. They would then make their way across the hills to their homes near Donard. I was still unhappy about Kevin remaining in the camp, but I had to wait until later that day, when General Holt had gone from the camp, to make my move.

The first thing I did was enlist the help of Hugh Vesty and Sam, both of whom Kevin admired. So we commenced on a three-pronged attack.

I held the Protection scroll out to him, but he said: 'No, Michael!'

'You have your Protection,' I told him. 'No one can harm you.'

'I want to stay *out*,' he protested, stamping his feet like a spoilt brat.

'God, I'd surely like to be going home to some home cooking,' contributed Sam.

'Wouldn't we all!' Hugh Vesty added weakly.

'Your family will hold me responsible for your safety Kevin,' I told him, 'and I can't vouch for that. No man can guarantee another man's safety in this...'

He interrupted me.

'''Tis my sister you are interested in, not me!'

This met with whoops and jeers from my two so-called allies, and I had to turn on them. 'Citizens, I'll thank you not to trivialise this very serious situation!'

'Oh now surely,' said Sam, 'love is never a thing to be trivialised.'

'The Doyles will never accept you as a husband for their daughter Michael Dwyer,' Sam told me, sympathetically.

'Of course they won't!' Kevin shouted. 'Why? Because they are loyalists and despise republicans. My father is a lackey and a coward and I hate him.'

None of us saw the clatter coming, but the sound of the slap resounded when Sam's hand connected with Kevin's face. As the boy's cheek reddened his eyes filled with tears. He stuttered an intake of breath and blew out the air to stop himself from blubbering.

'Never, ever speak in that way about your father. Do you hear me boy?' Sam looked at him sternly and Kevin nodded. Then Sam turned to Hugh Vesty and told him: 'Bring the horse, Hugh Vesty.'

Hugh Vesty brought a horse that was ready-saddled. Sam lifted the boy and set him on the mount. I handed Kevin the Protection.

'Be our eyes and ears Kevin,' Sam told him. 'Your contribution will be a very important one lad: in many ways more important than what we do here. You will be able to save lives and direct us as to how to bring down the enemy. Will you do this for us, Kevin?'

The boy nodded.

'Good man!' said Sam, and slapped the rump of the horse.

Kevin rode off, and I tell you he was not the happiest soldier in Ireland. We watched him ride for a while and then Hugh Vetsy started to coo to me: 'Uh-hoo! Mary Doyle!'

I thought about giving him a dig but he was an All Ireland wrestling champion, if indeed such a title legitimately existed. Though, in fairness now, he did ground anyone who came up against him.

Now there had been a report of a troop of Yeoman Cavalry from Talbotstown, some miles to the north, earlier in the day. Sam pointed out that that would mean that the barracks at Talbotstown would be lightly guarded at best, presenting us with an opportunity.

'Muskets, powder and ball!' said Hugh Vesty.

'They will be there aplenty,' I said.

We got a raiding party together speedily; it included Sam, Hugh Vesty, Arthur Devereux and Martin Burke. There were some like the Halpin brothers who did not want to ride with us because General Holt was not there. I pointed out that the General put me, as captain, in charge, and that I was sure he would want us to use our initiative, adding that we were in dire need of arms and ammunition. I wasn't going to order anyone; volunteers was what I wanted.

We set out early that afternoon.

Our approach to the barracks was screened by a row of ash trees. So when we first saw the two heads it looked as though they were suspended in mid-air, because we couldn't see the spikes with the trees in the way. But there they were, fresh and still dripping blood, one foxy and one blond. For a moment we were transfixed, staring at the heads, as dumbly as they stared back at us. Sam broke the silence with a shout of 'Kevin!' and we wheeled our horses round and galloped north.

Now I needed to keep *my* head!

By now Kevin would have had his Protection signed at the British Army camp and be making for home. What we needed was a vantage point on the mountains which would give us best view of the trek Kevin would take. I knew of such a place, but it was going to be easier to get there on foot than on horseback.

So we left our horses and scrambled across the last couple of miles of rough terrain.

We heard them before ever we saw them. There was a peel of laughter followed by a scream. As we edged forward and prepared our weapons we heard more: 'Please don't. It is my Protection!' cried Kevin's voice. We all sighed with relief, because at least he was alive. 'Eat it!' shouted a voice that I knew belonged to one Colbert, a captain in the yeos and as bad an egg as ever was laid. 'Your companions did and they seemed to find it extremely tasty!' he added, which was met with more laughter. 'Once you have consumed it you can then choose which one of your own body parts you would like to eat. A finger goes very well with parchment. Have we any suggestions?' There were plenty of suggestions and much laughter from those cursed yeos.

By now we had them in our sights and could see that they were tearing bits off the Protection and forcing Kevin to eat them.

There were six Yeos in all, and I knew we would have to take out two to equalise the fight. That is where the human battering ram was to be employed. By now we were within about ten yards of them and I whispered the orders. Hugh Vesty had huffed and grumbled his way over the rough terrain, but like most heavyweight wrestlers he had great speed over five to ten yards.

'Hugh Vesty, you take down the nearest two, there.' They had their backs to us. 'Sam, can you hit the fella by the horses?' He nodded that he could. 'Leave Colbert to me. Arthur, take one of the pair behind him. Hugh Vesty will move first. As soon as he's on his way, Sam, you open fire. Then we'll at them. Are we ready?' Sam and Arthur indicated that they were, and Hugh Vesty stared straight ahead at the Yeos. I tapped him on the shoulder and told him: 'Go!'

He didn't move.

'Now for God's sake man!'

Stock still he was. By now Kevin was gagging on the last pieces of paper and Colbert was drawing his sabre.

'Move, Hugh Vesty! Go!' I hissed.

'I can't,' he whispered.

'Why?'

'There's a dog!'

We all looked. None of us had seen it but, sure enough, sitting in the arms of one of the Yeos was a scruffy, little terrier.

'You couldn't call that a dog,' said Sam.

'More like a dirty ol' mop,' I told him. 'Move!'

He wouldn't budge. Sam took aim and shot the Yeo by the horses. As the two nearest us turned I came up and gave them a volley from the blunderbuss. Sam and Arthur ran into the others, firing pistols as they went. A ball from Colbert's pistol caught Sam in the shoulder, but I caught Colbert full in the face with the butt of the blunderbuss, and I heard bones crack and saw teeth fly as I connected. The dog ran yelping from the scene, and Hugh Vesty, better late than never, rushed headlong at the master and laid him out. We had disabled all of them quickly and efficiently. Kevin Doyle vomited emptying the contents of his stomach, which included most of the damned Protection, on the battle scene.

General Holt returned to Whelp Rock that evening and brought his good wife Martha with him, and that was timely because she was able to dress Sam's wound, which turned out to be not that serious. When we told him what happened with the Protections the General said: 'It is just as well, then, that I brought writing materials with me.'

'Why so, General?' I asked.

'Because we can write our own Protections,' he replied.

Everyone laughed at this, except Arthur.

Truly it was no joking matter. We could offer our own Protection to the poorer inhabitants of County Wicklow. We could guarantee them that if their persons or property were assaulted we would get satisfaction from the perpetrator. The real battle was for the allegiance of the people, and most of them knew that we had their best interests at heart.

If an individual or family was accused of aiding our cause it was agreed that they would claim that such aid was extracted by force, and if any of us were caught and interrogated we would back up that claim. With this arrangement I was confident that we would survive in the mountains until the French arrived. Our General was determined that no instance of intimidation, whether it was by shooting of persons or stock or damaging of property, would go unpunished. Every time the house of a republican sympathiser was burned we would torch the house of a yeoman; so reprisal led to reprisal, which led to even further reprisals.

It was about a week after these events that Arthur Devereux returned from a visit to Dublin with the news that a French fleet had landed in Killala in County Mayo. It was a small force, no more than a thousand men, and Mayo was certainly not a republican stronghold. After a victory at Castlebar the force was completely defeated at Ballynemuck in Longford. Arthur Devereux was convinced that, in time, a larger fleet would arrive and that we should continue to hold out, but our General was doubtful about this. I was with Arthur in believing that we could hold out for a long time in our mountain fastness, and should continue the fight. After all, we effectively controlled a sizeable portion of County Wicklow. That was our republic.

We waited for the General to speak.

'It is not enough,' he said.

'I know we all wanted more, much more, but we have what we have and that we should hold,' I advised. 'If we continue with our campaign others will join us. And the French will come General. They will come!'

Arthur was convinced of that too, and he knew more about what was happening in Paris than any of us.

Joe Holt is an older man than me, not in good health, and even then he had a wife and children. No, he was doubtful about going on, and Martha, loyal wife though she was, did not relish the idea of living indefinitely on the run. At this stage the General did not outline what future plans he had in mind for himself and I did not press him on that point. For myself, I believed in the new republic then and there in those Wicklow hills and I was prepared to die for it. It seemed only natural to me that I should want a wife and, God willing, children, to be part of my life in this New World.

It was Martin who spotted her wandering in the glen, and told me where to find her.

She sat by a stream, feet dangling in the water, a bundle by her side. The green cloak she wore on the fateful day was also by her side. She wore a simple white dress and no hat, so her long black hair hung loose. I watched her for a moment and felt as I had on the morning of the twelfth day in the church at Donard.

I called her name. She turned to me, stared at me for a moment and started to weep. I went towards her, but she got up and ran to me. She threw her arms round my neck and I held her as she sobbed. Then we kissed and kissed again, and embraced fiercely, all in a mixture of sadness, anger and desire. We fell to the grass, locked together. Her sobs began to subside as I stroked her hair. She said my name twice and then: 'You must never ever leave me again.'

'I know.'

'Good.'

'I had to...'

'I know. And you got him.'

'Yes.'

'And his head is on a spike.'

'Yes.'

'Good.'

We were silent for a while. Then she said: 'She was sweet as sweet could be.'

'She was.'

'Poor little thing.'

'Your family?' I asked.

'I have no family any more. We did not survive it. We could not. I know my father is a stubborn man and wrong in so many ways. But he is my father and I love him. Every day I tried to do right. To be dutiful. Sometimes it lasted an hour. Sometimes less. Then he would say something or I would say something, and it would start; the accusations, the anger, the resentment. My poor mother so worn down. The only end would be for me to leave.

We all knew that. They would have preferred a match for me. Had people in mind. But I didn't want that. Couldn't do that. I walked away. Over the hills and down the glens.' She laughed. 'Mountain Mary!'

"Mountain Mary' is right.'

'So, here I am Michael Dwyer.'

'I'm glad.'

'Are you?'

'Of course.'

'It is not the way I wanted it to happen. No girl would want that.'

'The times we live in.'

'Yes. And what will we do?'

'Our best.'

At that we both laughed.

She had brought some bread and fruit with her. We sat among the heather for a while and ate, enjoying the summer sun. The bees were busy all round us. We had moved farther up the hillside now and all around us was pure purple. And yet we could look across the glen at another hill which was green and yellow with gorse, then up towards the stony summit, brown and grey. We wondered that a scene of such peace and beauty could harbour so much violence and hatred.

I told Mary that my beliefs had not changed, and all the principles I had expounded by the stream and in the letter I still held firmly. She informed me that she was glad that I did.

'My father says that Cornwallis is a man for peace.'

'Yes, he wants to see us pacified, because he is a man for empire. Divide and rule is the tactic. He has no right to complain about the atrocities of the yeomen. They would not exist but for the likes of him. Your father may think himself safe, but he is not, because now no Catholic in this province is, and it is not Cornwallis and his soldiers that will protect them but Joe Holt and the rest of us.'

Then we walked and talked about our new republic, and how it would all be achieved by the end of that year, and looked forward to the new century and the children we might be blessed with.

As twilight closed in we walked into the camp at Whelp Rock. It was not, of course, an army camp in the usual sense. There were no tents, and at night every man wrapped himself in whatever clothing he had. There was little shelter, only some small caves and trees.

Mary was not welcomed with open arms there, but she was hardly aware of this being so relieved to see her brother. I was pleased that Joe Holt's wife Martha was there. Her presence was not appreciated either by the men, but Joe Holt would not send her away, and none of them would cross the General any more than they would cross me. That did not prevent some ribald banter. Martha Holt soon put a stop to that. Mary was pleased to make Martha's acquaintance, grateful that there was another woman present.

Martha was older that Mary of course; a settled, sensible woman, but refined, and conservatively dressed, always wearing a mop cap that covered her ears.

After the introduction Martha turned to me and said: 'You'll get a priest Michael Dwyer, and arrange everything properly.' I assured both Martha and Mary that I would indeed do that.

The Holts had a lean-to farther down the mountain, and Martha decided that Mary would share that with her for the time being. When I offered to help Mary with her things Martha told me that I could stay where I was. Joe Holt was to bed down in the cave with the rest of us. On hearing this Martin remarked: 'It is an ill wind!'

'It is an ill wind we'll have to endure tonight for sure,' said Hugh Vesty.

Joe Holt turned on them, saying: 'Don't bloody laugh about it. It is a condition I have. I can't help it.'

I had to put a stop to the disparagement of Joe Holt, because the General must have suffered greatly from his stomach but, during all the terrible travails he had to endure, I never once heard him complain. The following day I would have to look for a priest.

Chapter II
Michael celebrates his wedding and recalls the dreadful fight at Dairenamuck

Strictly speaking I should have gone to Father Reilly, who would have been the Parish Priest at the time, if you considered the cave at Whelp Rock as being my official residence. But he was not a man sympathetic to our cause. When his church was burned to the ground a few months later, he would change his mind. The Parish Priest of Donnard, where Mary came from, and where by rights we should have been married, could never bless our union because of the stand taken by Mary's parents. Indeed any priest who was to conduct the service would not only be going against the wishes of the bride's parents but would have been challenging the authority of his Bishop as well, because all the Catholic hierarchy were against the United Irish movement at that time. In the end Father Richard Murphy of Imaal agreed to marry us.

When I returned to the cave, I found Joe and Martha busy with pen, paper and ink. When I asked them what the business in hand was, Joe told me: 'You know this General Craig is offering a £300 reward for my apprehension?'

'Yes, I've seen the notices.'

'Well now *we're* going to put up posters offering £600 for *his* apprehension.'

That was typical of Joe Holt, and it was those kinds of gestures that endeared him to the locals, who found the very idea that we had that sort of money highly amusing. Although he differed from the rest of us in terms of class and religion, I always considered him a good Wicklow man and a true revolutionary. I wasn't to know at that stage that Joe had already made up his mind about the future for himself and his family.

Obviously, it was not possible to invite Mary's parents to the wedding or even to tell them when and where it was to take place, because they would have informed the authorities. I would have been arrested, and Mary sent back to her family home. It was some small consolation that, in Kevin, she would have at least one member of her family who would be present on the bride's side. Now we were faced with the strange prospect of the bride's younger brother giving her away.

Rumours spread quickly that the wedding party was some kind of Bacchanalian debauchery, but nothing could be further from the truth. Father Murphy presided over a very dignified sacrament, and Martha Holt and the ever-serious Arthur Devereux bore witness. I could not help but laugh when Arthur congratulated us both as 'Citizen and Citizeness Dwyer'. Although I passionately believed in our status as citizens rather than subjects, I was never completely at ease with this convention among United men of addressing each other as 'citizen', but that is a fault in me and not in them. My own parents were at the wedding, and thought me a lucky man to have Mary as a bride. They considered her to be an absolute treasure.

Joe Holt took me to one side and held out his hand to me: 'Well citizen, will you continue with this fight?'

'To the death, General,' said I.

'Well you'd better take command of our little force then.'

'What do you mean?'

'I'm finished here now Michael!'

'Joe?'

'We are going to depart, Martha, myself and the family.'

'How?'

'I will surrender myself.'

'Jesus Christ!'

'My wife knows Mrs LaTouche, who has some influence with our Member of Parliament Mr Hume.'

'You are guilty of a hundred or more capital offences.'

'I know.'

'They will march you straight to Kilmainham Jail and from there to the gallows.'

'We'll see.'

'Your wife is a friend of Mrs LaTouche? How do you think that is going to help you?'

'Terms.'

'Enlighten me here Joe.'

'Free passage for me and my family to the New World.'

'Jesus Joe, you are either mad or...'

'Or what?'

'Mad, mad, mad!'

Now if I was angry with Joe it was because he told me all this on my wedding day. Unfortunately we had raised our voices and the wedding guests heard our argument. It was not really a heated exchange, but those who heard it did not forget it. Such disagreements, when fuelled by drink, inevitably exaggerate themselves, and Joe and myself had had a skinful each. And why not? Didn't I have a double cause for celebration? In one day I had become a husband and commander-in-chief of our forces in Wicklow, now the only republican enclave that was still holding out. Even Mary had a couple of drinks that night, but I got cross with my own mother who accused me of plying the bride with a coaxiorum.

John Cullen was a great republican and, despite his age, contributed more to the fight than many of the combatants. What his age was at this time I do not know because he would not tell. When asked he would always say that it depended whether age meant how old you looked or how old you felt. I'd have to say that he looked ancient but he acted terrible young. He was a giant of a man who wore his silver hair tied back and was very proud of his massive white beard. John lived in Knockgorragh, in the townland of Ballyvoghan, between the ford at Knickeen and the Black Banks. Knockgorragh is a rounded hill covered with bracken, and on the eastern slope, environed by beautiful whitethorns, stood John's old house. It was there that Mary and myself spent our wedding night. The house was heavily guarded that night, and there had been a strong armed presence at the wedding as well, because there was a real danger of attack. I have to admit that the sense of danger added to the intensity of my joy on that day and that night.

We had fresh eggs and handsome bread that John had baked himself for breakfast. 'Twas as happy a meal as I'd ever consumed.

'What is the summer going to bring you, John?' I asked.

'Take a look up there,' he said, pointing to the roof. 'She won't last another winter.'

'Are you going to replace the lot?'

'Have to. Throw out the old thatch out and put a new one up.'

'Or maybe you could just leave the old one there.'

'Amn't I telling you, it will not last the winter.'

'No no no! Leave the old one there and construct a new one maybe six inches above it.'

He slapped his hand on the table. 'Cripes boy, that's the best idea I've ever heard. Sure, you'd be able to hide a whole battalion up there.'

'I was just thinking of a few muskets, John.'

That was the first of many nights Mary and I spent at John Cullen's, but at all times I placed a guard outside the house.

My first duty as commander was to change our main hide-out or headquarters from Whelp Rock to a cavern on Camaderry Mountain, which is nearly opposite the upper lake at Glendalough. This had been excavated in former times in the quest for minerals. The mountain, and especially on its southern slope, is riddled with old lead mine tunnels, but most of them are flooded during the winter months and would have been useless as shelters. There is one dry tunnel that measures about ten yards from its inconspicuous entrance to the edge of a perpendicular shaft. An old wooden beam is positioned across the top of the shaft to which a rope was attached, and by this means only could descent and ascent be made. It was the ideal hide-out, but hardly suitable for a woman, especially one who was newly-wed.

During what was left of that summer, Mary and I spent the occasional balmy night together on the hillside until we watched the dawn across the lakes, but mostly she stayed with friends or relations of mine, where I would visit her from time to time. This was a risky business and not comfortable for either of us, because she could never spend too long in one place. Some of the men thought the way in which I conducted my relationship posed a serious security risk, and there were mumblings of discontent. One of their number, a man by the name of Kearns, challenged me openly on this, and when I dismissed his concerns he persisted, to my great annoyance.

He was determined to prove his point. One night, when Mary and I were in bed in the house of a friend, Kearns approached the guard outside the house and said he wanted to see the captain. He moved silently to where we were sleeping, put his hand to my throat and said: 'Now, you see how easy...'

He stopped when he felt a touch of the muzzle of my gun, and realised that if I squeezed the trigger he would never have any progeny, but God knows that would have been no great loss. We heard no more from Mister Kearns, and for years Mary and I still laughed when we spoke of that incident. In those days we laughed frequently; at what, I have no clear recollection. We were happy and, in time, she was as committed to the republican cause as I ever was. Her brother Kevin's political education proceeded at an even faster pace under the tutelage of Sam, who introduced him to the writings of Tom Paine, James Madison and Jean-Jacques Rousseau.

Not all of the men took so kindly to a republican education. One day, on returning to the old mine on Camaderry, I was greeted with Hugh Vesty kneeling on Arthur Devereux's chest and applying considerable manual pressure to his Adam's apple. When I finally managed to pull the wrestler off his man he informed me: 'You know what Mister know-all is after claiming now?

'What?'

'That Oliver Cromwell was a republican!'

'Hugh Vesty, confine yourself to fighting, but be clear who is friend and who is enemy. Oliver Cromwell wanted a state without a king. That made him a republican.'

'Well by God,' said he, 'Oliver Cromwell is certainly no friend of anybody here, or if he is they have no damn right to be here.'

'No, he is not a friend of anyone here. He hated the Irish. He hated Catholics.'

A professional army will have a regime of drills and other routines, vital to keeping the soldiers occupied when they are not in the field or on the march. But we had to be quiet and keep a low profile, hiding in cramped conditions for long periods, and sometimes living miles apart and awaiting the call to action. This made it very difficult to maintain discipline and keep an eye on all the fighters.

The two Halpin brothers, who had witnessed this altercation, were helpless with laughter. I told them that I saw no humour whatsoever in the situation. I never liked the Halpin brothers, with their pointy noses on their chinless kissers. They were devotees of Joe Holt and never took to me as their leader. I kept them close and hoped that if they didn't like me, they would at least fear me. They did what they were told but never used their initiative while under my command. Instinctively I knew that the brothers should be kept apart. Insofar as I could, I sent them on separate missions to different parts of the countryside. They knew what I was doing, and they never liked it. So it was when I organised a detail to seek out places of concealment; I left J.P. Halpin to protect the entrance on Camaderry and I sent T.F. Halpin with Arthur Devereux down to Glenmalure.

In many ways we were like mendicant monks, depending on local charity to survive. Mind you, we never begged! We were also more or less nomadic. Although we usually had a headquarters, we changed it regularly and we did not all stay there all the time. We were a light, mobile army whose ability to scatter for days at a time and then regroup was fundamental to our success. For this to work we had to have caches of arms and food stored in diverse locations. We used the many caves made by man and nature for this purpose, but we also dug pits and moved large rocks as the need arose.

At the onset of winter it was particularly important to have a good supply stored up, and judging by the berries on the rowan trees the winter of 98/99 was going to be a severe one. Kevin Doyle went with Sam MacAllister over to Lug na Coille, and I went to Knockgorragh with Hugh Vesty and Martin Burke to see how John Cullen's false roof was progressing.

John had done a great job. The house looked exactly the same inside and outside, yet there was space enough between the two roofs to hide, not just arms and ammunition, but a couple of men as well. He had even acquired an impressive new hound to help guard the place. If I had known this I might have had second thoughts about bringing Hugh Vesty with me. John, a great dog-lover, had no patience with the wrestler's phobia. When we arrived he insisted on introducing the new hound to each one of us and it was sad to see Hugh Vesty trying to hide behind Martin Burke and myself. The poor man was in dire need of a drink when we got into the house, and mightily relieved when John left the dog outside.

Although John seemed contented for a man living on his own, I always made an effort to spend time with him whenever I visited. His reliable supply of very fine *poitín* made the times there pleasant indeed, and once I'd spent half an hour there I'd want to spend the whole night sitting by the fire and swapping stories. In all the years of visiting John he never told me where he got his grog, and that was typical for a man who really could keep a secret. The drink was very strong and the host insisted that we take plenty of water with it. Indeed, if you took a cup of water even the day after you'd had a feed of it, the spirit would be rekindled.

Water takes its toll, and it is bad for a man to retain it. So I went out from time to time to water the daisies as did John and Martin. Hugh Vesty never stirred and we were acutely aware of his discomfort. Finally he said: 'John, I need to relieve myself!'

'Who is stopping you, boy?' asked John.

'The bloody hound is!' Hugh told him.

'Go out of that, he won't touch you!'

'Will you not tie him up?'

'That'd be cruel, Hugh Vesty.'

'Or bring him into the house, just while I go out. I'm scared!'

'This is a good opportunity for you to grapple with that foolishness, and put an end to it once and for all.'

'But they smell fear off ya!' Hugh whinged at him.

'We'll all be smelling something else off you soon if you don't go out.' John laughed.

Hugh Vesty went as far as the door, and then he stopped dead, turned to us, and said: 'John did I ever tell you how Michael here dealt with the cavalry at Hackettstown?'

'I think you may have,' said John.

'As we forded the river we could see the cavalry lined up a short distance from the opposite bank, ready to charge. I thought this engagement, which was our first mind, would surely be our last. Tell ya they looked impressive with their spurs and their helmets and their swords. Michael turns to Martin and myself and asks us to come with him. And we had no idea why, had we Martin?'

'Would you stop hopping from one foot to the other and go out and pee!' said Martin.

'You can recount it on your return,' John added.

'Where did he take us but into a field that had a fine herd of cattle in it. We rounded 'em up and the boul'' captain told us to discharge our weapons, which we did. Well... The bullocks charged forward in a desperate stampede straight at His Majesty's mounted troops! Oh you should have seen them John, the pride of the British Hussars scattering before an onslaught of prime Irish beef!' Hugh Vesty laughed as he danced and the rest could not help but find humour in the poor man's discomfort.

'And now he sends me to my death!' said Hugh Vesty, edging towards the door, and at that point didn't the dog start a ferocious fit of barking.

'Jesus I told you, he can smell the fear even from here,' he cried.

By now we were sore with laughter, but then John quietened us, saying: 'He's not barking for no reason, boys.'

He went to the door, looked out, and turned immediately, shouting: 'Up between the roofs, quick! It is that bastard Colbert with a troop of Yeos!'

Hugh Vesty jumped on the table and lifted up, first Martin and then myself, and helped push us through the gap in the roof. Then we pulled Hugh Vesty up with John pushing from below.

We had barely got the spare thatch back in the gap when the door was kicked open, and the sound of a gunshot put an end to the barking dog.

It was a tight squeeze. We could hear every sound from below, and I was worried lest they could hear our breathing or our hearts beating. Colbert's speech had been badly impeded by the blow from my blunderbuss.

'In there, that door, quick,' he said, and I heard someone move towards the bedroom and kick the door down. At the same time the back door came in. There was now much pulling and dragging of furniture and then Colbert said: 'Up!' I deduced from this that John had been sitting on the settle by the fire. The sound of the settle being searched next, and then what I guessed was the yeos coming out of the bedroom, which was confirmed by a 'Yes?' from Colbert.

'He's not there,' said the yeo.

'Where is he?' asked Colbert.

'Who would that be Captain?' said John, calm as you like. Then a terrible crunch and groan as John was obviously hit with some force. It seemed like an eternity before he said: 'Unarmed old man is about your level Colbert. Come on! Put the gun down and stand toe to toe with me and we'll see what you're made of!'

A loud crash as the dresser hit the floor, and then other objects being thrown and smashed. John was quiet now. I was desperately concerned for him, but if we had made a move we'd all have been killed. Then there was silence until Colbert said: 'There is nothing here.' And with that we heard them move towards the front door.

Hugh Vesty did not so much burst as leak profusely. We heard it pour onto the table below.

'What's that?' said Colbert, menacingly.

'I leave bowls of water up there for the... the pigeons.'

'Pigeons?'

'They are inclined to knock them over,' John replied.

There was a shout from outside the house: 'We've got one of them, Captain!'

Colbert and his men moved outside and my heart sank as I heard him say: 'Well, if it isn't the young man with the Protection. But this time with no protection whatsoever.' Kevin never spoke, but I knew it was him; what I didn't understand was what the hell he was doing outside John Cullen's cottage. Colbert continued: 'It would give me the greatest of pleasure to flog you, but that would spoil things for Doctor Trevor, and I am sure the good doctor will be delighted to welcome you to Kilmainham Jail. He likes a young boy to be fresh and clean and unspoilt. Mount up!' Then we heard them ride off.

Coming down from between the roofs was easier then getting up, and I was mightily relieved to see that John was on his feet.

'We'll replace everything you've lost,' I told him. He bent down, picked something off the floor, handed it to me and said: 'You'll not be able to replace this.' It was a tooth. I washed his wound as the others salvaged what they could from the damage caused by Colbert and his men. John wanted to know if his hound was dead and Martin went and confirmed that he was. I told John that I would replace the dog and that Hugh Vesty would bury the dead one. There was no objection voiced to this. Now I didn't want to leave John in so desperate a state, but on the other hand I wanted to get back to camp, because I did not for the life of me know what Kevin Doyle was doing outside John Cullen's house.

Sam came towards us as we approached the camp and asked after Kevin. I told him that Colbert had taken him to Kilmainham, and for the first and only time I saw Sam MacAllister weep. While being patient with Sam in his distress, I needed to know what Kevin was doing in Knockgorragh.

Sam recovered and began: 'We were on the east slope of Lug na Coille, Kevin and myself, moving large rocks to uncover an opening that was broad enough maybe to accommodate a man. I wondered if it had been a grave in bygone times and whether we might find bones there. Anyway we stopped to get our breath and were looking across Glenmalure. Kevin saw them first, way in the distance, the troop of cavalry. Well, we watched them for a while and noticed them stop and talk to somebody. I had a spyglass with me and when I looked through I recognised the man they were talking to as J.P. Halpin who should have been guarding the cave at Camaderry. They didn't talk to him for long, but went off to the south at a gallop. Obviously the information they got was that you were over in Knockgorragh and that is where they were riding. There was no chance of me making it Michael, across the hill, dragging me leg behind me. He wanted to go and we thought it was your only chance, but it has turned out to be the worst curse-of-God decision I ever made in my life.'

'You did right Sam,' I told him. 'You did what I would have done myself.'

'We were sold, Michael. By Halpin. There is no doubt about that,' he said, 'and I want the rat. I want him dead.'

'Where is he?' I asked.

'Below with his brother and the rest of them, going on as though nothing had happened.'

'You are certain it was him?'

'No doubt whatsoever. We need no judge or jury for this Michael.'

'No, we do not Sam. But I'll be the one to do it.'

Nothing further was said. When we entered the mine the men fell silent, and I think they knew from our aspect that something serious was in progress. The two Halpin brothers sat together, as they usually did, and as I approached them I told J.P. to stand. Then I killed him with my knife, turned to his brother, and told him to bury the corpse.

I had done exactly what Joe Holt would have done, or indeed any leader of fighting men in the same situation. I had no real choice in the matter. This man had betrayed his comrades, put all our lives at risk, and the entire movement in jeopardy. Justice had to be seen to be administered; it had to be clear to the men that I would not tolerate informers, and that they would be dealt with in a summary fashion. This was the first execution I carried out, and I hoped to God I would not have to do it again.

Eventually T.F. Halpin managed to drag the remains of his brother J.P. away from the cave at Camaderry.

I don't regret what I did, and I won't apologise for it. He deserved to die. By killing in public I had shown them all that this was the price for disloyalty. It may have saved all our lives. The only mistake I made was letting the T.F go free. But what could I do? There was no proof that he had done anything wrong, or intended to do anything wrong, and therefore it would have been unjust to harm him. Mind you, if I had known the trouble and torment the same man was going to cause me in the future...

It was now important that we undertake two initiatives which would seem to contradict each other. We had to take some kind of action in retaliation, and we had to scatter. Although the old mine was ideal for our purposes we could no longer consider it safe. We would all now have to find our own individual hiding places and, once I had found a suitable headquarters, word would be sent through the usual complex channels.

The actions we took were usually reactive, the most common being an ambush, but that required a full complement of men and some prior knowledge of troop movements. Once we knew the road a troop was travelling we would send two men out against it. When these men were noticed by the soldiers they would feign fear and surprise, wheel their horses round and gallop off. The troop of course would give chase, and continue to chase until they galloped into an ambush. This simple method worked extremely well for a surprisingly long time. In the present circumstances, though, planning an ambush would have been out of the question.

Assassination of individuals or the destruction of property were the other alternatives. Harvest was over, and all the farmers, and Colbert was a farmer as well as a soldier, had their crops in. We would set fire to his barn. Some suggested that we set fire to his dwelling as well, but I opposed this. The man had children, and taking their lives would have been morally wrong and tactically stupid. Forcing the family to leave the house at gunpoint would have been too dangerous for them and us, and it would have required more men than we could safely spare. It would need only two or three people to torch the barn, and Martin, Sam and Arthur were keen to accept the task. That pleased me because they were the three most loyal and reliable men under my command.

Although the mine was an excellent concealment it had the disadvantage of awkward access, which on this day was a serious drawback. All arms, ammunition and supplies of every sort had to be taken from there and hidden in diverse places. This long and difficult task had to be done while being aware of the fact that we were liable to come under attack at any moment. It was dark night before we had accomplished it.

Then I had a job before me that was going to be more difficult than any of the work we had done that day. I decided to leave it till the morning. That night I spent under the stars, but I did not sleep, and at dawn I set out for a certain house in the townland of Camara, where my wife was staying.

From the way she hurried towards me I thought she may have already heard about Kevin, because bad news can travel mighty fast across the hills of Wicklow. When I saw the smile on her face, though, I knew that she didn't know.

'I have news!' she said joyfully.

'So have I,' I responded glumly.

She waited, I hesitated, and so she continued: 'I am with child. We are going to have a baby.' In the excitement I forgot about Kevin and flung my arms round her.

'This will be the first born citizen of our new republic!' I shouted.

'I'm pleased you are so happy.'

'Of course I am happy. I am overjoyed. But wait till I tell my mother. Can you imagine?'

Now that was tactless, and I could see that it hurt her.

'Perhaps they'll feel differently now that there is a child on the way,' I said, meaning her parents of course. She gathered her strength, determined to enjoy the moment, and told me: 'At least there is Kevin. If nothing else they will have an uncle.'

I could not bring myself to speak. She continued: 'Now, I do want to tell him myself. Where is he? Can you bring me to him?'

'I'm sorry,' I said.

'What is it?'

I told her exactly what happened.

'They'll hang him,' she said.

'No. They will put him on trial.'

'Or court-martial?'

'Not any more.'

The court-martials, or military courts, had dispensed rough justice in Wicklow during '97 and early '98, and sent many people to the gallows, but by his time they had been phased out, almost entirely.

I told her: 'No, he will get a trial and they will need witnesses.'

'Oh, they will have witnesses.'

'Any witness they have we will get. Nobody will testify against your brother, I guarantee you that.' Although I said this forcefully I could see that she set no great store by my guarantee.

'Could he be rescued?'

I thought my silence conveyed how absurd I felt the question to be, but she persisted. 'Well?'

'Nobody has ever escaped from Kilmainham.'

'I have lost him then?'

'I'm sorry.'

She wept and I tried to console her, but to no avail. Once she recovered, breathing deeply, she said slowly: 'I will go back to my parents.'

'No!'

'Throw myself on my father's mercy.'

'You will get none.'

'I must try.'

'Please! You can stay with my parents.'

She was silent.

'You like my mother.'

'Your mother is wonderful.'

'Good.'

'All your family treat me well, very well indeed.'

'Now that you are going to have our baby they will treat you even better.'

'What will they charge him with?'

'Treason, sedition, maybe even murder. Who knows?'

'All carry the death penalty.'

'Yes.'

I told her that we must not give up and that things might not go against her brother. The present situation was volatile, and who knows what the eventual outcome might be. We must hope for the best but be prepared for the worst. Mary knew about the Holts and thought that we might perhaps go the same road, but I told her that I had no intention of surrendering, and that we must hold out until the French landed.

'And when will that be?' she asked.

'I don't know,' I told her.

'We could wait for the rest of our lives?'

'No.'

'When will you know if they are not coming?'

'We will know.' I tried to assure her.

She was quite right of course. There had to be a way of knowing when or if the French were coming. I needed to give her hope and celebrate the prospect of a spring baby.

'I am what you married Mary. You know what we stand for. You agreed,' I told her, 'and you cannot turn your back on that now! It is for our children to inherit a just society that I fight. You know that.'

'Do the poor people here have anything more or less than poor people anywhere in the civilised world?' she asked.

'Less than most and more than none,' I said. 'This isn't just about Ireland, it's about the world. The whole world is changing! Look what has happened in France! An unstoppable tide will sweep away all the crowned heads and noble titles and level the ground for all men as it always should have been. I believe that Mary, I believe it passionately. We cannot give up.'

Thank God I managed to carry her with me. We went together to a quiet place where provisions had been concealed, and ate and drank. The rest of that day we sat close together and shared our dreams of the future.

When darkness fell we went together to my parents' house. First we told them the terrible news of Kevin's capture. This was greeted by a flood of sympathy from my mother, who promised to offer up prayers day and night, in the house and in the church, for his safety. My mother believed that God was merciful and would surely deliver Kevin, who was as mild and well-mannered a Christian as she had ever come across. She beseeched Mary not to lose hope.

My father was even stronger in his reassurance that Kevin would not be executed because the British now wanted to reach an accommodation with the local population and not cause further agitation. Kevin, he said, would most likely be given a prison sentence, in which case they could well transfer him to Wicklow jail, and by God we could spring him from there! Whether or not my parents truly believed this I was not sure, but their optimism certainly infected my wife, and it was with confidence she delivered her other and better news.

This was greeted with hoots of delight from my sisters Cathy, Etty and Mary, who were wildly excited at the prospect of a child being born into the house. The decision that Mary should give birth in the Dwyer house was taken without even consulting her, but she did not disagree as she was carried along in the excitement. Suggestions were already being discussed as to where Mary should sleep and give birth and where the baby's cradle should go. Much to my surprise my three brothers James, Peter and John became just as exercised about these matters. Indeed John, who was handy with the hammer and saw, started to make rough sketches of the cradle he was going to build. Nobody considered, even for a moment, the extra burden this might be on the family. We farmed twenty-four acres of mountainous land, and that yielded barely enough to hold the bodies and souls together but, as my mother would be quick to point out, we were better off than many people in the country at that time. My father stated that it was an event that called for him to 'push the boat out' and so the bottles were opened and the grog passed round. The night was spent in songs and story, but I had to leave before dawn in the knowledge that I would not be able to pass many more nights in that house during the months to follow.

The prospect of parenthood had me more passionate about the cause, but more deeply concerned about the likelihood of victory. This is why I sought out Arthur Devereux that day. Arthur could not be certain of what was happening in Paris, and the organisation of the United Irishmen in Dublin had been severely damaged by the revolution. A new structure had not, as yet, been established.

'The power in Paris now rests with the army, citizen. The Directorate is depending on them not just for security but for financial support as well.'

'So, they will hardly want to go warring in Ireland then?'

'On the contrary, they may be well disposed towards war and the income that activity in another country can bring. Above all, they want to defeat the British.'

'That all sounds like conjecture to me, Arthur.'

'Well, there is only one way to be sure,' Arthur said.

'What would that be?' I asked.

'I'd have to go to Paris to find out,' said he.

So it was decided that Arthur Devereux should visit Paris and find out for us what our prospects were for French aid. When Hugh Vesty heard this he said he was glad Paris was going to be cheered up. The hope was that Arthur would return within a few weeks and our situation would be clarified.

He set out in October '98, but by mid-February '99 he still had not returned. During this time I rarely saw my wife because I had to stay 'out' and avoid detection.

The way I avoided capture was this: I never slept in a house, always in a hiding-place or in the open air, and in wrapping myself in such covering as I carried I was always able to do so even in the severest weather. I always had some bacon and such of provisions in some concealment to which I never ventured except in the case of absolute necessity. If it snowed I made my way to a concealment while the snow was falling still, defacing the marks of my feet as I went. While the snow lay on the ground I never moved. At other times I was accustomed to go to any cottage, always without any previous notice, with a cocked pistol in my hand. I made the owner to give me full intelligence of all that was happening in the country, and to give me such provisions as the house could afford and as I chose to demand. Having done so I went off, first saying to the owner of the house to be sure and give immediate information of what he had done. Before any pursuit could be made I would be seven or so miles off. I had to live in that manner for that time, and it tested me sorely. This is how we all had to live. There was hardly a man among us who was not wanted by the authorities, and most of us had a price on our heads.

The other Halpin brother had now been taken into custody and housed in Kilmainham jail. We suspected that he was giving information to the authorities because many of our concealments had now been discovered and the food taken. It was a severe winter that year. We somehow lasted through December and January, but as February crept along our plight became desperate. I made the decision that we should all meet up, or as many of us as could safely assemble. For this to be possible I had to find a place which I knew to be secure, a location that nobody, or very few, could know about or suspect.

The families in Dairenamuck had been recruited by Holt during his time, and I had never used them as safe houses. The townland of Dairenamuck is near the south-eastern corner of the Glen of Imaal. There are three farmhouses convenient to each other there. The first was occupied by a family called Hoxey, which was about thirty perches distant from Connell's. The Toole's house—this was a family related to my wife on her mother's side, but they were estranged from the rest of that clan because of their republican commitments—was in between the two. The three houses were connected by a pathway.

On the night of February 15th 1799, myself, Sam MacAllister and ten others billeted ourselves in those three houses. Now it was even more dangerous for families to help us at this time, because landowners had been urged to evict any tenants they suspected of harbouring rebels. And most of those who helped us were tenant farmers. Ned Lennon and Thomas Clerk, who was known as the Little Dragoon, were accommodated at Hoxey's. Wat McDonnell, John Ashe, Patrick Toole, Darby Dunn, John Mickle and Hugh Byrne (that's Hughie the Brander) were at Toole's, while myself, Sam, John Savage and Patrick Costello were at Miley Connell's, which was the farthest house from the road. As we had made our way there from our various concealments the snow had continued to fall, which meant there would be no clear trail to follow.

Miley Connell had two daughters and a son. Both of the daughters were dab hands on the fiddle and Miley insisted that they entertain us, which they did to our great joy. The wine and whiskey flowed and it had the makings of a great night. Now Sam liked a drink, but he knew when to stop and I respected him for that. It did not surprise me when, at a certain point in the night, he stood up, stretched and said: 'Time to cork it!' Nobody argued. We said our goodnights and retired.

The woman of the house had prepared a bed each for Sam and myself in one of the rooms, and oh, it was a pleasure to lie in warmth and comfort. Despite the comfort we did not sleep immediately, and that was partly because we wanted to savour it and not waste it by sleeping through it, although we had work in the morning.

The action we had planned, which was the first in a while, would be against a new British regiment. It had been stationed at Hackettstown with the objective of putting manners on the local troublemakers. They were the 1st British Highland Regiment of Fencible Infantry, who were lads with a reputation, and not just for wearing kilts. Sam mused on the irony of young Highlanders, whose grandfathers were probably 'out' in the '45, coming to Ireland to quell a rebellion. One way or another we were going to give them a right Wicklow welcome in the morning. Our information was that they were to march through Imaal and then cross into Aughavanagh by way of the Ballynabarna Gap. We would lead them into an ambush at the Gap.

On the subject of changing loyalties in conflicts I teased Sam that the Ulster Presbyterians fought on the Williamite side at the Battle of the Boyne. He countered that they loved liberty more than their country. I came back at him then with the Cave Hill Oath, where Wolfe Tone, Henry Joy McCracken and Samuel Nielsen swore 'Never to desist in our effort until we have subverted the authority of England over our country and asserted her independence.'

'Never you mind about that,' he said, 'I have always put my republicanism before my nationalism. Many Presbyterians do Michael. I remember sitting with my mother and watching the bonfires blazing on the hills of Antrim in celebration of the victory at Bunker Hill. Oh yes, Northern Presbyterians were the flower of Washington's army.'

There were seven in my family, and that was not a large family for that time and place, but Sam was an only child. Neither of us could identify with the other's childhood. By now his mother had moved to Dolphin's Barn in Dublin, where she managed to procure occasional work.

'Why do we fight?' he continued. 'Of course for all the principles of republicanism and freedom, but also for the exhilaration and the glory and the challenge of the conflict. But for me there is something else, another reason why I go to war.'

'Why, Sam?'

'For the sake of the home-coming.'

Silence for a while and then I continued: 'Still, I like the company of men, the loyalty, camaraderie, banter...'

'Tenderness.'

'Yes.'

We listened for a time to the absolute quietude of the snow. I knew that Sam would like to have spoken to me about Kevin because that weighed heavily on the man, but it would not have been right for me to have broached the subject.

We heard the voices before we heard any footfalls, and quickly we extinguished all lights in the house. I looked out and there they were; about a hundred of them in kilts. I cursed Patrick Hoxley and Lawler who, despite the inclemency of the weather, volunteered to stand piquet duty. Maybe they had been surprised; it was not difficult to sneak up on a man in the snow. But then, how did the enemy know we were here? It was not a question for that particular time, but I could not get it out of my head. We could not have been spotted on the way there, and very few people knew of our association with the Connells or the other families, as we had never used them before. But the houses must have been watched.

Hoxley's was surrounded by about thirty soldiers. I heard a voice, whose owner identified himself as Captain Beaton, ordering the men inside to surrender or they would set the house on fire. There must have been a dozen children in that house and their screams were frightening. Ned Lennon then shouted that these people were held against their will, and to let them out first. The Captain ordered that all arms be handed over before anyone would be let out. There was a pause during which the screaming continued, and then I saw the door opening a little way and a rifle being handed out, butt first. The children shivered and cried in the snow as Ned Lennon and the little Dragoon came from the house, hands held above heads.

The same performance was repeated at the Tooles' house, but the response was not so immediate this time and it was clear that a disagreement was taking place regarding surrender. Toole could be heard telling them that the women and children should be left out and that the men would not surrender, but then a woman's voice shouted over him saying yes, they would surrender, all of them. The soldier told them that their lives would be spared if they came out, and that all the men of the party would be Captain Beaton's prisoners. 'Then let the Captain come in and speak to us,' Toole suggested. In answer to this the soldier told him that everyone had better come out immediately or the house would be set on fire. A window was opened and the arms were handed out. Then I heard the captain say: 'One more!' as they moved towards Connells.

While all this was taking place Sam and I primed and loaded every firearm that we had, Savage and Costello did the same and Miley Connell prepared a carbine and a pistol of his own. I told him to open the door and let his daughters and his wife out first and then follow them with his son.

'I'll send out the women sure enough, but Miles and I will stay and fight,' Miley Connell told me, and there was no talking to the man. We opened the door and Mrs Connell and her two daughters, carrying their fiddles, their most prized possessions, went out. As this was happening I shouted: 'These people have been held against their will and you must not harm them now!'

Captain Beaton then shouted in return: 'Michael Dwyer, surrender in the name of the King and your life will be spared and those of your men.'

'Our lives are in our own hands,' I replied, 'and if you want them you can come and take them.' On hearing this the Little Dragoon shouted: 'Up the Republic! *Erin go braugh!*' but a soldier put a pistol to his head and pulled the trigger. His blood spattered the night attire of the screaming women. Sam then took aim, and his shot caught the executioner square in the chest, who, falling backwards, joined the Little Dragoon on the snow. Captain Beaton ordered that the women and children be removed from the line of fire. They were herded into a barn a short distance away.

The Connell house was a solid stone structure with a thatch roof, and I had learned at Hackettstown how hard it was to dislodge an enemy from a stone structure. Nor would it be easy to set a thatched roof on fire when it was covered in six inches of snow. They would need artillery and they had none. They had numbers, yes, but we had a defensible position. While they were still in the open I knocked another one down with a shot, but if I did, Ned Lennon got a belt from a musket which sent him spinning. The Captain then ordered his men out of the range of our fire. Some of them entrenched themselves behind a cow-house which protected them from our fire. The cow-house was across the yard, to the right of the door of the house, and they found means from behind this outhouse to pour a constant stream of bullets through the door and windows. Now the fire-fight began in earnest. Some of the soldiers took up positions on the high ground to the rear of the house, but it was much more difficult to get a clear shot from there.

Miley and Miles did the reloading and the four of us fired through the windows. We were well-supplied with ammunition and I was confident that we could last for a very long time, while having to accept that the Highland soldiers were not going to go away. Indeed, if the fight did last long enough they could order reinforcements, and we had no intention of surrendering. Although nobody said so, all in the house knew that we were unlikely to leave it alive. It was a small cottage, and because the fire was coming into such a confined space, we were in as much danger from ricochet as we were from a direct hit.

Young Miles was the first casualty. As he handed Sam a musket he placed himself momentarily in the frame of the window and straight away took two shots, one to the throat and the other to the face. He bled profusely from both of these wounds, and he gurgled and choked on the blood until he could breathe no more and expired in his father's arms. Miles said a prayer into his dying son's ear, and then prayed quietly over the body.

He was deadly quiet as he primed and loaded the carbine. Sam came to take the weapon from him. Miley held on to the piece.

'Now Miley, take you my musket, and ready it. Give me the carbine!'

'That is my gun Sam, you load your own now.' The voice was quiet.

Miley knelt on the carbine and readied a pistol.

'Don't let him out the door!' I hissed at Sam.

Sam moved to the door, but Miley headed for the window.

'Bastards! Bastards!' he shouted as he discharged his weapons. He took maybe three or four bullets from them before he fell and I carried him to the table while Sam and the other two kept up as constant a fire as possible.

I propped up his head and tried to get him to sip some whiskey.

'I think I got one of them Michael,' he gasped, 'I think I did.'

'One of them? Man dear, you knocked out two of them.'

Of course he hadn't hit a thing but he nodded and said: 'Oh my God... please Michael... oh my God, I am... please...'

Then I understood that what he wanted was to say an Act of Contrition. I whispered it for him.

While trying to cope with all this we had neglected the rear of the house, and some of the Highlanders had come down from the high ground and managed to throw several burning faggots in through the window. They also fired a number of shots and caught John Savage in the back. Costello ran to the window and dragged one of the Highlanders through. He took the Scottish soldier's own scían dubh from his stocking and cut his throat. By now a slime of blood covered the floor, and every time we moved we slipped in it. The back door was on fire and a clamp of turf by the hearth was also ablaze. Now there were only three of us left to get the fire under control, load the weapons and shoot at the Highlanders. As the house filled with smoke, breathing became more and more difficult. Sam's first wound came from a ricochet which caught him in the hand.

'Jesus Michael!' he said, and I thought he was referring to the pain from his wound, but he was looking upwards at the inside thatch where sparks from the turf had lodged causing it to burn. Firing a weapon was now very difficult for Sam, and when another bullet shattered his shoulder it became impossible.

Pat Costello could hardly breathe at all and his eyes shone with panic through a face covered with blood and dirt. 'We'll have to make a dash for it Captain,' he said.

'No Pat,' I told him. 'You'd hardly be through the door before they'd cut you down.'

Gasping and coughing as he spoke he told me: 'The old lungs will give out boy. A bit of a weakness there anyway.' It was pitiful watching him panicking and fighting for breath.

'Oh funt it all to hell,' he said, 'I'll take the curse of Christ bullets.'

With that he opened the door and went out. As he staggered towards the haggard he took bullet after bullet after bullet.

It would be fair to say that Sam and myself had now reached the limit of human endurance, and I was the only one returning occasional fire to the Highlanders.

'They think there is only one of us left alive,' said Sam.

'Well, they ain't too far wrong,' said I.

'There is still some hope for you Michael. Run now!'

'No Sam, you'll be grand yet.'

'Stop that foolishness and do as I tell you.'

I feared what he was about to suggest, but knew that it was right.

'Load up your blunderbuss,' he told me, and I did so. I helped Sam to the door and he managed to stay upright there, leaning more than standing.

'Get you on your hands and knees. And when I tell you, spring!'

I crouched down and waited. Sam opened the door, presented himself and shouted: 'Let's see you spring!' Sam was torn apart by a hail of shots, and as he fell I sprung through the doorway and legged it round to the back of the house.

Two Highlanders then came towards me but they made the mistake of staying close together, and so the blast from my blunderbuss knocked the both of them over. I ran now as fast as I could through the field at the back of the house trying to put distance between me and them before they had a chance to reload. As I ran I heard breathing and footsteps behind me. I looked round and saw that one of the Highlanders had given chase and he was fast. It was better for me not to turn and deal with him because when he was that close the others might not fire. As we got farther away I let him gain and gain, and then I stopped suddenly, stepped aside and tripped him. The trip sent him up in the air and landed him on his arse. A hit from the butt of the blunderbuss stretched him. The troops at the cottage fired but I was already too far away.

As I ran I looked down at my bare feet and guessed that some of the blood on them must be my own. All I was dressed in was my flannel drawers. The snow had stopped falling now and I was making clear crimson tracks all the way. If I was to survive I had to make for a stream. I had now come over the brow of a hill and down the other side and I could see the Little Slaney down below me. I rolled down the hill and into the shallows of the river. I followed the course of the river until I came to Seskin near Camara where I made for the house of a relative of mine, one Thaddeus Dwyer.

I was in a pitiable state when I arrived there, without raiment, without hat or shoe, and my feet bleeding profusely. Thaddeus' wife heated some milk for me but when she turned round to put it in a vessel she saw soldiers outside. Thaddeus had put a charge in my blunderbuss, and I went out. There were two soldiers in the yard, but when I presented my blunderbuss to them they raised their hands. I signalled them to throw their muskets away and they obliged. As I backed away from them I kept my gun trained on them, but I did not wish to risk the noise of a shot because there were likely other soldiers nearby. At the far end of the haggard was a high ditch and if I got to the other side of that I knew I would have good cover. There was no time to delay and I ran for miles and miles through what was mostly woodland, which kept me hidden, until I got to Stranahely. There I turned up the course of Hairy Man's Brook over Cavanaghs Gap, and thence to the remote village of Corragh at the Head of the Douglas Water. I hoped and prayed that the good people there, known to be loyal to our cause, would shelter me, which indeed they did.

It was going to take me time to recover and I knew it would be safer to do that in a less populous location. I sent a message to John Cullen, believing that my safest place for recovery would be between the two thatched roofs. A message came back from John warning me to stay away because his house was being watched day and night. Worst of all he'd had another visit from the yeomen, and this time they bayoneted the thatch in the roof. This was alarming, not only because one of our most effective concealments was now of no further use, but because it was proof that somebody close to the leadership was giving them information. I swore that I would uncover the traitor who had betrayed us. Soon I was well enough to go back on the land, and although the good people of Corragh were very kind indeed, it was a risk to them and myself to be staying among so many people. Therefore I returned to my old life, living on the move, as I had now for many long years.

Chapter III
The first citizen is Christened and Michael takes a drink.

The children had gathered round Hugh Vesty who, although he was young to be a true *seanachaí*, had some talent as an actor and knew how to dramatise a tale. So he told them stories of the Red Branch Knights and the Fianna, of Glas Gaineach and the King of Spain, Cud Cad and Micad, but the story they requested over and over again was how the cavalry were routed by the cattle at the Battle of Hackettstown.

When he begun it they jumped up and down. He would have been the main attraction but for the bundle Mary held in her arms, who was my dearest Mary Anne, the very first free-born citizen of our tiny republic in the Wicklow Hills. She had not cried once that morning in the Parish Church of Imaal when Father Murphy poured the water on her head, crossed her forehead with the oil of chisum, and dabbed the salt on her tongue. We had to celebrate her Christening. My mother did not like such celebrations being referred to as 'wetting the baby's head' and so I referred to it as nothing other than we were planning a get-together. A message had been sent to Mary's parents, informing them of the birth and inviting them to the ceremony and the celebrations, but alas they did not answer. It was heartening for Mary that so many people were at the gathering with gifts and good wishes. It was a great risk holding such a party, but the need to mark such a great event outweighed the danger, or so we felt.

It was a welcome release for many reasons other than the birth. It had been a very hard, long winter and the spring had been sluggish, but now it was a sunny, uplifting May Day. Many of the people present had spent the past months living on the land, sleeping in the open, or in rough shelter where they could find it, and foraging meagre rations. So a chance for a square meal, plenty of drink, good company, a song, a story and a dance, was like a gift from heaven.

Finding the right location took much searching and calculating. A house would have been too vulnerable and too small for the number of people who needed to be there. A decent haggard with a spacious barn nearby for weather cover would have been ideal, but its position in the landscape was crucial for security. So the hooley was held at a place near Brittas, which had a commanding view of the countryside. Piquets were posted all round and no arms were permitted beyond them. It was becoming increasingly difficult to know who was friend and who was enemy.

Hugh Vesty sat beside me while he took a rest from his story-telling.

'Very few knew of our connection to the Connell's in Dairenamuck,' I said, 'and fewer still of the concealment in John Cullen's roof.'

'It had to be somebody very close to us,' he said.

'Do you have any suspicions?' I asked him.

'I surely do.'

'And?'

'Top of the list: Arthur Devereux.'

'Ha!' I waved that away.

'Where is he?'

'In Paris. Or on his way to Paris. Or on his way back from Paris. I don't rightly know.'

'Exactly!'

'What?'

'He could be anywhere.'

'Such as?'

'Comfortably lodged in Dublin Castle for instance.'

'Nonsense!'

'Why?'

'Arthur is more committed than any of us.'

'He is close to them Emmets.'

Hugh Vesty was referring to Thomas Addis Emmet and his young brother, Robert. Thomas, a surgeon and a lawyer, was one of the leaders of the United Irishmen who was in jail in Scotland at this time.

'I'll have nothing said against them.'

'Ah now, Michael.'

'But for Thomas Addis Emmet my family would not have the patch of land they work today.'

'Which proves my point. He must have influence with Hume and the rest of the gentry to get that lease for ye.'

'He is a surgeon. He is...'

'To the Lord Lieutenant of Ireland.'

'Not any more. He is in prison now, for God's sake.'

'Is he?'

'Hugh Vesty?'

'He wasn't taken at Oliver Bond's house with the rest of the leadership was he?'

'No but...'

'And he wasn't lodged in Kilmainham Jail.'

'No.'

'So, where is he in prison?'

'In Scotland. You know that.'

'Yes? Isn't that damned convenient.'

'Hugh Vesty, Arthur Devereux is not the rat in our midst.'

'No? Do you know where them Emmets are from originally?'

'Yes. Cork.'

'I rest my case.'

At this point, to my relief, my mother approached us and suggested that I might be neglecting my wife and child.

I went straight to Mary and asked her if I was neglecting them. 'No more than you are the whiskey and the wine.' she told me.

'Sure, I couldn't get near you up to now with the crowds round ya,' said I.

She assured me that she was only jesting, and I assured her that we would have the rest of our lives together. I told her that is what I was fighting for but I was aware that she nearly lost me a couple of short months ago. Neither of us wanted our children to be part of a family that had no property and no say in how their country or their lives were run. Those rights would never be given to us, so we would have to take them, and if that was going to happen in our lifetimes it would have to be by force. 'Sometimes I wonder if we know who our enemies are,' she said.

'Oh yes, we do,' I told her. 'Our enemies are the forces of the crown, and anybody who aids or abets those forces. They may disguise themselves but that is who they are.' The brief conversation was interrupted by folk coming to congratulate us and tell us whose eyes, ears and nose Mary Anne had. This was not easy for the new mother because she did not know when the three of us might be together again. It was one thing Mary putting her own life at risk by meeting with me covertly, but putting my baby girl in jeopardy could not be countenanced.

'I do so wish we could walk into a farm of our own and live and work and have more children and grow old together. A dream!'

'Just like the republic,' she said.

'Oh no!' I said. 'That is not a dream. In that I am not a dreamer Mary!'

I now had to move away from my wife and my daughter, because there was somebody of great importance to whom I had to devote some time.

After Dairenamuck when Sam had been buried, and of course I was not able to attend his funeral, my mother invited his mother to leave her place in Dolphin's Barn and come and live at our family home. Although Mary never said so I do not think she was too comfortable with this arrangement because she felt that Sam had been, in some way, responsible for Kevin's capture. If she only knew the love my dead friend had for her brother! Fifty bullets had been taken from Sam's body, or so I had been told. Fifty bullets! All for me. His mother was small and thin, but if you thought her weak you'd be wrong. When she held my right hand in both of hers, the grip was as strong as any man's. 'I'm very sorry Mam' was all I could think of saying.

'I know you are Michael, I know you are,' she said.

'Greater love no man ever had,' I said.

''Twas not just for yourself he gave his life,' she said.

'I know that. 'Twas the cause.'

'Surely. It took him over. It consumed him.'

'That it did.'

'Once he read those books there was no stopping him. I told him it was a dream, nothing more, for I did not believe that you could change the order of things. What happened in America and France changed my mind on that.'

'And Saint-Domingo,' I said, and didn't really know why I said it.

'What's that son?' she asked.

'A colony in the West Indies,' I said, 'where the black slaves revolted and overthrew their white masters.'

'I declare,' she said, 'but isn't that the world turned upside down, rightly.'

'Rightly indeed,' I said.

Somebody handed me a whiskey then and it wasn't the first of the day or even the tenth.

'Sam was never a one for strong drink,' she said.

'Oh a temperate man,' I told her.

'The ruination of many,' she said. 'It killed his father.'

'Did it? I didn't know.'

'And he was a good man.'

'Well they say now that it is a good man's fault.'

'What balderdash!'

'Ah sure, 'tis only talk Mam, and we have to be saying something.'

'You mind yourself with that stuff Michael Dwyer. My son didn't save your life so you could wreck it with hooch.'

'Erra now, we are only wetting the baby's head, welcoming my first born into the world.'

Just then Miley Connell's two daughters arrived with their fiddles, and I was mighty glad to be able to excuse myself from the company of Sam's mother. The last thing I needed that day was a Northern Presbyterian lecture on the evils of drink. I brought the Connell girls over to see the mother and child, and they both had a hold of the baby and agreed she was about the most beautiful thing they had ever seen. I explained to Mary who they were and the part they and their family had played at Dairenamuck. Mary gave each of them a hug and told them how sorry she was for their terrible loss. I told them that I was honoured that they brought their fiddles and led them over to the other musicians, because I thought it was high time the music began. My orders to the musicians were very clear: jigs, reels, slides and polkas, but none of those sad shut-eyed laments. Save those till later when the night would be drawing in and we'd be getting a bit maudlin. Hugh Vesty came up to me again. He wanted to talk, but I wanted to dance.

'A word, Michael.'

'A jig first.'

Now, Hugh Vesty dancing a jig was surely a comical sight. His belly bounced in counterpoint to the tapping of his feet, and this drew much laughter and hoots of encouragement from the assembled company. He was light on his feet for such a big man, but I had to lead him gently to a chair when the dance was over. Once he got his breath back he said: 'Joe Holt.'

'What about him?'

'That's who you think it is.'

'Ha?'

'The spy.'

'No.'

'Why did we move from the old mine once he surrendered? You knew he was going to make a deal.'

'We moved from the old mine as a consequence of the wedding party where there was an abundance of drink and too much loose talk.'

'He must have given them something to buy his freedom.'

'Is he free?'

'Well, they didn't hang him, and he was the one connected to the Connells.'

'Yes but the idea of building a false roof at John Cullen's came after Holt had already surrendered.'

'I hate to have to say this Michael, but your brother-in-law knew about the roofs at John Cullen's.'

'But Kevin didn't know about the safe houses at Daire-namuck. They were Holt's contacts.'

'True.'

'I'll tell you who knew about them, though.'

'Yeah?'

'Halpin. I should have finished him when I killed his brother.'

'Maybe so. It troubles me night and day Michael.'

'It troubles me too, but it cannot prevent us from continuing with the war, otherwise the spies will have won.'

'Perhaps we'll finish it this summer.'

'Perhaps. Much depends on the French.'

'Can't do faic without them.'

'We can hold out.'

'Yes, but for how long?'

'For as long as we like. For the rest of our lives if we must.'

'Ah now, Michael.'

'Why not? It's a stronghold we have here. A true stronghold. These hills are peppered with caves and mine-shafts. The summer is coming on and we can make as many of them as possible secure and habitable. There is a queue of young men waiting to join us now. That fight at Dairenamuck, even though it was a defeat, has acted as an inspiration to many of them. If we organise ourselves in these mountains we will be invincible; they will not be able to shift us without artillery and they have no way of getting that up here. That is what I am saying: this is our little Republic, here today.'

'I don't know.' He groaned.

'Don't you have the stomach for it?'

'Careful now Michael!'

'You go on whinging like that and anyone will doubt ye.'

I knew what was coming now: a tirade about the mighty deeds of the Byrnes. How they drove King

Richard II insane and off his throne, and how they har-
boured Red Hugh O'Donnell when he escaped from jail.
And he didn't let me down. He beat his chest.

I hoped I wasn't as drunk as him, but I think I was.

"Tis not about courage Michael. You know that. It is
about future security!'

'What has happened Hugh Vesty?'

He looked around furtively and then whispered: 'I've
met... I've seen someone!'

'I knew it. I knew it!'

'Keep the voice down now Michael. Saw her at the
Flowers of the May procession. Caught her eye just for
an instant, but I knew. I'm telling ye boy, bolt of lightning.'

'Good man!'

'Now Michael, this is to stay between the two of us!'

'That goes without saying.'

There we sat. Two boys with their secrets. Sure, we
could have been back at school. Naturally I was happy for
my friend, but I was also a trifle worried because I knew
just how malleable he might be in the hands of a woman,
but there was nothing wrong with that as long as it was
the right woman.

'You've made enquiries no doubt.'

'Naturally.'

'And?'

'Not prepared to divulge at this point in time.'

Well, he wasn't going to get away with that, let me tell
you. 'Just the two of us. Come on now. I want to know
everything: seed, breed and generation.'

'She is one of the Burkes from up by Leitrim.'

'She's related to Martin so?'

'First cousin.'

'Which Burke's is she?'

'John Joe's daughter.'

'Ah I have them now. A fiery man, but sympathetic to our cause. They say he'd have taken up arms but the wife wouldn't let him.'

'They have a rake of children, Michael.'

'True. Have you made an approach?'

'No, but I know she's not promised to anyone. What have I to offer though?'

There was a terrible sadness in the voice and, in truth, my heart went out to him. 'No more or less than myself,' I said. He thought about that for a while, and then replied: 'Not many like Mary Dwyer though.'

'Hugh Vesty, don't underestimate the women and don't underestimate yourself either. Talk to John Joe. Meet with the girl.'

'I will, faith.'

'God willing, it will all come out right.'

'God willing.'

Then he stretched out his big hand to me: 'Between ourselves!' I took his hand and assured him: 'You have my word.'

'I'll give you something for your word so,' he said, searching in his satchel and bringing out a small bottle. 'This is nectar squeezed from the finest, fermented Murphies in the County Wexford.' I took a sup and it went down like oily cream.

Oh what a gathering that was in the little haggard in the Wicklow Hills. There was old John Cullen, proud of his bruised and battered face gifted him by Captain Colbert, steady and erect Martin Burke, drink in one hand and the other clasped behind his back, Miley Connell's daughters fiddling frantically through their grief. Heroes every one! In the great tradition of Niall of the Nine Hostages and Con of the Hundred Battles, Sam of the Fifty Bullets and Diarmuid O Duimhne of the Mighty Member, and the women too, Brigid of the Churches, Deirdre of the

Sorrows, Maebh of Connaught and Sile of the Gig. Oho, boys oh boys! I let a joyous roar out of me then that could have been heard in Dublin Castle, but I didn't give a damn. I went and asked me wife to dance.

She said no.

'No Michael, not like this.'

'Well, if I can't dance with my wife, I'll dance with my daughter!' and with that I went to take Mary Anne in my arms.'

'No Michael! No! Take your hands off her when you're in that condition.'

I stopped. My mother was looking hard at me. So were some of the others.

They all stared at me.

I stood shamed.

PART 2

Chapter IV
Michael is inspired by Robert Emmet. But revolution turns to tragedy on the streets of Dublin.

'That's the second robin now for ya!' said Sarah (Byrne as she now was), and she tried to interest little Philip in the new caller to our cave, but Philip was more interested in his mother's breast than in the robin, and he fought to keep his place like a true wrestler.

'Where's the Daddy at all?' she asked her son, who seemed to care nothing regarding the whereabouts of Hugh Vesty.

'Do you know how they got the red breast?' she asked nobody in particular, and did not get an answer. 'Ah come on, sure everybody knows that story.' She went on, and I swear she raised both her arms in the air. Some set of jaws baby Philip must have had on him! 'When our Lord was on the cross, Jesus on Calvary, the robin, who was a bird of the air, took pity on him. So, didn't he fly down and land on Our Saviour's hand, and tried with all his might to pull the nail out of there, but of course the little creature couldn't budge the thing. All he got was his breast spattered with the blood of the Lord. And as a mark of gratitude God ordained that, from thence forth, robins should have a red breast.'

After the silence Mary said quietly that she thought it was a lovely story. Martin Burke then remarked that it was unusual to see robins this high up, and it was at this point I walked to the mouth of the cave. It was near the summit, with a commanding view of the hillside that was covered with gorse. So I looked down over the multitude of yellow flowers growing out of green bushes on a hot, dry summer's day, and I thought it must have been because my mind was full of images of blood and red breasts that I discerned patches of red among the bushes far below. When I realised they were moving I was snapped out of my reverie suddenly.

'Flint, steel and straw!' I shouted.

Thank God, the wind was to our back. As the gorse took light I ordered the women to cover the babies' faces and everyone to wait until the fire had spread before we started to scatter. The Highland regiment crawling up the hill cursed their luck, and I thanked the God who made robins.

Hugh Vesty had gone to Dublin more than a week since and, although I did not let on anything to his wife, I was worried about him. Now that our latest hide-out had been discovered I would somehow have to get a message to him that would redirect him to a certain shebeen in Glenmalure. Mary, now pregnant with James, had to be promised that I would drink no more than wine before herself and Sarah set off for safe-houses.

The problem with this shebeen was that to tolerate the place at all you needed something stronger than wine, because you could be suffocated with the smells of damp and mould. The quality of the liquor though was just about worth the discomfort. The first thing I heard in there was a rumour, and let me tell you that at that time rumours were more plentiful than robins in the County Wicklow. This rumour was that Hugh Vesty Byrne had been arrested in Dublin, interrogated and sent to Wicklow jail. There seemed to be a number of corroborating witnesses to this story which led me to believe that it was true. I now had to concentrate my mind on how to get him out of there but I kept my own counsel for the time being because there were a number of individuals present in the drinking den that I did not fully trust. Mind you, it wasn't safe to trust anybody in those times, but sure we had to take a risk now and then otherwise nothing would be achieved at all. So, I sat by the fire, nursing my glass, contemplating the problem and trying to work out a plan to free my old comrade.

I needn't have bothered.

Now, bear in mind how malodorous this place was when I tell ye that I smelt Hugh Vesty before I saw him. A groan went up as he entered the establishment and called for a glass of the hard stuff, but Johnny the Keep told him he should go and wash himself first.

'I'll wash you now,' Hugh Vesty told him, 'and hang you out to dry by your two splayed feet if you don't fill me a large measure and quick!'

Once he'd taken a sup I asked him where he had been.

'In Wicklow jail,' he told me

'How did you escape?' I asked.

'Through the sewer, of course!'

'There's a sewer in Wicklow jail?'

'Yes, and it goes down to the sea.'

'And you fitted in it?'

'Well, I wouldn't be here if I didn't, would I?'

'How did you get into it?'

'Some slabs had been loosened. Malachy Moran got down there a few weeks back.'

'Malachy never got out.'

'Did I say he did? It was a tight fit, and wet and smelly, but I made me way along until I came to a great mass of a body that completely blocked me way. Malachy himself!'

'Sure Malachy is a quarter of your size.'

'He was drownded Michael and his body had swelled up. Jesus I'm getting more of a grilling here than I ever got from the interrogators in Dublin Castle.'

'Go on.'

'I had to push poor Malachy ahead of me every inch of the way right down to the beach. Christ, but I was glad to breathe fresh air again. And the beach was clean. No decapitated corpses washed up! The fishermen's action must have put a stop to that. Wasn't that the most inhuman practice that the yeos ever thought up, ha? I mean hanging a man is bad enough, but throwing the decapitated corpse into the sea? And they call themselves Christians. The local fishermen were right to stop going out. Sure anyone eating fish in Wicklow was halfway to being a cannibal. Ha?'

Hugh Vesty was nervous as he prattled on, but I let him sweat for a while.

'So, what did they ask you in Dublin Castle?'

'The usual.'

Then I told him about the events of the morning: the Highlanders and the fire.

'So that is another hide-out discovered,' he said.

'Yes.'

'Somebody must be talking.'

'Somebody is talking all the time, Hugh Vesty.'

'Well, if I find out who it is I'll kill him, and I'm sure you'll do the same.'

I took his glass from him, refilled it, and brought it back. He did not have much information on the powers that be in the United Irish movement in Dublin, but everyone's hope was that another rebellion was being planned by the leaders in Paris. Formal structures were no longer in place and each group was meant to be autonomous, raising its own funds and administering its own justice. That certainly made sense to me from a security point of view. In the meantime, all we could do was wait for the bold Arthur Devereux to return from Paris.

Hugh Vesty got up then and said he wanted to join his wife.

'Well, Jaze Hugh Vesty,' I said, 'you better have a wash first or she'll be asphyxiated in the act!'

If I had known back in '98 that I would have to wait five years for Arthur Devereaux I might not have signed on for it. Of course these were five years on the run. The strange thing about living on the run is that it means stopping in one place without moving for very long periods. Then there were times when a whole group of us would be stuck in the same spot, unable to move, communicate or make any noise at all as we waited for an ambush or such. In other words, to be good 'on the run' you had to be very good indeed at standing still. This was not a facility that came naturally to children, nor should it. We were a family of five now: Mary Anne, Peter, John and the parents.

The most significant events in those few years were undoubtedly the births of my two sons. Yes, Peter and John, the sons of Michael came forth and thrived. Their mother was heroic and I was proud as proud could be. Of course I loved my daughter Mary Anne, the first citizen, as much as ever, but sons are special to a man. Sons mean strength and continuity. In those years I was in my prime, and feared no man in the County Wicklow, while a great many feared me. But the prime of life does not last forever and a man will weaken with age. It is then that he relies on the strength of his sons, and I knew that in my latter years I would be able to walk the land without fear, flanked by Peter and by John.

Kevin Doyle, in Kilmainham all this time, never met his nephews or his niece either, but they would always be told of their uncle's bravery and the sacrifice he was forced to make. Although the children brought great joy to Mary, nothing could compensate her for the loss of her brother.

Sure, on long summer days we had the best of times, running free in our own little republic, but sadly my lasting memories of those days are of partings, when the children would have to be whisked off because of an impending danger, and I had no patience with the screams of protest. So yes, I wished for an end to those days, but I also I feared that end.

There were often scattered reports of Arthur Devereux's having landed in Dublin and taken the road to Imaal, but experience taught me to ignore them. Instead I resolved to wait until I could see him for myself, could feel his firm two-handed shake, and could look deep into his eyes and know the truth. 'Are you with me until death or liberty citizen?' God bless him, he was the best of us, that little man who never smiled, but drew many a laugh from his fellows. And that is what we did when, at long last, we saw him make his way across the glen. We laughed. There was nothing particularly funny in his progress, as he led his heavily- laden horse so determinedly towards us.

'God, I hope them bags is full of silks and satins for us Mary,' Sarah remarked.

'Powder and ball might serve us better,' was Hugh's rebuke and, God forgive me, my hope was for a flagon of brandy. The bundles contained none of these things. Mind, when he first unpacked them I thought they might indeed have been clothes for the ladies because all I could see were bright greens and golds. It transpired that they were uniforms. Emerald green uniforms with intricate gold braiding.

'This must be yours, Hugh Vesty,' said Sarah, grabbing the most decorative of them.

'No,' Arthur told her, 'that's Michael's. It has the gold epaulets of a Captain.'

'Ha?' she inquired.

'The gold on the shoulders there, called epaulets,' he said holding the uniform up to me.

'Oh Michael!' Mary appreciated it.

'I'm not wearing that!' I told him.

'But it was made for you, citizen captain,' said he.

'Arthur, if you think I'm running round the hills and glens of Wicklow in that get-up, setting meself up as target practice for every half-assed yeo in the County you must be madder than I thought.'

'No, Michael,' he whispered, 'you don't don it 'till the day of the rebellion.'

Hugh Vesty picked up a uniform and asked: 'Was this made for me?'

'Yes,' Arthur told him.

He struggled but could not get his bulk into the jacket. 'Ah now, Arthur,' he said 'shoot the tailor.'

Sarah grabbed the jacket off him and wrapped it round herself, declaring: 'That is a grand bit of stuff. It'll surely keep the cold out at night.'

Arthur was not pleased and said testily: 'These are the uniforms of the army of the new Republic, please do not mock them.'

'Don't you come over here Mister high-and-mighty all the way from Paris and tell us what to do and what not to do. We have been fighting here boy, fighting the forces of the Crown, that is what we have been doing. Not swigging coffee and fitting on costumes, like some people,' Sarah told him, wagging the sleeve for her jacket, because she couldn't get her finger out.

'That is not fair now Sarah,' I said.

'Oh, yes it is Michael!' Mary joined in the fray. 'What blow has been struck for the new republic anywhere else?'

'We all know that,' said Arthur. 'We all know what you've been doing, and but for ye the movement would have folded long ago. Every time the French have wavered we've been able to come at them with the news of an ambush or some other victory achieved by the Wicklow Chieftain Michael Dwyer and his men. That was the kind of news to make a difference to the likes of Napoleon Bonaparte. What a general, Michael! The world has never seen his like. An extraordinary man, but still a man of the people.'

'Will we meet him?' I asked.

'When they land, you will,' he told me, 'and that will be the day that I will smile; when I see Napoleon Bonaparte shake the hand of Michael Dwyer.'

'Still Arthur, I would have preferred field pieces to uniforms.'

He assured me that that would happen in time. We had not yet fed and watered the man after his long journey, so we now attended to his needs. Later I talked with him on his own, but I was somewhat troubled by his proposition, and I told Mary so that night.

'But why doesn't Emmet come here instead of you going to Dublin?' she asked. 'Security,' I told her, and she understood that. Our security could be compromised even more than his by Emmet coming to Wicklow, but all my instincts rebelled against going to Dublin for a conference with all the leaders, because '98 had been betrayed by just such a meeting when the house was raided and the chief conspirators taken away in chains. I didn't know young Emmet, but I knew and respected his brother, and Arthur could not disclose the names of the other leaders.

"Tis you should be in charge Michael. You were the one doing the fighting when they were sitting around smoking their pipes. Not one of them stood by the people and defended them,' Mary said, and she had a point. 'They are dreamers, Michael. You are a soldier commanding your own troops.'

Later, as I looked at our sad stock of weapons that were stacked beside the gleaming uniforms, the truth of Mary's statement was brought home to me. No, I had not ceased to dream, but I was trapped in a conflict that had become petty and parochial, driven by the very sectarianism that Sam had warned against. The uniforms were of no use but the weapons, sad and all as they were, could still kill and maim. The most broken-down was the most over-used: my blunderbuss.

It had been a year since the weapon misfired and blew my right thumb off. Yes, I know that was partly due to my haste and the bad light in the tavern that night, and yes, the strength of the hooch. I cannot remember what that fight was about now. Some sectarian slur. It was all petty and parochial then; the right to walk down a particular boreen or to cross some disputed stream. Every action taken had to be met with a more forceful reaction. The burning of a barn had to be answered by the burning of a house, and the shooting of a cow by the slaughter of a whole herd. What all this had to do with Tom Paine and The Rights of Man, or Liberty, Equality and Fraternity, was often difficult to discern. But fancy uniforms were not the answer to the problem. Before I could throw my lot in with young Emmet I would need something more practical.

Arthur must have read my mind because it was not long before he arrived in the middle of the night with a creaking cart that had been dragged through the byways of south County Dublin into the Wicklow Mountains.

'Feast your eyes on this, citizen!' he said, drawing back the cover. And they shone in the moonlight, all brass and polished walnut, the muskets and the blunderbusses.

'Now citizen, that is more appropriate,' I told him.

'Will you come to Dublin?' he asked.

'I hate the city,' I said.

'Not to the city; to Rathfarnham.'

'That is close enough to the Wicklow border. Alone?'

'Whatever you need for security. Two or three perhaps.'

I knew I would go, but I did not give Arthur an immediate answer because I had to talk to my comrades and my wife. Mary was aware that my going to Dublin would change everything, and she feared for my safety, but agreed that we had no choice and resolved to be positive. Her one request, no demand, was that I stop at no taverns along the way. 'If you have drink taken Michael, they may get you to agree to something you'll live to regret.' I didn't argue with that and I gave her my word, even though drink was the one thing that helped me cope with the pain of my lost thumb, and tolerate the constant loneliness of the campaign.

We spent a happy night together, Mary and me, and I felt strong setting out for Rathfarnam in the morning. Staying away from drink for the journey was not difficult because the feeling of isolation that had so plagued me for years at last abated. Somehow when I lost Sam, I lost perspective, but the struggle now made sense again, and on that ride to Rathfarnam I felt connected once more; connected to the great American revolutionaries, to the United Scotsmen across the Channel, and Russell in Hamburg or God knows where, and the new French regime that was conquering Europe.

As we approached Rathfarnam we had to skirt round a major building project. The military were constructing a road, which they intended to extend all the way through the Sally Gap, and by Glendalough into Lug na Coille. Such a road would make it easier to move soldiers and artillery. No matter what happened with Emmet, our little republic in the hills would not be invulnerable for much longer.

Now, I only ever thought I was Fionn mac Cumhaill when I was very drunk, but Emmet was a man who, even in his sane, sober senses, was convinced he was the reincarnation of one of the heroes of legend. He welcomed me and told me he was honoured to meet me, and that took up more than a dozen sentences. I knew this was going to be a very long meeting. Finally he asked me what I wanted and I told him: 'Once that door shuts behind me I want nobody to leave this house until I have departed.'

'Of course Captain, I understand...' he commenced, and I interrupted him with: 'I am not asking for your understanding, citizen Emmet, merely your agreement.'

'You have it,' he told me.

That settled, I accepted the brandy I had been offered. No, I had not stopped at a tavern on the way, but I knew I would have to stay awake for this conference, and brandy would help me in that. There were five others present in the room but Emmet told me that 'for security reasons' he could not tell me their names, and I didn't bother to inform him that I knew their names anyway. They were all veterans of the '98 campaign, and I was pleased to see that a man called Quigley was the quartermaster, because there was no better man for that crucial job. Robert Emmet's plan was based on the success of the French Revolution. He planned the rapid capture of several strategic buildings, gaining him control of the city and, once it had fallen to insurgents, nineteen counties would revolt. There was nothing new in this plan, and for me it relied too heavily on the rabble. These buildings could only be captured through the use of overwhelming force, which meant large numbers of fighters assembling in crowded places, having first traversed the crowded city with their armaments in full view.

'No captain, my plan is for elite groups of veterans to gather in private houses located close to their objectives, where they'll be given firearms and special equipment. *They* will move first on an agreed signal and the main force will follow'. He then showed me a hinged pike, and I had never seen the like of it before. It could fold away and easily be concealed under a greatcoat, and these and other weapons would be distributed at the last moment from secret storage depots around the city.

My feeling was that this could be successful if the depots were both secretive and numerous enough, and the elite groups skilful enough.

'Would you care to lead the attack on Dublin Castle yourself, Captain?' Emmet asked, putting me on the spot.

'Nothing I'd like better,' I said, 'but if I am to commit to this enterprise, that might not be the best use of me and my men.'

For three days and three nights, during which I did not sleep, nor did anybody leave the house, we discussed the plan. I came to the conclusion that it was a good plan, indeed a very good plan. I grew less suspicious of Robert Emmet as time went by and I realised that all the verbiage was not a cover for duplicity. The man was simply overeducated, leaving his head full of all kinds of old stuff. His knowledge of the country was impressive enough all the same, and he had a very clear picture of what was happening in each county, even distant locations like Cork, Kerry and Clare. Local commanders were only given information on their part in the rebellion and only those in that room at that time knew the whole plan. There had been no mention of French assistance for some time, and when I asked Emmet where they stood in all this he was silent for a while, an unusual posture for him. Then he said: 'I believe they will come, but we will have to proceed on our own. The Autumn will suit their purposes best but the garrison in Dublin will be at its weakest in the summer, and I wonder if we can keep all this secret long enough to accommodate the French. At the first hint of discovery we will have to move, because this is *our* revolution citizen and not another front in Napoleon's war against the English. We will however need firearms from France to carry this out. I think myself that it would be most convenient for them to be landed on the Wicklow coast. Would this be appropriate?'

'Guns are always welcome in Wicklow,' I told him, and added: 'You can trust me.'

'I know,' he said, and then he had the courage to add: 'I do hope that the rebellion in Wicklow will not be used as a pretext for insurgents to repossess lands that have been forfeited by them.' I looked at him for a long time, and he held my look without flinching.

'You have my word,' I told him.

He then read out for us, *The Manifesto of the Provisional Government*, and I urge you all to read this fine proclamation because nothing more succinctly expresses our grievances and aspirations. But I wish most of all that you could have heard him read it, and you would know that this was an actor who could have graced any stage in Dublin or London. He was not a tall man, but when he spoke he somehow gained in stature as he strutted and gesticulated. I had been three days and three nights without sleep when I heard it, but I had to admit (privately of course) that the young man was a true visionary. Attached to the proclamation were thirty decrees that directed how the new republic would be established.

The ride home was arduous.

I awoke to joy as I was greeted by four smiling faces: Mary my wife, Mary Anne, the first citizen, and Peter and John, the sons of Michael. If I felt sick in my head from all the brandy I did not notice. All the best sleeps I had in those days were in John Cullen's and I was grateful now for this free time with my family in that house, even if it did mean having six men on piquet duty. The memory of her honeymoon in this place was sweet to Mary, but now tinged with sadness because it was here that her brother had been taken into captivity. Kevin was now in New South Wales, transported thence with Holt and Halpin. It broke Mary's heart when the authorities refused permission for her to visit her brother before he departed. He never got to see his nephews or his niece, and Mary would never see him again. That was hard.

Most of that day was spent looking at the rain, which did not cease for hours, but all that mattered was the closeness and the peace. No doubt it was punctuated by Mary Anne's fantasies about her life as a princess, and what she would wear and what her handmaidens would wear. There we were enduring all kinds of hardship for the new republic, and my daughter wishing she was royalty. That evening when the weather had cleared and wife and children were escorted to my parents' house I stayed with John Cullen.

I told John about Emmet's request to raise an army and march on Dublin but I did not reveal the details of the plan. John said: 'Wicklow will not rise for Robert Emmet but it will for Michael Dwyer.'

'How many men could we raise?'

John and I felt confident there could be at least five thousand ready and able to fight. That was a great many lives to have on my conscience.

'And do we get to fight in Dublin?' Curley Casey asked as he lifted a collar onto a massive white Clydesdale. I did not bother to ask him how he came by such a fine animal.

'We march on Dublin once the lads there have secured it.'

'Hmmm!' Curly, so called because he did not have a single hair on his head, emitted something between a groan and a growl. As he fixed the tack he did not look at what he was doing, or at me, but stared straight ahead past his house as though he expected an assault from God knows where or whom. This was most disconcerting, and I think it was meant to be.

'Problem?' I asked him.

'Like to be first there.'

'Why?'

'Before all the rich pickings are gone.'

'Emmet won't allow plunder.'

'Oh!' and he paused in his work, 'Emmet is giving the orders, is he?'

'No, I am.'

'And you'll stop us will ye?'

'Yes.'

'Rich!' he spat as he moved round the horse to tighten the girth. Now he stared over his fields and past his herd with the same concentration.

'We have to be an example to the rabble in Dublin, Curly. Establishing and maintaining order will be vital.'

'Once we have won we get the old ancestral lands back, is that it?'

'Not immediately, no. There will be a prohibition on transfers of landed property, and everyone continues to pay rent until the National Government is established. But all church lands will become the property of the Nation immediately.'

'You see Michael, I wonder if we are not just going to replace the English with the likes of Emmet, and all the other Protestant professionals and merchants.'

'No. We will *all* have a vote. No more tithes. No more established church. Absolute freedom of worship. All faiths living together, respecting and being respected.'

'You think that will work?'

'It must.'

By now he was ready to put the horse to the cart. I lifted one of the shafts and he the other, and we hooked on the chains from the breeching.

'When?' he asked.

'By the Autumn.'

'Firearms?'

'We expect shipments. I'll see you get delivery.'

'All right.'

'How many will volunteer from here?'

'Volunteer? They will do what they are damned well told and like it. I run these townlands Michael, and my word here is the law no matter what Dublin Castle says. Nobody makes any money or contracts any business without a contribution to the local army council of east Wicklow, which monies I collect and hold on their behalf, as you do in your territory.'

He looked at me now for the first time and I asked: 'How many men?'

'Six hundred, you have my word.'

He extended his hand and I shook it.

'All or nothing, then?' Mary asked when we were in bed together one morning in a safe house, a rare event in those times.

'Does not have to be,' I said.

'But if it fails?'

'It is a good plan, Mary.'

'I do not doubt that, husband, but it is war and so much can go so wrong so easily.'

'If he takes Dublin, we will hold it and we will not be dislodged, whether the French land or no.'

'If he does not take it?'

'Then we will not move.'

'Ah!'

'So you see. Safe, either way.'

'I married the smartest man in the seven parishes,' she said, and I didn't argue with that. So, we kissed, but then she was silent for a while.'

'What?' I asked.

'I think,' she said, 'after this nothing will be the same again.'

'Probably not.'

I talked about Emmet's manifesto and the concept of the new republic, and how all the British officers and soldiers captured would be taken hostage, and held until ours had been returned.

'Even those who have been transported?' she asked excitedly.

I read from the manifesto: 'The intention of the Provisional Government of Ireland is to claim from the English Government such Irishmen as have been sold or transported by it for their attachment to freedom, and, for this purpose, it will retain as hostages, for their safe return, such adherents for that Government as shall fall into its hands. It therefore calls upon the people to respect such hostages...'

'So, I may see him again?'

'Kevin? If we win, you will.'

'Well, what are you lying about here for?' she asked and gave me a push.

That day I stole a race horse and rode like blazes all the way to Rathfarnam.

This visit was shorter than the last and very tense. But now, considering the weight on his shoulders, Robert Emmet was holding up remarkably well. When I told him that I would be able to commit five thousand men to the effort he embraced me warmly, but I repeated my condition that I would not move until he had taken the city.

'I want two hundred good Wicklow men to be part of the fight in Dublin. Each of the neighbouring counties is making a similar commitment,' he said pointedly.

Shaking the head, I pondered and waited, but I knew this was an excellent opportunity to give Curly Casey just what he wanted. 'You have them,' I said.

'And I need a diversion somewhere in the south County to draw some troops away from the city.' I agreed that I would come up with something.

The signal was to be the firing of some rockets which would be seen from the Dublin Mountains, and then an agreed signal would be relayed from there to us in Wicklow, and we would march. Emmet was thinking of using rockets not just for signalling, but as a weapon. Fired directly into a column of troops, think of the damage they could cause! At this point he showed me one of his exploding planks. This was a beam that had the centre cut out, and was then lined with explosives and stuffed with shrapnel. These were to be laid across some of the roads and bridges that the military would use. The beam would be picked up and tossed to one side, and the impact would cause a charge to be set off, exploding the plank and wreaking havoc.

I had refused the brandy offered to me when I arrived, but now he offered me a drink for the road. 'Deoch an doras, as you'd say yourself?' I told him that I did not speak the language, but that I looked forward to having a drink with him in Dublin Castle once he had declared the Republic. Emmet came outside with me and admired my horse. I was going to sell it to him, but changed my mind and instead I returned the animal to its owner when I got back to Imaal. If Emmet could fire your imagination he could also stir your conscience.

It felt to me like the whole country knew a rebellion was about to break out, but nobody was doing anything about it, and it was rarely referred to in company unless for practical or tactical reasons. When the trees blew in the summer wind it seemed that they were heavy with the secret that had been told to them again and again, and soon, very soon, it would be known by all. Would the rebellion break out before the plan? We watched and waited. Men spoke gently to their wives and children, treasuring these times with them because any hour could be the last. I had much to do each day and I was glad of that. For Mary the time weighed heavily but I felt her support wherever I moved. She believed so passionately in the rightness of the cause, and even spoke of being reunited with her parents. Her father would surely accept the new status quo once he, as a Catholic, for the first time had the right to vote, and of course Kevin would be returned from New South Wales, and there'd be good times in the old country again. We watched for signals or for riders coming from Dublin.

To begin with the news was good. There were peace talks between the English and the French, but it was clear that both sides were gearing up for a new outbreak of war, and the English garrison in Dublin was now at its weakest in six years. Only one further cart-load of firearms reached us, and a very small shipment had been landed on the Wicklow coast. Curly Casey had taken possession of these because he would be the first to move. The news from the other counties was good as well, and it looked as though Robert Emmet's plan, in which I always believed, was indeed coming together. But then, when that fateful July morning dawned, I saw Arthur Devereux galloping across the glen, and knew by the cut of him that something was wrong.

He dismounted, sweating and gasping, and told us: 'There has been an explosion in one of the arms depots in Dublin.'

'Which one?' I asked

'Marshalsea.'

'Christ, that's only the biggest,' I said.

'The authorities had not discovered it when I left,' Arthur puffed, 'but they may have done by now. We must bring everything forward.'

I mounted and rode east for Curly Casey. Oh, he was ready and willing and I knew that there would be few who could match him and his men in close-quarter fighting.

'You will split up,' I told him. 'Twos or threes if possible. Stagger the departures and use every highway and byway.'

'And did you teach your grandmother to suck eggs before you left Imaal this morning?'

'This is not an east Wicklow cattle raid,' I told him, 'but a proper war.' That stung. 'You know the designated taverns in Thomas Street and Cut-Purse Lane?'

'Yes chief.'

'See they go easy on the hooch.'

'I hear you've sworn off yourself.'

'For the campaign.'

'I salute you for that, Captain.'

'Thank you citizen.'

I had told him about the explosion at the Marshalsea depot, and we both knew that it was impossible to predict what situation he would face in Dublin.

The muster in Wicklow was well-organised and went according to plan. We waited for the signal rocket or for Arthur Devereux to come and tell us that all had failed. Hours turned into days, and nothing happened.

In the end it wasn't Arthur who rode to us with the final news, but one of Casey's men. He told us: 'Everything that could go wrong with the plan did go wrong. Curly is captured and Robert Emmet is on the run. Ah sure, it was over before it ever started. We waited for rockets and signals, but there were new rumours every half hour. 'It was postponed'. That was the official word. But then fighting broke out anyway. Next thing we know Emmet is on the street. Uniform, sword, fancy hat, the lot. But the rabble! Fucking city rabble. No, that's not fair! There was men from Meath and Kildare among them. And all right, yes, there was Wicklow men there too. Dragged Lord Killwarden from his carriage and piked him on the street. Yes, that most liberal and popular of all the judges, on the filthy street. Oh Emmet didn't know anything about it. Army moved in. Shot some, arrested more. Most escaped, but the swoops will start now.'

'Emmet? I must find him.'

'I'd say he might find you first, Captain.'

'No Michael, distance yourself from it. We agreed!' was what Mary said when I told her I had sent people out to try and contact Emmet.

'But it is not over,' I said.

'You know it is,' she told me.

I did not add at this point that I had offered Emmet my protection and invited him to come to the Glen of Imaal. It transpired however that he turned down my invitation, but the messenger informed me that Emmet remained confident that the organisation in Paris would stand firm and we should regroup because he was certain the French would land in the autumn. But I knew Robert Emmet would not last on the run without my protection, and I suspect he did not come to Imaal for fear of putting me, my men and my family in jeopardy. Make no mistake, he was a gentleman. The most foolish thing the English ever did was putting him on trial, and the next most foolish was his execution.

News of his trial was brought to us almost daily and the tactics of the prosecutor outraged us. Because there was so much dismay evident in the country over the death of Lord Kilwarden, the authorities expected support for their crude vilification of Emmet. This was a sorry miscalculation, and yet another example of the English inability to take the pulse of Ireland, or even to discover where that pulse might be. Curly Casey had already been dispatched—hanged and beheaded—and it was an east Wicklow man who had witnessed his leader's demise who told us what he thought Emmet's sentence was: 'Hung, drawn and quartered.' We were with the Byrnes when this news was relayed to us, and Sarah greeted the news with a scream, and continued with a tone that was something between fear and relish: 'Jesus, Mary, he'll be drawn on a hurdle to be half-hanged, and then he'll be taken down and sliced before his own very eyes, and his insides will be taken out and burnt and him looking on, and then his head will be chopped off and he'll cut into quarters. That's the sentence so.'

Arthur Devereux went to Dublin for Robert Emmet's execution. I was tempted to go to Dublin with Arthur, but I listened to Mary's advice and stayed in Imaal.

When Arthur returned he told us of the events of that dreadful day: 'They would not let him wear his green uniform, in the same way as they refused to recognise the commissions granted to Wolfe Tone in the French Army. Fear of giving us any kind of legitimacy I suppose. He wore a black velvet stock and a pair of hessian boots. The gentleman revolutionary, indeed! He was accompanied in the carriage by two clergymen, Grant and Gamble. They took the longest possible route from Kilmainham to Thomas Street, crossing the Liffey at Island Bridge, and then along Connyngham Road, Parkgate Street and

Barrack Street. They were lined, these streets, Michael, Dublin had turned out. I followed it every step of the way, which was easy because the pace was so slow. They crossed the river again at Queen's Bridge, and he looked into the Liffey for the last time and said something. I did not understand what it was but a man beside me thought he heard him say: 'Ebb tide'.

'The crowd was packed tightly along Bridgefoot Street, but it was in Thomas Street that the real throng had gathered, and the procession could now only move at a snail's pace. It was three o' clock. Two and a half hours to get from Kilmainham Jail to Saint Catherine's Church on Thomas Street! The scaffold had been erected outside the church, a massive wooden structure, as close as possible to where Kilwarden had been killed. That act was anathema to him. You know that Michael, he abhorred it. They knew that, and the thousands and thousands watching knew that. The scaffold was guarded by the 21st Regiment of Scottish Infantry, but it was very high and the platform was clearly visible, as was the evil-looking noose. Twenty minutes elapsed before he alighted from the carriage, flanked by the clergymen.

'When he ascended the platform he called out to the crowd: 'My friends I die in peace and with the sentiments of universal love and kindness towards all men.' Two times he was asked if he was ready and two times he said 'no'. He looked into the crowd and seemed to be searching for something. Then the whisper went round the crowd: 'It's Michael Dwyer and his mountain men. That is what he is waiting for. They'll rescue him yet.' On the third time of asking the board was shunted and he fell. Hung there, choking quietly for a minute, no longer, but then suddenly he struggled violently and a gasp went through the crowd. He subsided and was taken down. His head was cut off and it was held aloft.'

'Ah Jesus now. I mean, he didn't expect our men to go galloping through...' Sarah started, but I left before she finished.

I knew where I would do it, and had known for some time. Well, not for that long because it had only been two months. Murt Murphy's shebeen was my den of choice. This was better than a tavern because it was quiet and private, and unlike most other such establishments it was clean and well-ordered. It was a room, a kind of parlour I suppose, joined to the main farmhouse. Murt was a giant of a man, and the premises opened and shut at his whim. You obeyed his rules or you departed very quickly. Most important of all you knew what you were getting to drink, where it came from and how strong it would be.

'Brandy is what I'm used to now Murt,' I told him.

'Paris would be the place for that Michael.'

'I think I'll go there so.'

'You'll have a drop of the craytur first?'

'Ah sure, I might as well.'

The drink was served and then, silence. Murt was a true gentleman, but he had no fancy britches. His wife was a lady in boots and an apron who talked only of the animals, the crops and the children. No questions were ever asked. Sometimes the drink does not numb the pain, but it allows you to take it in your arms, nurse it and make it better on your own. That is how it was for the first hour or so. I was alone. In time people would wander in, but by then I would be ready, unwound and maybe even a little loquacious. Murt was standing behind the counter, thick arms folded across his barrel chest, and I realised that I must have been staring at him for several minutes.

'So...' he said, and it was difficult to discern whether that was a question.

'Sad old time,' I said.

"Tis over then…' and once again this might or might not have been a question.

'Not at all.'

'Oh?'

'You'll see French troops here yet. Have no fear.'

'Oh, I have no fear. As long as they keep fighting the English I have not a care in the world.'

'That a fact?'

'Price of barley has almost doubled this year, and what they're paying for butter you wouldn't believe.'

'Go 'way?'

'Oh yes sir, we prosper.'

'Do ye, now?' I gave the question enough weight to convey that it was not rhetorical.

He met me though, putting his ham fists on the counter and leaning forward while he held my look: 'That we do.'

After a pause I said: 'This is no time for business.'

'No, that time is gone now.' he said, but I did not take the bait. He continued: 'So, what do you think?'

'Ha?'

'Of the drop.'

'As good as I've tasted.'

'He is a master craftsman. Oh, that he is, sir!'

'Long may he continue.'

'Oh, that he will as long as he's let.'

'And who decides that?'

Murt laughed: 'You never lost it chief, you did not sir.'

'And I don't intend to.'

Murt's laughter continued, as the door opened and a weak voice announced: 'God save all here.' I turned and said: 'And God save you kindly, Muiris O'Donnell,' to the timid little harper who stood in the doorway with his son Tomas, a good foot taller than he, who carried the precious harp wrapped in hides.

'Welcome both,' said Murt.

'Mister Murphy, give the travellers what refreshments they desire and I'll settle the account.'

'Ah, the Chieftain himself!' said Muiris.

'In the flesh, sir!' said Murt serving them the drink.

'How is the eyes with you, Muiris?' I asked.

'I can see shapes is all,' he told me.

'It hasn't affected his playing, mind,' young Tomas assured us.

'That was a sad loss in Dublin,' Muiris said.

'It was then,' I agreed.

'I went to mass for him,' Muiris continued. 'I know he's a Protestant but it'll count just the same, I'd say.'

'I'm thinking of putting a notice over that door: No politics and no religion,' Murt stated.

'What'll there be left to talk about so?' asked Muiris.

'Or sing about, for that matter,' Tomas added.

The place filled up soon enough because word had gone round that Muiris was there, and myself, I suppose. Murt rubbed his hands together at the thought of the money he would make. It was a good night to begin with as far as I can recall, because I was in and out of awareness. Muiris' music was sad and sweet as ever, and helped to purge my pain to some extent. The conversation was cautious and I took little part in it. Folk avoided the topic of what happened in Dublin and what might now happen in Wicklow and throughout the country. There was enthusiastic talk of bumper harvests and the money that would be made, but some were wise enough to temper their enthusiasm because they knew I would be coming looking for my cut. The usual *ráiméis* was talked about the prophecies of Colmcille and Pastorami and when exactly the destruction of the heretics would be brought about in

Ireland. I took no part in any of this as I drifted slowly towards the oblivion which was my destination that night.

People came and went as distant shadows and echoes. At one point I was aware of how solid and strong Murt Murphy was behind the counter. Just as solid but suspended a few feet away from him I saw the head of Robert Emmet, still bloody, and the eyes looked at me with unbearable sadness. 'You must not scream; you must not scream!' I told myself. I must have banged the table because people asked me if I was all right or what did I want. 'A martial air,' I said, 'something rousing for us all to sing. I have had enough of all this morbidity and negativity!' Muiris struck up a march, 'The Rising of the Moon', and the company joined in with gusto. Once that had got underway I went out to the yard to relieve myself. The moon indeed had risen, but Robert Emmet's head hung beside it and the eyes looked down on me with compassion as I pissed on the steamy cobbles. When I returned I feared to look anywhere in case it might appear again, and drink, drink and more drink was the only thing I thought might keep it at bay. I did see it again once or twice, but only in the periphery, and somehow that was even more frightening. Eventually I fell out of consciousness.

The sun was streaming through the windows as I awoke, dry and half-blind with a thumping pain. Murt came through from the kitchen and asked: 'Well Michael, how is the head?' I panicked at what he meant by this. Had he seen... No! Did I say something? Was this a sneer?

'What do you mean?' I asked and he just laughed, just laughed at me. Then all the anger and tension and frustration focussed on him, and I shot out of my chair straight at his Adam's apple, which I grasped with all my might to tear from his throat. It took big Tomas the harper's son, two farm labourers and Murt's wife and children to pull me off him. Once they'd pinned me down Murt went behind the bar to fetch something, and I was sure 'twas going to be a hurley with which he was going to lay into me. But no, it was a poster of me, a new one, looking like a mad dog, and a reward of five hundred pounds was being offered.

Murt whispered, angry and hoarse: 'Do you see this, Michael? Do you know how much education this would buy for my children? And I am tempted now Michael, very tempted. Your day has come and gone, and I want you out of here. Go home, Michael Dwyer!'

Chapter V
1803/1804 was a harsh winter and Michael relates how he made the best of a bad lot between Beresford and Hume

I walked the horse. Home? Not an easy concept for me to grasp. Home for me at that time was not so much a place as a set of people: my wife and my children. With them I felt the peace and security so central to the idea of home. We were not nomadic like Muiris and Tomas, because we stayed in one region. Someday we would have a dwelling that would be ours, but where or when such a place might be, I could not tell on that September morning. That day the stopping-place was a cave on Lug na Coille, where peace and security awaited me. Whatever hovel or dug-out we were holed up in those days Mary, God love her, arranged things in such a way that it had some little feeling of being a home: she would set out makeshift tables and chairs, which were rocks and sods in reality, and always placed her little statue of the Virgin in a corner with such flowers before it as were in season. On my way I stopped at a mountain stream and washed my face, which was painful but purifying.

As I approached the cave I knew that whatever else may await me it was not peace, because I could see my wife pacing up and down, hands on the hips. Now in those days she was tolerant of my binges as long as I stayed away from the family when I was on them. So, I knew it was not anger at me.

'Trouble?' I asked.

'Arthur and Sarah!' she told me, holding up the fists and shaking her head in anger.

'What is it this time?'

'He praised the child but refused to bless him. She is in a thundering rage, and he is as smug and stubborn as always.'

'Hugh Vesty?'

'Gone for provisions.'

'That's something.'

You see Sarah was convinced that Arthur had the evil eye, and what he had done now was proof positive of that fact. As we all know, the way those with the evil eye curse a child is by praising it without blessing it. Arthur had said Philip was a grand lad, but did not add 'God bless him' or 'God spare him' or better still 'God bless him and spare him'. 'Tis a simple and polite thing to do, whether you believe in piseogs or not. On the subject of faeries and the other world I remain neutral, but I certainly would never cut down a faerie tree or go digging up land in a faerie fort. Sarah believed that the Sidhe were ever present, and they lived in their world and we lived in ours, but they could see everything that went on in our world, whereas we rarely got a glimpse into theirs. Every time she saw a swirl of dust or heard a rustle in the grass it was a faerie. There was nothing I could do about Sarah, so Arthur was the one I had to confront.

'No, Michael!' was his starting point.

'It is only a couple of harmless words Arthur. 'God bless' or whatever.'

'I do not believe in God, Michael. I am an atheist.'

'Arthur!'

'As long as we are mired in this kind of superstition we will never be able to take our proper place alongside the other nations.'

'Please Arthur, just do this thing before Hugh Vesty gets back.'

'I am not afraid of him.'

'That's the problem Arthur. He'll break your neck.'

'I'll have a pistol primed and loaded.'

'Excellent! You'll kill Hugh Vesty and then I'll kill you, all over a couple of simple words.'

'It is the principle.'

'This is tactical. Just look at it that way. We are on a war footing and we cannot afford to be shooting one another. Do it!'

Reluctantly Arthur went into the cave to speak to Sarah, and Mary came to me, put her arm round me and thanked me. She asked me if I'd had a good time on the tear and I told her I hadn't. Apparently she had not had a happy time either and we agreed that perhaps there was a lesson in that.

'There is a new poster doing the rounds,' she told me.

'I've seen it.'

'£500 is a fair sum.'

'No arguing with that.'

'So?'

'What?'

'The future?'

I said nothing and so she continued: 'We can't last forever.'

'I know. Once that damned road reaches here they'll be able to wheel artillery up and our fastness will be no more.'

'It will take a while for the road to get here.'

'I know. Let us hope the French reach us first.'

'You are convinced that they will come?'

'I don't know, but I can't see an alternative.'

The silence lasted for some time. I knew this was a conversation that had to take place sooner or later and I was conscious of the fact that my wife had been restraining herself from putting pressure on me. She looked away now and waited. Mary had been stalwart through all the years and now she did not want to express her deepest fears.

'Talk to me,' I said.

'I love you and I don't want to watch you die. We are a family and we are happy when we are together. But I don't think we will ever be able to be together, here in Ireland. I'm sorry, I have lost my belief, my confidence. You are my husband and I will stand by what you want, but now it will be against my better judgement. Consider it carefully for the sake of our children.'

It was the rightness of what she said that made me angry. I shouted: 'You want me to surrender to give in. Everything we've... All for nothing!'

'No, it won't have been for nothing. What you achieved has given you a reputation outside this country, and there are places where you would be welcome.'

'For instance?'

'America. Oh, I think you would get a mighty welcome there.'

'A revolutionary hero!'

'Exactly! A true republican hero!'

She had opened the door to a future I had never imagined, and now she enticed me further: 'A republic, Michael, where we would be free and equal.'

'You think Hume would give us such terms?'

'They want to put an end to this rebellion, and you are the last remaining obstacle to that. The English don't want to be building roads and sending in armies. They just want you out of the way. Let us ask Hume at least.'

'If I ventured near Humewood I'd end up shot or in chains.'

'I'll go. There is no price on my head.'

'I won't have that.'

'What do you suggest?'

It was now time to be realistic and so I woke myself from dreams of the green fields of America. I said: 'I cannot desert my men. They have stood by me always.'

'Do you put loyalty to your men before your family?'

'Wife, do not force that choice on me.'

'I'm sorry.'

'I'll talk to them. Sound them out at least.' And I closed the conversation with that.

When scheduling tasks I always chose the most difficult first, and so resolved to speak to Arthur before the others.

There are times, although they are rare, when I dislike somebody on sight, but that happened with the Frenchman. Immediately I saw him standing with Tennison and Arthur I knew I'd get more respect from the horse he rode in on. He had a big hook nose on him and a long, scraggy French neck. He sniffed about him with disdain and disbelief. Now the weather wasn't with us, I'll grant you that: a murky November day had decided to present itself at the end of September, and the dank, heavy mist clung to clothes and flesh. The two horses that himself and Tennison had dismounted snorted plumes of steam.

I'd known Tennison for a number of years. He had been sworn in back in '97, fought in Kildare in '98, and made it to France at the end of that year. I shook his hand and welcomed him back. We expressed our mutual regret at the demise of Napper Tandy, who had died in France the previous month, and then Tennison handed me a sealed letter from the leadership in Paris. I suggested that we retire to a safe tavern, where I might read the letter and write a reply.

Well if the Frenchman didn't like the great outdoors of the County Wicklow he hated the inside of Johnny Mac's tavern even more. He dusted the bench with his gloves and coughed at the smoke of the old turf fire. When asked to take off his fine expensive riding coat, so that he might feel the good of it once he got outside, he refused. Perhaps he was afraid it might be stolen. He turned down strong drink saying he would only have wine, and when he tasted the wine he spat it on the fire. The rest of us downed a couple of stiff ones. The Nose then mustered all the English he could in one broken sentence. Not that he spoke through his nose, mind. Ah no, he did that through another part of his anatomy entirely. Anyway the gist of the sentence was that it would be an easy thing to kill a drunken man with five hundred pounds on his head. I told him to wait a few hours and see how easily a drunken man could kill a Frenchman with a big nose on *his* head, but I think the joke was lost on him. He rambled on in his own tongue for a while and Arthur told me later that he was bemoaning the prospect of any young Frenchman giving his life for such a God-forsaken place.

The letter assured us that the French still planned a landing of at least ten thousand men, and they wanted guarantees from us that we could match their force with a United army in Ireland. As soon as such guarantees were received they would send us a letter by return informing us of the proposed date of the landing. I felt I could give such guarantees, but could I rely on the French? Obviously this brought an answer from the Frenchman to the effect that the debacle of the rebellion in Dublin did not inspire them with confidence in us. I told him of course that it would not have been such a debacle if we had received the thousands of muskets promised us by the French. He retorted with the fact that the French managed their own revolution without outside help. At this I had to explain to the man that the French revolutionaries were able to get their national army on their side, but that the army in this country was not an Irish army but an English army of occupation. I further pointed out that there was a situation of religious conflict in this country which did not pertain in France, seeing as how they persecuted, killed or banished all the Protestants from their country long ago. It is probably just as well that the argument took place through interpreters because that process took some of the heat out of it.

The end result was that no blood was drawn, and I gave them my letter to take back to France. Obviously all this meant that dreams of America had to be postponed, which was a bitter disappointment for Mary.

I had met Beresford in my youth, but had no clear picture of him now. He was from Waterford, but had spent much time in Wicklow before joining the British army. His service in India gave him experience of subduing insurgents and conducting a campaign in mountainous terrain. All in all Brigadier General W. C. Beresford was the ideal man to lead the hunt for Michael Dwyer, and I waited with interest to see what his first move would be.

I found out when I saw John Cullen's blue drawers. John never revealed how this same garment happened to be dyed blue, but blue it was—pure cobalt blue. They were easily visible, and John hung them on a line to the front of his house as a signal for us to stay away.

When we saw them on this particular day we hid and kept watch on the house through a spyglass. As John came out of his door to go to his reek of turf he was accompanied by a young man who was dressed as an ordinary labourer. Another young man then appeared in the doorway soon after. So Beresford had billeted soldiers in John's house. He did the same with just about every safe house we used in Imaal and Glenmalure. Every time an occupant of one of the houses (male or female) went anywhere they were followed by a soldier. On every pathway or pass we used he placed an armed guard, day and night, every day of the week.

His plan was to choke us. This forced us to move only on foot and through the most difficult terrain. In reasonably mild autumn weather this was a hardship which was bearable, but in the cold and snow of winter it might not be tolerable. But, please God, the French would arrive before then.

October came and went but we heard nothing from across the water, and it certainly didn't take that long for my letter to get there and a reply to get back to Wicklow.

Despite the dire scarcity of food, Hugh Vesty seemed to broaden rather than shrink, and found hill-climbing more difficult than ever. And if it was tough on him in the summer it was harder still once the winter frost started to set in. On that November morning in 1803 the conditions were treacherous indeed as Hugh Vesty slipped and stumbled his way up the Wicklow Gap where some of us had huddled. 'Jesus, Michael, Jesus!' was all he could manage to say to begin with as he gasped for breath. 'Take it easy now Hugh Vesty,' I told him, 'nothing can be that bad!'

'Oh 'tis Michael, 'tis.'

'What?'

'Early this morning, a large force, horse and foot, came into Eadstown and surrounded the houses. They took everyone.'

'My father?'

'And your mother, and your sisters Etty and Mary Neale.'

'My wife?'

'She wasn't there.'

'Thank God. Well that's an end to it now.'

'Michael! If your father knew you were throwing in the towel because he was arrested he'd tan your hide.'

I had to accept that Hugh Vesty was right. Thought, not action, was called for now. Beresford wanted me on my knees before him, begging for mercy and pleading for the release of my parents and family. The move he had made now was against all the laws of war. But there was a strange contradiction in all this: they believed that we had an army of 25,000 men in Wicklow, ready to mobilise at a day's notice and yet they refused to recognise us as a legitimate force. They treated us as criminals and never as soldiers. Of course the truth is that we were just a raggle-taggle group, who were fast-moving and dangerous. If we had donned Emmet's uniforms and marched in ranks we would not have lasted a wet day. That Mary and the children had survived the raid was a great consolation, because Mary was by this time wanted on a charge of high treason. She would not just have been detained at His Majesty's pleasure, but could have been sentenced and hanged by a military court martial. This was her status because of her association with the movement. I regretted this but she always accepted it, believing as I did that the principles of liberty and equality were worth fighting and dying for. Martin Burke had been taken up a week before this and just such a threat hung over him.

The snows came very early that winter, and by the beginning of December it lay several feet deep on the higher slopes. It was high up in a disused mine-shaft that I huddled with my wife and three children, and now another on the way. We made the decision in silence. Mary asked: 'When would you like me to go?'

'It had better be soon,' I said.

She would go to the house of a yeoman called William Jackson, known to one and all as Billy the Rock. Despite our opposite allegiances we had cordial relations with this man, and that was rare indeed in a place so bitterly torn by sectarian hatred. Billy would take her to Humewood to see William Hoare-Hume M.P.

There were tears and screams from the children when she left, but I had enough food to keep them warm, and there was enough left in a bottle to keep me calm and civil. I was a patient man who could spend days lying in a wet ditch waiting to ambush a troop of cavalry, but the hours waiting for Mary weighed more heavily on me than any other time spent waiting. What if they kept her? What if Jackson decided to hand her over to Beresford instead of Hume? The hours went by and something close to panic started to grip me as we huddled together in the cold of the mine-shaft.

It was still light when I saw her ascending the slope. Putting Mary Anne on my shoulders I carried the two boys in my arms and set off to meet her. I shouted at her not to climb any farther, as a fall in her condition could have had serious consequences. She waited but moved on the spot because it was mighty cold.

'He's agreed,' she said.

'To America?' I asked.

'Yes. If we throw ourselves on the mercy of the Government, he will guarantee America. But it must be confidential. Not a word to anyone, not even Billy the Rock.'

Billy the Rock was a dour class of a man, with dark brows, black beard and a slow, perpetual shake of the head as if he were surrounded at all times by doom and gloom. Strangely, though, he had a great way with children, who adored him. He treated them with this casual but kind attitude which put them at ease. We stayed that night, the 13th of December, with the Jacksons, and were most grateful for the hot food and the warmth of the fire. The family farmed a smallholding of very poor land and managed to survive with the extra income Billy earned as a yeoman. I counted eight little Jacksons that night, but there were probably more, and by the look of the woman of the house the birth of another was imminent. What would become of them all in time? I wondered. Conversation with Billy was stilted, and confined to farming and the weather. They would take care of our children the following day while we went to Humewood for the surrender.

For such a crowded house it was as neat and well-ordered as any I have seen. Above the fireplace was a substantial curved beam of black bog oak, and some of the household goods were neatly arranged on this. The pots hung from a crane over the fire, and this could be swung in and out with the greatest of ease. Even the keep-hole by the fire was tidy, and before we left I hid some money there which Billy would find it in a day or two. As I shook his hand in gratitude and farewell I had the stark realisation that I was saying goodbye to Wicklow.

On the evening of the 14th of December we met with Hume at the Three Bridges, on the road immediately outside the Talbotstown gate of Humewood. Hume brought just one yeoman with him for security and I handed over my sabre and my blunderbuss as a symbolic gesture. Hume asked me if I understood that the terms of the surrender were that I throw myself unconditionally on the mercy of the Government. I looked at him in silence and then he added: 'I need you to confirm that you accept that before I say anything else.'

'I do accept,' I told him.

'Very well. You have my personal guarantee that your life will be safe, and I will secure free passage for yourself and your dependents to America. Is that satisfactory?'

'Yes.'

'Good. Then I would like to offer you the hospitality of my humble abode while we settle the details and await your transfer to Dublin.'

Humble abode? I have not seen the likes of it before or since. Clean rushes on the floor, a high, vaulted ceiling over a massive oak table before a roaring log fire. We had venison and sauces, wine, and brandy that was as good as Emmet's. I told him I wanted my mother, father and other relations freed from jail and he agreed to that. Mary asked that we not be separated from the children for any length of time, and he said that they could be lodged in Kilmainham with us. The brandy and the wine had given me courage and I said: 'Of course, all this is dependent on my main men getting the same terms.' There was a long silence while Hume chewed and swallowed what was in his mouth. Mary's look at me was as sharp as the knife she held in her hand, and which indeed I feared she would lodge in my chest.

'Whom?' he asked.

'Martin Burke, already in captivity, Hugh Vesty Byrne and Arthur Devereux. And their wives and families of course.'

'Very well,' he said, 'but I cannot guarantee them passage to America; however if they throw themselves on the mercy of the Government their lives will be spared.'

Our host dabbed his lip and cleared his throat, which led me to conclude that there was an awkward question coming.

'I believe Robert Emmet gave you a uniform,' he said with studied casualness.

'He did, but I never wore it,' I told him.

'And where might it be now?'

'I have no idea.' But of course Mary did know where it was, and she offered to locate it for Hume if he would like to see it, or indeed to have it.

'I should like that very much,' he said.

To this day I do not know what he wanted with the uniform, which I assume is still in his possession.

The following morning we had a visitor—none other than Brigadier General Beresford. He was in the hallway congratulating Hume when I came to join them.

'Dwyer!' he barked at me.

'Beresford!' I growled back at him.

He seemed aghast at such boldness, but he was out of luck if he was expecting any forelock-tugging or knee-bending. We took coffee together and he asked if he might be permitted to enquire as to the number and deployment of my troops, and I told him I would answer honestly and to the best of my knowledge.

'Now they tell me in Dublin,' he began, 'but I suspect this is something of an overestimation, that you have 25,000 men under your command.' I laughed. 'No?' he asked.

'Put it this way general,' I told him. 'There are three noughts too many in that figure.'

'But surely you were to bring force of several thousand to Dublin in July?'

'I had no hand, act or part in that madness. I was approached, yes, but gave no commitment. True, some men from Wicklow did go to take part in that debacle, but they are all now either dead, fled or in chains. What would I be doing with 25,000 men in God's name? Even a hundred would be an encumbrance. You know that.'

'That is what I told them. Small and mobile, that is the kind of force we are looking for.'

'And you were right. We are but a handful and now we have surrendered and thrown ourselves on the mercy of the Government. All of us!'

'I see.'

As he sounded a little doubtful, I thought then a bit of plámás might reinforce my point. 'Your tactics were absolutely correct sir. You squeezed us and flushed us out. Now it is over. We lasted a long time and we terrorised the populace into helping us. No one gave us aid willingly. Please God there will be peace in the old county now.'

Mary went to bring the terms to Arthur and Hugh Vesty, and she would come with the children to Dublin, and they were to lodge with us in Kilmainham Jail.

Chapter VI
Here he tells us of the old jail days in Kilmainham—the family all together in one place for the longest time.

Two days later I left for Dublin with Hume, flanked by a troop of his cavalry. These same soldiers were somewhat disgruntled because they did not get a share of the reward money that had been put up. Hume allowed them to take a glass or two at the various stops I demanded on the way. I would like to have visited all the taverns and shebeens I frequented in Wicklow, but sure we'd still be there if I'd done that. We had a few in Donnard, a couple more in Blessington and the last drop we had before entering Dublin was at a tavern in Rathfarnam. News of our coming had gone ahead and many country folk waited on the way to wave me goodbye.

There are few aspects of society I hate more than city rabble, and they were out in force when we arrived in the capital. Unusually they were not all of one mind. Some tried to show their support by shouting 'Erin go Braugh' and 'long live the republic' while others hurled obscenities at me, accusing me of robbery, murder, and such. As I was well-numbed at this stage these insults did not bother me. But when some gouger shouted: 'You left Robert Emmet to die, ya Wickala bastard!' I nearly threw myself into the crowd.

We rode into the courtyard of Dublin Castle, and I was taken before Alexander Marsden, the Under-Secretary of State for Civil Affairs, to be interrogated, but this process was soon abandoned because they felt I was too tired and fraught. The truth is I was stoscious drunk. That night I was very glad to get to my bed in Kilmainham.

I was sad to have left Wicklow, of course, and there were so many friends to whom I would like to have said a final farewell, in particular dear old John Cullen. My parents and the rest of my family I would get an opportunity to meet with before setting off for America. The other person on my mind that night was Sam MacAllister, whose mother had recently passed away. Was I leaving behind the traitor who had revealed our safe haven in Dairenamuck and brought about the death of my friend? I was tortured by the debt owed to this man who had given his life for me, and that could only be settled by the death of a rat.

After a couple of days they deemed me to be in a fit state and they brought me back to Dublin Castle to be examined. Marsden was there with Standish O'Grady and another gentleman who wrote down everything that I said. It was difficult for me to discern how much they knew already, and so I had to stick very closely to the truth while giving away as little as possible. They wanted to know about my involvement with Emmet and how I first met him, and I told them that I had received a message from Emmet through Arthur Devereux requesting to meet him in Rathfarnam at an appointed time.

'Now I never meet anyone at an appointed time, and I told Arthur to inform Emmet that I might come to see him, perhaps in a couple of months.'

'But you went there sooner,' Marsden said.

As he seemed to be aware of that meeting I told him about it: how I demanded that nobody should leave the house while I was there and how I did not sleep for the three days and nights. Yes, Robert Emmet said he had 60,000 men and he intended to surprise and take Dublin, astonishing the Government in the process.

'Obviously I concluded from this they wanted some of us to support him.'

'And did you?' Marsden asked

'I promised to assist Emmet when they should be in possession of Dublin for 48 hours, and that I could engage for 800 men and in that event bring 5,000. Sure they could not perform their part and I thought I might as well promise anything.'

I said all this in a most casual way, feigning disrespect towards Robert Emmet. To have revealed the truth about my admiration for him, and the esteem in which he was held by my followers in Wicklow would have put many in Imaal and Glenmalure in danger of capture and interrogation. This was the story on which myself, Martin, Hugh Vesty, and Arthur had agreed. We all admired Emmet and believed that the plan could work. To have committed all our forces to the fight in Dublin at the beginning would have been foolish. Emmet knew this. In the event of failure in Dublin I had to keep my force intact and wait for the promised French landing.

'Did he reveal the names of any of the other leaders?' Marsden continued.

'He did not then, but boasted of the secrecy with which they acted. If the same Emmet had brains to his education he'd be a fine man.'

'If you felt so negative towards the venture why did you support it?' he asked.

'Well now to be perfectly honest...' I began.

'Please!' he interjected.

'I thought the whole business might draw troops away from Wicklow to Dublin and afford us some time in peace.'

They seemed now to change tack and asked me about '98. I had no problem in giving them full information on my part in that, and explaining that the continued violence was mostly of a sectarian nature: 'Look, the people were told the Orangemen intended to murder them and the loyal were afraid they were to be massacred by the people, and troops were sent into the country. On their approach the people fled, the houses were found empty and thus both parties were confirmed in their belief.'

They then proceeded to ask me about Thomas Russell, a friend of Wolfe Tone's and one of the leaders of Emmet's rebellion. As Russell had been executed a couple of months previously I felt whatever I revealed could not harm him, and so I told them that Russell felt he could raise the north but I did not think that, up there, they liked the idea of a French invasion. 'You see many people promised to support Emmet who had no intention of making good on those promises. Even if there was an invasion now Wicklow would not rise, and if Robert Emmet had succeeded I could not have brought him more than 26 men!'

I doubt if they fully believed that last statement, but sure it kept them thinking. My feeling was that I didn't do too badly at my cross-examination at the Castle. I certainly did not incriminate anyone, and hopefully succeeded in removing suspicion from many. I do not believe that any-one has ever been interrogated at Dublin Castle without generating rumours that they have turned traitor, and I was no exception to that, but anyone with any sense knows that the source of such rumours is the enemy.

Kilmainham was the most modern of jails with great iron stairways and walkways. It was well-supplied with privies, but the pumping system and pipes had been faulty for years and at times the stench could be offensive. We were lodged in the first class section but Hugh Vesty and the others were put in the second class.

We did not know how long we would be lodged in Kilmainham, but we hoped our stay might be brief. For a family who had been on the run for five years, the 'crude confinement' of a prison cell is a welcome shelter from the elements. To us there was nothing crude about the accommodation. There was as much space as we needed. And beds! Imagine! Two iron beds with mattresses, and a blanket and a half on each of them. Our cell was maybe sixteen feet by sixteen, and contained three chairs and a table as well as a shelf for storing our belongings. Mary Dwyer, consummate home-maker, soon turned the cell into a luxurious hotel room. There was a great comfort in knowing that we would not want for food or drink as the rations were very generous: one and a half pounds of meat a day, a pound of bread, and two naggins of whiskey for me. All I wanted to know once we had moved in there was how soon we were going to get out, but Mary convinced me that I should enjoy the respite, which would build up our resources for the long journey ahead. The two naggins of whiskey a day made acceptance fairly painless.

Most fathers are not lucky enough to have such close involvement in the bringing up of their little ones, but as the days turned into weeks turned into months, that early period in Kilmainham became the most fascinating and happy time in my life. Mary Anne was a capable four year old, Peter was a sensitive, dreamy two and a half, and John was a pushy baby, who took his first steps in the prison cell and became a truculent toddler. All the while Esther grew in the womb. Big sister bossed the boys around of course but they were never as malleable as she would have liked. Baby John poked and pulled relentlessly at his brother, who would take the abuse calmly for long periods, but when it went too far he would turn on the baby, which was dangerous because Peter had a vicious temper.

There were stories and games, squabbles and reconciliations, day after day, but educating children within the limits of a prison cell was not easy. Apart from spiders and maggots there was little of nature to be seen. Where we were given our daily exercise there were no trees, and my memory is of the five of us, Esther being in the womb then, huddled together in a corner of that bleak yard as the rain poured down. I know it cannot have rained every single day, but that is my memory.

It was preferable that we get the breath of air and the exercise on our own, because the likes of what was lodged in the felons' section I would not have considered suitable company for my little ones. Mind you many of the people lodged in the first class section looked down their noses at us. Sure, aren't we all happy as long as we have someone to look down on? The heavy door to the cell remained locked to us, there was one small window which was barred and the four grey walls wept.

The beds creaked, but that did not keep us from our tense, whispered love-making. Thankfully the children were all sound sleepers.

The notorious Dr. Trevor did not make an immediate impact on me, but he was a man who revealed himself in stages. I realise now that he was sneakily sizing us up as a predator would his prey during those early encounters. His complete baldness made him seem younger rather than older because of the 'baby' features of his face, rosy cheeks and wide, brown eyes. He ignored me to begin with but smiled salaciously at the children, asking their names and ages while cooing at them in a most womanly fashion. The look he gave Mary seemed to imply that there was something he had to say about her but not yet. He always carried a cane, which seemed more suited to chastisement than an aid to walking. At all times Trevor was accompanied by a big brute of a man, 'Dunne the jailer', whom the doctor introduced again and again as 'Mister Dunne, who cut the head off Felix O'Rourke at the jail in Mullingar'.

I knew that Trevor was going to provoke me and I also knew that I would be able to dispatch Dunne as long as I got the first strike in.

One morning Dunne brought the day's provisions as usual, but there was no whiskey. He left quickly, closing the door before I had a chance to notice this. I shouted after him, but he didn't come back. In the mornings back then I could be very jittery and was inclined to dry-retching. Mary always made sure that there was a drop left from the previous day and once she had nursed this into me I would be okay, and she had done the same on that fateful day. 'Now Michael Dwyer,' she said, 'this is the provocation and you are going to have to muster up all your strength and courage, because whatever happens you must not react. That is what they want. You understand?'

Of course I understood, but that did not make it any easier. As the day wore on I grew more fearful. Later, as polite as could be, Mary requested of the guard who left us out for our exercise to speak with Dr. Trevor. By the day's end however nobody had come to see us. I passed the night in sweat and panic.

When Dunne came with the tray the following morning I was half afraid to look at it, but I knew in my heart that the whiskey would not be there. At this stage we were not sure if Dunne was a mute and Mary spoke to him assuming he was. She placed herself between Dunne and the door: 'Now, Mister Dunne, this is most important: we need you to tell Dr. Trevor that we must speak to him regarding our daily provisions which were agreed as part of our terms. Will you do this for us, please?'

It was clear that he had heard her, but clearer still that he did not intend to reply. A tense moment! If she didn't move he would push her aside and if he pushed her aside I would react. Mary bless her saw all this and moved to let him pass.

Mary Anne, God love her, sensed that it was not a day for playing with Papa, and she helped her mother keep the boys occupied. In the afternoon I heard Trevor's voice approaching the cell, and I panicked as he passed and went on. I ran to the door and shouted: 'Doctor Trevor, I need to speak to urgently about my terms.' He shouted back, but kept on walking: 'Your terms? Your terms! I know what your terms are better than yourself. You have no terms at all. There is no robber or highwayman could make better terms than saving his life.' Anger gave way to despair. That night as I lay down I shook violently and the next day was worse than the one before.

It was noon when Trevor came to see us with Dunne. Straight away he went to the children, laughing and joking, and playing peek-a-boo. Then he turned to Mary and me: 'Is there some unhappiness in this my favourite family? Pray tell me the source! For I do so despise discontent beneath my roof.'

Mary made a clear signal to me not to say or do any-thing and she spoke quietly and carefully: 'It is about the supply of spirits.'

Silence for a moment, and then Trevor spoke with feigned surprise: 'Oh the supply of spirits! Yes, yes, I've been able to solve that.'

'Oh good we are pleased,' Mary said with a smile.

'I thought you would be,' Trevor said, and nothing more.

I could not bear the silence and asked as gently as I could: 'How? How did you solve it?'

'It was a mistake,' he said flatly.

'How do you mean?' Mary asked.

Trevor answered, speaking paternally: 'Your agreed allowance was one naggin of spirits per day. Erring, so to speak, on the generous side, I gave you two naggins of spirits per day.' Here he shook his head and waved his index finger back and forth. 'Quite wrong! And must be corrected. Therefore, if I continue, for as many days as you have been here, to give you no naggins of spirits per day, then you should be able to return to the correct allowance of one naggin of spirits per day. Understand?'

'No,' I told him.

'Do you understand, Mr Dunne?' he asked the gorilla in the doorway.

'Aye!' was the reply.

Then Trevor said, with a shrug of the shoulders: 'If Dunne understands it, believe me, it cannot be made any simpler.'

The anger, the shame, the craving! But I had to stay in control and I muttered: 'I want... I need...'

Gently but viciously mocking he continued: 'You need it? Come, come Dwyer...' Then, holding his cane between his index finger and his thumb, he placed it under Mary's left breast and lifted it up. 'Surely there is enough sustenance for you in this!'

Mary grabbed Trevor's cane and lashed him across the face with it. I was stunned and so was Dunne, but I reacted first and launched myself head down at the big man, ramming into his belly and leaving him winded on the floor. Trevor had managed to get hold of Mary, who had layed into him with the cane, and he pushed her to the ground. I caught him from behind, stuck my thumbs in his eyes and started to gouge. Dunne had recovered and grabbed me round the neck. Through all this Trevor was shouting: 'Guards! Guards!' Now they arrived and three of them pinned me in a corner as Trevor lashed Mary with a cane and the children tried to protect their mother as she tried to protect them. Trevor drove mother and children from the cell, screaming: 'Get out of here, bitch! Into the streets! And take your brats with you. May you starve, may you rot. Or sell your hole to a manky sailor. Are ya as good a ride as yer brother, are ya?' Mary screamed and tried to throw herself at him, but the guards bundled them all out.

I'd never been in irons before, which, considering my career to date, was remarkable. The pains from the beatings were far worse than the weight of the irons, but in time those wounds healed while the irons got heavier day by day. Isolation and waiting were states to which I had grown accustomed over the years, but I would have swapped those days in the dungeon for a lifetime in the soggiest old ditch in the County Wicklow.

To begin with I was dazed and confused; it had all happened so quickly, like an episode in a nightmare. I pleaded with God to give me the time back. Why was I so slow? I should have sprung immediately Mary's person was touched by the cane. Sure, I would still have been beaten and put in irons, but wife and children may have remained in the comfort of the cell, fed and sheltered.

Where were they all? Where did they go to once outside the prison gates? Mary knew nobody in Dublin. If only I could have given her addresses of houses in the Coombe or Taverns in Thomas Street where she would have been given shelter! What of the child in the womb? Would the baby survive this ordeal? And if she went into labour would the mother survive the birth? Why had I been so slow? Had the inactivity of the months in the cell softened me so much? Or was it the damned drink again? Well I swore off all that there and then. 'Twas a bloody curse.

A lump of bread and a mug of water were my daily rations. On the second day, when Dunne handed them to me, Trevor, who was in the doorway, let out a sudden roar which caused me to drop the bread into the slimy water that covered the straw on the floor. I kicked the damn thing away from me and spat in their direction. 'Ah now,' said Trevor, ' 'tis only a country bumpkin would do that. Look at him, the man who has his wife fight his fights for him. And tell me is she familiar with the city? Well, if she survived the first night she'll be familiar with it now. I am told that there are sailors who pay good money to have their way with a woman fat with child. Perhaps she will be lucky enough to meet one of them. At least they'd eat for a day or two. Mind you, she'd probably lose the child. On the other hand she could offer the little girl. What's her name? No, no, don't tell me. Mary Anne! That's it. Many a wealthy pervert would pay a fortune to get his hands on that. Could solve all their problems. Hmm? Anyway think on it.' And he was gone.

My guess was that Mary would go south towards Wicklow, but that was a long, long way, and over mountains mostly. I prayed. It was all I could do, but it was something at which I was not practiced. I believed in a God, yes, but I rarely thought about it. My religious observance was kept to a minimum. I went to Mass whenever I could and confession once a year. Mary was quite different. She prayed morning and night, went to Mass regularly and observed all the rules. Religion was central to her life. To divert my thoughts away from worry about my nearest and dearest I concentrated on America.

Over and over again I imagined the journey and the arrival in the city, where I would be greeted with speeches and toasts as befits a hero of the Republic like myself. But we would not stay in the city. Oh no! Always we went to claim some rich, hilly land, which I would defend against man and beast. And we would be citizens, free and equal to all around us. My children equal to everyone else's children, and nobody with title or entitlement above us. And I would lull myself to sleep as I saw us ride together across our land, each on his or her own good horse, bought and paid for. Mary Anne the first citizen, whose beauty was the talk of the territory, Peter and John the sons of Michael, one tall and dignified, the other broad and powerful, followed, if she is a girl child, by the beautiful Esther, and the proud parents bringing up the rear would be so content.

I was lulled in this dream for what must have been the thousandth time when Trevor opened the door and Dunne came and released me from my irons, all in silence. They walked and I followed, along corridors and up stairs, still silent. We came at last to what had been our cell and the door was open. My escort walked on and I walked in. I could not believe what I saw there: Mary with the three children and a baby in her arms. It was indeed a girl child and we called her Esther. There were hugs and kisses galore, and hundreds of questions. Mary told the story.

'I don't know how we got to Wicklow, but we did. You should be very proud of your daughter and your sons, because there was hardly a word of complaint out of them. We got milk and some bread from country people on the way—people not much better off than ourselves, truth be told. Isn't it always the poorest of the poor who are the most generous? But then, I suppose, they are the closest to the Lord. I collapsed on the steps of Hume Hall and when I woke again I was on a day-bed by the fire. These three were in the kitchen being fed. I told Mister Hume what had happened but he seemed to know about it already. Now he was very kind to me, but it was clear that he did not want me there. I told him we had expected to be boarding a ship to America within weeks of being lodged in Kilmainham, but now we had been there for several months. He was silent for a while, then he told me the news, which shocked me and I know will sadden you greatly. 'You are not going to America,' he said. I raged at him and said those were the terms of the surrender, and he couldn't just change his mind. The man said that he had not changed his mind, but the American authorities had refused to let us in. I didn't believe that but he told me I could ask for a meeting with the American Consul James Wilson and put my case to him. Straight away I resolved to do that.

'Billy the Rock took us in a cart to Dublin, and your sister Etty, God bless her, accompanied us. We arrived, just in time, at a house in the Coombe, where I gave birth to this gorgeous bundle, God be praised. 'Twas an easy birth. Anyway I did not delay too long before heading off to see the American Consul, who was a little rat of a man Michael. He told me that the American Government's policy was quite strict about accepting Irish brigands into their country. 'How dare you sir,' says I, 'my husband is no brigand!' You know what he said? 'He is a murderer, a highway robber and a bandit.' I tried to be as restrained as I possibly could Michael. So, I said to him: 'My husband is a soldier in the army of the republic inspired by George Washington and modelled on the words of Mister Paine and Mister Masden. You welcome French revolutionaries, drenched in the blood of the massacres they committed in Paris, and now you will not let in one decent Irish man.' Of course he told me that he hadn't made the rules, but he wasn't for budging, Michael.

'Now it appears that we are to go to New South Wales. Not as convicts mind, but as free people, and we will be granted a tract of land. They will also give us £200.'

At this point Dunne came in with the day's provisions, including the whiskey, and, I tell ye, I was very glad of the drop. Mixed-up feelings now as I was happy to see the family again, but stunned by the news about America.

'Free people in New South Wales? Is there such a thing?' I asked her.

'Oh, yes!' she replied.

'But it is a penal colony. At the very least we will be subjects of the crown, watched day and night. All dreams of the republic, gone.'

'They will offer nothing else.'

'We had terms, Mary.'

'I think Hume offered terms it was not in his power to fulfil.'

'I would never have thought him a liar.'

'I believe he was sincere.'

'Sincere?'

'Yes, he believed he could deliver what he promised. He was prohibited. Perhaps he, in his turn, was deceived.' She sighed. 'We'll never know.'

'That's for sure.'

'Well there is one good thing about New South Wales, one truly good thing. I will see my brother Kevin again.' I remained silent, and she continued, more tentatively: 'Will that not be simply wonderful?'

'Of course,' I muttered.

A suspicion had started to grow which I really did not want to recognise, and so I turned my attention to Mary Anne and asked her if she had seen her grandparents, and she told me what a wonderful time she had, not just with them, but with her uncles and her aunts and all her cousins. She would be so sad to leave them as we were going such a long, long way to this place New South Wales, and we might be able to see them before we go, but then maybe never again.

'Did your granddad have any stories for you?' I asked.

'A great one about how Diarmuid rescued Finn from the White Nation,' she replied.

'Is that the doleful knight with just one eye?' I asked.

'Yes, and how he lost his eye and his smile.'

'That is gruesome.'

'Yes!' she replied and then we were silent for a while.

The suspicion would not go. I took another drink, which I hoped might quell it, but it was like throwing gunpowder on a fire. Mary broke the silence:

'What is it?'

'What is what?'

'Michael!'

'Please!' I said. 'Let us enjoy this. Yes?'

'Of course. But you have gone all...'

'What?'

'I feel I've upset you—done something wrong.'

'No.'

'Good.'

'Well... America!'

'I know.'

We were silent for a while and then I said: 'It's just...'

'What?'

'Nothing.'

'Please Michael, this should be a happy time.'

'That is what I said. I said we should enjoy it but you started an interrogation.'

'You were sulking!'

'How is my mother?'

'What? She was good. Warm, emotional! You know. Worried for you. Sorry you weren't with us. Sad, of course, sad that we will be going such a long way.'

I sighed: 'New South Wales!'

'I'm sorry,' she said.

'Are you?' I asked.

'What do you mean?'

'You'll see your brother after all.'

'Yes, and I'm pleased about that.'

'Hmm...'

'What's wrong? You like Kevin? You look forward to seeing him?'

'True, I do like Kevin. I feel responsible for him. And if we were ever misfortunate enough to end up in New South Wales I'd be delighted to see him.'

'There is no choice here Michael.'

'This American Consul, what day did you see him?'

'Wednesday. No, Tuesday.'

'Which?'

'Definitely Tuesday.'

'What time?'

'Two in the afternoon. What is...'

I interrupted: 'Who minded the children?'

'Etty, of course! What are you implying?'

'And what did he look like?'

'I told you, a little rat like man. If you want to accuse me of something, Michael, say it.'

'I think it suits you well enough to go to New South Wales, but not me.'

'Are you accusing me of subterfuge? You think I made this up?'

'Did you?'

'Jesus Christ, Michael!' Mary screamed and the children cried, but that did not stop her. 'I nearly died carrying them all to Humewood. Nearly died! And I stood up for you Michael against Hume and against the consul. Raged on your behalf. Then I gave birth, brought you back this beautiful child, and this is what I get.' She had started to cry now and the children gathered round her to comfort her. I had another drink.

'Yes, drink your drink. That is what got us into this trouble in the first place,' she sobbed.

'What got us into this trouble was you assaulting the prison governor.'

'You failed to defend my honour! You froze.'

'Temper! You could not control your bloody temper!' I shouted. Mary Anne now wrapped her arms round my leg and the boys clung to their mother. We both drew breath and patted the children. Then, to myself, 'New South Wales!'

'I know. I'm sorry,' she said quietly.

'I would not have come in for New South Wales. I came in for America.'

'Oh, Michael,' she continued lovingly, 'we were frozen, hungry, isolated. No more safe houses, a long winter before us, five hundred pounds on your head, and then your parents and brothers and sisters put in jail. There was no choice; you had to come in.'

I knew she was right, but my dreams had been shattered, the dreams that had kept me alive as I starved and bled in the dungeon. As usual Mary read my thoughts: 'I have had time. I'm sorry. Devastated, I know. So was I. The thought of Kevin I clutched at like a straw. Sure, we don't even know where he is or if he is even alive. It was just something to hope for.'

'I understand,' I said.

'We will have our own land, our own farm, our own little republic. The place of Michael Dwyer, the Wicklow Chieftain. Who would touch us? There must be hundreds of Irish there already, and we'll have Arthur, Martin, Hugh Vesty and Sarah with us. We will be a force.'

'I'll think about it,' I said.

We were quiet for a while. I laughed to myself.

'What?'

'I'd say he'll have that scar for life.'

'Oh, it's a beauty, from eyebrow to chin.'

'You caught him square.'

'I did, boy.'

Esther sucked. We smiled as Mary continued:

'All kinds of rumours about him outside.'

'Trevor?'

'They say he is for the chop. Inquiries and investigations are underway. They say: 'Misappropriation of funds, maltreatment of prisoners'. All kinds of carry on.'

'Oh now, I'd like to be a witness at that trial.'

'Wouldn't you just.'

Mary remained convinced that Hume had not tricked us, but I didn't trust him; in fact I didn't trust any of them. It was going to take a long time for me to get used to the idea of New South Wales, and apparently I didn't have that long, because the decision had been made and Hume would come and inform us when a suitable ship was ready.

It was some weeks before Hume arrived. Full rations had been restored in the meantime, and we did not see Trevor as Dunne saw to our needs in more or less complete silence. The centre of attention during this time was Esther, and Peter seemed to spend much of each day just sitting and staring at her, contemplating, I assume, not just the beauty of his sister, but the mystery of creation and the wonder of birth. John kept fetching presents for her—shoes, clothes, cutlery, crockery, anything that he could find in the cell. Sometimes his displays of affection were worryingly boisterous. Mary Anne preferred to be in my company. She was hungry for stories and very keen to learn to read and write. I acquired a slate and chalk and was able to start her on that journey.

The subject of New South Wales was avoided, but we knew we had to face it because Hume could arrive at any time. Here we were in a prison cell enjoying life, sure couldn't we be happy anywhere? Comfort and complacency sometimes go hand in hand, and I thought I had suffered acutely enough for long enough to be entitled to some peace, and there was great peace in the lack of responsibility that went with our present life. It was an unreal existence, in many ways made mistier by the whiskey. I had not given up on America, however, and I intended to challenge Hume on the matter and appeal to the appropriate authority, whatever that might be. In the dreamier times, late in the day, Hume would come to me with an apology for the misunderstanding and with an explanation that the minion in Dublin had acted in ignorance and once President Jefferson had been made aware of the error he had issued a personal invitation for the famous Michael Dwyer to come to the shores of America, where a hero's welcome would await him.

Alas, when Mister Hume entered our little cell it was obvious that it would not be so. I have never seen a man so awkward with children as the same Hume. He really did not want them to be present for this interview but there was no cure for that. Dunne brought a stool for the gentleman and Hume, having sat, dismissed the jailer, who left reluctantly. He cleared his throat several times before he spoke: 'I see you are restored to your former comfort.' Mary thanked him profusely. I said nothing. Baby John tried to climb on his knee and as Hume did not seem to care for that arrangement I took the lad in my arms.

'Now,' Hume began, 'you are both accused of high treason and there can be little doubt as to your guilt. That is a crime which carries a mandatory death sentence, as you know. However, be that as it may, you threw yourselves on the mercy of the Government, and the

Government promised that your lives would be spared but that you would be sent from this country. I know your choice of destination would have been America, but that has proved impossible despite my best efforts. All I can do is to offer my apology for that, which I do hope you will accept graciously.'

'America was part of the terms,' I told him. 'I would not have come in for less.'

'Then you would not be alive today.'

'Oh, I'd be alive, you may be sure of that.'

'Please that is of no relevance now.'

'You broke your word. That is what is of relevance here.'

'I spoke in good faith. I was not to know that the Americans would not accept you.'

'Why didn't they, so?'

'Because of your record.'

'Because I fought with the United Irishmen?'

'Obviously.'

'And what about Thomas Addis Emmet? Haven't they let him in? Sure, he was way higher up in the movement than me.'

'You cannot possibly compare yourself to Addis Emmet. He is an eminent physician and lawyer.'

'And protestant.'

'For pity's sake Dwyer, you robbed, you racketeered, you burned down homes, and heaven knows what else.'

In raising his voice he had upset the children. He was aware of that, and not comfortable. Lowering his voice again, he continued: 'New South Wales it has to be. I'm sorry. New South Wales or the gallows.'

Mary said: 'We will go there, of course.' She looked at me and I nodded.

Now instead of being relieved Hume was more tense than ever. He got up and started to pace the cell. For some reason I had this image of him pacing Hume Hall at night dressed in Robert Emmet's uniform. After a moment, he spoke:

'Now I know that perhaps you would like to take the children with you...'

'Like? Perhaps?' said Mary.

'There is a difficulty,' he continued. 'The ship on which you are to travel, The *Tellicherry*, is essentially a convict ship, and the captain, Captain Cuzens, believes, quite rightly, that it is unsuitable for the transportation of children and will not take them.'

'Then we will have to go on another ship,' said I.

'You do not seem to understand,' he said, 'I am not outlining choices for you here. I am telling you of the decision of the authorities.'

Mary shouted: 'I am not going without them!'

'Go, you will and must. There is no choice.' He was obviously a man performing a task that he did not relish, but I felt no sympathy for him. Hume sat and sighed; 'It is possible that the children could be sent on at a later stage on a suitable ship.'

'Can you guarantee us that?' I asked.

'No, I cannot make such guarantees.'

'And who can?' Mary and I asked in unison.

'The Agent of Transports.'

'And who is that?' I asked.

'Dr. Trevor,' he replied.

We knew that this was a conversation we could not have while the children were awake. I dozed off, and Mary woke me once they were asleep. 'I am not going without them,' she said, and I told her that we didn't have a choice. 'Couldn't we make a break for it?' she asked, and I shook my head.

'But there'll be plenty chances between now and getting on the ship,' she protested.

'No Mary, we'd never mange it without help from outside. That we do not have!'

To be honest the thought of going back on the run seemed even less attractive than a long sea voyage and a few months in a strange place without the little ones. That was not my wife's view. 'Look at all the situations you have escaped from over the years Michael; surely this is no more difficult than the worst of those?'

'This is very different,' I said.

'Will you think about it?' she asked.

I told her that I would, but that we would need to proceed as though we were going along with the plans for transportation, and that would mean talking to the Agent for Transports. That realisation stunned us into silence and we spent a fitful night. The following morning when Dunne came with the provisions we asked for an interview with Trevor. As was usual with Dunne there was no way of telling whether or not he'd taken in what was said. The day went by but nobody came and at exercise time we asked the guard if he would pass the message to Trevor. At least he nodded. Trevor still did not visit that day.

The following morning I thought it might be wise to try a more obsequious approach, and so I said to Dunne: 'Mister Dunne, could you please inform Doctor Trevor that we would be most grateful if Doctor Trevor would be so kind as to find the time to honour us with a visit.' Dunne nodded his appreciation of this before he left.

Trevor arrived in the early afternoon and he stood in the doorway with his hands clasped behind his back. I stood before him and said quietly: 'Doctor Trevor, as you know, we are to be transported to New South Wales, but the Captain will not allow us to bring the little ones on board. We would be deeply obliged to you if you could arrange for them to be transported to New South Wales on an early ship.' He was silent and just cocked his eyebrow and looked at me. 'Might that be possible, sir?' I asked with as much humility as I could muster. He thought for a moment, and then turned and left, slamming and locking the door behind him.

'What class of an answer was that?' Mary asked.

'I think he wants an apology,' I told her.

'He wants me to apologise?' she asked.

'Us. I think we will have to,' I said.

Trevor's next visit came after much requesting and cajoling of the jailer Dunne. He assumed the same stance in the doorway. Mary began: 'Doctor Trevor I wish to apologise most sincerely for the hurt I caused you... and... and...'

'Your impudence!' said he.

'Yes, of course, that,' Mary said and then Trevor turned to me and said: 'And your husband for assaulting me with my own cane?'

Jesus he doesn't want anyone to know that he was whipped by a woman!

'Indeed sir, I am deeply sorry for striking you.'

He relaxed at this point and moved into the room. 'So you are to leave the little ones behind, and you would like the good doctor to see that they are put on board a ship bound for Botany Bay? As soon as possible, I assume?'

'If possible sir, please!' I said.

'Possible, yes it is possible. But it is so much to ask. And who would accompany them? Your mother?'

'My sister, I think.'

'Hmm! I see.'

'Would you be able to do that?'

'I would be able to, yes. It is not a question of my ability.'

'What then?' Mary asked.

'Why, my willingness obviously.'

'And what might persuade you?' I asked. 'We could possibly raise some money, but not much.'

'Would I be so crude?' he cooed.

'What can we offer you?' I asked.

He looked Mary up and down and I shuddered. Then he looked at the children with the same salacious expression and I thought I would vomit.

'I am a man who has been mightily wronged in this place,' he said, 'and my character has been defiled with much calumny and detraction. How I have suffered! If you could find it within yourself to redress some of these slanderous slurs then I might be able to help you.'

'Tell me what to do,' I said. 'Should I write a letter, or...'

'Splendid idea, I'll get some ink and paper.'

And with that he was gone.

The letter was more or less dictated by Trevor, and it commenced with a eulogy on the dreadful 'doctor'. Then he demanded a recantation of all my republican and nationalistic principles. I had to write that my change of heart had come about because of his excellent tutelage and good example in Kilmainham. We were in his power and I would have said anything to extract a guarantee that the children would be sent on as soon as possible. I cannot remember the first part of the letter in detail but I can tell you exactly how it ended:

'With a heartfelt gratitude and fully sensible of how far I am from deserving any kindness from your Honours, I make bold to return you my sincere thanks for your kindness to me; and the consolation you gave me by promising your interest to send my children after me to Botany Bay; and your own humane mind will tell you there is nothing so distressing to the parents as parting of their children; especially one who has the misfortune to forfeit them and their country; and I declare to you that I never was sorry until now; for offending the Government until I see their kindness in forgiving the injuries done them and considering the wants of those that were guilty of such offences; now I am sorry to the bottom of my heart for having offended so good a Government and shall forever

*exclaim against any man or men if I hear any of them speak
or act against the Government; this I declare to be my real
sentiments at this moment and will till the hour of my death
for I never saw my error until now; as for my children I shall
leave it to yourself for it would be much boldness of me to ask
you for so great a favour and I so ill deserving of any; but I
sincerely lament for it and still hope from your humanity that I
may expect my children and shall find myself happy in
earning them bread and they and I shall be forever bound to
pray for your welfare. And I remain yours etc.'*

That nearly finished me but I didn't mind as long as it
was enough. It wasn't.

'Now,' he said, 'your companions, Martin Burke, Arthur
Devereux and Hugh Vesty Byrne are also lodged in this
jail, and I require a similar letter from each one of them.'

Although we had been in the same jail for several months
now, the authorities made sure that contact between us
was kept to a minimum. Hugh Vesty, who had Sarah and
the children lodged with him, had caused ructions from
time to time and ended up in irons more than once. I
never thought that I would have to show the shameful letter to anyone, but especially not my companions. This
would be more difficult than writing the document in the
first place. Martin Burke was going to be the easiest and
so I started with him.

'Jesus Michael, Jesus!' he said as he read.

'I know, Martin, but what choice did I have?'

'But it is such a betrayal, to our families, to our followers.'

'We can explain to people. People will understand.'

'You think so?' The enormity of what I was asking
now came home to me. If this was Martin's reaction what
the hell were the others going to say? I wanted to tear the
letter up or bring it back to Trevor and tell him I could
not stand by it.

'I am in his power now, we all are, what else can we do?'

'Cut his throat,' suggested Martin.

'I'd love to,' I said, 'but we would swing.'

Martin sighed and nodded.

I took the paper from him, saying: 'It was too much to ask. Going without the children will be heartbreaking, but the prospect of not seeing them again... well I don't think I could live with that.'

'Of course I'll write the letter. You are right. We have no choice,' he said, and I thanked him profusely.

Hugh Vesty on his own would have been easier to deal with than the Byrnes as a couple, but that was how it had to be. Hugh Vesty laughed at the letter and said nobody was going to believe it. I hope he was right. 'I don't want to go to this New South Wales place,' he said, 'It sounds quare beyond belief. And I don't want to be dragging the children there. Have you thought of the prospects of making a break for it Captain?'

'That is what Mary wants to do,' I said, 'but I don't see how.'

'On the way to the ship would seem like the best chance. They won't chain us because we are not supposed to be convicts.'

'We need assistance from the outside,' I told him. 'How are we going to manage that?'

'There is talk,' he said, 'of letting one or two people out to purchase supplies—farm implements and such. Probably the women. They will have to make contact.'

'I don't know if I'll be going out in my condition,' Sarah said, and I noticed that she was heavily pregnant. 'But I'm sure Mary will.'

'Good, good,' I said, 'I'm all for it. The thing is if we are going for a break then we mustn't arouse suspicion. So, I think it would be wise to continue to write these letters, and convince them that we are determined on going.'

'On the other hand,' Sarah piped in, 'if a famous warrior like Hugh Vesty Byrne writes such a grovelling letter won't the authorities be suspicious?'

'They know about my children,' I told her, 'and I assume you will want your children to travel as well.'

'Of course I'll write the letter, Michael,' Hugh Vesty said.

I thanked him and went to see Arthur.

Alone in his cell, he was silent once he had read the letter, and so I said: 'It is just tactical, you understand?'

'Is it?'

'Arthur, of course!'

'I would need a guarantee of that.'

'How do you mean?'

'Your word that our pledge still holds good—death or liberty!'

'There is talk of making a dash for it before we reach the ship.'

'That sounds more like death than liberty to me.'

'I agree. Then what do you mean, regarding the pledge?'

'I want the fight to continue wherever we may go, by whatever means are at our disposal.'

'Yes!'

'I need your oath on that, citizen!'

'You have it.'

He waited and then I said: 'I swear that I shall remain true to my oath as a United Irishman in the colony of New South Wales or wherever we may go.'

'Then I'll write your letter,' he said.

I thanked him and left.

Mary was silent when I returned after completing what I thought was a successful business on behalf of the family. But the whole experience was degrading and humiliating. At least now there was a good chance that the children would be sent out promptly to this new place. My sister Etty would come with them; I was sure of that. Mary said: 'I love you, Michael, and it would break my heart to be parted from you, but I don't think I could live without my children.'

'I think an escape attempt now would end in tragedy. You may forget it!'

'No, I am going to ask Hume to let me stay behind with the children. Then I could accompany them on the first suitable ship. That is a reasonable request. And what difference is it going to make to anybody? You are used to being parted from the children for long periods. But I have never been separated from them. No, I couldn't bear it. I want to ask Trevor to arrange a meeting with Hume.'

There was no surprise in Trevor's answer to Mary's request: 'Parliament is in session at present and Mister Hume will be in London long past your date of departure. I have my orders. You are both to be transported, that is the sentence, and you must trust me in the business of your children. Now with regard to allowing you Mrs Dwyer to take time in Dublin City to purchase clothes and farm implements, there will not be time for that expedition and you can get what you need in the City of Cork as it is in that harbour you will board the *Tellicherry* for New South Wales. I have arranged for your husband's parents and sister to come here to say their farewells and take over the care of your children.'

Chapter VII
Sad farewells and a very long journey. Michael tells us of the great sacrifice he is going to make for his family.

A hot July sun beat down on the prison yard. 'Twas the only fine day I remember there. Etty and my mother and father met us in the yard as there was a mite more space and freedom there than in the cell. Mary was quiet and she left it to me to explain to the boys and Mary Anne what was happening, and I think I managed to treat it as lightly and optimistically as possible. Of course I lectured them on how well they should behave for their Aunt Etty and Mary Anne assured me that she would keep her brothers in line and look after her baby sister. Esther remained in her mother's arms. Trevor was nowhere to be seen during all this, and it was Dunne who came and gave the gruff order to put an end to it. My mother took Esther from Mary's arms. It was like tearing the heart from her bosom.

As they left, Mary collapsed into my arms and I helped her back to the cell. We were quiet in the cell that night.

Mary did not weep; that would come later but now she was dazed and still distant from the dreadful reality. In fact the first tear was shed by me in the middle of the night at Esther's usual feeding time when Mary's breasts grew so sore that she had to express some milk.

On the cutter *Camden*, which took us south to Cork, she wept, and refused to look at the Wicklow coast as we sailed by it. The whole East India fleet was at anchor in Cork harbour when we sailed in. I had never seen so many ships in one place—there were over forty, and they would accompany us on the first leg of the long voyage.

I asked permission to shop for provisions in Cork myself, and failing that to accompany my wife, but the Captain of the cutter insisted that she go on her own. As she stepped on the boat to take her ashore I had a terrible dread that I might not see her again, and that she would start walking north to Wicklow and would not stop until she dropped. But as the sun began to set behind the city I saw the longboat laden with tools and clothes approach. She was glad of the diversion this necessary work afforded her and she accomplished it with her old strength and efficiency, and most of the £200 we had been given was still intact.

170 convicts were to sail on the *Tellicherry* and I had the devil's own job persuading the doctor not to shave our heads along with the others. She was a vessel of 468 tons and 14 guns, manned by a crew of 40. The general cargo included 160 gallons of Holland Gin, 150 casks of porter at a dozen bottles to the cask, as well as several of kegs of rum. Well, a man would not be short of a drink, anyway. There were provisions for the colony brought on board as well, including innumerable casks of salt beef and salt pork, firkins of butter and household goods. Space was at a premium on board and Captain Cuzens, who commanded this convict ship, put the ship's hospital

at the disposal of ourselves and our wives. This kind gentleman hoped there would not be an outbreak of fever on the voyage—a common occurrence on such journeys.

The *Tellicherry* was a large bark, with all three masts square-rigged. It was thrilling once we left Cork harbour and caught a wind. Splendid though she was, the vessel was always at the mercy of the elements whose power she had to harness. Nobody could say for certain how long the voyage might take, but probably about six months. The vastness of the space all round us made me dizzy after the months of close confinement, and I wished I could be happy with the freedom.

The weeping continued long after the lactation had ceased. The weather was balmy and we were permitted to spend some time on deck, where there was some space as long as you stayed out of the way of the sailors going about their work. On the second day out Mary came to me and said: 'Jesus!' and then again, 'Jesus!' I asked her what the matter was and she told me: 'Sarah Byrne is pregnant.'

'I know,' I told her.

'You know? How long have you known?'

'Since the last days in Kilmainham.'

'All that time you knew? Why didn't you say anything? Why didn't you tell me?'

'It slipped my mind. So much was happening.'

'What is she going to do? Or what is the captain going to do when he finds out? I thought she'd just put on weight the way she does, but she must be a good six months gone and that means that she will give birth on the voyage. He can't have children on board the ship, so what is he going to do? Ha? The captain? Will he put them ashore on some isolated island and let them take their chances with the cannibals?'

'They'd have some feed for sure,' I laughed.

'This is very serious Michael,' said she. 'I'd better go and talk to her and you should talk to Hugh Vesty.'

When I did talk to Hugh Vesty he didn't seem to want to discuss the prospect of the child other than to say that there wouldn't be a problem. What concerned him most at that time was how he was going to get used to rum as the grog of choice.

Mary's encounter with Sarah turned out to be even more peculiar, as she assured Mary that the captain knew about the pregnancy and did not have a problem with the prospect of the child. It seemed odd, and Mary wondered if we should confront the captain. I wasn't so sure. It was quite possible that Sarah was lying about the captain knowing, and approaching him might bring matters to a head. We both resolved to say nothing for the moment, and to stay calm. In a couple of days that calm was to be shattered.

I thought I was hallucinating when I saw him first, but there was no mistaking the big Byrne head on him and his mother's foxy hair. Sarah and Hugh Vesty were walking the deck with their five-year-old son Michael. How did he get there? Where had he been until now? Mary and myself rushed to them and asked at the same time.

Sarah started: 'There are no restrictions...'

But Hugh Vesty interrupted: 'He stowed away.'

Young Michael piped up: 'I was down in the hold with the prisoners. It stinks down there so it does.'

'You stowed away on the cutter and then got on board this vessel? Did ye help him or what?' I asked. 'But ye'll all be put ashore at the first port of call. Or worse still the poor lad will be sent back on his own. Has the captain seen him yet?'

'Sure they'll have to know eventually,' Sarah said to Hugh Vesty. I've never witnessed Hugh Vesty be more— what can I call it?—aggressively defensive.

'We left Philip behind ye know. So ye're not the only ones to be separated from their children. Trevor made us promise that we would keep him hidden from ye 'till we were well on the way.'

'What about the captain?' I asked.

Hugh Vesty shrugged: 'He didn't seem to mind.'

'The lying bastard,' said Mary, and strode off to the captain, who was on the bridge. She started the shouting before she even got to him. 'Rotten, lousy liar! Liar and coward! What's wrong with my children? Eh? How come you let that brat on board and not my little ones? Ye are all the same. Deceitful dogs!'

At this she hurled herself at the captain, and two soldiers got to her before I did. Then, of course, I jumped on one of the soldiers. Martin Burke and Arthur Devereaux came running to pull me off him. All through this Mary screamed hysterically: 'Turn round your ship! Go back! Go back! My babies! My boys and girls!'

In a while the screaming became a sobbing and a whimper. Then the captain spoke: 'I am under instructions with regard to you people. Any trouble and you are to be chained in the hold—you, madam, with the female prisoners, and you sir with the rest of the convicts. This incident I will overlook, because you have indeed been deceived, but not by me. I would have welcomed your children on board. The decision to keep them in Ireland was made elsewhere and I shall most certainly complain to Dublin Castle for using me in their dirty work.' Then he turned to me and said: 'See to your wife for the rest of this voyage Dwyer. And be warned!' He finished with a sharp jab of his forefinger and returned to his work. I put my arm around Mary and led her away, but when we got to the lower deck she pushed me from her.

'Don't touch me. Leave me alone. You let us down; you did not protect us. Trevor made a fool of you, Michael!

Now go away from me. All of you keep away. You do what you're good at Michael, sit on the deck and drink rum with Hugh Vesty Byrne. Drink. Drink.'

I did sit down, and Hugh Vesty did approach me with his crock of grog, but I turned and said to him: 'No more booze. I will not drink again until I have my children back.'

'Well 'tis there if you want it,' he said.

'How could you do that, Hugh Vesty?' I asked. 'How could you conspire with Trevor and lie to me?'

'I had no choice Michael,' he said. You know what they can do.'

God knows with what they threatened him, and I did not ask, now feeling ashamed as well as angry.

'You know what New South Wales is famous for?'

'Convicts?'

'Dogs,' I said. 'Mad, wild dogs, the place is only bloody crawling with them!'

Madeira Island looked quite magnificent—huge cliffs and majestic mountains covered with the finest of trees. After eleven days out this was our first port of call. Mary had become distant and quiet, glaring at Sarah Byrne and glaring at the captain. The captain, God love him, would come to Sarah from time to time, concerned about her condition. As I looked out over the island Mary came to me with Arthur by her side.

'We have a plan,' she said.

'Oh?' I asked.

'We can bribe a sailor to row us ashore at night. We have money, Michael, and money will get us a berth on a boat to Portugal, because this is a Portuguese colony; that is what Arthur told me. Once in Portugal it will be easy to get to France, will it not Arthur?'

'Well it would take some time, but it could be done, yes,' Arthur said, but it was very clear that his heart was not in this enterprise.

'Once in France we will be safe and Arthur has contacts there. We can get from there back to Ireland to the
children, or find some means to contrive to get the children over to France. Well?'

A sailor, who had been standing nearby, moved off
and he must have heard every word of this.

'Arthur, you should know better,' I said, as gently as I
could manage, because I knew he had been under fierce
emotional pressure from poor Mary. 'We would be shot
before we reached the shore, and as it is we will be lucky
not to be sent below in irons for planning an escape.'

I put in a formal request to see the captain later that day
and he agreed to receive me in the evening. His office
looked like something that did not belong on a ship—it
was more like a room in Humewood or Dublin Castle; all
polished oak and shining brass. He sat at a table, reading
notes and writing, and seemed loathe to take his eyes off
this work and focus on me. I coughed.

'So?'

'Firstly captain, I would like to apologise for our out-
burst the other day, but you must understand how
distressed we were to discover that Doctor Trevor had
mislead us. In truth I still don't understand the reason for
the deception.'

'I think you will find that it was due to events in the
colony rather than the situation in Dublin.'

'The colony?'

'Yes, where you are to be taken.'

'I see,' I said, but I didn't at all.

I continued with the formal speech I had prepared:

'My wife is distraught, understandably, and she enter-
tains unhappy delusions about jumping ship and finding
her way back to Ireland. These are not serious intentions
but symptoms of a troubled heart and mind. I assure you
I will prevent her from making any such an attempt.'

'Sorry?' he said, his attention having drifted back to the writings on the desk. 'Oh yes, splendid, good man!' Then he picked one of the papers and asked: 'Would you spell pooka with a double 'o' or a 'u'?'

'Beg pardon?' I said, completely lost. He showed me the paper, pointing to a line that said: 'The smallest and perhaps the nastiest creature of the she is a puka.' My guess was that he was testing whether I could read or not, but where the nonsensical material had come from I had no idea. 'Well 'she' is wrong. It should be 's' 'i fada', or 'sidhe'; oh fada is an accent. Yes?'

'Ah, I see. Wrong language, of course. Very interesting. Doesn't Sarah, Mrs Byrne, have a most impressive knowledge of your folklore!'

I didn't disillusion him by telling him that she probably made it up as she went along, and the more mutton broth and sweet cake he fed her the more extravagant the stories would become. Having been off the booze for a few days and having a little more room to move about I was feeling physically strong and I had a desire to be tested further. To this end I was going to ask the captain if he would give me some work on the ship. I thought the pulling and the hauling might keep me strong, and I would have loved to experience the thrill of climbing up the rigging. But standing there talking to him I changed my mind, because such a request would have placed me in an order beneath my host and that I believed was a place where I did not belong.

'Is that a hobby with you?' I asked.

'I am interested in peoples,' he said. 'You fought long and hard for yours.'

'I did that,' I said.

'Ah, well, pity! Will that be all?'

I thanked him and left.

The next leg of our journey was to take six weeks, and it was on the way to Rio de Janiero that boredom set in. Every day I became more restless as the novelty of sailing started to wear off. In time, I began to feel more confined than in the jail. The ship would have been about twenty feet by a hundred. Now, I know that is not small but it was a space we shared with a couple of hundred other people. Most of these—the convicts confined to the hold—were in chains. Obviously my situation might have been far worse. The convicts were regularly brought on deck for exercise and air. The state of all of them deteriorated dramatically as the voyage progressed, and we avoided being on deck when they were there. Mary and myself could not bear to look at them, and dreaded meeting their eyes, especially as some of them were known to us.

The food was tolerable but monotonous. It had to be carefully rationed because we did not know when we might arrive at our destination. After a couple of months at sea I ceased to appreciate the coffee and ships biscuit in the morning and the tea and bread and butter at night, but one of the sailors advised me to 'enjoy them while they are fresh'. Well now, 'fresh' is not how I would have described them. I was pleased to discover that I had good sea legs and never became ill like Mary, Hugh Vesty and Sarah, and could not be called lily-livered by the crew. The boredom was the killer though. So, I was very glad when Mary approached me and said: 'Sure you might as well be drinking as not drinking on the voyage. As long as you stay off it once we reach dry land and the work starts.'

There is no better cure for boredom than alcohol; however in this instance I did most of my drinking on my own. I didn't want any rowdiness and I didn't want any conflict with Arthur and Hugh Vesty. Poor old Martin Burke was a true gentleman, but as brave a soldier as any of us. After a certain amount of tipple I could convince myself that everything was going to be all right; that Etty would arrive with the little ones within the twelve month and we would have a house built and land cultivated for them. Soon I would drift into the kind of fantasies I had conjured up while in the dungeon in Kilmainham, but I could not pretend that these imagined adventures took place in some kind of idyllic republic. Sometimes the rejection by America would rise up within me like some kind of emotional bile. It took another dram or two to quell these eruptions. So it went on until we reached the last stop before our destination.

The magnificent Sugar Loaf came into view and we had reached Rio de Janeiro. Boats came alongside manned by Portuguese, Africans and natives who were darker that the Portuguese but not as dark as the Africans. They were selling oranges, plantains, bread and more exotic fruit and vegetables. It was a rich and industrious place grown more prosperous recently since the discovery of gold, which added to the already lucrative production of sugar.

There was a great bustle at the port of Rio as the ship was supplied with all the necessaries, including rum. Mary did not express any desire to go ashore there, but I would like to have seen the city for myself. The place was so exotic and alluring that I might not have remained temperate, and God knows what other temptations would have presented themselves on the streets of Rio. In the end I was relieved when we raised anchor.

We were only a few days out of Rio, on the last leg, when Sarah went into labour. Mary and Sarah had stayed away from each other up to this point, but there was no midwife on the ship and Mary helped with the birth of Roseanna. Mother and child survived and were healthy. Captain Cuzens joined us for a drink to welcome the new arrival, and we all saw to it that Hugh Vesty got mouldy drunk, which was not a hardship.

It was then that the weather changed dramatically as the winds and the rains lashed the boat as we sailed into the Indian Ocean. All the hatches were battened down, but not before a few waves poured in and drenched all the clothes and the bedding. Well I lost my sea legs now, I may as well tell you. The storm lasted for a week and the hatches stayed down all that time. Lights were not permitted because of the danger of fire. We had to suffer in the dark. We had a couple of screened-in buckets which were used as toilets and we fumbled to find in the dark to be sick into them. They found us before we found them as they were tossed about by the ship. Never in my life had I been so ill. Mary and Sarah led the prayers and I think even Arthur joined in. We prayed that the storm would pass and we would arrive safely, but I also prayed that I would never, ever have to endure the like of this again.

The greater hardship was on the poor convicts down below, because they had been greatly weakened by the voyage thus far and, by now, were desperately sick. Even when there was no storm their conditions were deplorable. They were all chained by rings to one long bar, and the vessel for defecation and urination was at the end of this bar, but the ring could only slide along the bars, which meant the prisoners could not pass each other and obviously this lead to the most degrading complications. That three of them did not survive the storm was hardly surprising.

Mary had wept after the birth of the baby, but she was genuinely happy for Roseanna and Sarah. As we drew ever closer to New South Wales her thoughts turned to her brother Kevin. Would he know we were coming? Probably not. How would he have changed? What would his occupation be?

'Perhaps you are an aunt several times over,' I said.

'Oh my God, I never even thought of that possibility,' she said, clearly enjoying the prospect.

Joe Holt was the other person we would likely meet when we arrived, and I was confident that the old general would have thrived in his new country. Mary, of course, looked forward to seeing her old friend Martha again. Then there would be Halpin. Was he the one who betrayed us and caused the death of Sam MacAllister? I thought so and I certainly intended to question him on the subject.

Captain Cuzens had papers from Marsden at Dublin Castle for Governor King who was in charge of the colony, and I was confident that once these had been read and discussed with the governor we could hasten the transportation of our children to the colony.

PART 3

Chapter VIII
Sobering prospects in the colony. A year of clearing and building is achieved, but will it be to no avail?

When we did arrive there were no friendly faces to meet us. As the prisoners were divided up and marched to their allocated destinations we were escorted to the Governor's office, which was not in Sydney Cove but farther up the river at a place called Parramatta, one of the few places in this vast colony to have a proper name. Like most everything else in New South Wales, this seemed odd to us. In Ireland every small stream, bog-hole or insignificant hill had a name. Indeed some of them had two or three names. Here, most enquiries about the names of places were met with a shrug of the shoulder.

The settlement at Sydney Cove was a ramshackle kind of place. Hard to say whether it was an army encampment, a holding place for prisoners, or the beginnings of a new town. Many of the structures were of a temporary nature, or at least I hoped they were. Some of the cabins would have made the hovels of Glen Imaal look decent by comparison. There were some fine, brick-built houses as well, and public buildings constructed from the native sandstone. There was no order or sense to the place architecturally. The society appeared ordered, though, as everyone seemed to be marching as part of a file or a column, the soldiers sharp-stepping in their high-polished uniforms ablaze with colour, while the convicts pale and drab dragged their shackles. Only the pigs roamed free on the streets.

The convicts who came off the ship were as close to emaciated as made no difference, and the ones who had been living in the place were hardly in better shape. They were red-faced, bruised and cowed. I thanked the Lord we had come here as free men and women.

In contrast to the chaos of Sydney Cove, the Governor's place in Parramatta was a fine edifice built in cultivated parkland. 'Twas as splendid as any of the 'big houses' in Ireland, and inside it was furnished in the most up-to-date European fashion.

Governor Philip Gidley King was a heavy-set man who had difficulty breathing and seemed to live in a state of permanent exasperation. Once he had read Marsden's papers he dropped his hands in despair and looked heavenwards. Then he pointed to me and said: 'You are the last thing this colony needs now.'

'Does it say anything in there about our children?' Mary asked.

'Oh my God, you have children?' the Governor said.

'But they are in Dublin,' Mary told him.

'Good!' he said.

I thought it best that I intervene at this point because Mary, God love her, would become too agitated.

'No sir, you don't understand,' I began, and from the look he gave me I gathered this was not a good beginning. 'It was part of our terms that our children should come with us, but at the last minute we were told that they could not. The blame for this decision was put on Captain Cuzens who denies that he had any objection to the children. We must be told who made this decision and why, and whether the Agent for Transports in Dublin is going to send them on the first suitable vessel.'

'One more demand from you Mister Dwyer, one more suggestion of insolence and you will join your friends in the work gangs on Norfolk Island. I think it is a disgrace that you have been sent here as a free man and are to be given a tract of land. That is not how I would have treated an enemy of my country. Get out of my sight and I hope that I will not encounter you again during what is left of my term as governor.'

We were given a decent tract of land in a place called Cabramatta, and the land was wild but lush. Two convicts were appointed to help us, and we could draw down provisions from the government stores.

When we arrived at our allotted place, Mary said: 'Michael, this isn't a farm: it is a forest.'

Now most of the countryside was rich with growth, but none was more deeply wooded than our tract. Some powerful trees, cedar and eucalyptus mostly, and interminable tangles of bush round and about them. For the first, and probably the only time, we were glad the children were not with us. They would only have been in the way of all the work that needed to be done before there would be any sign of a farm and a home. This was a spur for the two of us. First we had to build our house and already a standard system had been worked out for this in the colony. Saplings were used to construct the main frame of the house. There was an abundance of them that we cut and trimmed, all about three inches in diameter. The two men were expert at it and I wasn't long getting the hang of it myself. 'Twas easy enough as long as you had the proper tools, and that we did. The roof was made of bark cut from the eucalyptus trees, and I believe this was trick they had learned from the natives, and it was as good as any thatch. It had to be battened down on the outside and more large saplings were used for that. It was important for the roof to be as broad as possible, with a generous overhang to give the maximum shade.

Out from one gable we built a brick and stone structure, with a chimney, and this would be the fireplace.

There was a plentiful supply of lime, but the timbers we had put in were untreated and I did not know how we would get a coat of plaster to adhere to them. They'd worked out a solution to that problem too. Each sapling was chipped with an axe all the way down giving you a rough surface that the plaster would adhere to. The house was divided into four rooms, which was better than the two-roomed house I was brought up in, or even the three-roomed place where Mary was reared.

'Twas quick work, but, as I say, the convicts were very adept at it.

One of the convicts was a man called Cronin from Cork, hangdog in his appearance, ponderous in his movements and very careful in his speech, and Mary asked him if he knew anything of the whereabouts of Kevin Doyle from Wicklow.

'I'm afraid Mam, he was a casualty of the Castle Hill debacle,' Cronin said solemnly.

'You mean he's dead?' Mary asked.

'No, he could well be alive for all I know.'

'What is this Castle Hill?' I asked.

'You could call it the last hurrah, I suppose, unless you intend starting something yourself Captain. No? Very wise.'

'Tell us what happened,' I asked, and so he did.

'It was a black boy brought the news of Robert Emmet's rebellion from Botany Bay to Sydney Town. Some American boats had landed there, whalers I suppose, and 'twas all in a newspaper they had on board. There had always been talk of rebellion here and plots and rumours of plots abounded, but no doubt the news of Emmet's rising brought it to a head. The man everybody wanted to lead it, naturally enough, was General Joseph Holt, but he wanted no part of it. He was well set up with his wife and children, and had no confidence in the success of a rising. Holt had seen enough of informing and treachery during his days in Wicklow. Mind you, some say he might have indulged in a bit of it himself, but you'll have your own views on that, Captain. Anyway he believed that if it was bad in Wicklow 'twould be worse here, where no conspiracy could escape detection.

'There were those who didn't agree with him, your brother Kevin among them, Mam, and they were led by a man called Phil Cunningham. Two years ago now in the month of March chaos broke out round Parramatta, Castle Hill and Toongabbie, as homesteads were raided for arms, houses set on fire and settlers—men, women and children—terrified out of their wits. Eventually the rebels, about three or four hundred of them, took the high ground at Castle Hill. They were confronted there by the New South Wales Corps under the command of Colonel Johnson. What you might call a 'stand off' ensued. White flags were shown and they agreed to parley. Colonel Johnson and a couple of corporals rode forward and Cunningham with a couple of his men went to meet them, all supposedly unarmed. But no sooner had they started talking when the bold Colonel Johnson pulled a pistol from inside his sash, held it to the Irish man's head and told him he'd blow his soul to hell. The two corporals did likewise with their opposite numbers. The soldiers moved back to their ranks with their prisoners and the Colonel ordered his men to open fire and charge, which they did, and men were killed.

'Erra, 'twasn't much of a battle. The Irish had very little ammo and less discipline, and those who hadn't fled were soon dead. The pursuit went on till night fell and the following day the court-martials, the hangings and the floggings started off. Oh man dear, 'twas like back home after '98. Didn't they herd a crowd of God-fearing Catholics into a barn and threaten to set it on fire in revenge for Scullabogue. Now Missus Dwyer, as far as I know your brother Kevin was not among the dead, and not among the captured. That means he is most likely a fugitive and has gone into the wilderness. Nobody will follow him into that place. Mind you there are those who say that if you traverse the Blue Mountains and keep walking you will get to China, and if you walk through China and on through Mongolia and Turkey and on through Europe you could get to Ireland if you had energy left for the swim.

'Joe Holt took no part in the rising, but that did not save him. Oh no sir. He was put on trial, found guilty of treason and sent to join the work gangs on Norfolk Island. That is one place you do not want to go Captain. I had a spell there myself and if hell is half as bad I hope God keeps me in a state of grace.'

Of all the peculiar things about this land, probably the oddest to us was the weather. If you could say of any place, 'it never rains but it pours' you could most certainly say it about New South Wales. No such thing as a mist or drizzle here or a light shore, but torrents. When we experienced the first lash of it, we thought maybe it was an ark and not a house we should have constructed. And it wasn't just the rain, mind, but thunder and lightning as well. The ferocity of the bolts was terrifying, and it was not unusual to see one of the great trees cleaved into flames which would be hissed out by the torrents. We were delighted when the house withstood the first storm.

The furniture we acquired was basic, no better than Kilmainham really, but we knew we would be adding to it in time. Tables and chairs were made by convict carpenters, and from the crude cut of some of the items you'd wonder if they had spent more time in jail than they ever had in their trade.

In the hearth we burned wood and not the turf that we were used to. Above the fire, the various pots and pans we had bought hung from hooks and chains in a set up so different from what we were accustomed to that Mary had a struggle timing the cooking.

Before we could accomplish anything in our new home I had to promise Mary that, in time, I would search the wilderness for Kevin. I knew in my heart it was an empty promise, because he was a wanted man in the colony and we would not have been able to hide him in our farm in Cabramatta. But at this point I did not want to deny her the hope of finding him because, God knows, she had enough to deal with in the separation from our children. Their names became our litany: Mary Anne the first citizen, Peter and John the sons of Michael, and the beautiful Esther. We sent a letter off to my mother asking her to put pressure on Trevor to make good his promise, and no better woman for the job, but knew it could take a year for the letter to arrive and a reply to come back. We had to accept the fact that we would be without them for at least that year, but we also knew that it would take that long for the place to be made right for them in any case. So, we had to get on with the sawing and the chopping and the hacking and the burning. The stumps and roots of the big trees became the bane of my life.

At the end of each day we talked about how the children would love this place, and we wrote to tell them about the strange and wonderful animals, especially the possums, the wallabies and the kangaroos who kept their young in their little pouches.

'So Saint Brigid's Day instead of heralding the spring is going to mark the beginning of autumn,' Sarah mused on a rare Sunday when we all had the chance to be together. 'And midsummer's night will be in the middle of winter! Talk about an upside down world. What will we do at all?'

'We could change Christmas Day to the 25th of June,' Arthur suggested.

'Sure you can't do that; 'tis Our Lord's birthday!' she told him, and then she whispered: 'I still don't know, after all this time, whether they are here with us or not.'

Nobody present knew what she was talking about, and so she mouthed the word 'Sidhe' assuming, I suppose, antipodean fairies to be blind.

'Sure, wouldn't any such spirits belong to the world of the native people?' Hugh Vesty suggested.

'God and aren't they a quare lot?' Sarah said, 'and do ye know sometimes I'm terrified of them. The looks! You know I think they have the evil eye. Is it legal to shoot them?'

'But if you shot one of them and he had the evil eye, wouldn't he come back to haunt you? Then you'd be worse off than ever,' I told her. Hugh Vesty gave me a murderous look for ribbing his wife, who, of course, was unaware that I was making fun.

It was coming up to Christmas and nearing the end of our first year in the colony. Arthur had brought a letter round to us, which had come on a ship that morning and they were waiting now for me to open it and tell them the news, but I didn't open it because I wanted to share it with Mary alone.

It had been a year of hard work and no drink for me, with nine acres of maize growing and another six cleared. I don't believe I have ever felt as fit or as strong in my life. Martin and Hugh Vesty had made similar progress, but Arthur did not care for farming, being more interested in agitation than agriculture, and he never missed an opportunity to further the cause.

'I know you would have preferred your children to step off that ship rather than just getting a letter,' he said, 'but I think you are going to have to accept that they are being held as hostages and they will be kept until the war with France is over. But citizens we are in an excellent position here because the French have forces at Ille de France, which is only...'

'Out Arthur!' Mary interrupted. 'None of that talk here. Get yourself clapped in irons if you wish but do not drag my husband with you.'

They left and we opened the letter.

My dearest son Michael and precious daughter-in-law Mary,

I am pleased to relate that the children are all in the best of health. John will go nowhere without the little dog Tansey and Peter is fast losing his fear of the cow. Mary Ann, who has always been keen on the idea of reading, is now attending Master O'Brien's school.

Now to the matter which I know most concerns you both. Last week I was finally granted an audience with Dr. Trevor of Kilmainham Jail, who is the most unscrupulous villain I have ever encountered. Didn't he down-face me and tell me he had made no commitment to you regarding the children and feigned ignorance of the whole matter. If I'd had a cudgel I'd have split him open, but that would have dashed all our hopes. In the end he did promise that he would arrange a passage for

*them, but it could take a long time and will cost a great deal
of money.*
*I write this in haste because I am told there is a ship bound for
Botany Bay in the morn and it is very difficult to exchange
news with you.*
*The children pray for their mother and father morning and
night, and we talk about you all the time. Believe me I will try
everything in my power to get them over to you.*
God bless you both. Keep well and safe.
Your loving mother.

'I curse the day we ever trusted the man!' Mary said
through her tears.
'We had no choice.'
'We could have chosen the gallows!'
'Mary!'
'Better that than a life without them.'
'Money, I think money might be the key. We are doing
well here. Let us continue to work. King is gone and there
is a new governor here. Perhaps we can work something
through him.'

There was a young officer in the New South Wales Corps,
Cecil Lomasney, originally from County Tipp.—a strap-
ping lad. I suppose you could call him handsome in a pale
blond kind of way. Anyway he took a great interest in me
and my doings in Wicklow during the troubles. He
enjoyed coming to visit our home and couldn't get enough
of my stories and Mary's cooking. I thought at first that
he might have been sent to spy on us, but that didn't matter anyway because we had nothing to hide. He claimed
to be very close to Colonel Johnson who commanded the
Corps and wielded great influence in the colony.
   Next time Lomasney came round we made sure he got
a good spread and a nice drop of wine.
   'And you never touch a drop yourself?' he asked.

'If it doesn't agree with you, you are better off leaving it alone,' I told him.

Mary asked: 'What about the new governor? We've heard nothing of him yet.'

'I should be very surprised if you haven't heard of him. His name is Bligh, William Bligh.'

'Once Captain of the *Bounty*?' I asked.

'The very same,' he said.

'A tough nut and a brave man,' I said.

'I fear he will not be well disposed towards the Irish,' he said.

'But your friend Colonel Johnson will have some influence with him?' Mary asked.

'That relationship between Colonel Johnson and Governor Bligh will not be very smooth I fear. The two men have very different views of the colony and how it should be run. And one is more stubborn than the other.'

'I had hoped...' Mary began to speak, but she did not continue. Cecil Lomasney looked at her with true sympathy.

I said: 'I think money in Dublin is the only thing that will solve it.'

'I believe you are right,' he said, 'this fellow Trevor is rotten to the core and money is probably the only enticement that will move him. But you are doing well. You are an enterprising man Michael Dwyer. Be bold. There is money to be made in the colony.'

'But you will use your influence on our behalf?' Mary asked.

'Certainly dear lady, but I do not want to hold out false hope.'

We found Lomasney's visit encouraging, and it was good to have a friend who was, so to speak, well placed. I took his advice with regard to enterprise and decided to invest some of the small profit we had made during the year.

Coming up to Christmas there would be a demand for beef, and we decided I should go to Sydney and purchase a cask of beef from a ship newly arrived and bring it over to the Hawkesbury where I would sell it in portions. Mary thought it was a good idea and we kissed on it. We embraced. I fumbled, but she pushed me away saying: 'I told you Michael, I do not want to replace them.'

'But we don't have to...' I began.

'... Exactly!' she interrupted.

'It has been such a long time, and it is Christmas.'

All she would give me was her blessing.

In Sydney there was all the usual bustle of Christmas, but in scorching heat, which was odd to be sure. My thoughts were in Wicklow with the children and my mother and I prayed that this would be the first and last Christmas without them. I paid more than I intended for the beef because seasonal demand had raised the prices. But I need not have worried because the call for the commodity in the Hawkesbury was beyond all expectations, and I had to fight to keep sufficient beef for our own needs. Every time I struck a bargain I was offered a dram to seal it, but I refused. The plan was to get home while it was still light, but after the day's work I was exhausted and parched.

My last customer was a north man called O'Grady, who claimed to have fought 'longside MacCracken, and he was glad of the beef which would 'set him up rightly for Christmas'.

'Now sir, I'll understand,' he said, 'if you do not want to be recognised as your former self, but I'd be honoured if you'd just let me shake your hand there.'

As we shook a friend of O'Grady's joined us, a Cork man called MacCurry. O'Grady declared to him: 'Do you know who we have here? The great Michael Dwyer himself in person.'

'Ah stop! Michael Dwyer? will ya stop!' MacCurry gushed, taking my hand in both of his. 'Well now 'tis an honour, sure as eggs is eggs, and 'twould be a greater honour still if you'd permit me to buy you a drink.'

'I'm sworn off it.'

O'Grady admonished his friend: 'Don't you be leading the good Captain off the righteous path, Mister MacCurry.'

'Ale is all I'm offering, Mister O'Grady. Sure ale isn't a drink at all boy.'

'But 'twill quench the thirst surely,' O'Grady agreed.

Neither of them laid a hand on me as I recall, but they marched me towards the premises and, on the way, one of them, MacCurry I think, threw some coins to a boy and told him to see to my horse. When the door of O'Brien's tavern opened I was engulfed by the fumes of men and liquor.

'Make way for Captain Dwyer!' MacCurry shouted, and 'Service if you please Mister O'Brien!' O'Grady added. O'Brien was a big tub of red lard, red face, red hair and hands that were redder still. His nose had been broken several times and his ears would not have looked out of place growing in a cabbage patch. '*Céad míle fáilte*,' he said, 'and what is your pleasure, Captain your honour sir?'

'Just a glass of ale,' I told him.

'A glass of ale is it?'

He minced the words as he went about his business. Any repetition of that trick and I'd mince him, let me tell you. My thirst was desperate and so I finished the ale in one swallow. No sooner had the empty glass hit the counter than there was a full one in its place, O'Brien telling me that a bird never flew on one wing.

If MacCurry was like some kind of hornet, hovering in one place and then darting to hover in another, then O'Grady was like a monkey, whose neck was endowed with extraordinary elasticity; he would look high up and far away from me and then swivel and dip so his face was right up to mine. One of them was always in front of me and the other behind but slightly to one side.

'Come here to me,' MacCurry started, 'where have you been keeping yourself at all? Sure there was great excitement and expectations when you arrived, but nothing since.'

'Now now, Mister MacCurry, a man is entitled to his privacy and to go his own way.'

'And I don't say nothing to the contrary, Mister O'Grady. Making an observation, that's all.'

As I looked back from MacCurry, who was behind me, O'Grady's face was only inches away.

'Is it true you cut the head off a cavalry sergeant at Ballyelllis? he asked.

'I did,' I told him.

'And would you do the same tomorrow?' MacCurry asked.

'If I had to.'

'Would you do it to one of Colonel Johnson's men?' O'Grady asked.

'I intend to keep the peace here,' I said. 'My war is over now.'

'But supposing, supposing...' MacCurry began.

'We will suppose nothing here,' I said, sharp as I could.

To be truly honest I do not know how the rum got into my hand, but it was there and I drank it.

'What would you have done differently at Castle Hill?' MacCurry asked, adding 'That's a fair question. Don't answer it if you don't want to.'

'I'd have done nothing without ammunition anyway,' I said.

'Ah 'twas the lack of ammo scuppered it all right,' somebody said, who was neither MacCurry nor O'Grady.

'Emmet had ammunition and no guns and you people had guns but no ammunition. Maybe we'll get it right some day,' said I.

After the third rum I stopped, confused and angry. A point of no return!

I was supposed to have sung a song that night, a disaffected one if you don't mind, and done and said a great many other things of which I have no recollection. All I remember is falling down a deep, deep chasm, and at the first light of dawn waking on a bench in the corner of O'Brien's Tavern, all alone. It took me some time to work out where I was and longer still to unravel what had happened; no bruises, bloodstains or skinned knuckles, and so probably no fighting. Grappling with my self-disgust I got to my feet as O'Brien waddled in with: 'Hair of the dog, Captain?'

'Fuck you and fuck your drink!' I replied, 'Where's me horse and cart?'

'Outside sir, outside! Sure who'd tamper with the mount of the great Wicklow chieftain?'

There was barely a hint of mockery in the voice, and certainly not enough for me to give him a thrashing. I went outside. The sunlight was bright and painful, but not yet too hot. Taking out my purse I checked the money and it was intact—a handsome profit. So, no damage to anyone except myself. I climbed on the cart and slapped the old horse into a trot.

The road, if you could call it that, was bumpy and dusty, and the consequent rattling of my frame was painful, but the dust was the greater annoyance as I sniffed it and breathed it in. A fierce fit of coughing came on me that racked my body, and it got so bad I had to pull the horse up. Fearing I might throw up everything I had consumed last night—which would have been no bad thing by the way—I got down off the cart. The coughing turned into spasms of dry retching which brought me to my knees. There I was kneeling at the roadside in this piti-ful state and the horse turned his head to look at me, clearly thinking me the greatest gom in creation. In time the spasms subsided, and I rested for a while before con-tinuing with the journey, but now at a much slower pace. My mouth was dry as dry could be and the sun was get-ting hotter. I started to sweat and shake a little.

Now, truly I have never in my life been afraid of any man, nor did I have a terror of death, and while I never liked pain I'd accept and bear my share with fortitude. But now I experienced real fear for the first time in my life, and this fear was all the more disturbing because I had no notion what I was afraid of. One thing was certain though: the only cure for it was alcohol. One or two would put me right again.

The nearest place was Martin Burke's house and, although Martin was not much of a drinker, I was sure he would have a bottle in the house, given the season that was in it. Sure calling to Martin Burke on Christmas Eve was indeed a charitable act given that the man was living on his own! Martin got married quietly, indeed you could almost say secretly, not long before the surrender. We met the wife all right, whose name at this point I could not remember, and she lodged with him in Kilmainham for a while, but she left and he had not seen her since. The rumour was that she suffered from her nerves and that this was probably brought on by her stay in Kilmainham. Anyway he did not see her before he left and had not been keen to talk about her since.

He greeted me with: 'Jesus Michael, I hope you don't feel as bad as you look.'

'I'm grand,' I told him. 'I just came round for my Christmas drink.'

'You're back on the sauce?' he asked.

'A man is entitled to a drink at Christmas, for God's sake. I worked hard enough for it.'

'No denying that Michael!'

We sat in the kitchen and he poured us each a measure of rum. It was a struggle keeping the first one down, but the second one settled me a little. I asked Martin how he was and he told me that he was grand, but I said I thought he must be lonely.

'I have a lovely farm here Michael,' he said, 'but I wish I had someone to share it with. I am on the lookout but, as you may have noticed, there are very few available young women in this territory.'

'But what about...' I started, but did not know how to continue.

'The fact that I am married already?'

'Well, yes.'

'I was hoping we could all forget about that little impediment. Sure who knows about it over here?'

'Well, I won't say a word.'

Looking around his accommodation I did not see the lack of a woman's touch, but then Martin is about the neatest man I have ever met. Although he never trained as a professional soldier he had all the attributes of one, and if a woman ever did come into this place she would have a very high standard to keep up.

'God save all here!' said a voice from the doorway, and we laughed as we replied: 'God save you kindly!' because we beheld HughVesty, struggling with his bottles and guns.

'Thank the Lord for male company!' he roared. 'Women and children are grand in their place.'

The guns were for whatever unfortunate dogs he might encounter, and the bottles were for drinking. We all drank his health and his family's health.

'Mind you,' he said 'I can't say a word now against my Sarah for, despite her complexion and the doing she is getting from the sun, this climate seems to really agree with her—I've never known her be so willing! All she wants to do from morning till night is canoodle and canoodle. I'm not complaining.'

'She is probably broody,' I said, 'looking for another baby.'

'We'll accept whatever God sends us,' he said.

'How anyone could bring children into this world is beyond me,' Arthur said, having entered without a greeting or a blessing as always. We showered him with both and he remained impassive.

'Is that it really though Arthur? Do you think the world is not suitable for children at all?' Hugh Vesty asked.

'And it will not be citizen until we make it so.'

'And is that why you stay celebrate?'

'Now he won't have much to celebrate,' said Martin, and Martin and myself laughed until we cried. Hugh Vesty was annoyed and Arthur just watched until things calmed down. Then he said: 'You mean celibate.'

'I can never say that old word.'

'You should have been a priest,' Martin said to Arthur.

'I hate them and all they stand for,' Arthur replied. And so it went on—religion and politics, anger, laughter and sentimentality—deep, deep into a night like so many we had back in Wicklow. Eventually Arthur and Hugh Vesty departed. Before dawn? After dawn? I have no idea. Martin put me to bed and I slept. Several times he tried to rouse me but I sent him away roughly. In the end I was forced to rise and go and relieve myself in the sunshine.

'Well Martin,' I said, 'at least I'll be home on Christmas day.'

'Michael, this is Saint Stephen's Day.'

'What?'

'You slept. I tried to rise you, but I couldn't.'

She was seated at the kitchen table and did not look at me when I arrived. I put the money on the table, but she ignored that. Silence was to be her weapon, which I dreaded more than a barney, and so I was relieved when she talked: 'For a time I prayed that you were alive, but then I began to wish that you were dead, knowing that some dreadful accident would be easier to accept than... the other! But from where you stand I can smell that it was the other.'

I mumbled: 'I'm sorry!'

Close to tears now as she continued: 'You disgust me! You are weak and you are disloyal. Altogether despicable! You deserted me on Christmas Day, just as you deserted the children in Dublin.'

'Don't say that!' I pleaded.

Now she started to shout, losing control: 'Protection? Protection? You never protected them! You never protected me!'

Hurt by that I moved towards her: 'That is a damn lie. Take it back.'

I saw the object just before it left her hand and managed to move to avoid it. It smashed against the wall, and as the pieces fell on the floor I could not work out which item of crockery it was. A bowl or a cup? The next missile, an iron pan, could have taken the head off me if it had connected, and so I moved to restrain her. Luckily I saw the cleaver just in time as she lashed out at me with it. She backed me out of the kitchen, onto the porch and down the steps, all the while swinging her vicious weapon—quality Wexford steel bought in Cork. Oh how I wished she had chosen silence!

'Go! Move! Out of here! Go on!'

I moved, pausing when I thought I'd gone far enough. But if I did she started to throw stones, well rocks actually. One of them hit me right on the knee, and I thought it had shattered my kneecap. I had to keep moving until I was out of range, and she has some throw let me tell you. Glad to find a stump of a tree to sit on I took a look at my leg which was bleeding profusely. Then the pain started and it was vicious. But the turmoil in my heart and my head was worse. I looked back and saw her slumped on the steps, her shoulders shaking with sobs.

She was a good distance from me, and I had no intention of hobbling towards her just yet. For a long time she sat there crying as I sat nursing my knee.

I heard a sound like thunder behind me, and when I looked I saw a dust cloud. Eventually I could make out some riders. They were not soldiers of the New South Wales Corps, but Marines under the direct command of Governor Bligh. Three of them drew, cocked their pistols, and levelled them at me. The other two, holding chains and manacles, dismounted. 'Michael Dwyer?' one of them said.

'Who wants to know?' I asked.

'You are under arrest, by order of his Excellency Governor William Bligh.'

'What is the charge?' I asked.

'Treason, sedition!' said one.

'And that's just two of them!' said another.

By now I was in irons and they lifted me onto a spare horse, paying no heed to the agony I was in with my knee. As we rode off I looked back towards the house and saw Mary running and shouting: 'Michael! Jesus! Michael!'

Chapter IX
The four are tried and convicted. In the penal colony Michael gets an opportunity for bitter revenge.

They put me on board the *Porpoise*, a vessel which was anchored in Sydney Cove. This was in fact the very ship which had brought the new governor, William Bligh, to New South Wales, and he was convinced that his arrival in the colony prevented an outbreak of rebellion. I had always respected Bligh and thought that the mutineers who had set him afloat should be condemned for their cruelty, but now I wished that they had finished the job. I assumed that I would be taken straight to Van Diemen's Land, a place of which I had heard much and not a bit of it good. Now however I was informed that I would be put on trial along with Martin, Arthur and Hugh Vesty who had all been put in jail in Sydney. The news of the trial was a source of great consolation to me, not because I held out any hope for getting justice, but because it might afford me an opportunity to speak with Mary. If we were to part for a time, or indeed forever, which now seemed almost certain, then it would be easier to part on friendly terms.

Once a year! One small mistake, and it had brought this disaster on our heads. But no, Bligh had his sights set on us anyway and he didn't need my drunken foolishness as an excuse to put me away. What had I said or done that night in O'Brien's place? The problem was that anybody could accuse me of having done anything during that time and I would have had no defence. I knew for sure who the two principal witnesses were going to be and I was sorely annoyed with myself for letting them walk me into such an obvious trap. Be sure of one thing, they were two dead men now no matter what protection they had been promised. Never mind my foolishness, what about theirs? Unless, of course, they had been assured that I would be executed along with my companions.

Yes, I said I had no fear of death, but death while still estranged from my wife I did not want to face. I had no idea what her feelings towards me were then, and I had no way of finding out. True she had run after me shouting my name, but whether that was out of concern for me or anger at what I had done was hard to say. I'm not saying that she didn't have every right to be angry, and very angry, but I did not intentionally hurt her. A man has to have some outlet and there were too many restrictions on me altogether.

A list of the charges against me had not been read out to me yet, but treason and sedition had been mentioned and what constitutes those crimes on a given day in this place anybody can decide. What else was to be added? I had woken out of sessions with gaps in my memory before now, but my drinking had been done in secure company back in the Wicklow days. The night in O'Brien's had been spent among strangers, some of whom, for all I know, could swear that I had murdered somebody before their very eyes. Could I actually have killed somebody and not remembered it? I know such things are possible in a drunken haze but the like of it had not happened to me before. Always a first time!

No, if Hugh Vesty, Arthur and Martin had been taken as well then it must be political. Life in the colony had been marred by neglect and false expectation in London; Governor King had never wanted myself and my companions under his jurisdiction, not on the terms we had been granted, anyway. Dublin and London had wanted to be rid of us with the minimum fuss and were happy as long as we were not their problem any more. I honestly do not think that they saw the danger in transporting so many Irish revolutionaries to this place, a policy that could lose them their colony. Bligh saw the danger of course. He had already lost a ship to mutiny and he did not intend to lose a country as well, but he was hardly going the right way about it. Many thought New South Wales a godforsaken place, but wouldn't God have to be in a place in the first instance in order to forsake it? And there was no evidence of divine influence ever having touched this territory. As a natural optimist I tried to be positive about the place, but being clapped in irons takes that away from a man.

What kept me going when I had been chained down in Kilmainham was the prospect of freedom for us all in America. Now I had to conjure up some other happy outcome to my captivity. Agitation made the chains feel heavier and the wounds smart more sharply. God forgive me I was never a one for prayer, a consolation to many in a predicament such as mine. No, I had to paint an optimistic picture and live in that landscape. So I saw myself delivering a speech from the dock that would make Robert Emmet's sound like a penny ballad, and the jury and the judges would be moved to tears at my plight. They would set me free, make me a hero of the colony and send a ship straight to Dublin to bring over my children.

As I was being escorted from the *Porpoise* I was handed a page from the Sydney Gazette by an officer from the New South Wales Corps. When I read it I was filled with hope.

Such hopes were dashed immediately I entered the courtroom because this was not a court operating under the laws of the land, but a military tribunal or court-martial where summary justice was dispensed and the death sentence was most common. Although it was chaired by Judge Advocate Richard Atkins, the court was made up of military people, led by Lieutenant-Colonel George Johnston of the New South Wales Corps, and included another lieutenant from the same corps and four naval officers, one with the unforgettable name of Cadwallader Draffin. The charges were vague enough to convict the most innocent—treason, sedition and conspiring together to murder certain figures in authority and overthrow the lawful Government.

Before we entered our pleas of not guilty, Arthur suggested that we should refuse to recognise the court, and I had to dissuade him from that course. There might be some chance of freedom if we went through this charade of a trial but none if we did not. We were not allowed legal representation. The prosecution called their witnesses and once they had finished with them we were allowed to cross-examine.

The witnesses on the first day, who included Edward Abbot the Parramatta magistrate, outlined rumours of rebellion they had heard about croppies planning to overthrow the Government. It was explained to the court that croppies were: 'disaffected persons, opposing the lawful Government of the country, and using arts to excite and raise a tumult and rebellion against the state.'

The evidence was poor indeed and consisted mostly of half-overheard conversations reported by third parties. The only piece of written evidence was supplied by a man called Squires, a sworn enemy of Arthur, who had written in a letter to Doctor John Harris that 'he (Arthur) had been up to Parramatta on the Saturday for his provisions and was told there that Dwyer was going to the Hawkesbury with a cask of beef to see what he could do with the people up the country.' Now the only phrase that could possibly be interpreted as being potentially incriminating was 'see what he could do with the people up the country.' And Squires admitted under Arthur's cross-examination that the most logical meaning of the phrase was the potential selling of beef to the people of that area, and of course there was ample evidence that that was what I was doing at the Hawkesbury.

At the end of the first day I was feeling very confident indeed and inclined to believe that this trial might be something more than a charade after all. Although I knew in my heart of hearts this was most likely a false hope, I had to hold on to it and concentrate on strategies for our defence. We would be permitted to call witnesses to prove our innocence, but we were not allowed to speak to them beforehand. This meant that I would have to make some very careful choices, but that was for another day and for now I had to concentrate on the prosecution witnesses.

The first witness on the second day was that nervy little Corkman MacCurry, who constantly shifted from one foot to the other, like a hen on the stubble. He alleged that he had met me many times before my Christmas visit to the Hawkesbury and that I had planned all sorts of dark deeds with him. All through his examination by the prosecution I only took my eyes off him to note the dates and times of our many mythical meetings. He avoided contact with me, but had the misfortune to catch Hugh Vesty's eye at one point, and I thought the death stare he received would cause him to soil himself in front of the court. Then they asked him about the night in O'Brien's tavern and the extent of my intoxication. His answer was: 'Michael Dwyer is famous for being able to hold his liquor. Sure didn't he drink brandy for three days and three nights running with Robert Emmet and plan a revolution?'

When it came my turn for questioning I asked him if these meetings he had with me were just the two of us or did he have witnesses. He said it was always just the two of us, but once there was somebody else.

'Who?' I asked.

'Well I couldn't say because he was some distance from us.'

And that reply must have had the court thinking that this man might be just as shifty as he appeared to be. I had nothing further to ask him at this point but I made it clear that I would be calling witnesses to confirm I could not have met him on the dates and times he had specified; furthermore one of these witnesses would be Lieutenant Lomasney of the New South Wales Corps, who had been visiting my farm on one of the dates in question.

That monkey O'Grady was the next to be called as a witness, and he seemed much more confident than his friend.

The prosecutor asked: 'What was the nature of your conversation with Dwyer?'

'We asked him about the Castle Hill Rebellion.'

'And he said?'

'How he would have done it differently.'

'How?'

'By making sure he had plenty ball and powder before taking the high ground.'

'Did he then outline to you his own plan for a rebellion?'

'He did sir.'

'Could you outline that for us please?'

O'Grady stretched himself up to his full height and spoke like a well-prepared pupil: 'He was to instil into the minds of his countrymen a certainty of gaining their liberty. First they would destroy the Governor, whom they would ambush on his way to the Hawkesbury. That's good country for an ambush up there sir. That was to be the signal for the commencement of a general insurrection. The New South Wales Corps were to be surprised; the leading gentlemen of the colony were to have been killed, at the same time the *Porpoise* and shipping was to be seized, and a general massacre to take place.'

'And did he ask you to take part in this conspiracy?'

'Oh yes sir, but we wanted nothing to do with it.'

'What was Dwyer's next move to be?'

'He was to go to Martin Burke's house where he was to meet with Arthur Devereux and Hugh Vesty Byrne to put the final touches to the plan, so to speak.'

The prosecutor had finished with him and I took over. I asked him first of all if he knew who I was and whether he had any knowledge of my long campaign in Ireland; indeed he did and had.

'The key to the success of such a campaign was its covert nature and my ability to identify and root out spies and informers. Yes?'

'If you say so.'

'Did it not seem odd to you then that I should go into a tavern and in front of a crowd of people, most of whom were not known to me, and divulge an entire plan of an insurrection? Well?'

'That is what happened.'

'Do you really expect people to believe that?'

He shrugged. O'Grady's cockiness was laughable.

I paused, looked through my papers and recommenced: 'When you approached me that day at the Hawkesbury...'

'... I didn't,' he interrupted.

'Pardon?'

'You greeted me and asked me to come for a drink.'

'But I'd never met you before.'

'Indeed then you had.'

'When and where?'

'The Hawkesbury once and here in Sydney.'

'With whom?'

He shrugged. 'Different people.'

'Can you name any of them?'

'Not off hand.'

'How very convenient. Can you read?'

'Eh... yes.'

I handed him the newspaper cutting: 'Could you read this article from the Sydney Gazette for me please.'

He started to read: 'Conspiracy to overthrow...'

'Just the section I have marked, please.'

He read on: 'they were to have destroyed the Governor on his way to the Hawkesbury, which was to have been the commencement of the general insurrection. The New South Wales Corps were to have been surprised, the leading gentlemen of the colony were to have been killed at the same time; the *Porpoise* and other shipping were to have been seized, and a general massacre was to have taken place.'

'Could you read the date on the paper for me please.'

He was silent. I asked for the newspaper to be shown to the judges and the clerk of the court took it to them.

'Your honours will note that the article was published some months before the encounter at O'Brien's tavern.' Then, turning to the witness I asked: 'Is this not the same plan I was supposed to have outlined to you that night?'

'Very like it, yes.'

I let my anger show. 'What?!'

'It is.'

'What?'

'Just about the same.'

'Do you think I'm a fool?'

'No.'

'Do you think their honours are fools?'

'No.'

'No further questions, your honours.'

Johnston told O'Grady to step down.

Their next witness was O'Brien himself, and I thought this confirmed my suspicion that he was part of the conspiracy. The prosecutor asked him how much I had to drink.

'Little enough, but the little he had did for him.'

'What do you mean?'

'That he got very drunk very quickly.'

'Come now we have just heard that the man's capacity was legendary.'

'When you've been off it for a long time the first drop can hit you a fierce belt.'

The prosecutor decided to change tack very quickly: 'Did Dwyer sing that night?'

'He did.'

'And was the song disaffected?'

'Disaffected? No, but it should probably have been disinfected. 'Twas as bawdy a ditty as ever I heard.'

This drew much laughter from the court. The prosecutor had no further questions, but I had a few of my own.

'When asked what I felt about an uprising, what did I say?'

'That you'd have no part in it. That you wanted to live peacefully on your farm.'

'Was I asked many times about rebellion that night?'

'You were.'

'By whom?'

'O'Grady and McCurry.'

'And by no one else?'

'No.'

'And my reply was the same each time?'

'Yes.'

'Even when I was drunk?'

'Yes.'

'And how drunk did I become that night?'

'Too drunk to move. I had to carry you to the bench where you slept.'

'And the following day?'

'You left as soon as I arose.'

'And you thought?'

'He won't get far in the heat of the sun without a cure.'

'Thank you Mister O'Brien.'

I was pleased with his testimony. That ended the case for the prosecution.

The first witness I called in the morning was Lieutenant Cecil Lomasney, and he testified that I had given up any notion of rebellion and that my principal purpose in life was to get my children over to the colony from Ireland. He emphasised what industry I had shown and the progress I had made in improving my holding. The Lieutenant also confirmed that I was with him on one of the occasions when MacCurry claimed to have encountered me.

The next move we made was a serious mistake. Arthur and the others wanted me to be called as a witness for the defence. The purpose of this was to confirm under oath that I had renounced all my republican ambitions and allegiances. As I was the senior or commanding officer they felt that it was my place to do this. The court should hear from my own mouth that I was an innocent man, or so I thought.

It was a simple enough matter and we dealt with it briskly. As I had been called as a witness, of course, the prosecution could now cross-examine me. This was not something I particularly feared—what harm, since I arrived in Australia, had I done? But they grasped the opportunity.

He began:'You consider yourself a good family man?'

'Yes,' I replied, worried about where this was going.

'Your wife and your home come before everything else.'

(Well now I had an inkling)

'Yes.'

'Would you consider Christmas an important time for the family?'

(Now I knew.)

'I suppose...'

'... Indeed probably the most important date in the whole year for the family? Hm? Would you agree that that is so?'

(What could I say?)

'Yes.'

'But you didn't spend this Christmas at home?'

'No.'

'And what pressing business prevented such an up-standing family man from spending Christmas at home?'

I was stumped; didn't know what to say, and he let the silence go on for a moment before he urged me: 'Come Mister Dwyer, we are waiting.'

'Foolishly I became intoxicated. I was unable to travel on Christmas Eve.'

'You were unable to travel on Christmas Eve? A man whose capacity for alcohol is legendary and who is famed for his physical stamina was unable to travel—by horse and cart mind—the short distance from just outside Par-ramatta to his home in Cabramatta, because he was intoxicated?' At this point he shook his head and shrugged his shoulders, and I could cheerfully have wrung his neck. He continued with an exaggerated show of patience: 'Very well, let us accept that most unlikely

version of events. The following day—Christmas day—
you were able to travel, yes?'

'Yes.'

'So, you went home?'

'Look it wasn't exactly...' and I just did not know what
to say.

'Answer the question, please Mister Dwyer. Did you
go home?'

'No.'

'What more pressing engagement prevented you?'

'I went to Martin Burke's house.'

'Whom did you meet there?'

'Martin Burke.'

'Nobody else?'

'No.'

Well, he was surprised at that one: 'No? Remember
Mister Dwyer you are under oath. I will ask you the question again. Did you meet anyone else there?'

'Later, I met with Arthur Devereux and Hugh Vesty
Byrne, later.'

'Why did you go to Martin Burke's house?'

'I had a sick head from the drink and I needed a cure.'

There was much laughter, which was not to my liking
but the prosecutor enjoyed it. He pressed home the
advantage:

'Indeed, well may you laugh! No Mister Dwyer, I put
it to you that you did not go there for a cure, which took
twenty-four hours and had to be witnessed by three other
individuals.'

'But you don't understand...'

'... I would suggest to you, Mister Dwyer, that the reason why you and your co-defendants preferred to spend
your Christmas time together rather than with your wives
and families was not because you had all been drinking
and then somehow fortuitously landed in the same house.
It was because you were plotting together.'

'We were not.'

'You thought that at that time of the year you would be unlikely to be detected, didn't you?'

'No.'

'You would have the court believe that you and your friends just happened upon the same house, at the same time, and all just happened to prefer to spend your Christmas together than with your families? Is that your testimony?'

'It's not a crime to be a bad husband or enjoy a drink.'

'It is not. No, you went there to be the chief conspirator in the most dastardly plot to be hatched in the history of this colony, to overthrow His Majesty's legitimate Government and murder His Majesty's principal representatives. And that, I can assure you, *is* a crime. That is what you were doing there, isn't it?'

'No, I did not. We did not...'

'... I have no further questions for you.'

And with that, he sat down.

After that demolition all that remained now was for me to deliver the closing remarks of the defence, and I had had ample time while in irons on the *Porpoise* to plan my statement.

'I am guilty your honours: guilty of neglect, guilty of indulgence, guilty of inflicting the most severe injury on the one I love, and no punishments that your lordships might hand down would be adequate for those crimes. However, those are not the charges on which I appear before you. It is alleged by two individuals, who claim to have met me many times and yet cannot produce one witness to verify this, that I publicly boasted of a planned revolution, and that I then met with Martin Burke, Hugh Vesty Byrne, and Arthur Devereux to devise a plan that had been published in the Sydney Gazette some weeks previously. Is this the behaviour of four insurgents cunning enough to outwit the British Government for five years? I will not insult your honours' intelligence by pursuing that argument. My aim since coming to this colony has been to live peacefully and by my industry to accumulate sufficient wealth to bring my four children from Ireland to be united with their mother and their father, who miss them so desperately every hour of every day. Those who know me even moderately well will testify to that fact.'

Arthur then rose to address the court and my fear was that he would launch into some republican diatribe which would hang all four of us. He didn't. Instead he pointed out, quite rightly, that no evidence had been brought against himself and the other two, not even evidence of the flimsy and crooked nature that had been brought against me.

The court now retired to consider their verdicts. We didn't know whether we would have to wait hours or days, but they took not much more than forty-five minutes. The verdicts were read out.

Arthur Devereux—not guilty
Martin Burke—not guilty
Hugh Vesty Byrne—not guilty
Michael Dwyer—not guilty

I have rarely felt so relieved and elated. Colonel Johnston told us we were free to go. A guard came and took off our chains, and I embraced my comrades as we went out into the clean air.

I knew Mary would be outside the court, but could not see her at first because the crowd was being held back by soldiers. These were not soldiers from the New South Wales Corps, but Royal Marines who stood threateningly with bayonets fixed. I saw Mary in the crowd and ran towards her, but I was stopped by one of the Marines who pushed me back with his musket. As I retreated I got a vicious blow to the kidney from another rifle and this brought me to my knees. Before I could move I was in chains again and being bundled towards a wagon with the other three. This time we were all taken to the *Porpoise*. We had to wait two nights and a day before we were told our fate.

Bligh did not have the courage or the courtesy to bring the news himself but sent a lieutenant instead, who told us that the Governor had summoned an emergency meeting of a bench of magistrates who had now reviewed the evidence and found us all guilty. We were to be sent to the penal settlement on Norfolk Island and to join the work-gangs there. When I asked how long the sentence would be, the marine told me we would be freed if or when the Governor saw fit. I demanded to see my wife before we set sail, but this was denied me. So now I was to be sent to a place that could not have a worse reputation, for an indefinite period, perhaps for the rest of my life, with no sign of friendship or forgiveness from Mary. And she would be destitute, because now she would lose the two labourers who had been assigned to us and she would not be allowed to draw supplies from the Government stores.

Holt was at Norfolk Island, and for some reason that seemed to give me a glimmer of hope. Hope for what I wasn't sure, but the General had been here much longer than us and somehow I thought he might help me find a way to communicate with Mary and perhaps even help her in her pitiful plight.

I knew that MacCurry reminded me of somebody, and when I arrived on Norfolk Island I realised who it was, because one of the first faces I beheld there was the little pig face of T.F. Halpin. Memories of Sam MacAllister came flooding back, and I resolved then that I would achieve something during my stay in this terrible place. Joe Holt informed me, however, that it was nowhere near as terrible as it used to be. Flogging was still the favourite pastime there and it seemed that every prisoner had endured their share of it.

'What about yourself General?' I asked.

'They wouldn't dare Captain!' he replied. I must say that the General's attitude lightened my heart.

'Keep yourself to yourself, and your nose out of other people's business,' he advised. 'They do not like us here, but they do fear us, and some of them—King in my case and Bligh in yours—cannot accept the fact that we are free men and not common criminals. Mind you I made the mistake myself when I first arrived here of associating with one Maurice Margarot, the most seditious man in the whole colony.'

'An intelligent and brave man,' Arthur interjected.

'Stay away from him or you will finish your days at the end of a rope,' Joe told him.

'He is a great champion of our cause!'

'Your cause perhaps, but not mine.'

Arthur was shocked and stared at Joe in disbelief.

The General laughed and continued: 'All I ever wanted was to regain possession of my farm in Wicklow, and that is still my ambition. And I have great hopes of achieving it. I can make money from my farm here and make money from distilling. Oh yes, money will buy you most things here. When I first arrived on this damned island I asked Mister Jones, who was the chief jailor then, if I could pay someone to do my work on the gangs here, but I failed to persuade him. Other than that money has got me most of what I wanted, and I have people working on my behalf in Sydney and I hope to get back to my place in Parramatta soon. Then I will work on getting a free pardon and my passage back the Emerald Isle!'

I told Joe how worried I was about Mary's destitute state, and he assured me that Martha and their son Joshua would help as much as they could.

'Joshua must be nearly a man now,' I said.

'Man? Didn't he work his passage over here?'

'He never did.'

'As a sailor, yes sir! But the treatment he received from that Captain Salkeld was a salutary lesson. I had paid him sixty guineas for the boy's passage and he had entered him in the ship's books as a sailor and thus he had been living with the seamen and was entitled to wages and I ought to have received the money back I paid for his passage.'

'And did you fight it Joe?'

'You may be damn full sure I did. I got an order served on Captain Salkeld for the return of the sixty guineas I had paid for the boy's passage and his pay as a seaman.'

'No better man.'

'You have to know the sort of country this is, and I knew it before I ever set foot on it. The first sight that greeted me as we sailed past Pinch-gut Island was a skeleton hanging from a gibbet. That was sign enough for me.'

Hugh Vesty had not joined our company because he neither liked nor trusted Joe Holt, and Arthur had left because of the slur on Maurice Margarot. So, it was only Martin and myself who listened to Joe's advice.

'You will have to fold up your bedding and take it out to the yard with you every morning and there it will stay even if there is torrential rain all day, and that is what you sleep in that night. Whatever else you do, don't complain. Because one complaint will earn you twenty-five lashes, and that punishment is dished out on the spot and I tell ye lads they draw blood on the first stroke here. Once you have taken your twenty-five you join your gang and do a day's work, same as everyone else. The floggers here are arrant cowards, for cowardice always equals cruelty— fellows who dare not face a brave foe but would cut a submissive captive to mincemeat. I saw a man called Fitzgerald receive three hundred lashes one day, during which Doctor Mason used to go up to him occasionally to feel his pulse, it being contrary to law to flog a man beyond fifty lashes without having a doctor present.'

'Well isn't that a consolation anyway,' Martin Burke interjected sardonically.

'The bones were laid bare, let me tell you.'

'You have painted a clear picture for us all right Joe. And thank you for that,' I told him.

'The only strategy is to find a way out of here lads and I am working on that project. Money oils the wheels and I have some of that. Not as much as some people think now, but that is all to the good. You see the word has gone round that I have the rank of a General, which is true, but they do not know in what kind of an army I attained that rank.'

Never before had I known Joe to be so loquacious, but he must have been starved of good company because most of the inhabitants of that sad island were thieves, rapists or pickpockets, and Joe would not be happy associating with their like. True there were some Irish 'politicals' there as well, but attitudes to Joe within the movement were complex. There was a widely-held suspicion that he may have been a traitor, and a resentment that he had not led the rising at Castle Hill. He was a General with a well-earned reputation for being a canny campaigner, and he was the most senior member of the United Irishmen in the colony at that time. Mind you, he made the right decision. If he had led that revolt it is not the guards of Norfolk Island who would have greeted him but Saint Peter at the gates, and Joe planned to live many more years.

He did manage to get off the island. How or why we did not know, but one day he was no longer there. We could not ask those in authority what had become of him because that would have been considered too audacious.

Thanks to Joe's advice we managed to stay out of trouble. It was a hard life indeed. Each morning, once we had folded our beds, we marched to the yard outside the house of the chief jailor and then divided into two gangs. The gang leaders would lead their respective gangs to where they were directed and each man would be given a task there. The best plan was to finish your task as quickly as possible as this would leave you time in the day to work for yourself and earn extra provisions, because what we were allotted was not sufficient to support a body. Five pounds of flour was the allowance for each man, and he had to work and live for seven days on that. If a fella returned early from the public labour you were liable to be sent to the that part of the estuary they called 'the Cascade' and launch a boat, where you could be kept until ten o'clock at night without having tasted a bite of food for the day. Then it was back to the jail, soaking wet from head to foot, and you went to bed like that, because there was no time left in that day to prepare your food. Life on the run in the Wicklow mountains was rarely so cruel, and here if you stepped out of line you were severely punished.

A young lad from Cork, not yet twenty years of age, was made to work with a twelve pound iron attached to his ankle. He was forced to wade into the sea up to his waist to fetch some articles dropped from a boat. The poor lad collapsed eventually and was dead within two days. I added that young man to my prayers every night, because if anyone deserved eternal rest it was he.

Yes, I prayed, not an occupation to which I was accustomed, but here everyone prayed. I prayed that Mary was praying for me, and prayed the little litany I knew she recited as well—Mary Anne the first citizen, Peter and John the sons of Michael and the beautiful Esther.

But how could a man who prayed have so much hatred in his heart? All my hatred was focused on one person, whom I blamed for all our ills. I prayed for the hatred to abate, but every time I saw him it welled up inside me. When I knifed his brother all those years ago I should have done the same to him. That was an action taken in war. But this? What would this be but murder?

'Murder without question,' Arthur said, as the four of us sat picking at our measly slices of bread one night.

'What if we try him?' said I, 'try him as four United Irishmen, pass judgement on him and execute him.'

'You have obviously passed judgement already,' said Arthur.

'We are not fighting that war any more,' added Hugh Vesty.

'Well I am and Arthur is. I'm sure Martin is not going to renege on his oath, are you?'

'So what is the charge?' Hugh Vesty asked.

'Informing,' said I. 'Revealing to the enemy where we stored our provisions and the location of safe houses, thereby causing the deaths of Sam MacAllister and others.'

'I don't believe he informed.'

'Well somebody did.'

'And I believe that somebody to be Joe Holt.'

'That is just bigotry Hugh Vesty, pure bigotry.'

'Did he not admit himself that he didn't believe in the cause, and that he only joined the movement to get his farm back? Didn't he say that, Arthur?'

Of course Arthur agreed that he did, and I had to come to the General's defence again.

'No, Joe Holt is loyal and no matter what his reasons for fighting he was the most committed and professional among us. He would not inform. Halpin's brother, we know, gave information, which damaged us very seriously. The two of them could not have been closer. Once he had buried his brother, what did he do? He went to the authorities.'

There was silence for a moment and then Arthur spoke: 'This is personal Michael, nothing more. What could it achieve for the cause?'

'To show that we are still here. A force, even in this dark place, and nobody should cross us.'

'But Michael, many times over the last year I have come to you to talk United business, and asked you to meet with Margarot, and you sent me away every time.'

'True, but this arrest has changed all that. I am a father, Arthur, and was more concerned about my children than anything else, but now I know that we will never get justice from the English. We know the man is guilty. Let us see that he gets justice. What do you say?'

Hugh Vesty answered first. 'I still say if you are going to hang anyone, hang Joe Holt.'

'Martin?'

'Don't do it Michael. Put it to one side. I am thinking of your survival now. How are you going to kill a man here and go undetected? It is too great a risk. You will end up hanged in this Godforsaken place. None of us want that.'

'Sam MacAllister gave his life for me. I swore on his soul and on his mother's soul that those responsible would be brought to justice.'

'Sam was shot by soldiers of the Crown Michael. If you want to take your anger out on anyone take it out on them instead of inviting them round for tea,' Arthur said as he held my look.

'I'm using that man Arthur, for my own ends.'

'As long as he doesn't end up using you or... anyone belonging to you.'

'Say what you mean you po-faced prick!'

Martin saw the danger as I squared up and he stepped in between us.

'Gentlemen, you come to blows here, and you'll end up being flogged to within an inch of yer lives.'

A moment's thought and we both saw the sense in that; we took a breath and stepped back. Hugh Vesty came and put hands our shoulders: 'I tell ye boys it is going to take every ounce of strength God gave us to survive this place, never mind anything else.'

I knew he was right and I did try just to live every day as it came. We were a ragged ghostly lot marching and working in the blazing sun that scorched and bleached us. As a republican I believed that all of us are created equal but as a country man I could never take to the city rabble. By now, however, I felt sorry for all of us. Each day seemed to get longer than the one before it, and the tasks were so menial that they never taxed the mind in any way. From early morning we dreaded the midday sun, and when it did reach its full power that cursed ball of fire seemed not to move for an eternity, day after day. You wanted to scream with the heat and the tedium but woe betide any man that did.

Not a day went by without a flogging, and those perverted floggers loved their work; indeed they seemed to need it every day. The typical sound of this colony was not the call of any of its exotic wildlife but the lash of the cat-o'-nine-tails. The punishments, of course, had to be witnessed, and keeping the bit of food a fella had to survive on down in the stomach became an effort for some as we stood in the blistering heat. Even the days when there was a welcome breeze would be ruined as specs of blood and scraps of flesh could be blown into your face. How could a God look down on such a place and believe that what he had made was good? For our part we prayed that he might send some deadly poisonous mist or cloud to annihilate all who dwelt here.

In time it wore a man down into a state of useless apathy. But I raged against this and cursed all those who had brought me here. I cursed Colbert and Hume and Beresford. I cursed Trevor and Dunne and that damned American Consul. I cursed King George of England and Governor Bligh of New South Wales. I cursed O'Grady and MacCurry, and yes, above all others, I cursed T.F. Halpin.

Yes, it always came back to Halpin, and he was the one within my grasp. Day in, day out, I never took my eyes off him. He noticed, naturally enough.

One day when I was seated in the hut he came and stood over me. It took some time for him to summon the courage to speak. 'Let me make one thing clear. I did not inform. I swear by Almighty God that I gave no information regarding the locations of supply dumps or safe houses to anyone at Dublin Castle or Kilmainham Jail or anywhere. That is the truth of it. It would not be wise for you to move against me in this place, and I know that is what you want. But those in charge know your feelings towards me and if anything should befall me here you will pay the full price.'

He walked away, and I had to restrain myself from strangling him then and there.

Hatred can kill a man but it can also keep him alive and it is hatred that sustained me through those terrible days on Norfolk Island. Obviously I should have listened to the advice of my comrades, but I was confident that I could contrive a way of getting the satisfaction I craved. It would have to seem like an accident—that much was clear. Over days and weeks I observed Halpin's routine, and I began to see a way.

The Halpins were famous poachers back in Wicklow and, like most who plied that trade, they knew countless ways of getting fish out of a river. T.F. carried on this practice in the colony and in Norfolk Island. On the days when he finished his public work early he would go to a river and catch fish, either to supplement the meagre prison diet or as a commodity to sell or barter. This was to be my opportunity. Like most poachers, however, he had almost a sixth sense to detect when he was being watched.

The day came when we all finished early, and Halpin slipped away quietly to make for the river. I followed at a distance and kept well hidden. There was long grass on the bank that overlooked the river and I managed to crawl on my belly through this. He approached the river cautiously, looking about him all the time. But as he was about to kneel down to his nets he stopped suddenly and turned to look in my direction. I swear he did not see me, but he ran from the river as quickly as he could. When I arrived back in the hut he gave me a look that told me he knew the game I was at. I would have to wait and wait I did.

It was a long time before he slipped away for the river again, and the next time he did I did not follow, neither did I on the time after that nor the time after that. Indeed I let him go and fish several times in the hope that he would become complacent. Which indeed he did!

He seemed as cautious as ever when I followed him again and looked around just as much, but as soon as he knelt and bent towards the river I was on his back.

Nobody fights so fiercely as when they fight for their life. I had him by the hair of his head with my knee in the small of his back. Using both my hands I pushed his head under the water and held him there with all my strength. Halpin was no fool and he pushed himself away from the bank into the river. Near the bank it was only up to my waist, but in the centre there was a very strong current and it was into that he was trying to drag me. I resisted with all my might and held him down. He pushed his head towards me trying to butt or bite, but I managed to hold him off and his movements started to get weaker. I could not stove his head in with a rock because I did not want him cut as it had to look like a drowning. Then Jesus, what did I see but blood, blood streaming under the water. How the hell did I cut him? Then as his hands stopped beating I saw that it held a sharp piece of rock, which he must have had all the time, to use as a knife or a gaff, and he'd cut my arm with it. As it had happened underwater I hadn't felt it. When he was completely still and weak I let him go, and it was finally done. I blessed myself and said an act of contrition on his behalf. I am not a murderer and never was.

There were rumours in Wicklow that I was some kind of demented killer, but they were untrue. It was necessary for me to be ruthless with my enemies, because they were certainly ruthless in their war against me. There was a proclamation circulated long 'go to which my name had been forged claiming that I would pay £10 for the head of any Protestant and £20 for the head of an Orangeman. It was wiser at the time not to deny this because it added to my reputation, and my reputation got me out of more scrapes than my ability to fight ever did. But this act had to be kept secret.

I let the body float away before I tended to my arm. The gash was long and deep and it continued to bleed. My clothes were very ragged anyway, so tearing my shirt wasn't going to make any difference. I pulled it tight around the wound so that it would staunch it, and walked slowly back to the hut letting my clothes dry in the sun. Martin and the others asked me what had happened to my arm and I told them I had a fall.

Over the years I'd had many fitful nights because of the killing of Sam MacAllister, and my inability to find the informer who brought about this terrible tragedy. As I lay me down that night I hoped sleep would come soon but it did not. All night long I tossed and turned and fretted. Where was the relief, indeed the elation for having avenged that death at long last? It didn't come; it never came. Was it the danger of being found out that disturbed me? True, I was apprehensive about that, because the punishment would be certain death, and my death would leave Mary and my children in dire circumstances, because they'd lose the land and they would have every right to curse me for the rest of their days. But would they have cursed me more as the coward who let a rat live for fear of his own skin.

As I had anticipated, it was the following morning when Halpin was missed. Martin, Arthur and Hugh Vesty did not look towards me when his absence was announced, but they suspected that I was to blame. When a man went missing on Norfolk Island it was always assumed that he had tried to escape. Escape was virtually impossible from the island, but in desperation people tried it again and again, risking the terrible punishment that always followed. One of the guards came straight up to me and asked me if I had seen Halpin and I told him: 'No, I returned from work with these lads,' pointing at my four comrades who nodded their confirmation.

The deed was not mentioned between the four of us, but I knew that we would be questioned if the body was discovered. I'd had little time to weigh down the body before I would be missed, and, as I feared, it didn't take long for it to turn up. Hugh Vesty was the first to be called for questioning. When he returned he told me something that I suspected already—Halpin had informed the authorities on the island that I had threatened to kill him. During the next couple of days Martin and Arthur were called as well, but they did not call me. Days went by and still I was not called. Now I knew this was a ploy on their part, and I noticed that I was watched even more closely than usual.

One evening at the end of one of the hardest days work I'd ever done in this place I was called to the office of the chief jailor. This was a man who thought he was much cleverer than he truly was. He took the usual long pause staring at papers on his desk as I stood and waited. Then he said: 'Dwyer, we know you killed T.F. Halpin. You fought with him, stove his head in with a rock and then threw him into the sea.'

'No sir, I did not.'

'Then what did you do to him?'

'Nothing sir.'

'How did you kill him?'

'I didn't.'

'You killed his brother.'

'No!'

'And he informed on you to Dublin Castle.'

'His brother?'

'No Dwyer, T.F. who was a prisoner here.'

'Oh.'

'He revealed the location of a safe house and this caused the death of one of your gang?'

It seems T.F. had given a detailed account of the past. And isn't that just like an informer?

'Well now,' I said, folding my arms, 'did he indeed?'

'That is, you believed he did. I am not concerned with what happened in Wicklow all those years ago. I am concerned about what has happened here on my watch. I believe you to be guilty of murder and I have sent my report to Sydney informing them of my intention of carrying out the death penalty. Your friends, whom I believe to be accessories, will suffer the same fate. That will be all.'

The guard opened the door and I was ushered out. Now I wondered why they didn't just hang us here on the island, which is what normally happened when a capital crime such as stealing from the store was committed. I presumed that there was some apprehension about the hanging of four prominent United Irishmen because of the possible violent repercussions in the colony.

I decided not to tell my comrades that this death sentence had been passed on them for an act which I had committed against their strong advice. Best to wait until the last possible moment.

One morning when we had all gathered in the yard as usual the four of us were called out. We were marched in silence under armed guard to the harbour, and put on board a cutter. I asked one of the sailors where we were bound, and he told me: 'Van Diemen's Land.' At this point I told my comrades what had happened and that I believed that we were being brought to Van Diemen's Land to be executed.

'Then why are we not in chains?' Martin asked.

'And why is there no armed guard on this vessel?' said Arthur.

'Begob,' said Hugh Vesty, 'we could easily overpower what is here and take the boat for ourselves.'

'And we'd get far,' I said.

'Maybe as far as one of those exotic islands where dusky maidens would dance attendance on us?' mused Martin.

'I don't know about you Martin Burke but I do not find the thought of my execution at all funny. I told ye Michael! I told ye not to go after Halpin! We all did. Now it is going to be the death of us,' said Hugh Vesty.

'I don't think we're for the drop,' Arthur said. 'Much more likely that they will put us in the work gangs in Van Diemen's Land.'

My feeling was that Arthur was probably right. Van Diemen's Land was only beginning to be opened up, but already the work gangs there had a far worse reputation than those on Norfolk Island. Could something be worse than Norfolk Island? Oh Dante Alighieri was only trotting after King George's Government when it came to thinking up tortures and privations.

As we approached the harbour in Hobart I noticed a figure pacing who was dressed a lot like Mary, and the closer we got the more like my wife she looked.

'That is Mary, surely!' said Martin, and she started to wave. Why she was on the quay at Hobart none of us could fathom.

As we disembarked there were no soldiers or constables waiting to greet us, and we were able to embrace freely. She welcomed the others to the island saying to Hugh Vesty: 'Sarah and the children will be sailing across soon. You will have to be patient.' As we showered questions on her she held up her hands to calm us down. 'You will have to remain here on this island as free men until matters are finally settled in Sydney Town.'

She paused and looked at the four of us.

'Where do I begin? Yes, I will begin, I suppose, with O'Grady and MacCurry. Differences had arisen between Governor Bligh and Colonel Johnston, and other senior figures in the colony were involved as well. There was this movement and their aim was to remove Bligh from office and, I tell ye, the Governor had indeed become less popular by the day since you left. This didn't all have to do with your trial but that was a part of it, and Cecil felt this might be a good time for us to intervene...'

'Cecil?' I asked her.

'Lieutenant Lomasney. Believe me I would not be here but for him. In fact I should probably not be alive at all but for him. Now, others did help as well, and the Holts in particular—Martha and her son Joshua, who is a strong man now, and the General himself once he returned. It wasn't enough to save the crops because the convict help had been removed, but I was fed.'

'What about O'Grady and MacCurry?'

'Wait 'till I tell ye. On the Lieutenant's advice I went to see O'Grady's wife Una, who is a grand woman and God knows what she was doing married to that devil. If she could get her husband to swear that Bligh had told himself and MacCurry to tell those lies in court then this would help to discredit the Governor and, more importantly from my point of view, it would get you off that dreadful island. Oh Joe Holt told me about the regime there and you know him; he didn't spare any of the gory details. Martha had to stop him in the end because I became so upset. Where was I? Yes, Una O'Grady! So, I said to her: 'Be sure of one thing: General Bligh is on the way out, and if he goes, and go he will, Michael and the men will return from Norfolk Island. And where will your man be then? Legging it over the Blue Mountains to escape the wrath that will descend on him.' She wanted a guarantee from me that if her husband went with MacCurry to Major Johnston and told him the tale, you would not molest her husband once you were free. I gave her that guarantee most sincerely whether I was empowered to or not.

'In a couple of days the two rats were on their way to the headquarters of the New South Wales Corps when what should happen but they were shot dead. One bullet each, back of the head! Something of a mystery surrounds all this. They were not shot at close range with a pistol, but from some distance with muskets. The two of them were watched all the way by Johnston's men, and nobody is sure where the shots were fired from. The only people in the vicinity were a group of blacks and we all know that those fellas cannot use firearms. Logically it must have been one of Bligh's marines, but how the news of the traitors' confessions got to them I cannot for the life of me work out. I talked this over many times with Cecil, Lieutenant Lomasney, but we could not get to the bottom of it. He claimed that there was not a marksman of that ability in the ranks of the Marines. But you know there's always competition between the various regiments in that army. Anyway sure who else was going to profit by the deaths?

'So all I could do now was wait for events to take their own natural course. Every day resentment against Bligh grew in the colony and yours wasn't the only case where he overturned the verdict of a lawful court. That set the judges against him more and more. He had always taken a stand against strong drink and the rumour was that he was going to ban the sale of rum altogether in the colony, and you can imagine the uproar that would have caused. In any event he forbad the use of rum for bartering, and I'm not sure what anyone could have against that particular law. But now you won't find me having a good word to say in favour of the same Bligh. God knows he caused us all enough pain.

'The main man to stand against him was John Macarthur who, if you ask me, seems to own half of New South Wales, and 'twas he got the Corps to move against the Governor in the end. Mind you, according to General Holt that Macarthur fella exploited and cheated many members of the Corps. All the soldiers were given a grant of land you know, but most of them couldn't farm to save their lives and when the bold Macarthur offered them a gallon or two of rum for the parcel of land, didn't they sell it to him! What truth there is in that I do not know, but that is how Joe Holt had it. I never brought this question up with Cecil because I thought it might have been a touchy subject with the soldiers.

'Anyway, the day of reckoning finally came for Bligh, but now it was more like a festival than a revolution. The

New South Wales Corps led the way—cavalry and infantry trotting and marching to the Governor's house. Then came the band playing 'The British Grenadiers', and after them the populace and we shouting 'out with the tyrant' and 'off with his head'. Bligh's famous marines were nowhere to be seen because I suppose them buckos know which side their bread is buttered on. His daughter, Mrs Putland, was the only one fighting for him. There she was standing in the doorway shouting: 'Ye can't come in here, leave me father alone, what did he ever do to ye and where would ye be without him!' Major Johnson brushed her aside, God love her, and in he went. Now, and here's the best bit, but I'm not sure whether it is true or not, didn't they find the bold Bligh hiding under the bed. Anyway they took him away and he is deposed.'

'Where did they take him?' Arthur asked.

'To Hobart.'

'What? You mean he's here?' we shouted.

'Indeed he is and well-minded I'd say. Now Major Johnson has to go over to London and lay all this before the King, or whatever relevant person, who might be in possession of all their faculties, and competent to deal with such matters. Yes, I think that is how they put it. Hopefully then a new governor will be appointed and shipped over to us. Then, and not until then, can we go back to our home in Cabramatta.'

'Who is in charge now?' I asked.

'At the moment it is a man called Major Foveaux, and ye may have heard of him in Norfolk Island, because that hell hole was partly his creation. Oh yes, a black bastard by all accounts, and I mean black in the sense of evil and not in the sense of native. He is a law-and-order man which they feel is what is needed at the moment, but there will be someone else appointed temporarily until London has sorted it out and the new man arrives.'

'Are Sarah and the children safe and well?' Hugh Vesty asked.

'Oh, they're grand. It is just that there wasn't room for them on the transport I took over here. Well lads, enjoy the freedom of Van Diemen's Land. Ye'll have to seek employment to keep body and soul together, but I'll leave ye to yer own devices for I need to be with my husband.'

With that she took me by the arm and led me to an inn where she had reserved a room.

'Take your shirt off,' said she when we got there and I did.

'Now turn round.' I did.

'Jesus, you weren't flogged at all. I was expecting to see ye covered in great welts.'

'Are ye disappointed?'

'What happened your arm?'

'Bit of a fight.'

'And you got away with that?'

'I think so.'

'Very mysterious. Put your shirt back on; there's a lady present.' I did that.

'I have something to show you now,' said she with a smile.

'What would that be then?'

She handed me a piece of paper. The writing on it was somewhat slant and a bit crooked. It said:

> *Dear Mamma and Dadda, A letter for you. I hope you are well. We are. I am tired. We love you. Mary Anne Dwyer*

I read it again and again. We embraced and wept. For a while we just sat together and could not speak. Then Mary said: 'I want you to do something for me.'

'Anything! I mean anything.'

'Sarah Byrne.'

'What about her?'

'She's pregnant.'

'Pregnant? But we have been away nearly a year. Ten months, isn't it? How?'

'She had children to feed and clothe. It was desperation Michael.'

'Fucking whore. A wife and a mother, to do that.'

'She could not draw supplies from the Government stores. There was no one to help her. You know the problems between the Byrnes and the Holts.'

'To do that!'

'She did not have a choice.'

'And what about you?'

'Pardon?'

'Were you careful or just lucky?'

I should have seen it coming and ducked, but the clatter caught me smack on the cheek.

'How dare you!' she shouted.

'Well no bloody wonder! With your Cecil this and Cecil that and Cecil the God-damned other thing.'

'Jealous! Jealous! Don't be. He is a callow youth and not a man!'

My face stung.

'That really hurt, ye know.'

'You've had it coming since Christmas past. Never connected once then.'

'Never connected? You smashed my kneecap with a rock.'

'I did not. Show me so.'

My problem was I couldn't even remember which knee.

'It doesn't matter. It is all right now.'

'Smashed it! you said. Well show me!'

I rolled up the right leg of my britches, hoping there was a mark on the knee but there wasn't.

'Nothing!' said she. 'You know I think that Norfolk Island is after making you soft.'

'You have no idea,' I told her.

'So... anything? You said you'd do anything for me.'

That seemed a long time ago, but I agreed.

'I want you to tell Hugh Vesty about Sarah's condition and make sure that he accepts and looks after her and all their children.'

'I'll tell him Mary, but he won't have anything more to do with her.'

'You will see that he does.'

'I can't, and anyway he shouldn't. A woman to do a thing like that.'

'You can and you will. She is a virtuous woman is Sarah.'

'What?' I laughed.

'Oh yes she is. She hates what happened and what she did, but she did not see another way. Sarah is a good Catholic—better than myself. The torment and turmoil that woman is going through now, I would not wish on anyone. Worst of all there is no Catholic priest in the colony now and she can't go to confession. Do you know what that means to Sarah? This is what I'm asking of you and if you love me you will do it.'

'If he takes back a wife carrying someone else's child he will be scorned. He will be laughed at for God's sake.'

'Hugh Vesty Byrne, six foot four and a nineteen stone wrestler? Who is going to scoff at him? And you Michael Dwyer will make damn sure that nobody even thinks of it.'

'Very well, I'll try.'

'No, not try. You will do it!'

We found work and accommodation with a farmer near Hobart, and lived in a shack near his barn. It was a comfortable enough old shack for all that and now very dear in my memory. I had never been more in love with my wife than during those days in Van Diemen's Land, and after three months there Mary became pregnant. We were happy at this turn of events, but it did nothing to alleviate the pain of the loss of our four children left in Ireland, and now the possibility of getting them all over here seemed more remote than ever.

Without a doubt the most difficult task I had during that time was reconciling Hugh Vesty Byrne with his wife Sarah. When I told him of her condition he pushed me away and remained silent. I decided that the only thing for it was to leave him to it, and that he would talk when he was ready. Mary was not pleased with this circumstance, but I told her that we had to give the big man time and space. It transpired that he didn't need much of either, because late that night Martin Burke called to our shack to say that Hugh Vesty had already stretched two men outside a local tavern and was likely to do the same to anyone who approached him. 'The thing is, Michael,' Martin told me, 'that he won't say a word, and he refuses to tell either Arthur or me what the matter is. Do you know yourself?'

I told him that I did, but it was up to Hugh Vesty to reveal his own problem. When we got to the place we found him striding up and down inviting all comers to take him on—two at a time if they liked. Fortunately no constables had arrived on the scene as yet. Hugh Vesty had always followed my order, so when I commanded him to march away from this place flanked by Arthur and Martin he did so. When we got to the hut that Martin and Arthur shared I told him to tell his comrades what the problem was or I would have to tell them myself. He broke his silence with: 'You tell them so!'

'Hugh Vesty's wife Sarah,' I said, 'is pregnant. She had a choice between starvation for herself and her children or compromising herself in this way.'

'The bitch!' said Martin, and I was shocked into silence by this reaction from so quiet a man. But, after all, it had been my immediate reaction as well.

'Take that back Martin.' said Arthur. 'That's a fine way to treat a fellow citizen in distress. A mother has to feed her children, and that she puts before everything else. Do not blame the woman, but those who run this colony. They are the ones who compromise us at every turn and treat us as less than human. Where is she now?'

As Hugh Vesty was still inclined not to speak, I told Arthur that Sarah and the children would be arriving in Hobart, but she was afraid of her husband and had got Mary to tell me instead in the hope and that I would placate Hugh Vesty.

'If she sets foot in this place I will have nothing to do with her, because if I lay eyes on her I will not be responsible for my actions.'

'But you will have to feed and look after your children,' I told him.

'I do not have a problem with my children—just her!' said he.

Arthur added: 'As long as we live under the yoke of oppression we will be in such danger. If you throw out your wife or assault her they will have won. Do you not see that? The brave thing to do, the strong thing to do— and I believe you to be both brave and strong—is to take her back and forgive her. You must see that.'

Well said Arthur, I thought.

But Hugh Vesty put his head in his hands and groaned: 'I can't. I can't.'

'What are you going to do so?' I asked.

'Run away.'

'Where to?'

'I don't know. Into the jungle and hook up with the black fellas. At least they won't judge me. Everyone here is going to be looking at me and judging me. Always, always!'

'Nobody on this island knows your full circumstances, except those who are here, and nobody here is going to judge or criticise you or your wife. Isn't that right, Martin?' I asked.

'It is. I know I reacted angrily initially like yourself, but of course the lads are right.'

The big man sighed deeply and agreed that he would try.

And try indeed he did. When Sarah had arrived on the island with her children and the Byrnes were a family again it was clear that the balance of power within their relationship had changed radically. She no longer ordered Hugh about or scolded him at every turn, but went quietly about her business with head down and eyes averted. As Martin Burke put it, somewhat unkindly, she was chastened but hardly chaste! It was, Mary explained to me, that Martin was bitter towards women because of the marriage in Ireland that had gone so badly wrong.

Not that everything was plain sailing during the time in Hobart—far from it. We all had to work very hard just to subsist. Hugh Vesty had changed, lost much of his softness and was very quick to lose his temper, which got him into many scrapes. I feared that he might be arrested and sent back to Norfolk Island, and, sad to say, there was part of him that would have welcomed that.

Although the celebrations were muted he did seem to accept his new daughter.

There was nothing muted about the celebrations, though, when James was born to Mary and myself, as I drank my fill to welcome my new son and made sure everyone else got drunk with me. Yes, Mary was happy too with the new arrival, but it made her miss the others more than ever, and she kept Mary Anne's little letter with her at all times until it was tear-stained and wet with kisses.

I was even more impatient now myself to get the rest of them over but, by the looks of things, that possibility seemed more remote than ever. We would have a long way to go, but the appointment of a new governor meant that we could at least take the first step and return to our home in Cabramatta.

Chapter X

How they started from the beginning again and Michael is offered a position which may solve their problems or land them in even deeper trouble.

The sight that greeted us there can only be described as desolate. Drought followed by deluge followed by drought had laid waste all our land. We had to start again from the very beginning and put the three wasted years behind us. At least we were alive and together back in our home, had our 'convict help' restored, and we could draw supplies from the Government stores. We had learned much from our first year working this land even though that harvest had been lost due to my incarceration. The land had been cleared and so we could settle down imme-diately to ploughing and sowing.

I had never really felt that this land was mine until it was taken from me, or rather until I was taken from it. When I returned I truly took possession of it, and rose every morning with a great enthusiasm for my work. Crops needed more care and nurturing in this place than they did in Ireland, but we were equal to the task now. I had grown accustomed to the sun, and had developed a healthy respect for its strength. Not that I ever used a mirror over much now but I did notice that my hide had taken on a kind of a red raw look. Some said that this was partly caused by the consumption of rum but I know the sun was mostly to blame. Mary's complexion on the other hand took on a deep honey colour, which matched her blue eyes and black hair. That year brought a bumper harvest, and once it had all been saved our daughter Bridget was born. We disagreed as to whether she looked more like Esther or Mary Anne, and oh how we wished her sisters were there to greet her.

Hugh Vesty and Sarah's visits in the past brought chaos and colour, but now they just brought gloom. Sarah would stare straight ahead vacantly while Hugh Vesty looked down, consumed with interest in his boots. There was still no priest in the colony, and it would seem that Lachlan Macquarie, the new Governor, a Highlander, or a Hebridean to be exact, was not too keen to have one ministering during his term of office. In all other matters the man seemed to be liberal and forward-looking, and I resolved to go and see him on the question of the children. Sarah asked, if I did get to talk to him, to put in a request for a Catholic priest to be allowed in the community. I told her that I was concerned only about our children being brought from Ireland and cared nothing about priests, but Mary said: 'Don't worry Sarah, of course Michael will bring up the question of our being allowed to practice our religion if he gets to see the Governor.'

It took some time, but the Governor did grant me an audience. For a hardened professional soldier who had been through many tough campaigns, the man was extremely smooth and clean, and impeccably manicured, coifed and attired. His voice had a soft Hebridean lilt to it which put me in mind of Sam MacAllister.

'*Fáilte romhat, a cheannaire uasal,*' he said in greeting. '*Cloisim go bhfuil ag éiri go brea leat i gCabramatta.*' (I hear you're getting on well in Cabramatta.)

I had to tell him that I didn't speak the Gaelic and that put me on the wrong foot straight away. The man listened with what seemed like rapt attention to my story—head slightly inclined, long fingers touching the forehead as he nodded almost imperceptibly. I told him about Hume and his terms and Trevor and his assurances. When I finished he asked: 'Do you have a written undertaking of any kind from this Doctor Trevor?'

'No, there is nothing in writing.'

'I see.'

'I have worked hard since coming to this place.'

'Indeed you have.'

'And I've done no wrong. However, I've had grievous wrong done to me.'

'That was most unfortunate.'

'And I think I deserve... What I'm saying is I cannot make up for that time and how it has hindered me in attaining the main object of all my endeavours, which is to bring my children from Ireland.'

'I understand.'

'In view of this sir, could you not see your way to ensuring that they are sent out here speedily?'

'I regret that I cannot do that.'

'But you are the absolute authority here.'

'Here, yes. But I have little influence in Dublin or London.'

'They would listen to you. They would!' And now I was coming close to begging which made me very angry indeed.

'Even if you had money—and money is an impediment—I doubt very much that you would get a ship to take them while we are still at war. And at war with an enemy you have supported.'

'I don't support the French. I've never supported the French. I don't like the French. Republicanism, that is what I stand for. The rights of man!'

'It is an abomination sir, that flies in the face of God. You Irish should know that better than most, as priests, nuns and bishops are put to the sword by republicans. It is not right or natural and will never succeed.'

'What about America?'

'America is a country whose economy is based on slavery. Perhaps that is a prerequisite of your republicanism—Ancient Greece and Rome, Republics with systems based on slavery. Surely sir you do not support slavery?'

'The only thing I know of slavery sir is the convict ship that brought me here. Like most other such vessels it was designed, built and used in the slave trade that brought so much wealth to your country.'

My anger had shown through but it was greeted only with a hint of a smile, and a final: 'That will be all sir.'

Where I should have gone when I left the interview was directly home, where I knew Mary would be on her knees praying for a good outcome from the meeting with the Governor, but I was almost apoplectic with rage and needed something to ease the anger. The district I walked through was called 'Liverpool' but was more commonly known as 'Irishtown'. Every second building seemed to be a tavern, and they all looked welcoming. For the past couple of years I had tried to stay away from spirituous liquors with some success, drinking mostly ale or wine. What I would have liked now was a shot of John Cullen's *poitín*, but I would have to make do with Barney Dillon's rum. Barney's place was quiet, and as I entered a man at a table in the corner finished his drink and left quickly. I didn't get a look at him. Barney was his usual, congenial self. He had been ten years in Sydney and they had a child every year. He was a roguish sort of a chap, with black curly hair and a wicked twinkle. 'Tell me this and tell me no more,' he said, 'did that big friend of yours have a terrible time on that bastard island?'

'Fierce bad,' I said, 'but we won't talk about it.'

'And I won't be asking. I was enquiring only in the generality, you understand. But I have never seen a man drained so much of his spirit. And there is a kind of a bitterness there now—not good, now, not good!'

'He'll get over it—in time.'

'Sure doesn't it cure all, says you. I'm fond of ol' Hugh Vesty and I'd hate...' Barney stopped talking and obviously did not like the three men who came in. One was a tall, lean and muscular man, but it was hard to tell his age because you couldn't work out whether the lines on his face were scars or wrinkles. He said nothing but held up three fingers to Barney, who poured them out three shots and then scurried off to busy himself in another part of his establishment. Well I was in the mood for a fight. Nothing was said and nobody looked at anyone. The two lads threw back their drinks and the tall man sipped his. When he'd finished it he dusted himself down, straightened up, turned and looked at me.

'I hear you did for Halpin on Norfolk Island,' said he.

'Not a notion of what you are talking about.'

'And you let that Protestant bastard Holt go free.'

'I wouldn't call the General that latter to his face if I were you.'

'Ah, you are well in with the Prods all right. You have some round for tea and you go and beg favours off others.'

I slapped him hard across the face. Why I slapped him instead of punching him I do not know, but it was a mistake because it left him standing. The two lads were quick, and they dashed round me grabbing an arm each from behind. The lanky man kicked me where a man should never be kicked, and then he connected first with a right and then with a left to the head. I saw stars for a moment and then I saw his kisser right up against mine. 'How do you like that, 'Captain'?' He sneered, but then he screamed with pain as I bit into his nose with a grind and a growl. The two lads loosened their grip and as I freed myself Barney threw me a bottle. I smashed it over one of the lads' heads and the jagged bit left in my hand I shoved in the other lad's face. Exeunt all three screaming as I spat the gristle from my mouth.

'You haven't lost your touch,' Barney said.

'No, just me front tooth.'

The other patrons now emerged from the darkness, ordered drinks for themselves and plied me with whatever I was having. Drinks and questions were coming at me from every direction, and connections were established as each drinker discovered that he was related in some distant way to somebody in the tavern or at least knew a cousin of theirs from way back. It was pleasant to be feted as a hero again, and every man insisted that I drink the drink he had bought for me. It wasn't too long before it took its toll and apparently I was wanting to take my leave of the place a long time before I keeled over.

To this day I do not know the identity of the two men who wheeled me home on the handcart, and once they had placed it down gently in front of the house they skedaddled as quickly as they could. Mary, of course, got a desperate shock when she saw the state I was in, but then she didn't know that most of the blood was not my own. And if she was shocked at the sight of me she was even more shocked when I spoke, for I roared: 'That bastard Macquarie!'

'Jesus preserve us Michael, you're not after assaulting the Governor?'

When I recovered I told her the whole sad tale of the Governor's refusal to help and how I was assaulted in the tavern, leaving out the gory details. Then we looked at each other for a while, searching for hope, and painfully aware of our powerlessness. Obviously we delighted in the growth and development of James and Bridget, but every time they achieved something, overcame some small obstacle, we were reminded how the four in Dublin were coping without us. We would gladly have swapped the sunshine, comfort and freedom of this time for a few of the old jail days in Kilmainham. We had work to do every day and we were thankful for that.

So, early the following morning I was out stabbing at the hard ground with my hoe, sore and jittery from the previous day's exertions. I wasn't long at it when Mary called me, with: 'You'll never guess who is here!'

I couldn't.

'Cecil!' she announced, and that didn't fill me with joy.

The Cecil was there right enough, every inch the toy soldier, and he had brought his bride-to-be with him, a porcelain figurine in powder blue called Melissa. He shook my hand, but somewhat gingerly, because I hadn't washed it—just wiped it on the arse of my britches. Melissa backed away from me apprehensively keeping close to her husband-to-be. My face, of course, was scarred and swollen, but I wasn't about to offer any explanation for the wounds.

'I have heard so much about you,' Mary said to Melissa.

'And I about you, Mrs Dwyer,' said the doll in a voice that was surprisingly low and husky.

'We would not be looking forward to the upcoming wedding but for your good wife, Michael,' Cecil told me. 'Oh yes indeed, she was the one who persuaded me that I should bring Melissa over here.'

'That sounds as if you did not want me of your own accord, darling,' she purred.

'Oh no my dearest, had you not been willing to come here I would have returned to Ireland. You know that my sweet. But I believe in this country. I believe in its future. A man can prosper here. Can he not Michael? You are the living example of that. Look at what you have achieved despite all the adversity.'

'We would not have survived the adversity but for you, Cecil,' said Mary.

'Yes, we are indebted to you Cecil,' I said. 'Oh yes Miss, this man was a veritable knight in shining armour to my wife while I was incarcerated. He gave so much of himself and called whenever possible to see to her needs. Did you know that?'

'No Mister Dwyer, I did not.'

'So, have you fixed a date?' Mary asked hastily.

'Well we we're thinking of...' Cecil began but Melissa interrupted sharply: 'No, we have not decided yet.'

'I see,' said Mary, somewhat taken aback.

I wondered who was going to win the battle of 'should we invite the Dwyers to the wedding', and I knew Cecil the toy soldier was about to embark on a real war.

'Will you miss Ireland, Miss?' I asked.

'Perhaps in time, but not yet.'

'And where will you miss, Miss?'

'I am from Tipperary.'

'Ah, a fellow country person. Whereabouts?'

'Near Cashel.'

'That is the Earl of Llandaff territory.'

'Indeed our estate, farm, borders his land.'

'You will know John Mathew, then?'

'I have met the gentleman, yes, and his wife.'

'She is one of the Whites of Cappawhite.'

'Indeed, you are correct.'

'A fine family.'

'I agree.'

'You see, a connection established. Whenever two Irish people meet it is always possible to establish a connection. Don't you agree Cecil?'

'I suppose,' he said, and Melissa laughed. We waited for her to explain the reason for her mirth, and she did.

'I have to admit that I was somewhat apprehensive to meet you, Mister Dwyer.'

'And why was that?'

'Well, when I was a girl I was threatened with you when I was bold.'

'I could never imagine you being bold, Miss.'

'Oh now Mister Dwyer! It was "don't wander off or Michael Dwyer will come and get you". "Stop crying or Michael Dwyer will take you away." I thought you an ogre.'

'And now you've met me you know the truth.'

'Precisely!' she said.

Cecil then asked us if we had heard of the Governor's latest initiative, but Melissa corrected him saying: 'I think actually dear that it is Mrs Macquarie's initiative.'

'Well she may be organising the event but it is the Governor's idea.'

'Well, pray tell us what it is!' asked Mary.

'Well, he, she, they are giving a Saint Patrick's Day party, for the Irish,' said Cecil.

'Convicts!' added his wife-to-be.

'Not just convicts dear, but overseers, military personnel and settlers.'

'Are there Irish settlers?' she asked.

'Of course dear!' he said, rightly shocked.

'Oh how silly of me. Obviously Mister and Mrs Dwyer you are... em...'

'I hope you will grace the occasion with your presence,' Cecil said.

'We would be delighted,' Mary told him.

The Saint Patrick's Day party was a very tame affair. Now it may be that the Scottish definition of a party differs radically from the Irish definition, or it may be that Mrs Macquarie has her own idea of what a good hooley is. It was all very nice and polite, and there was no hard drink involved. She had rustled up as many singers and musicians as she could, but the best ones must have left their instruments behind, and those that had brought theirs would have been better off leaving their's behind. A Donegal man sang a come-all-ya in Irish that went on for about half an hour. Don't ask me what it was about but the Governor understood and appreciated every word of it.

Arthur did not attend, but Martin, Hugh Vesty and Sarah did. The Grecian style was in vogue that year among the women of Sydney and we were treated to a more generous display of flesh than usual. I asked Hugh Vesty what he thought of the show and he hissed: 'Bitches!' and I saw he was looking at the women with unconcealed hatred. Martin, on the other hand, was oodling. 'Mind you they don't show as much as the native women,' he pointed out.

Hugh Vesty, obviously keen to change the subject, said the Macquarie was going to allow horse-racing in the colony, and wouldn't that be a good day out. Martin wondered if women would be allowed to the event and Hugh Vesty hoped bloody not!

Sarah and Mary had been helping Mrs Macquarie with the festivities, and I noticed them talking intensely with the Governor's wife. They seemed upset when they joined us.

'Highfalutin madam,' said Sarah and spat. 'Black Protestants, they are all the bloody same!'

I asked them what had transpired and Mary began: 'Well, we were *plámásing* her husband and his liberal views and all...'

'You were *plámásing* her Mary Dwyer, not me,' Sarah corrected her.

'Now Sarah, this is of more concern to you than it is to me.'

'All right, I asked for that. Go on so!'

'"Well", says I to herself: "I suppose it will only be a matter of time before the Catholic Faith is officially permitted here".'

'And do you know what she said? Go on Mary!'

'Absolutely not!'

'Now imagine that! But that's not all. Wait till ye hear this. Tell 'em Mary!'

'"My husband", says she, "holds that the Popish Church is founded on superstition, and firmly believes that there should be but one religion in New South Wales—the Established, Reformed, Protestant Church".'

'Then why are they honouring Saint Patrick?' Martin asked.

'Didn't Mary ask her the self same question. And her ladyship says, bold as brass, 'Saint Patrick brought Christianity to Ireland, not Roman Catholicism'.'

'Are they saying Saint Patrick was a Protestant?' asked Hugh Vesty in complete bewilderment.

At this point we had to put an end to the conversation because the Governor approached our little gathering. He asked us if we had enjoyed the 'modest' celebration and we all murmured our appreciation; nobody complained about the National Saint's new designation. After some more small talk Macquarie drew me aside and asked me to come and see him the following day. My fear was that some half-nosed bastard had lodged a complaint against me.

It was with some trepidation that I set out the following morning, and I upset Mary by trying to discuss the eventuality of my not returning from the visit to the Governor. He offered me tea on arrival, which led me to believe that I was not in trouble. But then he remarked on my scars and asked me if I had been in a 'bit of a scrape'.

'The way it is, your honour, I have a reputation and men are frequently tempted to test the validity of it.'

'I'd say very few have got the better of you,' he mused.

'So far nobody has,' I told him.

'Splendid!' he remarked, which I found very strange indeed. Then he looked at me and struck a pose, head back, arms folded, like a professor about to dispense wisdom.

'It is now little more than twenty years old this... settlement. There, you see, we don't even know what to call it. It was conceived as a prison camp in the remotest corner of the world. We had lost America, our jails and prison hulks were full to overflowing, and Cook had found this place—New Holland! It was an experiment, or a harebrained scheme if you wish. Miraculously those who arrived on the first fleet survived, or most of them did. Great praise is due to Governor Philip for bringing them through those first years, when starvation was a real and terrible possibility. It is a cruel and unforgiving land this—you know this yourself because you tamed some of it. You have children who were born in this place—two now is it?'

'And another on the way.'

'I see, splendid! That is an investment indeed, in this land, in this venture. There are many Irish here now—some convicts, some convicts who have gained their freedom and rehabilitated to settle here, some free settlers, some deportees, like you and your companions, who have the status of free settlers, and others who have come here of their own volition. Yes, a great many Irish, and I consider you the chief among them.'

'No sir, that honour should go to General Holt,'

'Your General, as you call him, has no commitment to his country—to the venture—and he does not command the same respect of the people as you do. You are familiar with the district known as Irishtown. Your people—some of them, many of them, more and more as time goes by—have moved together into one place. They feel safe there. Unfortunately nobody else does. Now, to the point. I am reforming the police force of New South Wales. Indeed, what we have here already one could hardly call a police force. Will you join this new force as a constable based in the suburb of Liverpool and responsible for the area known as Irishtown?'

I had been wondering where this was going, and was not happy with where he had led me. I asked: 'You see me as the poacher turned gamekeeper, is that it?'

'Oh, much more than that!'

'Thank you, Governor, but I am happy on my farm. It keeps me fully occupied.'

'But you would keep your farm! Indeed, I would like to see you expand your farm. You will draw a salary and you can get help with the daily tasks on the farm. Yourself and your good wife will still run it. What do you say?'

'I'd like to think about it.'

'Of course, and you must discuss it with your wife.'

'Yes, and with...' I stopped.

'Yes?'

'Just my wife.'

'Excellent! I have not forgotten your original petition to me, regarding your children left behind in Dublin. If you accept this job it will certainly help that situation.'

'In what way?'

'In two ways. Your financial situation will improve, and you will be seen as having renounced your former rebel status.'

'I will always be a republican, Governor.'

'Believe what you like in your heart. We are all free to think what we please, but keep the peace in this land. You put up a brave fight, but it is over now. America didn't want you, and I suspect the French don't either. Not that you'd want to live in France I'm sure, which is certainly not a republic any more because it is ruled by an emperor. Or can a country be a republic and a dictatorship at the same time? Hm?'

'I suppose not.'

'Of course not. Here you will be a free man; a man of substance and of status. I'd like a prompt answer Michael.'

'I'll give you that.'

'Splendid!'

I was tempted not to tell Mary what he had said about the children in Dublin, because I knew she would find it difficult to see beyond that hope. But it would have been dishonest to withhold it. How wrong I was to have doubted her courage and loyalty.

'If you think it is too big a price to pay, I understand that. I am not going to ask you to renounce all your principles and beliefs. Your children would not ask that of you either. It has to be your decision Michael.'

I would have preferred a stronger stand of course. Indeed I would have preferred if she had made the decision for me. 'I took an oath, Mary,' I said.

'So did thousands of others Michael, but the venture failed.'

'What is this place, though?'

'Whatever else it is, it's our home now.'

'What will our children be? What will our grandchildren be? And the republic? Where is that?'

Then I articulated something which had been troubling me for some time. 'How is it that I feel less free here than I ever did in Kilmainham jail?'

She told me: 'There are four answers to that.'

She was right, needless to say, and we repeated our little litany together, and we wondered if James and Bridget and even the baby soon to be born would learn to say it before they ever set eyes on their brothers and sisters. My feeling of captivity came out of the enforced separation from my children.

'I should discuss it with my comrades.'

'No you should not.'

'They stuck by me through thick and thin. I led them into terrible dangers—put their lives at risk. I have to talk to them.'

'Talk to them by all means, but not until we have made a decision. Then you can tell them before you go back to Macquarie. What's the uniform like?'

'There isn't one, but you get a new suit of clothes every year, to keep you looking respectable.'

'That'll be grand as long as I can choose it,' she said.

I laughed, but then she asked a very pertinent question. 'Do you think you could demand of Macquarie that taking the job would be conditional on his getting the children brought over?'

'I don't know. It depends on how badly he needs me.'

'Irishtown is completely out of hand and getting worse. You are the one to keep it in order.'

'I'll try it then. But I'll speak to my companions first.'

'I'd prefer if you gave your answer to Macquarie first and then told the others.'

We agreed to disagree on that, and invited them to come and dine with us of a Sunday.

I was unable to see Arthur in person but he declined the invitation. Martin, Hugh Vesty and Sarah came. I had built a porch at the rear of the house which afforded very good shade and after the meal we sat there drinking wine like true colonials. My announcement had received a muted reaction, although Martin did seem to be very interested, but cautious about giving voice to that. After a spell of unsettling silence on the porch Sarah said to Hugh Vesty: 'Well, you're not joining anyway, and you may be sure of that!' Hugh Vesty agreed that he wouldn't be and she added: 'Oh no, I'll have no husband of mine parading round in an English uniform!'

'There will be no uniform. Well nobody's asked him Sarah, have they?' Mary put in.

'In the event!' said Sarah.

'Unlikely!' said Mary.

To relieve the tension Martin said: 'The constabulary of New South Wales!'

'Wales!' said Sarah, and spat.

'What's wrong with Wales?' Mary asked.

'Well now Mary, your one brush with the Welsh was the Ancient Britons. Or had you forgotten that particular episode from your past?' Sarah twisting a knife.

Mary replied, close to tears: 'Of course I haven't forgotten. That was very unkind Sarah.' And she wept. Sarah rushed to her, now in tears herself, and embraced her as she spoke: 'Oh Jesus Mary, forgive me, what am I saying? I am a bad lot some times. I don't know what gets into me. It is having no Mass and no priest and no confession. Not able to stay right at all. 'Tis a desperate way to be living. The Protestant minister was round at the house again yesterday, at us about coming to his service today. Sure we'd only be excommunicated if we did that.'

'Which he knows full well,' Hugh Vesty added.

'Oh you may be damn full sure he knows it. Isn't that what he wants—all of us cast out and turned into heretics. He has some chance, let me tell ye. Didn't he want to baptise Charles?'

'And Mary Agnes before that.' Hugh Vesty put in. Now Charles had been born a few months previously, but Mary Agnes was the child of Van Diemen's Land and the mention caused an unease. Sarah, who had disentangled herself from Mary by now, clutched her husband's hand but did not look at him. She continued: 'We baptised them ourselves of course, because that is allowed in the church if there is no priest available. 'Tis a great consolation to me to know that they are without sin, which is more than can be said for myself. What will become of me at all? If I was to die tomorrow? Oh Jesus!'

'Hush girl, there's no fear of you!' Hugh Vesty said firmly.

'Ah thanks Hugh Vesty, pet. You're a wonder. I have a great husband.'

'That'll do now!' he said.

Martin swiftly changed the subject to crops and stock. All three of the farms in Cabramatta were doing extremely well. But Arthur, whose farm was farther away to the north of Parramatta, had hardly put a spade in the ground yet. Sarah suggested that it was the lack of a woman and a family in his life that had made Arthur the way he was, but on the other hand Martin managed very well with no wife or dependents. But then Martin always intended to bring a woman into his house and Arthur, as far as I can recollect, never mentioned the subject.

'This is about getting our children over here. That is why Michael is taking this position,' Mary stated.

'Well then, you'd better make that a condition of your taking the job,' Hugh Vesty said.

'Oh he intends to do that,' Mary told him, and I wished she wouldn't speak on my behalf.

'While you're at it you could bring up the subject of a Catholic priest with your friend,' said Hugh Vesty with a sneer.

'He's not my friend!' I told him.

'Well your boss then, or whatever he is.'

Martin calmed things down with: 'He's all our boss, whether we like it or not. That's how it is.'

This move of mine was going to damage my friendship with Hugh Vesty; I knew that. But I also knew that it would mend in time. The damage to my relationship with Arthur, however, would be permanent, and that meant much more to me.

I rode out to Arthur's place, where I had not been since before our sojourn on Norfolk Island, and I could not believe my eyes. Not a tree had been felled; not a bush uprooted. It seemed to me he had done nothing. Dotted about his land were these bockety structures made of branches and the bark of trees, and wandering about were these natives, black men and women, some of them almost as naked as the day that they were born. Now I had seen natives about the place—never had any truck with them mind—but not so many together and never so bare. I rode up to the house where there were black fellas sitting on the steps, and Arthur came out to greet me; well to meet me, not so much to greet me.

'What the hell are these doing here?' I asked.

'The Bidjigal or the mia-miyas?' said he.

'What? What?'

'The people or the shelters, citizen?'

'Both! On your land?'

'Whose land?'

'Ha?'

'Is it mine?'

'Of course it is.'

'How?'

'It was given to you.'

'By whom?'

'Stop this.'

'King George of England was it Michael? Was it Michael?'

'What are you trying to do here?'

'And was it his to give?' He waited. I said nothing and he continued: 'We fought for five years to contest his right of dominion over the people and lands of west Wicklow, but when he lays claim to this place we do not have a problem.'

'This is different.'

'How?'

'You know it is.'

'You were always a republican first and a nationalist second. The Rights of Man, Michael! You and Sam MacAllister swore by it'

'But... are these men?'

'Jesus Christ!'

I whispered now: 'I thought the jury was out as to whether they had souls or not.'

'Believe me they have souls Michael. I have seen them and they are quite magnificent.'

'Anyway it won't be tolerated.'

'By whom?'

'The authorities.'

'Oh, you'll come and arrest me, will ya?'

Now he had me on the back foot and he looked away from me.

'You know?'

He nodded his head, but still did not look at me.

'How?'

'I have eyes and ears, Michael.' I said nothing, he looked at me, and I thought he might cry: 'Have you signed whatever you have to sign or taken whatever oath they ask yet?'

'Not yet,' I told him.

'Please reconsider it.'

I sighed but said nothing. A black sitting beside Arthur smiled at me. It was a kind of a sad but understanding smile, and I did not like it. I had always avoided eye contact with the natives. Not that I was afraid of them mind, but they did give me the creeps. Mary thought their children were lovely, but then all children are nice.

'It is a question of survival.'

'You want to ask these people about survival. The Eora could tell you a thing or two about that.'

'The what? You called them something else back then.'

'The Bidjigal,' he said, putting his arm round the darkie beside him. How could he do that to a savage covered in grease and dirt, with a bone through his nose and a bone through his hair? Made me shudder.

'The Bidjigal are Eora, but so are the Karegal, the Wanegal and the Kadigal.'

'Arthur, I am not interested.'

The black fella then said something to Arthur, in his own language, and Arthur replied. Then the savage said something else, and at this point I saw and heard something I had never witnessed before—Arthur Devereux laughed, loud and heartily. The native laughed with him. Once they had subsided Arthur said: 'He asked me if you were in the Rum Corps—that is a name for the New South Wales...'

'... I know what the Rum Corps is Arthur.'

'When I told him you weren't he asked why you had a rum nose.' They continued to laugh, too loud and too long for my taste.

'It is the bloody sun, okay!'

'I have not known the sun to have such an effect,' the native told me in perfect English. 'You continue to drink rum Michael Dwyer, and you will no longer be a great warrior.'

'The difference is—we can hold our liquor. Did Arthur neglect to tell you that?'

'I told them you were our Pemulwuy.'

'Who the hell is Pelumbee?' My mispronunciation caused general laughter.

'You have been in this country more than three years now, and you have never heard of Pemulwuy? He held out against the English longer than we did Michael. Twelve years and they couldn't catch him. He won battle after battle—at Parramatta, Lane Cove, Bridge End, and he burned crops and houses and barns. They sent cavalry and infantry after him, marines and soldiers. But they could not catch him, because this was his land and he knew it. Twelve years Michael! Imagine that!'

'How come I never heard of him?'

'If the English write our history, what will you be? A footnote—a criminal.'

I looked at these natives in a slightly different light now, but though I might admire them I could never get to like them. On the other hand, people who could make Arthur Devereux laugh must have something.

'They did this on their own?'

'There were some Irish with them, certainly at the battle of Parramatta, but they are all dead now anyway. For a while, King gave the settlers permission to kill any native on sight if they saw fit. So many dead.'

Arthur brought a jug of fresh water and we sat for a while in the shade. When I arrived here I had feared for his dignity, but now I feared for his safety and sanity.

'So, you refused to wear Robert Emmet's uniform, but you'll put on a uniform of the crown?'

'Shut up, Arthur! Anyway there is no uniform.'

'You made me a promise Michael. You gave me your word. If I wrote that letter to Trevor you would continue to be a United Irishman and work for the cause.'

'Whatever you have in mind Arthur I do not want to know.'

'It is their land, Michael.'

'Is it?'

'Well it is not a *terra nullius*.'

'A what?'

'God, you never got your pennies' worth from Master O'Brien.'

'I learned to read and write. That is all I need.'

'An empty land that belongs to nobody.'

'Well they haven't done much with it.'

'They have survived here, indeed thrived here, since the beginning of time. The first fleet arrived and the invaders nearly starved to death within the twelve month. Oh no, this is their natural place.'

'Anyway, I will continue to work for the cause in my own way. Our cause, not somebody else's.'

I cannot now recall the names of any of the natives I met that day. They looked fresher and healthier than the ones I met around Sydney and that was probably partly due to the fact that Arthur would not tolerate alcohol. They showed me all their various implements and weapons. All I wanted was a try of a boomerang, and although they didn't often use them in this part of the country they brought me one, and I found it an exciting and formidable weapon. Their greatest pride however was in their spears. These were small, lightweight and very sharp. Some were made more dangerous by gluing sea shells with a cutting edge to the point. Then they had an ingenious device which they called an 'umana'. This was a simple piece of wood with a socket at one end which engaged the butt of the spear. When released it propels the spear a great distance. This was their principal weapon in their war against the English, as they could release a shower of spears from behind cover, which would land on the enemy with devastating effect. An impressive weapon but not much use against field artillery.

Arthur sat shaking his head from side to side for a long time. Eventually I asked: 'What?'

He replied: 'Our cause? Is not that the same as theirs? You see, that's the problem Michael. As long as we care for our own kind more than for any other kind, there never will be peace. You would have so much to offer these people Michael—so much to offer.'

'I have children Arthur. Children change everything.'

At this, he merely sighed.

'So, what happened to him, this Pemulwuy?'

'They killed him eventually. Then they took his head away—out of the country. Same as Robert Emmet, really—no grave, no monument, no focus for future agitation.'

As I got up I offered him my hand: 'There is nothing for me here.'

'So, you will become a constable?'

'I think our people would rather be policed by me than by others.'

'True. But I think your appointment is a stroke of genius on Macquarie's part. Good luck.'

He took my hand and I said: 'Take care citizen.'

I rode home slowly.

The first thing Macquarie did at our meeting was congratulate me on the birth of our daughter Eliza. Despite this friendly opening I was nervous. It was all very well people advising me to make the transportation of our children a condition of my becoming a constable, but I knew that Macquarie was very unlikely to agree to that, and indeed it might not be in his power to do so. In any case I put it to him, and he did not dismiss it without consideration.

'I think your concern for your children is admirable, and you are right to fight to have them by your side. But that time hasn't come yet. In... I don't know... a year or so perhaps, when I may grant you a pardon and you become a free man, then anything might be possible.'

'I thought I already was a free man.'

'Technically, no. I have taken some time to study the cases of you and your comrades, and read the notes of Governor King and Secretary Marsden. You surrendered and threw yourself on the mercy of the Government. His Majesty's Government agreed that your lives should be spared, but that you would be exiled from your country for the rest of your life. You remain under that sentence. Once you are pardoned then you truly are completely free.'

'Even to return to Ireland?'

'Perhaps.'

This possibility had never occurred to me since coming to New South Wales. It may have been that Macquarie was holding out a carrot to me, which he could withdraw once I had outlived my usefulness. While I did think Macquarie was probably an honourable man I decided that I would not tell Mary about the possibility of returning to Ireland.

Macquarie continued: 'But that is all hypothetical and in the future. So far your conduct and that of your comrades has been... well... almost without blemish.'

'Arthur Devereux is not a farmer,' I told him, assuming that Arthur was the blemish being alluded to. 'He is a good man moved by the condition of the natives as any Christian should be.'

'Indeed you are quite right Mister Dwyer. I am myself concerned with the plight of the natives, whom we have discommoded by our arrival in this country, and who have always behaved in such a friendly and open fashion towards us, never mounting any opposition to our various projects. Why do you look at me askance sir?'

'Your honour, you fought a war against them.'

'Quite incorrect sir.'

'Truly?'

'There were, I believe, outrages committed by a small vagabond element within the local community. Such an element you will find in most communities. We offer them the gift of civilization. I intend to set up a school for the children, a farm for the adults where they will learn modern agricultural techniques, Mister Masden will look to their moral development and Darcy Wentworth, a fellow countryman of yours, will see to the betterment of their health. A great vision, is it not?'

I couldn't argue with it and so I just said: 'Yes.'

'Their way of life is finished, of course. These things inevitably come to an end. Culloden saw the end of Gaeldom in Scotland, but the Scottish people and the British Nation have marched on. Your own people and culture have suffered defeats, but as we speak an Irish man leads the British army in the war against Napoleon on the European continent.'

To be honest I could never dream of debating with Lachlan Macquarie, a man who was as passionate as he was articulate. Obviously I disagreed fundamentally with much of what he had to say, but it would have taken a Robert Emmet to argue our cause with him and I would have paid good money to see that debate.

Before he appointed me as constable, for which thankfully there was no uniform supplied or oath required, he had one further word of caution.

'You have a fatal flaw, Michael Dwyer, in common with many of your race, and a goodly few of my own, and I hope it will not come against you in this venture. Be temperate in your habits and do not let rum rule your life, as it seems to rule the lives of many in this country.'

I thanked him and reassured him before going to collect my cutlass and my rattle, the tools of my new office.

Mary was concerned about how I would feel in a role that made me effectively a functionary of the Crown, but I told her that I would not dwell on that aspect of it because it could deflect me from my principle purpose— the unification of our family. That was what I had to keep to the forefront of my mind—the day that my four Irish children would meet my two Australian children and we would all settle in our farm at Cabrammatta, which would be our very own new republic.

More people were now beginning to use the term 'Australia' to describe this new territory. The mood in the country had started to change slowly but noticeably since Macquarie took up office, and the transformation of Sydney had begun. Other towns were being built and roads were being constructed and all of us, convicts, freemen, Irish and English, were all made to feel part of it by the new Governor, even the natives.

Obviously I am not qualified to speak for them, and neither was Arthur Devereux, no matter what he said. I had to admit to prejudice. While I respected their rights, and sympathised with their cause, I just didn't like the look of them. They gave me the bloody creeps. Arthur's version of their recent history was completely different to Macquarie's and, although I respected Macquarie's reputation as an honest man, I could never trust him as much as I trusted Arthur. Arthur Devereux was the best of us, and I admired him as deeply as I did Robert Emmet or Sam MacAllister. Yes, I was concerned about whatever crazy initiative he was now about to take, and I knew it might end up with my having to defend him, but that I would do with my life. I was jealous that this man Pemulwuy could claim a better record against the British than myself, and concerned about how I would treat his people in my new job. If Arthur was right then maybe I had changed sides in this struggle. Maybe he was, and maybe he wasn't.

Macquarie saw part of my task as being a moral guardian of my area of Sydney, with particular emphasis on ensuring that the Sabbath was kept holy, peaceful and prayerful. God help the poor black fellas, they did not know one day of the week from the other because they worked from their own calendar, and why shouldn't they? Drink was an even bigger problem for them than it was for me, and many of my Sundays were spent keeping them off the streets. I don't know why they didn't stay out in the country, which would be their natural environment, but more and more they seemed to want to congregate in Sydney.

Mary now had to take charge of most of the farm work, but she was more than capable of managing this, having been brought up on a farm herself. Her father had the reputation of being one of the most progressive farmers in Wicklow. God love her, she had lost so much, Mary—the love of her parents, the life of her little sister Roisin, and her brother Kevin lost in the wilderness. She had now accepted that he was, most likely, dead. We did all we could to work and graft towards a common end.

You could say in my case that the word 'graft' had another meaning as well. Drink never cost me money during my time on the force because I was now given as much I needed, and that was a lot, from innkeepers and others who wanted to keep on my good side. Day-to-day commerce in Liverpool, Sydney was conducted through bartering, and I made sure that I got my cut of every deal that took place. Indeed it was like being back in Wicklow again in the old days, but with no enemy to fight and a clean comfortable house to go home to every night.

I was approached time and again by disaffected persons who wanted to tempt me into leading a rebellion in the colony, but I didn't see any sense in that. If we did pull off a successful coup, what were we to do? Declare an Irish Republic in Australia? Hand the land back to the

natives and go—where? America? That was what the
rebels at Castle Hill had in mind in 1804—overthrow the
authorities and take a ship to America. But that was no
use to me because America had already turned me down,
and my only chance of freedom was here. You could not
have freedom in a penal colony, but that was changing.

General Joe Holt was a happy man when in 1811 he had
been given an absolute pardon. He came to see us with
Martha and Joshua to tell us the news.

'And do you know what I am going to do Captain?'
he asked.

'What's that General?' I asked.

'I am going back to the Emerald Isle.'

'You never are!'

'Oh yes, we will,' said Martha.

'Well, I declare,' said Mary, 'but I did not think such a
thing was possible. Did you Michael?'

'I did not.'

'And what are ye going to do when ye get there?'
Mary asked.

'I am going to get my old farm back in County Wicklow,' said Joe Holt. 'We'll have money now to oil the
wheels of justice, and if I have to buy it off the gombeen
who stole it, so be it. I can sell the farm we have here, and
I've made enough from my other businesses to make me
a wealthy man.'

Joe touched his nose at me as he said this, and I knew
what he was talking about. General Joe Holt had been in
the illicit distillery business in New South Wales for many
years now. He was caught a few times, served his time, and
then always started up again. Rum was the staple drink in
the colony at the time, but many of the Irish still had a *grá*
for the old *poitín*, and Joe had perfected the art. He had
brought a bottle of his best stuff with him that night and

we finished it as we celebrated. Mary could not get over what was happening, and I was worried how this might affect her attitude to life in the colony.

Joe saw no future in this country, believing that it was opened up for criminals and, for the most part, run by criminals. Most of his neighbours were settled convicts and Joe's maxim was 'once a thief, always a thief'.

'But Joe,' said I, 'most of them stole to supply the necessaries of life to their families—loaves of bread, bags of meal, blankets!'

'Thou shalt not steal, Michael! No exceptions!'

'We stole to keep body and soul together on the Wicklow Mountains.'

'I never did citizen!'

The word 'citizen' he delivered as an insult and a challenge, but I was not going to take him up on that now. This was a celebration of Joe's good fortune and I did not want to spoil it, but I also had a plan hatching in my head which would require Joe's help, and so I did not want to remind him that his gains were ill-gotten, and that, although he may not have robbed during the Wicklow campaign, he tortured and executed people at random. He may be remembered as a fine general, and the rest of us as highwaymen and banditti, or maybe not. Anyway, he was an honest man in my book, and we drank his health, and their health, and our health. In the small hours of the morning we helped them onto their buggy and I said to Joe: 'I hope that horse knows his own way home.'

'Never fear, Captain,' he shouted, giving the horse a ferocious whack, and off they galloped.

As we lay in bed that night Mary said that she would miss Martha and talked of the Norfolk Island time when the Holts were such a help to her.

'Well,' I said, 'I think they may be of greater assistance to us now.'

'How is that?' she asked.

'We have money now Mary, perhaps enough to pay the passage of one adult and four children from Ireland to New South Wales, and enough left over to bribe whoever needs to be bribed in Dublin. It is going to take a capable person to handle these negotiations. I don't think my mother or my sister Etty would be up to the job, but Joe Holt would.'

'Oh heavens be praised. Would he do it?'

'I'll ask him anyway.'

'And I'll pray. Oh Michael I wish there was a priest here who could say mass for this, or a church where I could light candles. I must give this over to the Lord now, and pray for acceptance of His will. Yes, Joe Holt would be the man to do it. I agree. Oh Michael let me not keep thinking about it or I'll have them here in my head.'

'Lie quiet,' I said, taking her hand. 'We have suffered long enough. I think the time has come for release.'

So we lay together holding hands silently sharing these sweet, sweet, thoughts.

I do not understand why I had the dream that night, because usually it only came to me when I was troubled. I had been having it now and then ever since Norfolk Island. 'Twas a disturbing old nightmare and I couldn't make head nor tail of it. I am walking along by a river bank on a nice warm summer's day. Warm now, not hot. More like an Irish summer than the harsh heat of this place. A companion walks by my side. I don't know who he is but I know he is a friend. The ground now starts to get softer and softer. This is not unpleasant to begin with; in fact my companion and I take pleasure in the strange experience. Soon I am drawn down deeper and deeper and now it is hard to breathe. Then the ground becomes water and I am looking up to the surface—a long, long way up. I start to pull myself upwards, but my clothes drag me down and I have to work hard. Now I am nearly there and my head is about to surface, when two hands push me back down. I gulp and gasp and struggle against the hands but they are strong. There is a figure above me but I cannot make out who it is. It must be Halpin! But when the sun catches the figure I see that it is Sam MacAllister. Now his fifty wounds appear and blood pours from them into the river, and I struggle, drowning in the water and the blood. I think my lungs will burst and I wake up, sweating, terrified, unable to breathe.

'What troubles you, my darling?' Mary asked.

'Nothing,' I told her. 'Back to sleep now.'

Joe listened to my proposition carefully and then said: 'That bastard Trevor should have his head nailed to the wall.'

'That wasn't what I had in mind General.'

'Don't worry. No bad blood between us. He never crossed me and I never crossed him.'

'Glad to hear it.'

I told him about the letters Trevor had duped us into writing, and how he had fobbed off my mother when she came to see him.

'Oh, I'll be able to handle him all right, never fear. And if that is what you want I will do it for you, but...' And he stopped.

'What?'

'By the time I get over there, get all this done, put the children aboard a ship which will bring them here, you will probably have received an absolute pardon yourself.'

'So?'

'You'll be able to go back home.'

'I don't want to go back there Joe.'

'You tell me?'

'That's it.'

'And what about the God-damned climate?'

'I'm getting used to it.'

'Well your face looks like something you'd find on a butcher's slab.'

'Thanks Joe.'

'Let me tell you it is not to my liking—the climate now not your face. It is either drought or a deluge here, and I do not like such harsh extremes. I know we complain about the weather back home, but it is soft. Perhaps it is because I am older now, but soft seems good.'

'Will you do this for me?'

'Of course. You get the money together and I'll do what you ask.'

Getting the money together was not a straightforward task, because we did not have our own coinage or a bank of our own in the colony as yet, and most business was done through bartering or dubious notes of hand. Proper coin of the realm is what Joe would need in Dublin. But he wouldn't be going immediately and I would have plenty time to put it all in place. During this time I was pestered by Hugh Vesty telling me how foolish I was to be trusting Joe Holt, and how presumptuous the General was to think that he would get a warm welcome in Wicklow. If that wasn't bad enough, Mary started to have doubts about the wisdom of the plan.

I came home one evening after a hard day keeping the streets of Sydney civilised to find two members of the New South Wales Corps sitting in my parlour before me. One of them was known to me—yes indeed the bold Cecil—and the second was introduced to me as 'Richard, Dick to you, Burke'. The latter was stocky or squat depending on your point of view, and clearly a seasoned member of the Rum Corps, and probably one of those responsible for giving it its name. Dick had a habit of patting himself about the chest and thighs as if he might have forgotten something, or just to ascertain if he was all there, or indeed to work out why the hell there was so much of him there. Being unable to breathe through his nose he puffed and growled as he ate. Mary had put a plate of fruit and bread in front of them and had poured them out bumpers of General Joe's *poitín*. I hoped to God she hadn't told them where it came from. The same Dick told me that he was pleased to meet me.

'Ye gad sir they will be impressed back home when I tell them I met the great Wicklow Chieftain in the flesh. Oh now, they will, they will, they will. They sing ballads about you back there. Did you know that? Oh yes ballads no less.'

'We have a great idea for you Michael,' said Mary.

'Oh yes?' said I, worried about what was coming next.

'Lieutenant Burke is returning to Dublin soon and thinks he might be able to help us with our plight.'

'What plight?'

'Why the children of course!'

I sat down and waited for Mary to continue.

'The Lieutenant has some influence in Dublin Castle.'

'Friends in high places,' Dick added.

'And he feels they would have some influence over Doctor Trevor.'

Dick put in: 'Oh, I know they would. And he is not a doctor by the way, that is a title he took onto himself. He is bad egg sir, a bad egg.'

'The lieutenant has kindly offered to accompany your mother to see Trevor, then arrange a passage for your sister and the children and see them off. We would defray the expenses, obviously.'

I said in a measured fashion: 'That is most kind of you indeed Lieutenant.'

'Glad to be of service. 'Dick,' to you, by the way.'

'"Dick" it is then. The problem is that I have already made an arrangement with a close and trusted friend of mine. I could not possibly go back on that. Thank you, but I must decline your very generous offer.'

'But Michael the officer will be travelling very soon, and God knows how long we would have to wait for the Holts. I'm sure Joe would not mind.'

'Oh I'm afraid he would mind Mary. He would mind very much indeed.' I was firm as I said it.

Silence for a while, and then the rest of the officers' visit was spent in small talk, in which Mary took no part.

Once they had departed she asked: 'Why, Michael?'

'I didn't like the cut of him.'

'How?'

'I wouldn't trust him Mary. He'd have our money drunk before he left Rio de Janeiro.'

'It takes one to know one!'

'Precisely.'

'But Cecil vouches for him.'

'I don't trust Cecil either Mary.'

'Well I do.'

'There we differ.'

It was 1813 when the Holts finally set sail. We wished them God speed from the quay. All our hopes sailed with them.

PART 4

PART 4

Chapter XI
The Duke of Wellington brings bad news from Ireland. But God's Anointed also disembarks and the old Penal Days of Ireland are commemorated in the Colony.

In all my years as a constable I never once had to spring my rattle. The day Mick Dolan had a go at me was probably the nearest I ever came to it, and that was early on in my career. He came out of nowhere and connected with a kick to the small of my back, which is a sore enough place to get kicked. I was able to get hold of him easy enough though and soon had him face down on the ground. He let out a stream of curses at me, calling me every name under the sun, prefixing most of them with 'Protestant' or 'English'.

'You're in enough trouble now as it is. Do not add sedition to the list of possible charges, Mick. Why is a man who has only recently had a fine son born to him in such a state?'

"'Tis the same son has me in this state,' he told me, and I wondered how a baby could be the cause of such a fuss, unless the case was similar to poor old Hugh Vesty's here. In any event I couldn't fathom why the anger was being taken out on me. Poor Mick let me know quick enough.

'Your masters, damned heretics, are after taking my son and giving him a heretical baptism.'

'Ah sure now Mick one christening is as good as another.'

Mick was an assigned convict and his wife, who had recently given birth, had the same status. Since Macquarie had become governor he had insisted that all children born to convicts should be baptised. Since there was no Catholic priest to be had, the Protestant minister administered the sacrament, or the Protestant version thereof. This was the cause of much resentment within our community.

Mick calmed down eventually, and I stood him up.

'I'm sorry Michael. I got so angry and you are the first man I saw when I came on to the street. You'll take me to the guardhouse, or will it be the jail?'

'It would be the guardhouse Mick, because striking a constable is only a petty offence, but you'd get fifty lashes for it. You deserve every one of them for your foolishness, but I sympathise with your plight and I'll let it go.'

'You are a decent man, Michael Dwyer,' said he, and went on his way.

If I had known the pain was going to get so bad afterwards I might not have let him go at all. By the end of the day I was blinded by the damn thing. The cure for it was a few stiff bumpers of rum. In recent times I had been steering clear of the hard liquor, but there was no better man to deaden the pain and it worked on this occasion as well. The ride home at the end of the day, if not completely pain free, was reasonably comfortable. When I got there, however, I had quite a shock, because parked outside the front door was a coach that belonged to the Governor. As I dismounted I became concerned about the effects of the medicine I had taken before setting out. Although I only felt slightly light-headed I knew that the rum had a distinctly pungent odour. Macquarie had no tolerance for drink on the job. To lose the income and benefits from being a constable would have been a serious blow to our prospects at this stage, and I was acutely aware that I was soon to be considered for an absolute pardon. As I approached the door I was filled with self-loathing for allowing myself be oppressed by a lackey of the Crown like Macquarie, and the loathing turned to anger as Mary opened the door.

'Michael!' said she. 'Do you know who is here?'

'Himself.' said I.

'No, herself,' said she, 'and not a thing prepared or a child in the house washed.'

Seated in the parlour, playing with James, Bridget and Eliza, sat Elizabeth Macquarie, first lady of the colony of New South Wales.

'Constable Dwyer, forgive the intrusion,' said she.

'Your most welcome, ma'am,' said I.

'Your little ones are charming—so healthy and well-behaved. And more on the way from Ireland, your wife tells me.'

'Yes, ma'am we expect them any day now.'

'Aren't you blessed!' At this stage she had neither chick nor child herself, but rumour had it that she'd had no fewer than six miscarriages, God help her.

'The luck of the Irish, I suppose ma'am.'

'Yes, you have a unique ability to increase and multiply.'

'Ah sure now, give us a couple of generations and we'll outbreed the rest of Europe. Did you offer her ladyship refreshments Mary?'

'I have a little wine with water in it, thank you.' She showed me her glass. 'But I'm sure you'd like a tot of rum yourself. I know Lachlan always has a dram of *uisce beatha* when he has finished work.'

Mary brought me a drop of rum, which I sipped, grateful that the issue of the smell was now no longer a worry.

'I have arranged to meet my husband here. I hope you do not mind. We were touring the farms of the area. He should be here presently.'

'Splendid!' I said, and regretted saying it because it was a phrase I used to mock Macquarie's haughtiness, but never to his face.

In time the man himself strode in, full of bonhomie.

'Splendid Dwyer, absolutely splendid spread. A fine product of industry and invention, and I have seen many today. This land will be transformed in time—a profitable and happy place.'

'Thank you, Governor, and you are very welcome here.'

He accepted a glass of rum from Mary and we drank the health of the country.

'Yes! All in excellent shape. All except one!'

'Ah!' said I, having a good idea of which 'one' was not in excellent shape.

'Where is he?'

'Arthur? I don't rightly know. Gone into the wild with his native friends, I think.'

'He feels he has something in common with them?'

'They make him laugh.'

'How very frivolous!'

'Well, if there is one thing Arthur Devereux is, believe me it is not frivolous.'

'He is sorry for them,' Mary put in, 'because they lost their land and everything.'

'With respect Mrs Dwyer it is most emphatically not, nor has it ever been, their land. This has always been a true *terra nullius*.'

'What?'

'That's an empty land,' I told her; 'a land that belongs to nobody.'

'Oh they have traversed the land for many years, but they have never settled it or developed it as God intended. Too primitive to understand the sacred concept of property. As I have told your husband we will educate them and Christianise them. Who could wish for a greater gift?'

At this point I moved to replenish Elizabeth Macquarie's glass, and I must have limped or grimaced because he said: 'Have you sustained an injury, Michael?'

'Kick from a horse,' I told him.

'Should we give him fifty lashes?'

'No point in damaging a good horse.'

'Indeed.'

We then discussed the children's names, including the ones with whom we would soon be united, and he was impressed with their biblical origins—except Bridget of course—and Mary explained that she was our patron saint, stressing the possessive pronoun, in case your man would claim Saint Bridget for the Protestants as well as Saint Patrick. There was a lull at this point, and then the Governor returned to his favourite theme of the day, and went on at some length about how pleased he was with agricultural progress within the colony, and how well his policy of allowing convicts who had completed their sentences to settle and have some land had worked. He had been much criticised for this emancipationist policy, but now he was feeling vindicated and his wife assured him that he would indeed be remembered as the great emancipator.

Then Mary said, I think half to herself: ''Tis a pity we don't have a Catholic emancipator as well.'

At this point Macquarie became solid ice, and gave my wife the coldest, hardest look I had ever seen. I could have slashed him for that look. I could have smashed the glass

I had in my hand and rammed it into his jugular so that he might pump his life out on the parlour floor. I just cleared my throat instead. The good Governor then proceeded to give us a little sermon.

'As you know in 1803 Governor King allowed the Mass to be celebrated and Roman rights to be practiced. What happened next? In 1804 we had a Papish rebellion. Bloodshed, murder and mayhem in the colony! But for the bravery of the men of the Corps this great project could have been destroyed. That cannot happen again. I will not allow it to happen again. You are Christians as I am. I say let us unite in one faith, one religion, and that must be the national and natural religion for this great empire, of which we are all part.'

'Better still,' I said, 'if we all had the freedom to worship according to our consciences.'

The visit ended in what you might call tolerant tension. Once the Macquaries had departed I turned to Mary and said: 'Careful you do not lose me my position, wife!'

'Ah to hell with your position! With your 'Governor' this and 'ma'am' that... Get away out of that. And you better than the lot of them put together boy.'

I married a lion of a woman.

Folk said that I helped Martin Burke join the constabulary so that he would cover for me. True enough he did cover for me from time to time, but he was an excellent policeman in his own right—in the end better than me. This was a stressful time for myself and Mary. 'Twas going to take at least a year for Joe Holt to get to Ireland, meet with my mother, negotiate with Trevor and put my children and sister aboard a ship for New South Wales. By the end of the year we were starting to watch out for shipping, and that was probably very optimistic. But Mary had great difficulty containing herself as she bought clothes, made beds and fixed cots. So many of the early years of this colony had been spent waiting for ships to arrive from the other end of the world, bringing badly-needed food, live-stock, family members or new governors. Our plight was understood and sympathised with.

Despite all the support, on any given day I would get jittery after an hour or two of work, and the only thing to settle me would be a couple of stiff drinks. So I would sit in a dark corner of a tavern for a spell sipping my rum until it calmed me down and then I could go back to patrolling the streets again or working in the guardhouse. By midday, when I took a break anyway, I would need a top-up, just to steady the nerves again. Darcy Wentworth was the man in overall charge of the police force, but he was a busy surgeon supervising the building of a new hos-pital among a hundred and one other projects. So he did not have time to worry about the behaviour of every con-stable. Macquarie himself, however, was something of an all-seeing eye. Not that I was afraid of anybody.

I was very worried that something might go wrong with the transportation of the children and the effect this might have, not on myself but on Mary. Once the children had arrived then I would give up this drinking habit, which I knew to be unhealthy. But I needed the hooch to get me through this patch.

I managed to keep Irishtown relatively quiet and equi-table, and in time it was integrated into the new Sydney, which was now being ordered and developed as streets became named and houses numbered. Everybody had to have an address and a purpose in life, or in the life of the colony at least. I still preferred to administer my own jus-tice on the spot, but obviously arrests had to made, reports written and punishments administered so that we could justify our existence. In any event Macquarie and his administration seemed happy with our work. The

Governor had advised me to expand my agricultural oper-
ations and I took his advice, leasing more land and buying
livestock. Like many other political deportees from Ireland
I was attaining a certain status in Sydney, and once the children arrived I would be able to relax and enjoy that status.

The transport ship The *Duke of Wellington* arrived at Sydney Cove with many Irish on board. I waited with Mary
and our three children on the quays as we watched the
long boats ferry the people to shore. It had been a long
voyage, nearly five months, and the effects of the ordeal
marked the faces and bodies of the poor, bemused crea-
tures who clambered onto the quay, and we prayed that
the children—for we were certain they were on board—
had come through it alive and well. Obviously we were
not going to recognise them nor they us, but I was confident I would know my sister Etty. More crowds gathered
on the quays and more packed boats set off from the ship.
Apparently there were about two hundred passengers and
none had been lost on the voyage. This we gleaned from
conversations shouted between boats and shore. Still no
sign of a woman with four children! A yell of joy from
behind almost deafened me as some fortunate man spotted a relative. The throng grew and crushed this way and
that. Mary was in turmoil—and started to panic.

   A ship's officer had come on shore, but a crowd
pressed round him. I made for him though, moving aside
those who stood in my way gently but firmly. I presented
myself to the young man: 'Michael Dwyer... Constable!'
   'Ah, we have something for you,' he told me.
   'Thank God,' I said. 'Where are they?'
   'On board. We will get them to you presently.'
   'And they are safe and well?'
   He looked at me, puzzled. 'Pardon? Well, yes of course.'
   'All five of them?'

'Five? But, we have only three?'

'What happened the other two?'

'Sorry?'

'My children? What happened to them?'

'We have no children for you sir, but letters.'

We waited in silence—Mary in my arms, Bridget and Eliza in her arms and James hanging from her skirt—until the letters were handed to us. There were indeed three of them—one sealed and addressed to me from Joe Holt, a second addressed to both of us from my mother, and a third addressed to Mary, also from my mother. I took the letters and led Mary and the children away through the crowd.

'Home first,' I said, 'we will read them there.' Mary nodded her silent agreement and we set off.

Once home and settled I said: 'Joe Holt's first.'

Mary was silent, so I broke the seal. This is the letter.

Dear Michael,

I trust you and all your colonial care are well. The Holt family landed in the Cove of Cork after an agreeable enough voyage. It took a mere one hundred and sixty days, which I am told is not far off a record. The city of Cork is as busy and prosperous as ever, but we did not delay there too long. We resolved to visit Dublin first before making for Wicklow, and believe me that was a wise decision. I have a cousin who is a solicitor in Dublin whom I intended to engage in the matter of my property. We took a cutter up the coast to Dublin and at least got a view of Wicklow from the sea. Little did we know that this would be the last we would see of our native county.

My cousin, Terrence, a man not given to overstatement, said to me, when I told him of my intentions, that I could not and must not go anywhere near the County Wicklow and the Barony of Talbotstown in particular. When I asked him why he told me that I am a marked man, and would be shot on sight there.

I asked him why I would be a marked man in my own county, for which I have given so much. But Terrence, who in truth is only a young fellow, told me that he did not know what went on within the ranks of the United Irishmen and the various wars and feuds in Wicklow, but he was certain that there would be hundreds queuing up to take a pot shot at me if I showed my face there.

I thought it wise to take the young man's advice and not venture south to find out for myself. So I sent a message to Hume at Humehall asking him to meet with me. The good gentleman did not delay but made all haste for Dublin as soon as he got my missive. He came to our hotel, and before we even sat down to eat he told me that my coming to Ireland was a foolhardy move and if I went anywhere near Wicklow I was a dead man. As you know Michael I do not take kindly to threats, and I reminded the good Mister Hume of this fact.

He told me that Wicklow is at peace now, that it should remain so, and that if I went south now then that dreadful cycle of murder and reprisal would start all over again. He did not want to see that, and told me that he would not allow it to happen.

My memory of Hume had always been of a mild-mannered man, and I was perturbed to see him so agitated. I implored him to sit down and explain to me calmly what the circumstances were. He told me that I am considered to be an informer. He was not accusing me of anything himself, but merely telling me what the common view had become. When I asked him who believed this nonsense, he told me 'all the Catholic population'. Then he said the probable instigators of this story were the Byrnes and the Dwyers. Indeed reports had come from New South Wales that I was 'up to the same old tricks' there.

To say I was deeply hurt by this Michael would be a grave understatement. I have shown nothing but kindness and support to you and your family over the years, and I have done more for the cause of the United Irish movement in Wicklow than anybody else. And this is the gratitude I am shown!

Hume went on to point out that the Loyalists in my home county would certainly not welcome me because, God knows, I had shot enough of them. Hume clearly thinks I am a thoroughly bad person and he brought up to me acts committed in war of which I am not proud. He reminded me that I had executed an eleven-year-old boy who was a spy, and pointed out that the child had a mother and father and brothers and cousins and so on.

Sadly Martha and myself have resolved not to go to Wicklow and we intend to purchase a hotel in Dunleary and to try and make our living from that.

I hold money of yours and I should like to know what you want me to do with this. If you wish me to send it to you in the colony I will do that, or you can ask your mother to collect it from me here. I am sorry that I cannot be of help to you in the matter of your children.

Martha sends her love to Mary.
Sincerely yours,

Joe Holt.

My mouth was dry when I finished reading. I offered Mary water before I drank but she remained silent. I couldn't stand the silence myself, but I knew no matter what I said it was going to be wrong, but speak I had to. 'Damn the Byrnes. Damn the Byrnes to hell!'

'Not just the Byrnes, Michael,' she said quietly, staring at the letters from my mother.

'What does she say?' I asked.

Mary opened the letter to both of us and struggled to read it. Now, there was always a sadness in reading letters from home, but my mother's recounting of the children's doings was usually a source of consolation and joy to us. Not so on this occasion. As Mary read in a flat, mechanical voice about Esther's cow-milking and Peter and John's otter-hunting she might as well have been talking about strangers.

The tone and pitch of the reading changed when the letter took on another subject.

'We hear that hound of hell Holt has returned to Ireland. Hasn't that blackguard some neck to go showing his face in this country again? If he sets foot in County Wicklow he is a dead man for sure. Indeed there is talk of going up to Dublin and doing the deed there. More of a risk maybe but some think it might be worth it. I don't for the life of me know why yourself, Hugh Vesty and the lads did not do for him in Botany Bay. Rest assured the scoundrel who did for Sam MacAllister and countless others will not last long in this country...'

The letter concluded with a request for financial assistance, which was reasonable and understandable. Mary handed it to me with a gesture that said she never wanted to see it again.

Then she picked up the letter addressed to herself and opened it saying: 'What the hell is this about?' She read in silence for a moment and then started to weep. The sobbing and the choking did not allow her to speak for some time. I took her in my arms. Once she had the breath back she told me: 'Your little girl, Michael, the first one, is not a girl any more. She is a woman now. Imagine that.'

I looked towards the door and saw standing there the gauntest man I had ever laid eyes on.

'God save all here,' he whispered.

'God save you kindly sir,' I replied.

'I come upon you in an hour of sadness, but it is for such times we were made.'

Mary and myself composed ourselves as best we could and invited the stranger across the threshold. He told us he had just arrived on the *Duke of Wellington* and introduced himself: 'Jeremiah O'Flynn, ordained as a monk of the La Trappe reform, and I have now been secularised and authorised by the Holy See as prefect-apostolic to this territory of Bottanibe.'

'A priest?' Mary asked, more in disbelief than anything else.

'Anointed of the Lord,' he said.

She knelt before him and he laid a hand on her head. Then, in the same hoarse whisper, he intoned the full Latin blessing, making the sign of the cross above her head. I went on one knee myself for that bit. This same whisper I refer to became a kind of growl at times for pious, irate or humorous effect and could be projected across great distances.

Father O'Flynn was a skeletal man with a ferocious appetite for meat, potatoes, fruit, bread cakes, or indeed anything that was put before him, and in all the time I knew him he never gained an ounce in weight. That first day he put away a great feed, and once he'd wiped his lip he fell fast asleep where he was sitting on the hard chair by the table.

We crept around clearing the dishes and kept the children from crawling all over him. In time he awoke just as suddenly as he dropped off.

'Hup ou' that,' said he, getting to his feet and rubbing his hands together. 'Now, Michael Dwyer, can you direct me to this Scotch Governor of yours?'

'He'll do better than that,' said Mary, 'he'll take you to him.'

I hitched a horse to a buggy and drove the priest to the Governor's house in Parramatta. On the way he regaled me with tales of his days in the West Indies—how he fought with the Abbot at Martinique and fell out with the Archbishop of Baltimore when he was Pastor of Santa Cruz. Before we even neared the town of Parramatta I knew that Father Jeremiah O'Flynn would not find favour with Lachlan Macquarie.

I agreed to wait outside the Gubernatorial residence for him. As I sat in the shade the full import of the day's events enveloped me and I was sorry to have left Mary on her own with the children, but sure she would have it no other way. 'Twas difficult to guess how long the priest would be with the Governor and I started to calculate where the nearest tavern was and how long it would take me to go there and get a bottle, which would be the only medicine to slow my racing head—Holt, my Mother, this Priest, the children, the money! But I waited and waited.

Eventually the priest emerged, and I could tell by his demeanour that things had not gone too well.

'You'll lodge with us tonight Father,' I told him as he climbed on board.

'That is kind of you Captain,' he said, and then he lapsed into silence.

When we had travelled a mile or so he sighed and began: 'I do not believe that Columba did a very good job of Christianising those Scots. At least if that Governor of yours is anything to go by. He told me that I may return to The *Duke of Wellington* and take myself back to England. And this subsequent to my having informed him that my petition to minister here had been ratified by Bathurst in London. Not strictly true, but he had no immediate way of verifying that. I told him I had no intention of re-boarding that cursed vessel. At that he threatened to have me clamped in irons. Is not Christian tolerance a won-drous virtue, Captain? I thought it wiser to change tack at this point, and so I pleaded exhaustion after the long voy-age and a curiosity to explore this new colony, requesting that he, at least, postpone my deportation. Thank the Lord he did relent, and agreed to my remaining here for a few months, but on very strict conditions, to wit—I must not preach, say the Mass or administer the sacraments. I agreed of course.'

At this point he lowered his head and looked at me.

'Sometimes we must deceive to do the work of the Lord. But he will allow that for we do it in His name. Would you agree?'

'Well, I think Father that you would be the expert on such matters.'

The Reverend did not seem at all pleased with my reply.

'This may put you in a difficult position Captain Dwyer. You are, as I understand it, a law enforcement officer in the employ of the colonial authorities. Hm?'

'Correct.'

'So, what you should render unto Caesar may now seem less clear-cut.'

'Have no fear on that count.'

'Of course, you are a man well practiced in exploiting the contradictions in a system.'

'As long as we are discrete.'

'Indeed discretion will be vital. And I do promise to involve you as little as possible in my subterfuge.'

'Subterfuge is second nature to most of us now.'

'And one wonders if that is a good thing.'

'True for you!'

The rest of the journey was spent in my telling the new priest about life in New South Wales.

There must have been the best part of a hundred people gathered round the house as we approached—men, women and children. Some held lambs in their arms, others hens, and the priest wondered whether they intended offering sacrifices. I was very annoyed at Mary, who must have been the cause of this gathering. They crowded around the buggy as we arrived and offered their gifts to Father O'Flynn. A corner of the barn had been cleared out, and a table and two chairs set there to serve as a temporary confessional. Several individuals, Sarah Byrne among them, knelt in an orderly queue outside the barn. The priest had no option but to start work immediately.

I explained to Arthur and Martin what Macquarie's conditions were and how important it was for everyone to be aware of these conditions.

'He'll have to say Mass. Sure, don't a priest have to do that every day anyway?' Hugh Vesty asked, and added: 'So some of us might just keep him company from time to time as he says it.'

'We'd have to be very careful that we are not carted off to Norfolk Island or worse.' Martin said.

I told them: 'I can take no part in these clandestine Masses and sacraments, and I don't think either of you should be involved in the enterprise. We will be watched more keenly than most.'

As I pondered these matters I noticed a big, clean-cut Tullamore man who stood beaming at the spectacle of the confessional queue. William Davis was among the first of the '98 prisoners to be transported. A blacksmith from Kings County, his crime was forging pikes to be used in the rebellion. The man was pardoned back in '09 and set up a victualling business in Parramatta, but by this time he also owned a tavern in Sydney and had other business interests in the Colony. He had a big, open, innocent face but a shrewd brain ticked away behind it. If Davis was noted for anything it was his piety. When eating a biscuit or taking a drink of water he would bless himself before and after.

As I arrived at his side he turned to me and smiled: 'God bless you for doing this, Michael Dwyer. God bless you, sir.'

'At this point William my involvement in the venture has to cease. The good priest has been told by the Governor that he is forbidden to practice. You understand my position is a complicated one, and I cannot have the man living under my roof beyond tonight. Sarah and Hugh Vesty would be very keen to help, but they have a house full of children, and discretion is vital in this dangerous project. And, best will in the world, but Hugh Vesty would not be the greatest at the organisational end. On the other hand yourself and Catherine have neither chick nor child under your roof and you are, if you don't mind my saying so, blessed with great business acumen. This is the project for you, sir. Take the priest under your wing and organise the secret Masses and the sacraments for him.'

'An honour Michael, an honour!'

When Mary and myself finally lay together at the end of that, one of the strangest days in our lives, we stared at the ceiling in silence for a long moment.

'We should let my mother have the money.'

'Yes, that would be best.'

'And we are back where we started.'

'Again.'

'Best get letters to her and to Holt before the *Duke of Wellington* sails again.'

'Yes.'

'What a time for that damned priest to arrive!'

She sat up.

'Michael, that's blasphemy.'

'No, it is not. Very well, I should not have said it. Nothing against the man personally; in fact I like him. But the timing of his arrival...'

'Was meant! Do you not see that? It was ordained. The Lord sent him our way Michael to help us through this terrible time.'

'Then why did the Lord send the 'terrible time' our way in the first place?'

'It is not for us to question his ways.'

I sighed.

'Do you never wonder whose side he is on?' I asked

'He doesn't take sides.'

'What sense is there to any of it?'

'You must have faith.'

'I don't.'

'I could not live without it. Faith and prayer—that is where I get my consolation. You get yours from a bottle.'

'Not fair. It has been a difficult day and not a drop has passed my lips.'

'True. I'm sorry.'

'And it will have repercussions. The priest! You may be sure of that.'

The Governor wrote for a long time without so much as a glance at me. When he did look at me it was as much as to say 'what are you doing here?', despite the fact that I had been summoned to his presence.

'We have this pesky priest now.'

'Yes, Governor.'

'I don't want him causing trouble.'

'He won't.'

'Do I have your guarantee on that?'

I coughed. He changed his mind.

'That is an unreasonable request. Yes, I know. We have peace in the land Michael. With peace comes progress, comes prosperity. You can see that? Hm?'

He waited.

'Yes, Governor.'

'Splendid. We do not want, once again, the old antagonisms of the other side of the world played out here.'

'No.'

'Catholics taking pot-shots at Protestants and Protestants taking pot-shots at Catholics.'

Obviously I couldn't let it pass, but I spoke with all the restraint I could muster: 'That was not the matter of the conflict in which I was involved in Ireland.'

'It most emphatically was, sir!' The 'sir' delivered as a slur.

'It may be what it became, but that was not why I took up arms. Why any of us took up arms. Not one of the leaders of the rebellion in Ireland was a Catholic.'

'Free-thinking, dissenting, Francophiles. Traitors to a man. Oh, they manipulated you all right. Fomented hatred. Exploited ancient divisions.'

'It was you... the establishment who exploited the divisions.'

'You are coming very close to sedition now, Dwyer!'

I held his look, but I could see the threat of Norfolk Island in one eye and Van Diemen's Land in the other.

'Yes sir. Sorry Governor.'

'This venture will only work if we are all of the one religion—the Established Church with the King at its head and me as his representative here. You have so much to offer this colony Michael Dwyer, so much. Keep an eye on that vagabond priest. If he commences any of his mumbo-jumbo then he will be in irons until the next transport.'

I was about to remind him of the depth of people's religious convictions and how many would be willing to die for it, but I thought I had said enough. He would have reminded me of my fine position, my good salary, my well-appointed, richly-furnished house, my fine farmland. As I stepped out onto the streets of Parramatta I knew I was commencing on a life of subversion that might well border on insurgency. Even if I wanted it, there would not be a way out of it.

So began a time that reflected the Penal days in Ireland. Not that any of the Irish in New South Wales at that time could remember the Penal days, but all of us had been brought up on stories about them, and the stories, true or false, had been branded on our souls. Once again it was a time of secret passwords and illicit meetings at the rising of the moon. William Davis organised it but I facilitated it. I did not have the deep, unwavering faith of some of my countrymen, but I respected the depth of their devotion, and enjoyed the old thrill of deception and conspiracy.

Mass madness had overtaken the Irish, and it made my constabulary duties much easier. Masses were celebrated in backrooms of taverns and in upstairs rooms of houses in Sydney, and in the barns of remote farms at the Hawkesbury and beyond. A secret network was set up to inform people when and where a service would take place. As far as I know no spies infiltrated the network. The little congregations would arrive at specific but staggered times, and look-outs had to be posted outside the premises and on all the roads that led to it. It was my task to ensure that the New South Wales Constabulary did not come near these locations.

There was a backlog of baptisms, communions and confirmations to be performed. A record number of weddings must have taken place during this strange, exciting time.

I marvelled at O'Flynn's stamina, and came to understand his enormous appetite for food that boosted his energy from hour to hour. He shared a bottle with me on a number of occasions and enjoyed tales of the rebellion in Ireland. After all, he was but a lad in Kerry when those events took place. He had a strict cut-off point when it came to drinking, however, and he would indicate it by slashing the air horizontally with his hand.

'Enough is enough!'

'By God, for a Kerryman you have a poor capacity!'

'I've seen that stuff kill stronger men than you, Michael Dwyer,' he'd say, and I'd throw back my head and laugh:

'Yeah, but what a wonderful way to die!'

Then he would look at me with sad but piercing eyes, full of pity. Stayed with me to the end that look.

Hugh Vesty, Martin and myself would meet in a tavern now and then and reminisce about old times, drinking always to absent friends. Now that Arthur had removed himself, the meetings were less fraught than they used to be, and to be honest I missed the flare-ups between Hugh Vesty and himself. It was during one such gathering that Martin made his announcement.

'I think I will be availing myself of the good priest's services while he's here.'

'Are you to be born again?' I asked.

'No Michael, I'm to be wed again!'

'And who is the lucky woman? And lucky she is to be sure!'

'Phoebe Tunstall is her name.'

'Phoebe Tunstall? But isn't she...'

'Yes, she has two children already, but I love them all, and we will be happy.'

Hugh Vesty remained silent during all this. We allowed him room to speak, but he just threw back his drink and I called for another bottle.

'You must come to visit, all of you. Mary will be delighted. So, Hugh Vesty, why don't you bring your care round as well and we'll make a day of it?'

'Yes... I suppose,' he said, and then, holding out his big paw to shake Martin's: 'Good luck to you, boy!'

Right go wrong, Mary wanted the wedding to take place at our home, but I could not allow that. The risk would be too great, and Martin did accept the fact that it would have to be a very low-key affair. Phoebe's two children were by different fathers, and certainly one of these, a man to whom she was assigned as a convict but who never married her, was deceased. The parentage of the other child was less certain, and these circumstances made both Sarah and Mary concerned for Martin—would Phoebe be loyal and true to him? In earlier times Sarah would have expressed moral outrage at the state of affairs, but she was no longer in a position to throw stones.

There was but a brief pause in the ceremony when O'Flynn whispered: 'Does anyone know of any reason why these should not be joined together in Holy Matrimony?'

The ceremony was held in the barn of a sympathetic farmer, and there were lookouts posted all around. It was not unlike my own wedding in Wicklow all those years ago. In some strange way, though, the fact that the ceremony had to be both simple and secret made it all the more sacred.

O'Flynn wore his everyday clothes, the only priestly emblem being a stole which he would place round his neck. He travelled with a bag to the various locations where Mass was said and it contained all the necessary props—the chalice and paten, which could only be handled by the priest, the ciborium, the theca, the bread box, and the communion paten. Then the altar stone was brought by a member of the congregation. Obviously the stone had not been consecrated by a bishop, but one of our stonemasons had carved a cross on it. A carpenter had made a Penal Cross: a carved cross with a wooden figure of the Lord attached to it. It was very small, the horizontal sections being short, so that the priest could slip it up his sleeve if the ceremony were to be interrupted. Candles in black candlesticks were brought along as well, by Sarah Byrne, but the question of their suitability led to a confrontation with William Davis. They were only tallow candles and, according to William, not in the least suitable for the purpose.

'How the hell could the kind of candle make a blind bit of difference?' Sarah demanded.

'Indeed it does Mrs Byrne, a considerable difference. Wax candles, always wax candles!'

'Why so?'

'Wax is one of the most expressive symbols furnished the church by nature to express allegorically the holy humanity of Jesus Christ. Most significant is the virginity of the bees and the purity of the substance drawn from the nectar of the most exquisite flowers and compare these things to the conception of Jesus in the pure womb of Mary...'

O'Flynn interrupted: '...The Lord created the tallow maggot as well as the bee, William.'

Now, do not misunderstand me here, I had the greatest respect for the project pursued so diligently by William Davis, and all the assistance I gave him was given freely and in good heart. Why so moral and upright a man would go so vindictively against me in time I do not for the life of me understand. Yes, we had our political differences, but such differences should have been tolerated.

The dignity and fervour of the Catholics in the colony at that time attracted others to the Faith, and Father O'Flynn was soon making converts. It was probably seen as an anti-establishment movement and attracted disaffected people, of whom there were a great number in the colony at that time. Obviously Macquarie was aware that these gatherings were taking place, but he had to bide his time. He had no desire to have the New South Wales Corps ride up in the middle of a Mass, sabres drawn, to arrest the priest and disperse the people.

An opportunity would arise soon enough. And when it did it was from an unexpected quarter. The 48th regiment was stationed in the colony at the time and had many Catholics in its ranks. The Governor, ever the military man, had respect for the soldiers and so they approached him and asked him that Father O'Flynn be allowed to stay on in the colony and minister, as a priest, openly. Macquarie was pleased as punch with this opportunity and moved immediately to have O'Flynn deported forthwith.

On the 20th of May 1818, despite petitions from four hundred free Catholics, and some leading Protestants, Father Jeremiah Francis O'Flynn was placed forcibly on board the *David Shaw* and sailed away from New South Wales. He left behind a community, in one sense defeated and bereft, but also strangely renewed and ambitious. But he left something much more important behind. In a sacred lunala placed secretly and securely in a room in a tavern owned by William Davis, Father O'Flynn had left a consecrated host. This would be the focus of Catholic devotion in New South Wales in the years that followed— an important place of pilgrimage.

William Davis was proud indeed of the honour, and came to me, rightly, for advice on how to regulate visits and adorations.

'I know you will help us in this Captain, because this is the cause for which you fought so long and hard.'

'What cause would that be?'

'Why your Faith, sir. Fatherland as well, yes I know, but Faith first and foremost.'

'I fought for neither, sir!'

'But your oath?'

'No oath taken by a true United Irishman says anything about Faith.'

'Mine did.'

'Well, what class of an oath was that then?'

'To quell all nations and dethrone all Kings and plant

the true religion that was lost in the reformation.'

'Now William, I have never heard the like in my life.'

This was not strictly true of course because I had heard of such oaths been issued in Carlow, parts of the Midlands, certain towns in the west and even down in Kerry, but I wasn't going to say any of that to William Davis. These were wrong oaths and had nothing to do with what Tom Paine had written and Robert Emmet had died for. But I would help William Davis in this project, because I am a Catholic and I believe in the right of everyone to worship in whatever fashion their conscience dictates.

'I believe with Tone and Emmet in a society in which Catholic, Protestant and Dissenter can live in harmony.'

'True, that may be the best we can hope for in this country, but I still dream of an Ireland where the One True Catholic Church will be the official established religion.'

I did not comment on William Davis' vision of the future Ireland, but I assured him that I would lend him every assistance in keeping the Sacred Host secure but accessible to those who wanted to worship.

In the meantime, Macquarie had summoned me to his presence again, and I was concerned as always because I could never be sure what slip-up I might have made, even though I was careful and well-covered. I knew immediately I entered the office that I was all right as there was a broad grin on the Gubernatorial kisser and an expansive gesture from the Gubernatorial hands.

'Splendid news for you Dwyer!'

'Yes, Governor?'

'Today, you are to be granted a complete and unconditional pardon.'

I said nothing.

'Well man, what do you say? Stunned into silence are you? Most unlike you.'

'Thank you, sir.'

'Is that all?'

'No, I am, very grateful indeed, sir.'

The truth is I was not grateful at all for this pardon, because I think I did nothing for which I should be pardoned. I had fought a just war and had been defeated. There was no crime in that. No, in my heart I was not grateful. In my heart I was insulted.

Mary, on the other hand, danced for joy when she heard the news. At first I did not understand why, but then she told me: 'Because we can return to Ireland now. Because, at last we can all be reunited.'

Obviously I should have been prepared for this reaction, but it took me completely by surprise. I sat silently in my favourite armchair. It was a handsome, comfortable, winged armchair, stuffed with horsehair and covered with a fine woven wool in a rich yellow. There was a foot-stool covered in the same material, with similar cabriole legs in mahogany. As I sat I looked at the rest of the room, which was richly furnished with fine pieces for which we had worked hard, saved, and bought with pride.

'I think I'd like a glass of rum,' I said.

'And why wouldn't you? You are entitled to it, boy. And do ye know something? Given what's happened, I am going to have one myself.'

Mary went to the sideboard and filled two glasses from the decanter. I loved that sideboard, of polished English oak, with intricate carvings. Three drawers and three presses, all with brass knobs and brass hinges. She sat on the stool before me, and I asked how James had done at school that day.

'A rebel Michael, and he always will be. I don't want to dampen that in him, but it can't get in the way of his education.'

I agreed with that.

'But your news! How did you hear about it?'

Then I told her about being called to Macquarie's office, what he had said to me and what I had felt in my heart about it.

'It is just a means to an end Michael. A game that has to be played so we can get what we want.'

I finished my drink and stood. I held my hand out to her.

'Come.'

We walked together to the porch. It was twilight. The green pastures and the golden fields of corn stretched before us.

'Look at that!' I said. 'What a sight!'

'Indeed,' she said.

'And it is all ours.'

She sighed. We were silent for a while. Then she said: 'We could sell it, Michael.'

'For what?'

'Mary Anne, John, Peter and Esther.' And then a plea: 'Michael?'

'Look at it Mary. Look at what we have. And the house! All we have earned. What would we get in Wicklow for this? A bit of scrubland in the Glen of Imaal! If we could find anyone to sell to us.'

'We would have each other. All of us together, Michael. That is the dream.'

'No, Mary we will not go to Ireland!'

'Selfish!'

'No, *you* are the selfish one. The children's future, is that what matters?'

'Please, listen to me...'

'Is that what matters?'

'Of course.'

'Well then there is nothing further to discuss.'

'What about when Old Ireland will be free? What

about the new republic? They will never have that here. Here they will never be citizens. Subjects of the Crown, Michael! Subjects of the Crown!'

By now she was shouting.

I said: 'Fed, clothed, educated. No Lords, or Ladies, Half-Squires or gombeen men to look down on them. Heads held high! All of us! And here, this spread. This house. Our own little Republic. We will bring them here.'

'When?'

'Soon.'

'Soon! Soon! I am sick of soon. It has been 'soon' for years and years now, and still nothing.'

'I do my best. As God is my judge, I do my best. I expect promotion soon. There will be more money. If we have to, you go over and bring them back.'

'We will have money like that?'

'In time, yes. And now that we have been pardoned and the wars with France are over, Trevor and the Dublin authorities will no longer be an impediment.'

'We can do this?'

'We will do this.'

'Yes?'

'I promise.'

Chapter XII
He is promoted but given an unwanted task that ends in tragedy

Chief Constable Dwyer! Now you had to make an appointment to see me. I had three constables under my command, and they did the work while I signed the orders, reports and summonses. A dwelling had been made available to me in Sydney, but I continued to live at the farm in Cabramatta. This arrangement did not go down too well with the residents of the area known as Liverpool, of which I was Chief Constable. But I was able to maintain control of the area as long as I could stay in control of myself.

At a weekly meeting of myself and my three constables—Morgan, Bradley and Martin Burke—I sat down to listen to their reports, and the time seemed to jump in some inexplicable way to Bradley concluding his report. The three of them looked at me and waited.

'Very well then Morgan, let's hear yours,' I said.

The constable gave me a puzzled look and said: 'But sir, I have already read you mine!'

'Well, I know that. There are some points I would like to go over for... eh... clarification.'

'You want me to read the whole report again?'

'That is what I said.'

Then Martin said very quietly: 'But it is already midday and we should be patrolling the streets.'

'Yes, indeed,' said I, 'we can take this up at some future time.'

The three constables left but Martin came back in.

'What was that?' he asked.

'I don't know just... blank!'

'Be careful Michael.'

'Yes, of course! It was a fright, a shock.'

'There is already talk, Michael.'

'Talk?'

'About your level of intoxication while pursuing your duties.'

I held his look. He continued: 'All respect to your authority Michael—as ever. I owe you my life. I know that. You did not have to make it a condition of your surrender that we be afforded the same terms. You could have left us there in those Wicklow hills to be hunted down. I know that. But this will bring *you* down and I do not have the power to save you. Please, take care!'

I took Martin's advice, and when I finished work for the day I only had one bumper instead of my usual five or six. This turned out to be a wise move, for who should be sitting in the parlour of my house on my return but the bold Cecil, married by now to the porcelain doll, and we were still waiting for an invitation. He had been expressing his deep regret for what happened with Holt and the children, but behind it I detected a sneer that said 'You should have left it to my friend Dick when you had the chance.' He congratulated me on being one of the largest landowners in the colony, because between what we owned and leased there were now about one thousand acres. After more backslapping and small talk he came to the purpose of his meeting.

'You know there is now a road open across the Blue Mountains?'

'Haven't been on it, but heard of it,' I told him. 'Sort of like the Military Road but bigger.'

He laughed: 'No comparison, I assure you. We are, I mean the Governor is encouraging exploration and new settlements.'

I didn't know what any of this could have to do with me but then he came to it.

'Bushwhacking, as they call it, has become a serious problem and an impediment to progress. Folk travelling the road fear for their lives.'

'I'm sure now Cecil you'll root them out and hunt them down.'

'Rest assured we will. There is one group, made up almost entirely of Aboriginals, which is led by an old comrade of yours.'

'Arthur God-damned Devereux!' I said.

'I believe that is his name.'

'What do you want me to do?'

'I want you to ask him to come in.'

'Well now Cecil, you put that very simply and politely.'

'This is different to the usual bush-ranging as it has some hare-brained political motivation, which is about as mad as it is dangerous.'

'Are you asking me this or is it Governor Macquarie?'

'Truthfully Michael...'

'Please.'

'I petitioned the Governor to allow me to talk with you. If we, and by 'we' I mean the Corps, go after them, it will be a bloody confrontation. This could have unfortunate repercussions on the Governor's very successful policy with regard the natives. And obviously it would also have a rather unfortunate consequence for Mister Devereux.'

'If you manage to find him.'

'Oh, we will find him.'

'Arthur Devereux lasted five years on the run from the British, and they never found him. Now he has joined with veterans of Pemulwuy's campaigns and they evaded the British for ten years.'

'Perhaps.'

'No, Cecil, these are facts. If I was a betting man my money would not be on the Corps in this business.'

'You think you could find him?'

'Perhaps.'

'Would you?'

'I have my duties as Chief Constable of Liverpool.'

'You could be relieved of those, *temporarily*...' and then he added casually: '...in this instance.'

The implicit threat was hardly subtle.

'If I manage to bring him back to Sydney what will happen to him?'

'Well nobody has been killed, yet. At the moment he is a threat, no more than that. If he confesses to the error of his ways then there should not be any consequences.'

'All very vague Cecil!'

'I cannot guarantee that he will not spend time in jail but I can guarantee that he will not forfeit his life.'

'Will the Governor guarantee that?'

'I guarantee it on the Governor's behalf.'

That was not good enough for me, and Cecil knew this. He added: 'That is the best I can offer.'

'And if I refuse your offer?'

'Then a detachment of the Corps will be sent in pursuit of the insurgents...'

'... They are insurgents now?'

'Potential insurgents. If they are to be brought back alive it will be to dance on a gibbet.'

'What makes you think I care that deeply about Arthur Devereux?'

'Then you will do it for your own sake.'

That sounded like a threat and I did not grace it with a reply.

'Just how secure do you think your position in the New South Wales Constabulary is?'

He waited for an answer; I gave him none and so he continued: 'I hope you do not think that the Governor and Darcy Wentworth are blind or stupid. One of the conditions of your expedition would be that no spirituous liquors will travel with you. You can take a small number of men and some natives to track. Say goodbye to your wife for me Michael, and good hunting.'

After three days on the hunt I began to feel better, and actually started to enjoy the respite from the pressures of work and home. I was never cut out to be the Chief Constable of anywhere, and in my heart I knew I was not coping with the pressure. Now, I could have kept the district they called 'Liverpool' quiet and orderly if left to my own devices, but all these reports and trials and submissions had my head addled. Yes, I knew they were a necessity in a fair and civilised society, but I could never master them. Mary argued that I could if I tried because I had shown a good legal brain at my trial. She would hear no talk of my leaving the constabulary because the money earned was to go towards bringing the children over from Ireland. This same money had become a source of conflict between us because the correct sums were not handed over at the end of every week, and she argued that she had the right to demand accountability on behalf of the children. This led to some bitter battles between us. So now it was good to have a rest from all that and breathe the good air of this country that was both wild and vast.

Three recently settled convicts, one Scot and two English, rode with me and two native trackers. The trackers were very skilled at their craft, but I knew that we would never find Arthur and his little band. My hope was that they would find us. When we reached the territory in which Arthur was supposed to be operating I asked the trackers to go off and locate some of the local natives and try to get a message to Arthur, telling him that I had something I wanted to communicate with him to his advantage. After much difficult communication with the trackers, trying to convey this order as they bickered with each other, I deduced what the problem was: our trackers might not be able to communicate with the natives of this area because they spoke a different language. At which the Scot, who was called Murray commented: 'Desnae make sense. Wan native cannae ken wha' another wan is saying.' The two English men looked at each other and shrugged, not able to understand a word that Murray was saying. Of these two my mother would have said: 'English born and English bred, long in the legs and thick in the head.' God help them, like many transported to New South Wales these were petty criminals of the less cunning class who managed to get themselves caught.

When I thought about it I realised it should not have come as a surprise that groups of natives living so far apart for such a long time would not be able to communicate with each other. Sure isn't that the same as saying the French should be able to understand the Spanish and likewise the Dutch? Indeed some believed that this enormous country could well be the size of mainland Europe, and wasn't that a concept to grapple with?

Murray was a tightly strung individual who hated the natives—feared them and distrusted them. I never liked or respected them myself. They were lazy and couldn't hold their liquor, and the way they looked at me still gave me the bloody creeps. But, I had to accept with Arthur that they were men and as such entitled to the rights of all men. Their conquerors did not believe that. I respected the Aboriginals, as Macquarie called them, for their fight against the invaders. They were tricked of course because they thought the English had only come on a visit, and when they realised the truth of the situation they were outgunned. 'Twas dangerous for me to follow this line of thought for too long because I'd only end up siding with Arthur.

On returning from one of their sorties, our trackers told us they knew the area where Arthur and his merry men roamed free. They led us into dense forest, and I began to question my wisdom in trusting them. This was hellish terrain. You could not walk a yard without becoming entangled in some class of strange vegetation, and distances were impossible to calculate. A journey that might be two miles as the crow flies could end up being a ten mile march as you trudged down one side of a deep ravine and up the other. My three companions were supposed to have had military experience, but they showed little evidence of it. Murray became more nervous with every step, yelping: 'Who is there? What was that? Did you see that?' The two English grumbled to each other. While Murray was a fat dwarf, they were lanky and hirsute.

Nights were the worst, as it was then that I most missed my rum. When we travelled in open country I felt much better, but this entire expedition was still a sore penance. We felt we were watched at night, and certainly there was movement in the trees around us that could have been man or beast. Murray insisted on having a musket and pistol primed and loaded by his side as he slept, and the two English men and myself followed suit. For two nights the trackers were very tense and admitted that indeed we were being watched. Murray and the two English were rattled by this but it calmed me down, because, assuming it was Arthur, he would approach us sooner or later. Nights were cold enough and we lit a big fire, which seemed to attract more insects and reptiles than it repelled.

On the fifth night in the forest, Murray was more jittery than ever and now I wished we had some rum with us, because that would be the one thing to guarantee us all a night's sleep. To the west and very close by there was definite movement, and I whispered that we should all be calm and quiet. Of course this only made Murray worse. There was sudden noise and Murray discharged his musket into the darkness. We felt it had hit some creature. Silence for a moment. Then a bright flash and a loud report from out of the darkness. Murray jerked back gurgling as the bullet hit his throat. I knew it could not have been Arthur, who couldn't shoot straight to save his life, unless it had been some extraordinary fluke. Instinctively I fired at the source of the shot. I regretted it immediately. Who could it have been if not Arthur? Then I heard screams, but these were the screams of a woman. Jesus, don't tell me I've shot a woman! That is a thing I would never do. War is war and it should have nothing to do with women and children. We staunched poor Murray's wound as best we could, but we knew he would not last. I sat until first light not knowing whether I had shot Arthur or a woman.

During that long night Murray expired. He was a man killed by his own stupidity, which had led me into an act of even greater stupidity. I was certain that my bullet had hit the shooter, and I felt sure now that Arthur must have been the shooter. When I heard his voice at dawn I was mightily relieved: 'Michael, can we talk?'

'Show yourself slowly. No weapons!'

It wasn't so much the guns I feared as those vicious little spears the natives used. I didn't want to see a shower of them coming out of the sky. Arthur walked into the clearing, alone, bearded, tired and sad.

'Have you medical supplies?' he asked.

'Not much!' I told him.

'Alcohol?'

'None.'

He raised an eyebrow at me.

'Truly!'

'He is in bad way. He wants to see you.'

So saying Arthur turned and walked away and I followed. We came to the clearing that was their camp and the fire they had lit was hardly visible, but the place still seemed warm. A native youth lay on the dry ground, injured in the shoulder, and he was tended by an older woman. Arthur walked past these however and towards the fire. Another man lay by the fire, a younger woman by his side. He raised his head.

'Brother-in-law,' Kevin said, 'thank God it wasn't you. Who did I hit?'

'A Scotsman called Murray. God rest him.'

'I'm sorry. I shouldn't have.'

'Self defence. Sure aren't you one of Holt's top sharpshooters. Self defence.'

'Well he shot my other brother-in-law.'

'Your what?'

'This is my wife, Duveen,' he told me, pointing to the young black woman by his side, now weeping. She was probably beautiful, but the kind of beauty I could not appreciate. Then he pointed to an old man, wide eyed and sagely bearded, who held a child in his arms. Not an infant now. She was perhaps three or four years old. 'That is our daughter, Martine. Just look at her. Isn't she the head off Roisin?'

As the child wriggled, twisted and shook her head, even in the shadows, I saw what he meant.

'Mary will adore her,' he said, 'and she will understand why I chose the name Martine. I know you won't.'

would be accomplished—that for which we had spent twenty long years striving.

Mary and James tended me as best they could, but I resented that and wanted to be by myself. Then there was the smell—the terrible stench that went with the bloody flux. I abhorred that for myself and hated to inflict it on my family. Poor James, he did his best, supporting me and lifting me, but these were no tasks for a lad of his tender years. When I was his age war had not yet come to Wicklow and the First Fleet had not landed in this place.

I walked and crawled across the land, weak as weak can be. How long it took me to get there I could not say but in the end I arrived at South Head. In the beginning of the colony there was a flag pole erected here and a flag was flown when a ship was sighted. But Macquarie had ordered a lighthouse built and I sat beneath it on that last day. As I looked out over the calm sea no sail was visible all the way to the horizon. I knew they were out there, and I prayed that God would keep me breathing until they landed.

Looking around the harbour I marvelled at how much this place had changed in the years we had been here. From what? A wilderness of savages? Oh-ho Arthur would have jumped on me for that one. 'Republics, citizen! Primitive republics of which Tom Paine would have approved and they brought them the sophistication of monarchy.' True, I suppose because Macquarie demanded each tribe have a leader. One man placed above the others. One family granted more privileges than the others. But they had leaders of course. One at least that I knew of— Pemulwuy, who fought the British for ten years, which makes my five years of resistance seem only half as good. But I would never admit to that in public, nor would any of us. Vanquished and beheaded in the end like poor Robert Emmet, who never got to fire a single shot.

'Quiet now Kevin, we want to keep you alive for her.'

He shook his head and sighed. Then said: 'Three more children you have now?'

'Yes, three.'

'And they are mighty looking. I watched them from afar. Watched you all.'

'Why, oh why did you not come to us?'

'A wanted man is restricted Michael, you know that.'

'We would have shielded you.'

'I shot those two informers for you. Treacherous liars. I hope that was some recompense.'

I didn't have the heart to tell him the shooting of O'Grady and MacCurry actually set us back several months.

'Haven't lost my touch, have I?' he added.

'Indeed then you haven't.'

'That was my plan. Procure firearms and teach these as Sam had taught me. Just a dream Michael. Another republic, another dream! I am so ashamed. So sorry about Sam.'

'Sure we are all sorry about Sam,' I said, 'He was the best of us.'

'You don't understand. It was me. Trevor! I could tolerate very little. What he did was unbearable, degrading. Told him all I knew. Miley Connell and the houses at Dairenemuck, the food planks, the arms dumps. I would have told him anything, anything he asked.'

'But you could not have known about the safe houses at Dairenamuck.'

'Sure the Tooles are my first cousins Michael. Mad republicans! I knew that. Everything, Michael, I told him everything.'

I had to walk away. Turmoil in my head and not a tot of rum to cure it. Mary! She must never know of this. And she must never know that I shot him. 'But stop now!' I had to tell myself. 'Stop and tend to the boy.' Boy? Boy no longer. Not boy for a long time now. I walked back to the fire and sat beside him. He was weak, exhausted, but also desperate. The wound was bad, in the chest; not the heart, but the lungs and some of them veins around the heart and the lungs. Bleeding inside too, I thought, drowning. He would hardly last a day and we could not carry him.

He gathered all his strength and started to talk:

'I wanted to achieve something, a victory. I thought then you might... you might... but no, you could never forgive me.'

I looked at him and watched him struggle, but I could not say it. Instead I told him: 'Quieten yourself now son, take it nice and easy.' I talked to him of Wicklow days, of the Glen of Imaal and Lug na Coille, of Glendalough and the Sally Gap. Talked of Hugh Vesty and Billy the Rock, of Fintan and Rory, his murdered friends. At all costs trying to avoid a mention of Sam. Not easy because Kevin was Sam's shadow in those days. If Sam meant the world to me he meant the sun moon and stars on top of that to Kevin. But still I could not say it. Instead I went on with a lot of nonsense about *seanachas* and shebeens, about the harp restrung and the tree of liberty in bloom again. The rising of the moon, God damn it! Anything, except I forgive ya boy, be at peace. That was all he wanted. That was all he needed. What kind of a piece of work am I at all that I could not do that? I stroked his forehead and held his hand. Before he died, when the sun was at its height, he asked me if I would bring the child and the woman to Mary, and I told him that I would.

It was a few days' march in a blistering sun back to Cabramatta and so we had to bury him where we were. The two English helped dig a grave and I fashioned a crude cross with some branches. All through this the natives set up this low sorrowful moan that went on and on. Why could I not say it to him? After all this I went to the woman he had called Duveen and said: 'So Duveen, Kevin has asked...'

No sooner was the word out of my mouth than she put a frightened hand to my lips. Arthur said: 'When a man dies here you do not say his name.' I looked at him. He went on: 'It is a custom, citizen. Respect it!'

So, I told her it had been her 'husband's' wish that she and the child should come with us and she nodded in acquiescence. Then I turned to Arthur and said: 'Arthur, I want you to come with us to Sydney.'

He looked at me in silence. Before I knew what was happening the two English approached him with shackles, ready to clamp him. I let a roar out of me and grabbed the shackles off the first English, swung them with ferocity and connected with his face—a red splatter. As the second approached I swung the irons at his balls and as he went down I brought my boot to his kneecap. I was shouting, the English were roaring, Duveen was screaming and the natives huddled together. Arthur came and held me round the waist:

'Michael, for Christ's sake man, get a grip of yourself! I am coming with you. It is all right.'

Arthur helped the English men to their feet and started to tend their wounds. The natives looked at me with, what? Awe, disgust, fear?

The journey back was mostly in silence. I knew I had to square things with the two Englishmen or they might bring a charge against me. When we stopped I held out my left hand, palm flat, with two crown pieces on it, and I made a fist of my right.

'Now you can choose the left and keep your mouths shut, or you can have the right if you intend to blab.'

They chose the crowns.

'Saint Martin!' Mary told me. 'Sure isn't that the only black saint he'd know. As far as I know 'tis the only black saint that ever was. But sure he couldn't call a girl Martin. Do you understand? Anyway the one thing it proves is that he wanted her to be brought up as a Christian. So, it is up to us to honour his wishes. Why, oh why did he not bring them to us?'

'Well, he was a wanted man, and he didn't want to jeopardise our position.'

'My poor brother.'

''Twas him that shot O'Grady and the other fella.'

'Stop! Truly? Doesn't that make sense now! We should have copped that at the time, shouldn't we?'

'We had thought him dead.'

'But never at rest. At least now I know where he is lain. You will be able to find it again?'

'I think so. She'll know where it is anyway—Duveen.'

On hearing her name she smiled her beautiful smile. Mary had put her in a dress because when we arrived she wore next to nothing. Indeed now she didn't seem so much to wear the dress as just have it on. Like something had fallen from the sky and wrapped itself around her! Never completely comfortable in our home, in our society. To me she was easier to look at with the dress on. More feminine somehow, but still, I don't know, primitive and provocative even. Martine on the other hand was completely at home from when she came through the door.

We watched her now playing with Bridget and Mary said: 'Will ye look at the darling? The hop, the skip and the shake of the head. Black as jet but the absolute spit of her aunt.'

Mary would veer between joy at Martine to grief for her brother and back again every few minutes.

'If we got a proper coffin could we move his remains back here and give him a real burial?'

'Maybe. It is rough terrain. We'll see.'

'He fired first, you say?'

'Did I? Yes. No, no, I fired, we... we fired first. Hit one of the natives... her brother. He was hurt, but not too badly. Then Kevin fired and hit Murray, and Murray shot Kevin.'

'What? Murray fired at him after he'd been shot?'

'At the same time. I don't know, it was black night in the middle of the jungle. Confusing, fire-fights are always confusing.'

'Are you sure it wasn't Arthur who shot Murray?'

'Yes! No, it definitely wasn't Arthur. Please don't say that!'

'I know we do not want it said at his trial. But this is just between us. This is private. I want to know how my brother died, exactly. You are not telling me everything.'

My voice raised now: 'I am telling you all that I remember. There was... confusion.'

'Were you drinking?'

'No, of course I wasn't. There was no rum! Was Cecil here when I was away?'

'Cecil? Why would Cecil be here?'

'I don't know, do I? They tell me he is on manoeuvres or something, that he will be away for a while. I need to see him.'

'Why?'

'Because he was the one who promised Arthur would be safe. The Governor won't see me and so I must see Cecil before the trial.'

'Stop tormenting me about Cecil!'

I shouted: 'Life or death Mary. My comrade. I gave him my word. I gave it because that God-damned toy soldier guaranteed me!'

She broke down in tears: 'My brother is dead and all you can think of is Arthur, Arthur, Arthur!'

Duveen went to comfort her.

Perhaps if Arthur had just remained silent the outcome would have been different, but I doubt it. If he had marshalled a defence and called witnesses would the court have listened to him? Now, we will never know. He was charged with sedition, treason and murder, all of these being capital offences. Of course he would plead guilty to the first two without any reservation. Why had he come with me so readily? I had never lied to him, and when I guaranteed his safety—assured him that his life would be spared—he believed me. I had convinced myself that my promises to him were sound, and that I was right in trusting Cecil—a man I had not trusted since the day I met him. The Governor kept a dignified distance from the proceedings, ensuring that his integrity remained intact.

Once the death sentence had been passed, and he was taken back to his cell, I was not allowed to see him, for fear of further conspiracies and the fomentation of rebellion. This was not surprising because Arthur's speech from the dock was a call to arms for all the oppressed in the colony, black or white. I now try to console myself that that is why he came back to Sydney—to make that speech. And that he did not come because of my pledges and his own disillusionment with the ridiculous bush campaign for the rights of the savages.

Never felt more like drinking than I did that night but I abstained for Arthur's sake, so that I could stand strong and dignified before him in the morn when sentence would be carried out.

The sun was already blazing when they dragged him to the scaffold. In truth of course there was no need to drag him. The man would have walked quite calmly on his own. Before he ascended the steps he looked into the crowd until he found me and then he said, so I could barely hear: 'Goodbye citizen.'

They had the rope round his neck and the trap kicked open before he could step forward and declare his righteousness in the manner of Robert Emmet. He dangled, danced and defecated for a long time until at last he swung still.

I went to William Davis' House and knelt before the consecrated host in its timber tabernacle. Nothing!

I went then to the station house and threw the rattle I had never sprung onto the floor. I brought my boot down on it again and again until it was in smithereens.

A constable whose name I did not know came to the door of the station house. He handed me a letter. The letter was from the Governor, and it informed me that I had been dismissed from the New South Wales Constabulary.

'You are too late! I resign!' I shouted at him.

'And you'll pay for that rattle as well,' he said, and left.

Later that day, or maybe it was the next, not for the first time, I was wheeled home on a hand-cart. Duveen and Martine, God love them, were terrified, because they had not witnessed such a scene before. My own children knew to stay out of the way but were not unduly alarmed. 'I have left the Force!' I shouted 'I told them what they could do with their stinking job!'

'Well, once you are sober you may go back and tell them that you are rejoining.' Mary told me calmly.

'Never, never, never! Not after what they did to Arthur. Arthur Devereux, who was worth ten of them, a hundred of them, a thousand of them. Lying bastards and cowards. That Scottish prick afraid to show his face. Not to mention that Tipperary tit Cecil sneak Lomasney. Know where we stand now, don't we?'

It was at that point I saw for the first time that Hugh Vesty was in the house.

'It is true then?' he asked.

'Where the hell were you?' I asked.

'I didn't know. Didn't hear about it until today. Why in God's name did you bring him in, Michael?'

In a rage I threw myself at Hugh Vesty, but he held me easily and did not loosen his grip until I had calmed down.

'You never liked him, did you?' I said.

'Never liked him, but always admired him.'

'Yeah, yeah!'

'Let's get you to bed.'

He lifted me through to the bedroom and took off my boots.

'Holt never did nothing Hugh. Never told anything. I know that for a certain now. And T.F. Halpin, God forgive me we were wrong, wrong, wrong.'

Before he could answer darkness descended.

It was still the night when I awoke, but of what day I could not tell you. Dry, nauseous, pulsating pain in my head, I staggered through to the parlour, from where I could hear voices. Mary was there with Hugh Vesty and Martin Burke, sipping wine, if you don't mind. I took a look at Martin and said: 'As conspicuous now with your presence, as you have been by your absence.'

'I was sent up to the Hawkesbury. Some disturbance. It was nothing. Just an excuse to get me out of the way. Will you take a drop of wine?'

'Jesus Christ man, don't be disgusting. I am sick as a dog.'

'Sorry Michael.'

'I'll try a drop of rum.'

For some reason the lads found this amusing. My right hand shook so much I had to use my left to steady it so that I could bring the glass to my lips. They watched as I waited, praying I could keep it down. Finally Mary said: 'Martin has told me the truth Michael.'

I ignored that and talked to the two men: 'They promised me they would not take his life. Prison for a while
perhaps. No more than that. I was given their word.'

Hugh Vesty nodded: 'Sure didn't they give you their
word you could go to America. Didn't they give you their
word all your children could come with you here?'

'You must go to Macquarie Michael, ask for the job
back. We need the salary.'

'After this? I'd rather die first.'

'Arthur is dead now, there is nothing more we can do
about that,' she added.

'Enough!' I shouted.

'If you two are going to go at it I am leaving now,'
Martin told us.

'And poor Kevin too?' Hugh Vesty asked.

'A bloody mess, the whole job,' I said.

'Out there all this time,' Mary said, 'and we knew nothing about it.'

'He fought for the cause right up to the end, you
know,' said I.

'Sam would have been proud of him,' Martin said.

'Adored the ground he walked on,' Hugh Vesty said.

''Twas he shot the two informers after the trial,' Mary
told them proudly.

'He never!' Hugh Vesty said.

'Two muskets, one shot each, to the head. Two
hundred yards at least—imagine that,' she added proudly.

'Holt's sharpshooters boy,' Martin said.

'Michael what were you telling me about Holt earlier?'
Hugh Vesty asked.

'Ha? Was I talking about Holt? No recollection.'

'Remember Arthur and those God-damned uniforms?'
Martin asked. 'All the way from Paris.'

'Can you imagine frolicking round the hills of Wicklow
in them? We'd have dazzled them to death in our green
and gold.' Hugh Vesty laughed and we joined in.

After the laughter a lapse into silence. Martin broke it eventually: 'Isn't it quare just the same, a wake without a corpse.'

'Two grand men gone,' Hugh said, and then, turning to Mary: 'Will you write to your parents?'

'Don't know if they are alive or dead, Hugh Vesty. They finished with me a long time ago.'

'And the little black one is his they tell me?'

'Yes,' said Mary.

'Erra you can't blame the boy. If I was stuck out in the wilderness that long myself I'd say any bloody savage would do.'

The slap she gave him on his fat face gave us all a start. I grabbed her by the hair and threw her in a corner.

'Don't you dare, ever, ever, raise a hand to one of my comrades. You'll pay for this let me tell you.'

Hugh Vesty stepped in between us: ''Tis all right Michael. She is distraught. I didn't mean any disrespect to your brother Mary. He was a grand lad. The best out.'

After the silence Martin said: 'Arthur had a friend didn't he? French fella, some kind of a radical.'

'Maurice Margarot,' said Hugh Vesty.

'The very man!' said Martin.

'Oh he's long gone,' I told him.

'Dead?'

'No, back to France, or maybe America.'

So passed the time, talking carefully about the past, always on the edge of anger. And all I could think of was why I could not forgive him. It was not anger at the vilification of Joe Holt, or Sam's death with Miley Connell and the others, or even the drowning of Halpin. I simply could not do it, could not bring myself to it. I could not tell Mary. So it stayed stuck in my heart and my head, a torment like Lowry Loinsheach's secret of old. No one to talk to, no one to share it with. That is until Therry arrived. That was the man who would change our lives. But before Therry there was the two Scotsmen.

Chapter XIII
Michael finds himself a new profession, but all who know him believe that it may indeed be the death of him.

'This will not just be for the Irish, mind. Eh Mister Campbell?' Daniel Cooper asked William Campbell the Younger, who replied: 'Oh quite the contrary, Mister Cooper.' Cooper smiled at his partner's reply. It was a full-faced smile, teeth and eyes and all, but in a flash it went back to blank. Campbell's smile on the other hand was a closed mouth one, but he kept his bright eyes on me at all times, assuring me that he was truly smiling. Between them they were putting up two thousand pounds for the project.

'Oh indeed we Scots are just as partial to a dram as you Irish. And this would be a safe place to drink—a secure house,' Cooper said.

'And who is going to be foolish enough to cause trouble in an inn owned and run by the great Michael Dwyer?' his partner added.

'But open to every race as we say.'

'Except the blacks mind.'

'Oh well, of course, except the blacks. Nothing against them personally, mind but...'

'...They cannae hold their liquor,' Campbell finished his partner's statement. 'And they hardly have the wherewithal to pay for it.'

'Which, in the end, is the purpose of the exercise—the making of a profit.'

Silence for a while as I considered the proposition.

'So we extend our house by ten further rooms?'

'That should be ample,' Cooper agreed. and his partner nodded, adding: 'Now the source of the profit will not be the guests who stay but the patrons who drink.'

'Will they come?' I wondered aloud.

'There is no name better known than your own in this colony. It is time you used your popularity to make money,' Campbell assured me. 'The Irish will travel for miles so they can say 'I had a drink with Michael Dwyer, the Wicklow Chief!' You talk about your life back in Ireland, they drink, and we all make money.'

'No disrespect intended in this to the cause for which you fought so bravely,' Cooper now.

'None whatsoever!' his partner added, slapping the table, and then they waited for my reply.

'If I did want to open an inn, why would I need your help?'

They moved their heads closer together and then towards me.

Cooper spoke: 'We are not here to offer help to you, Michael Dwyer. Of course not! We are here to invest in a business opportunity. I know you are the wealthiest and most successful of the Irish who came here—the strongest landowner in the Liverpool area, and getting stronger. We have an import licence and can supply you with the very best at the keenest prices. Work has already commenced on our new distillery, and we also plan a brewery. The grape can be grown here. Wine produced. I know you believe in this country Mister Dwyer and I see you at the heart of its future. Others are opening taverns it is true, but we have something unique: you!'

So, I thought about this for a moment. There were many people who felt it might be a good idea for me to open a tavern. I would have been one of the best known people in the colony, and not just with the Irish. They liked a rebel in this part of the world, and many were impressed with how I had conducted my defence against the trumped-up charges Bligh had brought against me, and how that had helped to bring that tyrant down. I did not have the money to spare myself, but I had let it be known that I would listen to anyone who might be interested in investing in the business, and these two had come forward.

They were patient through my silence and Campbell spoke quietly:

'You are a busy man, expanding your agricultural inter-ests. It would be difficult for you to find the time and commitment this project will demand. With our help... contribution... it could be up and running in no time.'

'I will have to talk to my wife. It is our home.'

'But of course,' Cooper agreed.

'And then we can sort out the details,' concluded Campbell.

I had rarely raised my hand to Mary, and when I did it was always in self-defence. The pulling I gave her after she slapped Hugh Vesty had to happen. I could not allow her to smack a comrade of mine in company and let it go unmarked. This was not just because of the personal loss of face, but there was the danger that Hugh Vesty could have taken the law into his own hands so to speak, and that could have had terrible consequences. Mary under-stood all this, but it did not stop her from calling me a bully when I presented the conversion of the house into an Inn as a done deal.

'What is left of the fund to send me to Ireland to bring over the children?' She demanded, hands on hips.

'I've lent money here and there. People needing a dig out. You know what it's like yourself.'

'Who?'

'Different people.'

'Michael!?'

'This business venture will turn everything around.'

'It will destroy us.'

'No. You do not understand these things.'

'Ha!' she shouted dismissively.

'You should not question me. Not on these matters. We have done well. Success! Look! You can see it all around us.'

'I want to see my children all around us. That is all.'

'Soon. You cannot go yet, not with Martine and her mother here. You do not want to walk out on that. Money, profit, that is what will make all things possible. Say what you like, I know a bit about drinking.'

'Too much.'

'Then let us put it to good use for a change.'

'I fear for this, Michael. Truly I do. You cannot gamble when it comes to our children. You cannot.'

I took her in my arms, and soothed her as best I could. She sighed, surrendering to the inevitable. Then she asked:

'What more did Kevin say, before he... expired? Tell me all.'

The knowledge of her brother's treachery gave me an uncomfortable feeling of power. I prayed that I would never use it because it would hurt her more than anyone deserved. On top of that, of course, I was the one who shot him. So, I had to be careful when I spoke about his last moments:

'Told me it was a pity I was not with them—himself and the native rebels. They needed leadership, military leadership. Arthur, of course, could give them theoretical guidance on political matters, but he was never a soldier. Said I would have had so much to offer them—so much to offer.'

'Was that all he talked about?'

'No, of course not. He talked of Wicklow. Your parents. The campaign of course. The old comrades—Joe Holt, and Hugh Vesty and Martin.'

'And Sam surely?'

'Sam more than anybody else.'

'Did you tell him about the fight at Dairenamuck?'

'Oh, yes.'

'He had never heard an eye-witness account of that.'

As we talked we walked arm-in-arm out to the porch, and we had been conversing for a while before we saw him. He stood a few perches off, left leg straight, right foot resting against the inside of the left knee. A square of hide draped over his privates. A spear pointed to the ground, held lightly in one hand. Like he had grown there almost. Seemed taller now than when I had first seen him in their camp in the bush. The eyes and the beard lending him an aspect of a bard or even a chieftain. And I wondered if that was what he was—a chieftain of his own race.

'Come to see his grandchild,' I said.

'He has every right to do that, doesn't he?'

'I suppose.'

'He makes me uncomfortable, standing there and staring at us.'

'I think he looks just grand. You just have to get used to them Mary. It takes time is all.'

Like most natives we had known, and in truth that was few indeed, we could not pronounce his name. We called him 'Tom', because that is what the first syllable sounded like.

The building was well underway when Father Therry arrived, and during our first meeting he had to sidestep the movements of planks and wheelbarrows while he tried to speak above the hammering and the sawing. He could not have been more different to Father O'Flynn. This was a man blunt of manner but sharp of intellect. He had told us that 'proper accreditation had been afforded him in London and there was nothing Macquarie could do to stop him ministering'. He let me know at that first meeting what he felt about my politics. 'Physical force as a way of getting justice for Ireland is redundant forever. It did not work, it will not work, it cannot work. Yes, we must be tireless in our endeavours to secure political and religious freedom, but using peaceful means only. Very soon Catholic Emancipation will be passed in the British Parliament, and this will give us the right to have strong representation in the Westminster Government. That is where the battles will be fought now in the Irish cause and the Catholic cause. It will be slow and arduous, but we will prevail.'

Those working on the building had stopped to listen and so he addressed them directly: 'Ah now lads, do not let me come between you and the good work. Just as long as you all know where I stand, especially when you are swinging those planks of wood around.'

During the ensuing laughter he led me away by the arm, but made sure everyone heard his next sentence:

'Well Michael Dwyer, I am in awe at what you have achieved in this colony. Now tell me what you plan here.'

I told him about the Inn, and the Tavern that would be part of the Inn, and how I felt there was money to be made from the venture. He agreed with me wholeheartedly, and in the presence of Mary, who still had doubts about the project. Mind you she questioned every carpenter, plumber and mason about where every plank, brick or pipe was going, what its function was and how the finish would look.

Eventually we persuaded the priest to sit down with us and take a glass of wine with us—he did not care for spirituous liquors and had no time to eat.

'That Macquarie is a tough nut,' he said.

Mary told him: 'He is better than the last two governors, but very anti-Catholic.'

'Well, he'll have to put up with us now because he has been given his orders from London. You have had a few run-ins with him Michael I believe?'

'You could say that.'

'And he gave you the sack for drinking on the job?'

Mary tensed, but I didn't move.

'I was deceived. They went back on their word. And so the action I took led to a comrade, a dear friend of mine being hanged.'

'Yes, I heard about Arthur Devereux. You exercised admirable restraint in not taking up arms as a result. But your answer was the right one Michael. You showed them what you can do with industry and ambition. Isn't that right Mrs Dwyer?'

Mary was caught off guard: 'Eh... yes of course.'

'Now tell me about the children—the ones left behind in Ireland.'

So, we told him our sad story, and as we talked he took out pen and paper from his satchel and made notes. When we had finished he took one of Mary's hands and one of my hands.

'All I can promise in this is that I will do my best. You have suffered dreadfully the pair of you and deserve justice.'

Then he continued with a complete change of tone.

'Now to cruder matters! Money! I will be needing your financial assistance.'

'How much and what for?' I asked.

'Michael! You don't have the right to be questioning the priest on how he spends his money.'

'Now, it would be your money too, Mary. And of course he has the right. I am going to build a church right in the centre of Sydney Town.'

'I wonder what Macquarie will have to say about that?' I asked.

'Oh, the Governor has given me permission and will grant me some land. We will get started right away.'

'You can depend on our support,' Mary told him.

'"Saint Mary's"? How about that for a name?' he smiled and twinkled.

'Oh now, you can depend on our outmost and undying support!' I told him and he laughed again.

'In the immediate, is there anything I can perform for you?'

'My brother is buried in unhallowed ground some-where in the bush. I want him to have a Christian burial.'

'Where is this place?'

I told him where it was, two or three days' ride away, and the circumstances that led to Kevin's death (the version I had told Mary, of course).

'I will not be able to attend to that immediately but I will offer up the Holy Mass for the repose of his soul.'

Once we had expressed our gratitude for this he asked about 'the native mother and child'. Mary told him that Kevin wanted the child brought up as a Christian.

'Well, I will baptise the child, but not the mother unless she wants to and is willing to take instruction. I am not supposed to convert anyone from their own religion, but in the case of natives I think we can safely say that they do not have a religion. Now, if you will forgive, I have many more calls to make.'

With that he rose and shook both of us by the hand.

I accompanied him out to his horse and told him that I was in dire need of confessing and could I arrange a time and a place with him.

'No time like the present,' he said, and took a stole from his pocket, kissed it and draped it round his neck. As we walked from the house, he leading the horse, I told him what had happened the fateful night out in the bush—how I shot Kevin and Kevin's deathbed confession and, what troubled me most, my inability or unwillingness to forgive Kevin.

'But you can forgive him now?' he asked.

'It was a heartless, unchristian thing to do—to let the lad die like that.'

'His testimony did a great deal of harm?'

'And caused the death of my closest comrade.'

'If you forgive him, you must forgive yourself.'

'Nobody could have resisted Trevor's tortures. A man would say anything under that,' I said to him.

He told me to offer up a rosary for the repose of Kevin's soul and the souls of all the others sent to their maker before their time. The good priest absolved me and got on his horse.

'Drink is a good thing Michael. A gift from the Lord. The first miracle he turned water into wine. But respect it. Be temperate at all costs and see to it that your customers are too. Then this venture should go very well for you.'

'All that happened with Kevin. I could never tell Mary.'

'Nor should you. God bless you Captain.'

He rode off.

I did not fight at the battle of Harrow, nor did I ever claim to have fought at the battle of Harrow. The Inn at Cabramatta was named 'The Harrow Inn' in memory of those brave men who took part in that famous victory in Wexford back in 1798. The opening of the Harrow Inn was

for me a celebration of all that we were, and a new beginning, not just for the Dwyer family, but for the entire Irish
community in New South Wales. But there are those who
would argue that it all started to go wrong from that very
first night. I got carried away with the excitement; there is
no denying that.

Mary had come round to the idea, and started to
believe that it might indeed be the solution to all our problems. She was impressed with the enthusiasm of the
throng gathered outside our front door, but she did not
approve of the extravagance of my inaugural gestures. I
turned the key in the door and then held the key aloft in
my hand and declared:

'The doors of the Harrow Inn are now open and I give
you all my word that they will never, never close again.'

Then I walked to the well, displayed they key to one
and all, and dropped it into the well. This was greeted with
a mighty cheer.

Nobody paid for their first drink. Now to say that
nobody ever paid for any drink at the Inn is a terrible lie.
Mary, along with Messer's Cooper and Campbell, was dis-
mayed at my gestures of generosity. True I thought I was
Fionn mac Cumhaill of the Golden Hand, reminding
people that the strength of an Irish Chieftain, long 'go
was not in what he possessed, but what he gave away.

The interior was hung with banners—*Erin go Braugh*
embroidered in gold thread on a green background with
gold trimmings, *The Harp Restrung* and *The Tree of Liberty*
and then two battered Wexford hurleys which were
crossed and lashed together. I had asked William Davis to
make a couple of pikes for us, but he felt that that might
have constituted an incendiary act. And, God knows, the
man had a point.

Once the drink flowed the entertainment commenced.
There were stirring martial airs accompanied by much

table-thumping, long, shut-eyed, come-all-ye's that brought tears to the eyes that understood and which infected the eyes of those who did not. But the act that stole that night and many a night thereafter was performed by a young man called Brosnan from the County Kerry, who delivered in its entirety Robert Emmet's 'Speech from the Dock'. The young man sounded nothing like Emmet of course, but his rich Kerry accent lent a passion and poetry to the speech more powerful than Emmet's educated Anglo tones.

What have I to say that sentence of death should not be pronounced on me according to law?' he began, and waited for silence before he continued. The silence was intense. But this was not a passive audience and the first cheer of agreement came soon enough as Brosnan looked at each man in turn saying:

'A man in my situation my Lords has not only to encounter the difficulties of fortune, and the force of power over minds which it has corrupted or subjugated but the difficulties of established prejudice: the man dies but his memory lives!'

Brosnan allowed the cheer to happen, but before it degenerated into commentary he pressed on. The next interjection came on:

'I wish my memory and name may animate those who survive me!'

'Oh it does Robert it do!' some shouted.

Then a full-throated angry shout came on:

'A Government which is steeled to barbarity by the cries of the orphans and the tears of the widows it has made.'

And this changed to murmurs of sympathy when he:*'appealed to the immaculate God.'*

It was a long speech, but there was never a night when it did not hold its audience. No drink was served during the speech and when patrons had grown used to this custom they stocked up before it started. Every sentence had a resonance, some of which were quietly acknowledged, like:

'I wish to procure for my country the guarantee which Washington procured for America.'

Which was greeted with 'that is it, nothing more, nothing less'.

My name was evoked and my shoulder patted as he intoned:

There are men engaged in this conspiracy who are not only superior to me but even to your own conception of yourself, my lord; men, before the splendour of whose genius and virtues, I should bow with respectful deference, and who would think themselves dishonoured to be called your friend—who would not disgrace themselves by shaking your blood-stained hand...'

This was greeted with whoops and yells. And we were with young Brosnan all the way to the end. And at the end we grasped hands and clutched shoulders—men who would not touch each other in cold sobriety—and for the end we all joined in:

'When my country takes her place among the nations of the earth, then, and not till then, let my epitaph be written!'

Applause was clapped and tears shed while the next round was ordered.

So it was night after night at the Harrow Inn.

The man we knew as Tom never came near the house, nor did he announce his presence. He stood at a discrete distance and waited until he was noticed. Then Duveen and Martine would go to him, and the three of them would set off, usually at a trot.

Mary was very worried the first time this happened, fearing that she would not see her niece again, but they returned after a few days. Duveen's English improved all the time and we agreed that it was a good thing that Martine should meet her grandfather from time to time. The child grew speaking English, and in time would forget all knowledge of her native tongue. Duveen took instruction in Christian doctrine and Mary and myself agreed to stand as her godparents when the time came.

She was one of many natives brought to the Faith by Father Therry, and Mary sponsored several of them. The plans for the new Catholic church went ahead and, in a public ceremony, Lachlan Macquarie laid the foundation stone. Therry had become one of the most popular men in the colony, and not just among the Irish. But he was not pleased with the excesses that went on in the Harrow Inn and called me to task more than once about them. I had to remind him that he had no authority over me, but secretly I was very relieved about the sacredness of the seal of confession because of the terrible secret he did hold over me. That same cursed thing became like a gulf or a barrier between myself and Mary. I thought confession would take that burden from me but it didn't, not fully. But it wasn't always a burden because sometimes—and this is strange now—when we quarrelled it was a secret weapon, which I could unleash if she pushed me too far.

Martine was popular with her cousins from the start. They enjoyed the exotic novelty of her, and she would win a place in anybody's heart with her devilish ways and her wicked sense of humour. And if that did not conquer you then you would soon be won over once you saw her dance. What a dancer! She had those outside the family who despised her, but she had a formidable protector in James Dwyer, who was now coming into his teenage years.

Duveen was remarkably strong and could manage the work of any man. She was afraid of the cows, though, and Mary could never entice her to milk them. Apart from that they worked together in harmony and could communicate with ease. They shared stories of Kevin, animated and excited. But my abiding memory of them was sitting in silence, perfectly at ease, staring into the fire. Then, on occasions, for no apparent reason they burst into laughter, hysterical, uncontrollable laughter that took some time to fade out in ever-reducing giggles. I was never told what the matter was, and I think perhaps they did not know themselves. They were pleasing for a man to look at, very pleasing indeed.

Mary reared up on me once because I asked Duveen to clean out one of the spittoons from the tavern. I did not think that it was so dreadful a request because the aim of most of my patrons was so pitifully bad. But I agreed not to do it again.

I never stole from the Harrow Inn, but somebody definitely did. Mind you it would have been easy enough for a man to do because few days went by during this time without my having a number of prolonged blank spells. I'd come out of these not knowing who I'd been talking to or what I'd been saying. Folk must have noticed it but it was never commented upon.

The finances of the Harrow Inn never added up, and before long Cooper and Campbell stopped looking for a return on their money and started looking for a return of their money. I didn't think much of their chances and I had to run them off the premises more than once. Hugh Vesty cautioned me and Martin warned me that this could all have a very bad end, but by then I didn't care much and soon I would not care at all. My capacity for caring had been taken from me.

The scream woke me from one of my wide awake dreams. What I dreamed of I do not know. It was night and I was leaning on the bar counter. Maybe I was having a conversation and maybe I wasn't.

'Michael! Michael!' I heard Mary's voice coming from outside. I ran to the door, shouting for lights to be brought behind me. Illuminated by a lamp on the ground by the well Mary held the naked body of Duveen in her arms, and she was pleading with her to wake, to talk to her for Christ's sake, but the body was lifeless. When I got to them I saw no sign of blood on the body, but I could tell from the way the head flopped that the neck had been broken.

'A doctor!' she shouted, 'someone ride for a doctor! And constables.' Before I could say anything she added: 'She's been raped Michael!'

'How do you know?' I asked stupidly.

'Shut up. She has been raped. Get something to cover her.'

A young man, one of a group who had been drinking in the Inn handed me his jacket and I draped it over her. Two other young men had already mounted horses.

'Get Therry as well,' I told them and they rode off.

James and Bridget came from the house to see what was happening, but I ushered them back in and told them not to let Martine come out.

'She came out to draw extra water. She has done it before many times. Did you hear anything? She must have struggled. She must have screamed.'

At this the group who had gathered round started to melt away.

Mary could not get anybody to help her prepare the body for the wake and this hurt deeply. She looked as beautiful as ever though, stretched out in our parlour. Not many came to wake her. Martin, of course, and Sarah, but not Hugh Vesty. James tried to keep Martine out of the room but she did not want to leave her mother's side. Bridget and Eliza were inconsolable. Father Therry said Mass in the house for the repose of her soul. It was not a proper requiem Mass, and he did not give her the death rites because she had not been baptised. This meant that she could not be buried in a Christian burial-ground. This was hard for Mary to accept and she pleaded with Therry to make an exception because Duveen had after all been tak-ing instruction in Christian doctrine. In her heart Mary knew this was pointless, but she demanded to know from Therry what we were to do with the remains. He had no need to reply because the answer came unexpectedly but with great dignity.

None of us had heard them approach—four men and four women, and the men carried spears and shields. All wore cloaks of hide. The men stood to one side and the women approached the body. They lifted her shoulder high and walked through the doorway and out of the house. One of the men turned to us before leaving. He looked at me—bone in his nose, bone through his hair. Was this the same man who sat beside Arthur on the steps of his house all those years ago? When he spoke I knew it was.

'We take her to her place.'

As far as I know all Aboriginal peoples in Australia bury their dead in the area where they were born.

Martine screamed but Mary, who was bawling her own eyes out, held her tight.

As they marched away I saw him, tears glistening in the light of the torch he held, as they dripped into the white, white beard.

That was the only night the Harrow Inn did not open for business until it was closed forever.

This was as bad as any of the bad times in Mary Dwyer's hard life.

She had gone into Sydney to meet with Therry and regis-ter Martine as a member of our family, and returned towards the Inn later that afternoon whipping the buggy along at a gallop. Without even stopping to tie the horse up she ran into the tavern. Breathlessly she told me:

'It was Hugh Vesty! I've told the constables and he will be arrested. Has been arrested by now, I'd say. He'll swing for this Michael. He will swing for it.'

'Woman, woman, will ya calm down for a minute! What are you on about at all?'

'I met with Sarah and Hugh Vesty in town. And his face was scratched. Down here like that. And here like that.'

She ran a finger violently down each side of her face.

'His face is scratched and so he raped and killed Duveen. There are constables who believe it?'

'She was a strong woman Michael, the strongest I ever met, and it would have taken a powerful man to get the better of her. Only a wrestler could snap her neck like that.'

I could not believe that she was serious.

'Mary?'

'He was here that night wasn't he?'

'Well... eh... yes.'

'And he must have gone out at some point to relieve himself or whatever.'

'I don't know. Sure I was talking to him when I heard your scream. Been chatting to him for ages.'

She looked at me and it was the first time I had ever seen fear in her look.

'Then why did Sarah say that he had come home before sundown on that day?'

'Mary, I get days mixed up. They run into each other. I am busy. Pressure!'

'You are going to take his side in this, aren't you? No matter what happens you will side with him.'

'It is not a question of sides.'

'She was my brother's wife, Michael.'

'Wife?'

'He was a boy. Took up arms to follow you and Arthur and Sam MacAllister. A boy. Never spoke to his mother and father again. Suffered Christ knows what tortures in prison, and was driven into the wild when he came to this place. Then one good thing. She was the one good thing, Michael. Love! And that sweet, sweet, beautiful child. You *will* support me in this.'

'There will be an investigation.'

She screamed now: 'You will support me in this!'

She left in a hurry and I followed her to the door.

He was there again, closer than usual now, standing foot by knee, spear in hand.

Later that day Martin arrived as I thought he might.

'Official business?'

'More or less.'

'You won't have a drink so?'

'Ah. I'll have a tot of rum all right.'

'Good.'

He looked around as I poured. 'Jeez Michael, this place is going to the dogs.'

'Can't get good help.'

'You paid any of them debts recently?'

'Naw.'

'There'll be summonses against you from the court soon then.'

'I suppose.'

'So! Hugh Vesty?'

'What about him?'

'You tell me.'

'Leave this alone Martin, like a good man.'

'Thing like that. I didn't think he would be capable.'

'He's not.'

'Was he here that night?'

'I think so.'

'You think so?'

'If he says he was here that night then he was. If he says he left early then he left early, and if he says he left late he left late.'

'I see.'

'To be honest, I wouldn't know for sure.'

'What do you mean?'

'I had a few of those old spells. You know what I'm talking about.'

'When your mind went away and left you for a while?'

'Exactly.'

'That happening often now?'

'Every day.'

'Jesus Michael, you'd want to ease up on the old hooch.'

'I'll try. I do try though. Can't seem to whack it.'

'You'll have to.'

'What are you going to do about Hugh Vesty?'

'There is not much evidence. And I'd say he'd have his pick of alibis.'

'And what do you think Martin? Is he a guilty man?'

Martin paused and thought for a while before he decided to speak:

'No more or less than the rest of ye.'

'What the hell is that supposed to mean?'

'Could have been any of ye or all of ye. Amounts to the same thing. Unprotected girl in a den of drunken savages. Could have been any mouldy Mick going out for a slash who saw her there. Unprotected! And he, of course fully protected by the oaths of secrecy among the society of United Irish Drunks.'

He waited for me to challenge him on this. I didn't. He finished his rum.

'Thank you for the drink, citizen.'

And with that he left.

I was relieved to see that Old Tom was not standing there any more. I don't know why his presence troubled me more than any other aspect of this sordid business. But if such a thing had happened to a daughter on mine I would be mightily aggrieved as well.

When Hugh Vesty came in that night I ushered him into a corner, then I picked up a stool and rammed it into his gullet.

'The truth, Hugh Vesty. I am not saying I am going to do anything with it or about it. But I need the truth. Did you do this?'

'No Michael, I did not do that thing.'

'You are sure?'

'Yes, I swear.'

I put the stool down.

'And what about you Captain, are you sure?'

'What?'

'Are you sure you didn't do it?'

'Go to hell.'

'A man in Parramatta killed his brother in a drunken rage, but he had no recollection of it afterwards. Could not remember a single thing. You know the feeling Michael. You were in and out of the premises.'

'So you were here?'

'I left early.'

'What happened your face?'

'Clearing brambles.'

'So we will never know then?'

'No!'

Every time Tom appeared now he was closer to the house. I could see his face more clearly, but I could not read it.

'That is not good enough Michael.'

'It will be good enough for a court of law Mary.'

'Well then you will take the law into your own hands.'

'What are you saying?'

'Oh, are you not practiced at that?'

'Mary!'

'That is what you did to the Halpin brothers. That is what you did to the Welsh Sergeant who killed Roisin. For me. You did that for me. I ask you for this. I beg you for this.'

'He was my comrade in arms.'

'So was Arthur Devereux, your 'comrade in arms' and you led him to the gallows.'

I was not going to be drawn. I did not react. I remained calm and said:

'Be careful now, wife.'

'Or what? You'll break my neck and rape me? Ha! As if you could.'

'It is over Mary. Offer it up.'

'Oh it is over Michael. You and me. I do not want you near me. I detest cowards, you know that.'

I walked to the door to open it and let her out. He was standing there again, now closer than ever.

'What does he want?'

'He wants the head of the pig who murdered his daughter.'

'No.'

'He is looking at a coward. But we are not all cowards. My son James will do it. Few short years and he will be strong enough. He will do it for me.'

And she walked away towards the cows that needed milking.

She was wrong about Tom and what he desired. I knew that. Their ideas of justice were different to ours. During the days of the first fleet, Philip who was governor at the time, was a man of liberal attitudes to the natives. When a convict was brought before him who had stolen from the Aboriginals he ordered that the man be flogged, and invited the savages to witness the punishment. They were horrified apparently that a man should be so degraded and some ran to try and wrestle the whip from the flogger's hands. No, he did not want the murderer's head. But he wanted something. But what?

Brandy had not been distilled in the colony by this time and I kept a couple of bottles in memory of Robert Emmet. I picked one up and dusted it down, and walked towards the old man.

I presented it to him.

'I'm sorry. This is all I have to offer you. But it will help. Believe me it will help.'

He took it and I walked away.

The spider was the first episode. A small brown one, it was one of the harmless varieties—some of the ones here can give you a nasty sting. Now I felt the creature as well as seeing it. But when I went to scoop it up and throw it on the floor it had disappeared. This rattled me a little, I have to say.

The next incident was more disturbing. On a bench in the corner sat a woman and her two sons. Well I assume they were her sons, but in truth they could just as easily been her grandsons. Mind you having said that they did not bear any physical resemblance to her. She had a long, thin, pale face with dark, deep-set eyes. Her hair seemed to be black but I could not see it clearly beneath the shawl pulled up over it. The two sons were foxy and freckled. They could have been twins because the only difference between them was their teeth—one had none while the other one's protruded.

I was talking to Hugh Vesty when I noticed them. Now obviously I did not allow women to drink in the tavern, and I told Hugh Vesty that I was going to get rid of them. As I walked towards them I noticed that the two boys were nodding and smiling as if they were listening to some very pleasant music or a reassuring story. The woman's head also moved, but almost imperceptibly, and I thought perhaps she was humming and that is what the boys were keeping time to. When I came up to them someone to my rear called my name, and I turned.

'Who was that?' said I, 'what is it?' But no one paid me any heed.

When I turned back, the woman and her sons they were gone. I was staring at an empty bench.

I walked back to Hugh Vesty.

'How the hell did they get out? Did you see them go?' I asked him.

He gave me no answer but looked at me in a very concerned fashion.

Hugh Vesty came to the Harrow Inn now almost every day and Mary did not approve of this. She wanted me not to serve him or better still to bar him from coming anywhere near the premises. To me he was an innocent man and my closest friend and oldest comrade. I had no intention of budging on the matter and we rowed about it frequently.

James' fourteenth birthday came around, and there was no denying that he had been a very good lad, very helpful to his mother, and he did a man's work around the farm. So I had no problem in agreeing that he should have his heart's desire as a gift. It transpired that his heart's desire was a dog, and not just any dog but a big brute owned by a neighbour. Some said it was a cross between a bull mastiff and one of the native dingoes. Anyway, 'twas as savage-looking a creature as I have ever seen, but for all that he was placid. The dog roamed freely round the perimeters of our home. Hugh Vesty never again visited the Harrow Inn.

As for Old Tom, he did not stand at a dignified distance any longer but sat on the ground, sometimes near the well and sometimes by the steps to the Inn. I brought him grog from time to time and he seemed to appreciate this. Once or twice I sat with him and had a drink. I spoke but he never said a word.

The contraption I'd invented made the mornings almost bearable, when it worked. I had fixed a belt round my right hand, attached to the wrist so that it supported the weight of the hand, but in such a way that the palm of the hand was free. Like a kind of a basket I suppose. Then I tied a strong string to the belt. I ran the string round the back of my neck so that I could hold it in my left hand. The glass of rum, half-filled, could rest securely in the right hand while the hand remained completely relaxed. It was tension that caused it to shake, you understand. So when I pulled the string with my left hand I could raise the glass to my mouth and drink. If I was lucky I could keep the liquid down. On hot mornings this was not easy. By now I was no longer sleeping in the house but on a bench in the tavern. In the mornings the floor would be littered with dried vomit, overturned spittoons and blood, always blood.

The day Martin arrived I had managed to keep down two good measures and I was feeling more human than usual. He looked at me, full of pity.

'Fuck off!' I told him.

'You have to come with me Michael,' he told me.

'I am going nowhere.'

'If you are not in court you will be held in contempt and that could go very badly for you.'

'Whatever you say, Constable.'

'You'll need to clean yourself up. Mary won't help; she's adamant.'

'Mary don't do much these days except give out.'

'You are lucky she doesn't put a bullet in you.'
'Sure wouldn't she be better off without me.'
'Yeah, yeah!'

Well I very nearly was held in contempt, not because I did not turn up but because I found the whole proceedings hilariously funny. All these people looking for money, and I didn't have a penny to give any of them. Campbell and Cooper were there of course, saying that I had come to them to borrow money which was untrue because they approached me with a business proposition. Could I help it if the business did not work out? Yes, I drank too much. But isn't that what people came to the tavern to see? Isnt it? Michael Dwyer the great fighter, the great drinker? A woman called Stroud from whom I had rented some acreage was there looking for her money. She hadn't been paid in years, but then she'd never asked for it. 'Afraid to approach me,' she said. The one who angered me most though was William Davis standing there demanding the return of a few pounds I'd had off him. Self-righteous and vulturous!

Somewhere in the middle of the proceedings I went blank and I did not come to until everyone was being upstanding again. Martin led me away.

'Where are we headed?' I asked.

'You are for the debtors' prison,' he told me.

As a jail the debtors' prison hardly qualified. The room was clean and comfortable and I was well fed. It would have been better than Kilmainham if I'd had a supply of whiskey, but there was little hope of that. The guard did not introduce me to the other occupants and I thought it better not to ask. In truth they did not take up much room. I think the boys looked in my direction and nodded a greeting, but as they were nodding constantly anyway it was difficult to be certain. The mother, or as I say she could have been the grandmother, did not look at me at all. I sat myself down on the bed and said:

'Tis good to get in out of the heat anyway.'

It was not as though they did not hear me, I'm damn sure that they did. The woman was humming a tune or lilting, or at least I think she was. I could almost hear it but not fully, and this began to irritate me.

'Will ya sing up woman so I can hear the thing!'

No recognition!

If I could hear it properly I wouldn't have minded, or if it ceased altogether that would be better still. In time it became something worse than an irritation, and it started to grate and scrape the inside of my brain.

I cradled my head in my arms to shut out all sight or sound of them. But it was still there, the barely audible hum. I started to lilt and sing myself to block it out, and I had to get louder and louder. The guard banged on the door. I stopped, brought my head up to look around, and they were gone. Yes, I was relieved but still very apprehensive. The apprehension grew from fear to panic. I tried to analyse what my fear was but I could not concentrate. 'Twas like I was tingling with energy but dropping from exhaustion.

I prayed for night to come and when it came I wished it gone.

Curled up in the bed then waiting for sleep to come or dawn to come. Did not want to stretch my legs out for fear of something at the end of the bed. What that might be, I had no idea. Ever so slowly I stretched them anyway. Nothing happened. Then that confounded spider again, quick-crawling along my arm. Tried to snatch him but he outpaced my hand every time. Crawled along my shoulder, round my neck and down my side. Then he disappeared, but in an instant was crawling on my foot. Was it the same or was this another now? No, it was another because the first fella was now crawling across my chest. I grabbed for both of them but let go when another crawled across my face. Soon they were all over me. And the itch! The itch unbearable! I scratched and tore at it but just made it worse. Rubbed myself against the wall and then rolled around the floor. Tried to scream and made no noise like in a dream, but this was no dream.

I must have collapsed because I woke with a start when the guard opened the door in the morning.

'Jesus Christ what are you after doing to yourself?'

I looked and saw that I was covered in blood. There was blood on the floor and the walls as well.

'It was them,' said I like an imbecile.

'Come away now,' he said, 'come away!' And he took me by the arm like a child, that big, fat-moustached man.

Brought me to the hospital. Don't remember much about the hospital. Just a bed and a ceiling.

From the hospital back to the debtors' prison.

No one came to see me in all this time.

The deal with the debtors' prison made absolutely no sense. The person to whom you owed the money paid for your upkeep in the prison. If they could not meet their obligations you were expected to pay for yourself. If you did not have the means to so do, and let's face it most people interned in a debtors' prison lacked such means, then you were kicked out—so that is what happened to me.

James was not a talkative boy at the best of times, but on the journey home he would say nothing at all. No matter what I asked he would not answer but shooed the horse along. I was about to clip his ear for him but was afraid that I lacked the authority.

When we approached the house I thought I was seeing things again. Every item of furniture, crockery or utensils that we owned had been placed on the lawn in front of the house. People walked around them, looking at them, touching them. Bridget and Eliza clung to their mother and wept.

'What is this?'

'You know fine well what it is.'

Mary was way past anger now.

'All the stock has been sold and the crops. The land too, every perch of it. The house is to go up for sale next when this lot is gone.'

'Jesus!' I flopped into my favourite armchair, now outdoors, and looked about. Then this woman came along and said:

'Can I see that please?' So I had to get up.

'Thank God.' said Mary.

I followed the direction of her look and saw Therry galloping towards us. He was always galloping in those times. Sometimes he went through three or four horses in a day.

He dismounted and hurried towards us.

'This is the best I can do. The very best. They will allow you all to live in the house as tenants, but you will not own it. On Michael's death it will revert to the creditors.'

'Thank you Father. Thank you so much.' Mary grasped his hand.

Then she turned to me: 'Well you had better stay alive. In an ideal world it is not what I would want but you had better stay alive.'

'That means no hard liquor Michael. You understand?' Therry told me.

I nodded.

It was Brisbane who initiated the scheme soon after he became governor. We did not get an opportunity to see Lachlan and Elizabeth Macquarie, and their son young Lachlan, in person, but we joined the multitudes on the

quay and waved them goodbye. He had done legendary
work in developing the colony and now it needed free settlers. To this end a scheme of free passage was set up and
relatives of those already settled in the colony were given
preference. Needless to say we were over the moon when
Therry came to tell us that we had been accepted for the
scheme. Letters had been sent to Dublin and Wicklow so
that Mary Anne, John, Peter and Esther could, at long last,
board the first available vessel for Australia.

I thanked Therry profusely for this achievement, and
he agreed to dine with us that evening.

'Your own achievements are not to be scoffed at
Michael. You have conquered more adversity than most.
But I'd say the demon rum might have been your
strongest enemy.'

'You could be right there Father. Stronger even than
the might of the British Army.'

'Well those days are over now—fighting the British
Army. We will get justice in the old country in another way.'

'And how might that be?'

'In the Parliament at Westminster.'

'Some chance.'

'Ah now, Catholic Emancipation will be granted. Thousands of Irish Catholics will have the vote and then there
will be good men to represent them.'

'You tell me?'

'Oh yes. Young Kerry Lawyer, Daniel O'Connell. Making waves.'

'Is he a republican?'

'Eh... no... I don't think so.'

'Then he is not for me.'

'No compromise?'

'Not on that. Tom Paine got his way into my heart and
mind like nobody else did. Too many of my comrades gave
their lives. I may never fight again, but I will always believe.'

'No law against that.'

'There is not then.'

Mary Anne had got herself married by now, and she would be coming over with her husband.

'Isn't it just as well we had the premises extended and enlarged,' I said to Mary one sunny Sunday afternoon as we all sat together on the porch, looking over the land that we no longer owned.

'We will need the space right enough as we increase and multiply.'

'Will they be on the sea already Father?' James asked.

'They should be by now,' I said.

'And we will all have a party,' Bridget said.

'The party to end all parties.'

'My big brothers!' James said quietly.

'That is right.' said Mary.

'Do they wrestle?' he asked.

'You can be sure they do,' I told him.

'I'll not be able to match them.'

'What you need is practice,' I said. 'Get up out o' that.'

James had shown reasonable promise as a wrestler and Hugh Vesty used to coach him. But I knew a few moves myself.

'Now you need to use your opponent's weight against him.'

He gripped my shoulders and we wrestled. James moved in low, pushing hard and he wriggled his leg behind me. He heaved, and I had to go with him. I ended up on the ground. Mary applauded. James lay on top of me.

'Put your arms by your side,' I said. 'Now stiffen up.'

I caught him on the hips and lifted him until my arms were fully stretched. It was a great effort. Bending my arms, I left him down again. Then I lifted him again full stretch. The third time took a really mighty effort and by the fourth I was gasping for breath. I went for the fifth though and just made it.

'Get off me now boy. I need to sit.'

Breathing wasn't easy as I sat. Mary wiped the sweat from my forehead. I had said 'sorry' to her hourly to begin with and then two or three times a day. Trust was beginning to return gradually. So was my health and strength, and this meant that I could be industrious once again. This time I was determined that I would do everything properly and when my sons Peter and John arrived there would be some basis on which they could build. My mistakes would not have been in vain and I would do all in my power to ensure that they did not stray from the path of industry, unlike their errant father. Yes there should have been a thousand acres of farm land and a fine mansion waiting for them, but now they would have to build their own fortunes. With my help it would take no time at all. There was a good ten or fifteen years of digging and lifting left in me, and maybe another ten in a restful state, counselling and directing.

To begin with I would have to work for others and the ever reliable Therry found me employment. Pride had to be swallowed, but that was a diet I had lived on before. So, I put the head down and got on with it.

It was easy to sound optimistic, and sometimes I managed to convince myself, but a terrible unease could grow within me, and in no time that could grow into a full-blown panic. And that would paralyse me. In the middle of a task I would be immobilised. When would it end? Or would it end? That was the panic. Breathing deeply would calm it down in time, and I would be grateful to be able to continue to work and live. A lingering jitteriness would remain.

When I walked these streets—what—no more than a year or two past I was feared and respected. Now I walked in fear of the very streets themselves. The city had grown more mighty in the years since we stepped ashore. God bless Macquarie. Fair dues! They should have called the city after him in my opinion, not just the street. More and grander buildings had now grown up, built of the native sandstone, the old yellow block. That honeyed stone beloved of the sun. In a certain light it could indeed look like a golden city. So warm! And yet I feared its streets and those who walked them, feared them with a desperate nauseating fear. Oh, there was a cure. My body knew that. My heart knew that.

'Take another drink sir, and you may die!' a doctor had told me before I left the hospital. I could not recall his name. I could not recall what he looked like. Perhaps I had imagined him. Perhaps nobody said that at all. In which case a small tot of rum, that would still these awful tremors, might do no harm whatsoever. Such were the tricks my head played upon itself. He laughs at the horrors who never went through them. I felt so alone. Where were my companions? Dead! All dead because of me. 'Grand cause'. Grand cause? Grand cause, my arse! Oh, the old wrestler was still alive, but too much had come between us.

Family! Of course, yes. Reconciled almost, but never to be fully trusted again. But, I was needed. That was it. If I went, then the house went with me. 'And what would the robin do then poor thing?' What? Robins? Rhymes from the past! 'He'd hide his head under his wing.' Visitations in a cave, long 'go.

When not in the shakes I walked sometimes in bewilderment. Where had it gone? My one thousand acres? My well-appointed Inn? Surely a man could not drink that. Not *all* that!

And did they know? Those two Scotch bastards, did they know that it would all come tumbling down? Not

much use to them now is it? The people? The good will?
Lost and gone forever.

'Take another drink sir, and you may die.' Must live
now. Must needs become the Methuselah Man to save us
all. Live long enough for Peter and John to prosper. For
Mary Anne and her man to build a life, and for the beautiful Esther to have a decent dowry, and not be relying on
Father Therry for the 'wedding dollar' which he now lent
over and over again. The thrill at the prospect of the
reunion energised me. Oh that I could do more—earn
more. But if I did earn more they descended upon me for
their slice. Oh yes, the Shylocks did keep their knives
sharp at all times. Anything gained had to be hidden.
Never liked the poor mouth but it was a facility I had to
develop. Such a proud man in my day. And I drank in
pride in days gone by to celebrate my prowess. In the end
I drank out of shame for what I had become. So much
destroyed. And nothing restored? James, Bridget and
Eliza of course. And I had not forgotten Martine. Any-
time I saw Mary walk with her by the waters, skipping and
hopping, curls bouncing from side to side, I could weep.
What happened to her mother was the darkest deed of all.
There is not punishment enough in this place of perverse
punishments for the Irishman who perpetrated that. But
would I hunt him down, and seek him out for a summary
execution by my knife? In the end, of course, Martin
Burke was right: it could have been any or all of us. We
were the protected ones.

Immobilised again! Caught for breath! Let this gasp
not be the last. I had to hold on to life so that we might
hold on to the house. For dear life I held.

Had to leave the room when a temper came on me.
Through the bad times James had become the man of the
house. Mary treated him as such and oh that was a source
of sore annoyance. A young man now he was, protecting

his territory, and protecting her. Yes, at the best of times I found it amusing, and indeed I took pride in him. Days there were though when I came close to taking the head off him when my own wouldn't be right. We only had the house now, no longer any land to stamp off through. Oh, how our little republic had shrunk. I knew that in time, I would start to accept.

No sooner had I started though than the 'bloody flux' came on. Now I had always prided myself on the fact that I could eat and drink anything. Forever proud of my toughness, and the toughest part of me was my gut. In the debtors' prison and then in the hospital I had experienced, for the first time, some turmoil in the intestine, but that had passed. Slowly, I grant you, but pass it did. The bloody flux was much more aggressive and in a few days it was turning me inside out. The doctor told me to keep up the fluid intake. When I drank water I became a human sieve and I could not retain ale or wine either. The pain that came with this terrible affliction was as bad as I ever had, and yes, that does include having my thumb blown off by the blunderbuss.

The most effective cure for pain, I always believed, was brandy. It was an expensive commodity but Mary agreed we should acquire some. I took a slug. Well, it was like pouring vitriol on an open wound. I admit that I screamed. If brandy could not stem the bloody flux then it could not take me to oblivion either to escape the pain.

In the shortest time I was only skin and bone and there was precious little of the former. I sweated and rattled my way through days and nights, and I saw little hope of an end. That little hope I had was vested in the arrival of my children, now on the high seas. Yes, I thought Mary Anne, John, Peter and Esther would bring with them some healing balm. Just the sight of them might cure me. Well, it

'Please God, let me last until they arrive, from wherever they may be—Rio or Cape Town.' That far? No, I could not take the pain for that long. I begged Him then, as I could not take the pain, to please take me. Which indeed he did.

So I breathed my last, dirty and alone on a hillside. Not an uncommon condition for me.

Michael Dwyer died on the 23rd of August 1825. When Mary Anne Hughes (née Dwyer) and her brothers John and Peter with their sister Esther did arrive in Sydney they visited their father's grave in the Irish burial grounds.

The End.

Historical Note

This is a work of fiction, but most of the characters are based on real historical figures, and the events are based on real events.

Arthur Devereux, Kevin Doyle, Cecil Lomasney, Curley Casey, the various barkeeps and the native Australian characters are all fictional, as are some of the minor characters.

Michael Dwyer's Wicklow campaign against the British is all a matter of historical record. Whilst the character of Roisin and Dwyer's killing of the man responsible is fictional, it is firmly based on the reality of that conflict. The incident of Roisin's death is based on a similar incident involving the killing of a young girl in south County Down in 1798, which is documented. In the battle of Ballyellis, the historical Dwyer did kill a 'large' member of the Cambrian horse who was fleeing the scene.

The meeting between Dwyer and Emmet is historically accurate, as is his subsequent failure to support that uprising, and Emmet's demise. The historical Dwyer did indeed capitulate on terms that included his transportation to America—terms that were then breached, but the reasons why involve some speculation on my part.

The historical Dwyer was imprisoned in Kilmainham as I describe, and subsequently deported to Australia, leaving his four children behind. The letter he wrote therein is as I have quoted it, and it was all but certain to have been extracted from him under duress.

I have not been able to ascertain to my satisfaction the reasons why the children were left behind, but that they were is sure. If Cuzens forbad them to board the ship for safety reasons then why did he allow the pregnant Sarah Byrne on board and her son Michael? Some believe that Mary and Michael chose to leave the children behind, but I cannot reconcile this with the letters to Trevor that I have seen, nor with the fact that they repeatedly tried over the following twenty years to bring the children over. In short, I have taken my best guess as to what happened based on evidence that is sadly insufficient. To the best of my knowledge and belief, the scenario I have described seems more likely than any other on the balance of probabilities.

The historical Michael Dwyer was transported to Australia under the conditions described. It is true, however remarkably, that he became a free man, then a police constable, and eventually an influential landowner. Pemulwuy's campaign against the British occupation of Australia happened much as I have described it, and the various governors of New South Wales that Michael encounters are all real, and as accurately described as I have been able to manage.

Hugh Vesty Byrne was a real man, and a loyal friend to Michael Dwyer all his life. He was never suspected of rape. From all the documents I have been able to track down, it does appear that Sarah gave birth to a child who could not possibly have been his.

O'Grady and MacCurry were real people. In reality, though, they were never assassinated, but allowed to live.

As to Michael Dwyer himself, I have portrayed the man as accurately as I am able to do so. Some of his writings have been made available to me, and I have quoted from them faithfully. In particular, Michael Dwyer's description of how he managed to evade capture in Wicklow on pages 61-62 is a direct quotation of his own words.

The Dwyers contributed to the building of Saint Mary's Cathedral in Sydney, an area where several descendants of both Dwyer and Byrne still live to this day.